Third Eye Witness
Bearer of Truth

Kathi Bjorkman

Disclaimer
This book is a work of fiction. Places, Names, characters, and incidents either are products of the author's imagination or are used fictitiously. Any resemblance to actual events or locals or persons, living or dead, is entirely coincidental or fictitious.

Based on the Experiences of Marilynn Hughes
*Taken from The Mysteries of the Redemption: A Treatise on Out-of-Body Travel and Mysticism, Marilynn Hughes, Chapter Eight, The Out-of-Body Travel Foundation, 2003, SOURCES
The Mysteries of the Redemption: A Treatise on Out-of-Body Travel and Mysticism, Marilynn Hughes, Chapter Eight, The Out-of-Body Travel Foundation, 2003,
Galactica: A Treatise on Death, Dying and the Afterlife, Marilynn Hughes, Chapter Eight, The Out-of-Body Travel Foundation, 2003.

Dedication
I dedicate this book to my daughters Sara and Megan, who encouraged me to write a second novel.

.

Chapter 1

Seated across from each other in the darkened interior of a stretch-limo the two men entered into a low-voiced secretive conversation.

"So you've located it?" Well dressed with a foreign accent, the elderly man asked with eager eyes. "Are you certain?"

Younger than the other and in his forties, the American with non-descript features and short bristly facial-hair cast a reserved stare. "I said I'm almost certain I've located it. We can't know for sure till we retrieve them," he added.

Older by decades than the man in his forties, the European maintained a refined and rigid manner as he savored the moment. "Hmm," he uttered, exuding authority and an air of superiority with the coolness of an observant lion. "But you're sure this is the family that has it?"

"I can't find one better," returned the American sitting across from the man in charge. "Everything points to them."

"Is that right?" Grinning slyly, the older man didn't allow a response. "Then it goes as planned."

"I don't want anything to happen to the old guy," the younger of the two said. "He is scheduled to be out of town on an important business matter. There will be plenty of time to execute the plan."

Instilling urgency, the elderly man straightened his grin. "I warn you, we must locate this missing one." He looked out the deeply tinted window. "If you don't it will jeopardize everything. I mean everything."

Seemingly less assured, the younger man sounded, "How can that be?" With concerned eyes, he watched the older man.

Waving him off with arrogant aloofness, his gaze returned to the underling. "If, or when he decides to act on them, it will be just the proof needed to validate all of them. The world can't afford this to happen." Cynicism crept into his voice, "Stir men up and they think. Add anger and they rebel."

Throwing a strange look of start, the American chose his words carefully, "I didn't know so much was at stake."

"We have to secure these like the others," the old man declared with cool detachment. "Or they will end up in the courts. That's not what you want."

"That's not what I want," the American repeated.

"Deniability won't work a third time for us." His cold eyes communicated a stern message to the younger one. "Not when it includes this man's family."

Digesting the orders, the bristled-face man complied, "I understand."

"Do you? If you fail you'll go down before I will," the older gentleman said with persuasive conviction.

Acknowledging the seriousness of the matter, the younger man agreed, "I won't let that happen."

"Have you made sure you have what you need?"

"Of course." The young man nodded. "I have the man I need and his useful idiots."

"Make sure they never see you."

"That will not be a problem," replied the American.

Silencing him with a flick of his hand, the European glared at him. "It will be everyone's problem if you're caught. You were hired to protect our interests. It will come at a great price if you are discovered with these."

"I thought your financial connections were unlimited," the younger man questioned nervously. "You told me you were invincible."

"Yes, as long as we're invisible," sounding ruthless, the old man grinned evenly as the frank conversation took a turn. "So, you see we will not risk exposure."

Puzzlement washed over the American's face as the threat rang in his ears. "I see. How do I know I'll be safe from your men when this is over?"

"You're not safe without us," the old man warned as he clasped his hands together and rested them on his briefcase. "There are others determined to locate what you've found."

"What I *think* I've found," he corrected the distinguished man.

"Yes, so you've said."

"So we understand each other," the young man said with a quick lilt in his voice. "Right?"

Deflecting his words, the old man tilted his chin. "Let's just say you better be right because if you don't locate this and deliver it as promised," he shifted to a threatening tone, "I can't protect you anymore."

Following stunned silence, the younger man said tenuously, "Protect me from what?"

"From us," the elder man said scathingly. He handed the younger man the briefcase. "It's all there. You can pay for the help you need, and keep some for yourself. The rest comes when we receive our goods." Handing him a note, the man explained, "We need it here. We can't accept it till it arrives safely on this soil."

Chapter 2

"We're going to make it," Martine vocally assured the three women seated in her car. Seconds later her face squinted in chagrin as she saw another traffic light turn yellow. Reducing speed with the traffic ahead of her, she addressed her sister Jolene who was poised stiffly like a mannequin in the passenger seat, "It's not too much further. Please don't be upset. Not today." Mature in her forties, Martine was average height, blonde-haired, and normally self-assured. Today, she did not resemble or feel like herself.

Unable to control the angst in her voice, Jolene sounded suddenly, "You have to run them. You have to pass these cars, or we're going to stop at every intersection for the next ten miles." Taller, more refined, and much younger than her sister, the normally confident Jolene was emotionally fragile—verging on tears.

Bursts of smelly smoke belched from the old truck that blocked her view and slowed her speed. Reminding herself to stay calm, Martine replied as if she had been questioned, "I would pass him if I could. Getting us there safely is more important than not getting there at all—but I know we're not going to be late." Martine, the pillar of strength in her sisters' life, braked to a stop at another yellow light. "NASA wouldn't even have *The Right Stuff* to get around this moving menace," she added as she motioned to all the traffic in front of her.

"You think we're going to be there on time?" Jolene fumed. "I've driven from Phoenix to Flagstaff faster than we can drive down Indian School Road." She raised her lip in contempt. "This is pathetic. There must be forty red traffic lights—just waiting for us. I'm going to be late." She looked on in disbelief.

Glancing at the cars digital clock read-out to gauge her progress only added to the urgency—causing her face to wince. "Don't worry," Martine soothed her sister without hearing herself. She was preoccupied with her own concern of failing on such a momentous day.

Sandwiched in between rows and columns of cars, no other foreseeable options were possible other than tolerating the slow mind-numbing traffic delays. "Hey. This was your plan, not mine." Watching backed-up lines of cars take turns crossing through the intersection only made Martine feel more helpless and anxious. When her light turned green she hit the gas hard, clenched her jaw, and whispered her words, "Here we go." Speeding her car to fifty-five miles, she changed lanes and triumphantly passed the truck she had been stuck behind. Smiling demurely, Martine sighed her relief. "That's better." Mentally paralyze by the notion of being late on this day, of all days, revved her adrenaline. Frigid hands clutched the steering wheel as she kept speeding to rush the next lighted intersection before it flashed its dreaded yellow light. Moments after she made it through the intersection, she muttered in dismay, "Uh-oh. There's a cop behind me." Watching in her rearview mirror she saw the police car speeding up to her with its colored lights on strobe. Martine frowned and instantaneously revised her sighting, "I'm being pulled over." Automatically the three other passengers in Martine's car moaned and turned their heads to look out the back window.

Jolene went ballistic while the other passengers stayed silent. "You've got to be kidding me. Now we're going to be really late, if we even get there at all. What else could possibly go wrong?"

"You mean besides this ridiculous make-over I just got?" Martine was more disturbed by her recently acquired exotic airbrushed make-up and up-do hair style than a forthcoming traffic ticket. "Don't go nuclear. I'm sure it's fine. We know I was speeding a bit," Martine attempted to reassure her sister who was looking more like a glamorous Barbie doll than the Scarlet O'Hara she just morphed into. Engaging her right turning signal, she continued, "Maybe if you three hadn't made arrangements for hair and make-up at a place called The Hair Frolic with Gina the Hair Commander, we wouldn't be in this mess. He's probably pulling us over because we look like working girls—and you know what I mean," Martine said sarcastically to the three equally made-over passengers.

Halting her car to a complete stop for the wailing police car tailing her, Martine shifted her car in park and started searching for her purse among all the bags, shoes, shirts, pants, and coffee cups strewn about the front seat. "Anyone here have an FBI badge on them?"

"No!" The three said together.

Twisting around to look for her wallet in the back seat, she replied impatiently, "Then help me find my purse, or we'll be here all day."

Tossing the purse into Martine's lap, Jolene mused, "You're the only one that even brought a purse—I mean luggage. This is huge."

Forcing a smile, Martine said with a scolding edge, "Yeah, and luckily I did."

Jolene put her face between her hands and sniffled. "I can't believe it just got worse."

"Yeah, well at least I'm prepared with my credentials," she replied as she aggressively dug for her wallet inside the dark-cave full of the personal items that were never far from her side. "Maybe I can get us out of this. Of course if we didn't look like this he might believe it was an emergency." Seeing the cop approach her window, she rolled it down and greeted him sheepishly, "Is there a problem officer?"

Like a robot, he answered mechanically, "Yes, ma'am, there is." Standing straight, the faceless pillar could be heard clearly by everyone in the car.

Martine looked into the holstered gun that was inches from her face. "Seriously, what seems to be the problem?"

"Looks like there's a warrant out on this car."

Frenzied, Martine snapped "What? That's crazy. There's no warrant out on this car. There has to be some kinda mistake."

"No mistake, ma'am," his stiff autocratic voice replied.

Perplexed as another police car with flashing lights pulled in front of her car, she offered her identification to the officer. "Here, check again," she said.

Jolene leaned over towards the driver's window and shouted, "Excuse me, this is an emergency." Her eyes glittered from the tears that were forming. "You've made a mistake."

Leaning down to acknowledge both Martine and Jolene, the officer removed his glasses and smiled. "You're right, this is an emergency and we're here to make sure you get to the church on time."

Jolene gasped. "Bobbie? Is that you?" Jolene's watery blue eyes and white teeth sparkled from the sun hitting them.

"You bet it is."

Jolene obliged a smile. "What's this all about?"

"Like the National Guard we deploy quickly and are first on the scene. Let's move out ladies." Bobbie signaled the police car in front of them to get going. "You're not going to be late for your wedding, Jolene."

Martine looked straight ahead and sped off between the escort of police cars. "Looks like we're going to have a wedding today. I told you we wouldn't be late."

"Seems like you always have the answers. Well then, what if he doesn't like me after we're married?" Jolene blurted-out a new anxiety that took over.

"What if you don't like him after you're married?" Addressing the subject of Wade—the man who chipped away the wall around her sister's heart, Martine fired back again, "You're not alone in this." Knowing it was her job as Jolene's older sister and matron of honor to reassure her and settle her nerves, she continued playfully, "You know, marriage is like a fine wine."

"That makes sense," Eva, Martine's youngest daughter, laughed from the backseat.

"Yeah," Jolene agreed. "Explain that."

"Well," Martine said thoughtfully as she glanced at her sister—searching for a hint of how she was holding up now. "When the grapes are grown, the wine makers purposely stress out the grapes, by depriving them of water and subjecting them to an over abundance of sunshine. This weeds out the weak ones, so only the strongest and best survive. Those are the grapes that make the finest wine." Not hearing an objection, Martine continued, "The greatest love survives the harshest of conditions. Surviving turmoil is what makes a marriage strong. You and Wade Harding are both tough enough to be married till death pulls you apart."

"Martine, thank you." Jolene dab her tears. "Now you're messing up my face before he sees me."

"Don't worry. He'll like what he sees."

Chapter 3

Max, the name he used on the numerous computer blog sites that the heavy-set fifty year old man frequented, lounged on his sofa while surfing the internet on his laptop computer. Keeping a beat on politics as he listened to his favorite news channel was routine. Max, silver-haired with a ponytail, couldn't get enough information if he latched onto a topic that intrigued him—and plenty of them did. He loved to debate all his theories with faceless people that were as passionate as he was.

Basically recluse except for his part-time graveyard shift at the nearby diner, he used all his alone time to satisfy his aching desire to expose heresies and conspiracies. A consummate master in researching rogue political schemes, investigating unsolved mysteries, and exposing criminal exploits made him a popular personality on-line. He took the screen name 'Supermax' when fellow bloggers commented on how he took everything to the extreme—to the max. Right-winged and conservative the excitable Max was about to find another possible 'cover-up' right outside his own back door.

While simultaneously researching the net for more chat-sites on his latest fetish and getting today's political drama at the White House from the evening newscasts debates, his monotonous ritual was jostled when an incoming alert sounded from his TV—displaying a local news break-through. Hairs on his arms bristled as he followed the broadcast. Processing the disturbing flash report brought back some old memories, creating the urge to call his old high school chum.

Hoping Gordy would be home on Saturday night, he used his aged cell phone to ring-up his buddy. When he heard Gordy's somewhat inebriated voice he knew it was already happy hour—meaning Gordy will want to talk for hours. "Gordo!" Max blurted. "Checkout what just happened right here in Apache Junction, Arizona."

Gordy, who lived in lush Oregon, scoffed, "A sand storm?"

"Not exactly. They just identified the body of a missing Colorado guy. He'd been missing like three years before they finally found his body."

"Sooo?" Gordy's disinterested voice drawled.

"Yah. So guess where they found his body?"

Gordy grunted, "How would I know that?"

"It's the same place we went camping when you were here like five years ago."

"You mean Magic Mountain?" Gordy guessed.

"No," Max rebuffed. "They're called the Superstition Mountains, you dweeb. We thought we were gonna find the lost Dutchman's mine."

"Oh yeah. We sure thought we'd come back with gold. All we found was rock and scorpions though. So what happened to the guy?"

"Well," Max was jazzed that Gordy asked, "He was a Colorado guy in his mid-thirties that secretly came down to look for the Dutchman's mine. No one knew how much he had researched about the mines location until he went missing and they started investigating his life, looking for clues of his possible whereabouts and people that may be suspect in foul play. I mean they really looked hard for this guy when he went missing. All his belongings, books, maps, his tent, his jeep, his food, and his keys were found—just no body. There was an intense foot and air search done down here, but they never found anything until now."

Max and Gordy were also would-be prospectors infatuated with the tales of an elusive vast gold reserve hidden in the Superstition Mountains. Legendary or real, men have been obsessed since the mid-eighteen hundreds in finding this lost treasure. Dutch

Hunters have fueled more than 100 books and maps. Gold fever at this location has captured men's thirst for a hidden treasure that is according to history, both fantastic in size, and exceptional in quality—like no other mine ever claimed.

Located east of Phoenix, the rough mountainous region where people go searching—only to never be seen again alive, or at all, is a place of mystery and intrigue. The German man Walz that the mine is named after died in 1891 before ever revealing the location to anyone. It was a known fact that he mined in the Superstitions and returned to town with magnificent gold nuggets that he bought supplies with.

"Well, did they find any gold on him like some of the others?" Gordy quizzed.

"Nope, just his backpack, cell phone, and bones."

Gordy sobered up, "How'd he die? Where'd they find him?"

Max got serious. "You know. Same basic region we figured it'd be. His body was found only a half-mile from his campsite. They say he was wedged between boulders for three years until a couple hikers came upon his backpack. When they looked up the mountainside, they saw a boot and the boot lead to the bones. That's how they found the skeletal remains and authorities just identified the guy through DNA. But, Gordy, based on what I'm hearing, that could've been us—if someone pushed us off the trail. I just don't see how it's possible to fall off that path. And how could all these searchers have never seen him, or his backpack? And it's being ruled an accident."

"No way," Gordy hooted. "Another accident?"

"Yes way."

"I suppose you're thinking about going back in there."

Max hesitated. "Maybe."

"Don't even think about it," Gordy spouted louder.

"I'll get back to you, Gordo. Gotta get to work."

"Don't hang up . . . ," Gordy's voice trailed as Max disconnected.

Chapter 4

Martine rose from her chair with a glass flute in one hand—fizzing with freshly poured champagne, and a spoon in the other hand. Looking out at the glamorous array of guests that vibrantly decked the ballroom where they encircled round tables graced with floral centerpieces made of coral and cream colored roses, she used the spoon and glassware like a dinner bell to get everyone's attention. "Hello," Martine summoned. "Thank you for joining Jolene and Wade for their wedding celebration."

Glancing down to her left, she tenderly addressed her gorgeous sister Jolene who donned a diamond encrusted tiara attached to poofy layers of white mesh. "I am so honored to be sitting here today between you and my two daughters, on the wedding day of your dreams." Acknowledging her two daughters Eva and Alexa, Martine tilted her head down to her right and smiled affectionately. "And now for Wade, who couldn't be more well-suited for my baby sister, and who is a new addition to our family for as long as he'll have us," Martine sniffled her words with tears glossing above her cheeks as she connected with his handsome grinning face. Turning back to speak to the battalion of distinguished guests, most in service with the police department and local FBI, Martine spoke from her heart, "What do we know about love?" She paused as she scanned the crowd. "What makes love so powerful that these two survivalists that each packs their own guns and badges would even need anyone else to be with? I can think of a lot of reasons. Like, it's been around longer than any of us. It's existed longer than the United Nations." The guests all chuckled. "It's caused wars, and it's made peace, it's a source of compassion that brings people to-gether, it saves lives, and makes new ones. Love is so powerful that when we meet the right person we cannot resist the desire to make more love. When our souls meet their harmonic counterpoint it recognizes its chance to produce more love. We choose to create love because we can and must." Martine raised her glass and her voice as she turned to address the wedding couple, "May you never lie, cheat, or steal, but:

If you must lie, lie with each other
If you must cheat, cheat death
If you must steal, steal a kiss."

Everyone in the room rose to their feet clapping for the bride and groom till they also stood and kissed.

Wade picked up his glass and toasted his guests, "*Here's to those who wish us well and to those that don't' can go to . . .*" Wade's uncontrollable signature grin widened as he turned to kiss Jolene again while the boisterous group of fellow buddies hooped and hollered.

Martine and Jolene hugged tight and then Eva and Alexa em-braced them both. The four of them have been a family for years. With Jolene and Martine's parents deceased while Jolene was still in school, and Martine's husband James deceased after a tragic car accident, the girls only grew closer the smaller their immediate family became.

Eva and Alexa resumed their exciting conversation about all the handsome single guys in the room, especially the two grooms-men sitting at the opposite end of the long head table, Jolene and Wade made their way to the center of the room for their first dance, and Martine watched nostalgically as her beloved sister floated magically like a fairy princess in circling patterns with her new life partner, Wade. Jolene's exotic Grecian inspired wedding gown with crystal and pearl beaded sweetheart bodice glistened under the moving mirror ball lights. Twirling like a radiant white-robed goddess, her full-bodied skirt fanned-out, showing the fullness of its exquisite overlay of tulle lace with delicate embroideries smothered in fine rhinestones. Without words spoken a new memory was being formed, and a new beginning for all of them was emerging.

Unsuspecting of the events about to occur, Martine was oblivious to the dissimilar dark world of lies and delusions whirling in full force to the point of touchdown. Soon she would find herself engaged in events so monumental and consuming of her time and space it would be this moment that would capture the contrasting effects of deceptive beliefs and divine truths.

Reflecting on the spectacular ballroom elegantly decorated to suit her much younger sisters sophisticated personality, the whole extravaganza was an unforgettable extension of Jolene's captivating beauty.

"Excuse me," a deep voice and a cloud of expensive cologne announced a tall mustached man in a black tux. "Remember me?"

An unmistakable voice caught her attention. "Well hello, Mr. Mahoney." Martine turned in her chair, putting the familiar tone with the Director of the local FBI, and Jolene's boss. "I was hoping I'd see you," she said with a pleasant smile. "It's been awhile." She noticed how he looked so changed in his formal attire instead of casual pants and cowboy boots. His broad face and powerful build was handsomely displayed like she had not seen before.

"Yes it has, and call me John." He sat down in the chair next to her and gave her a reflective look. "I was hoping you'd be glad to see me again."

"Of course I am. You know the saying, *'absence makes the heart grow...'*"

John Mahoney interrupted, "Fonder?"

"No." Martine smiled large—accentuating her high cheekbones.

Mahoney flashed a disappointed look and tried again. "Stronger?"

Martine laughed, "No, I was gonna say smarter."

"Interesting," Mahoney lifted an eyebrow and nodded slowly. "You must be doing better."

"I am." She faced a sympathetic smile from him. "I think I'm finally operating on all thrusters. It really is an adjustment to lose a husband. I just don't understand why people want to get divorced faster than the latest jeans go out of style."

Mahoney, widowed himself, acknowledged her observation, "I hear yah. Never understood that myself."

Martine sipped her champagne as she viewed the complicated man she met a few years ago. She being raised in rural Southwest Colorado—where cowboys still rode tall in a saddle, contrasted Mahoney's upbringing from a tough Detroit area where you kept one eye on the weather, and the other on your neighbor. "Jolene will be very pleased that her boss could make it."

"I couldn't get here sooner, but I wouldn't miss my prettiest agents wedding," he said charmingly.

"She'll want to hear that."

Mahoney cleared his throat. "I wanted to tell you how beautiful you look, and those girls of yours—they're going to break some hearts tonight." Mahoney raised his amber colored cocktail to toast his proclamation.

Martine, pleased with the compliment, raised her glass and clinked it with Mahoney's while she observed both her daughters take to the dance floor with the groomsmen they were already familiar with. "Oh yeah, this is like Cinderella's ball. They're going to have a great time." Martine admired the transformation of her little girls into grown women outfitted in off-the-charts *pure haute couture* evening dresses. Their ethereal-muted-coral satin gowns with strapless wrap-around pleated bodices, accented with sparkling bracades of sequins and crystals, matured them both by five years.

"Well, I hear you're going to be staying in Arizona while Jolene and Wade are on their honeymoon in Hawaii. Any truth to that rumor?"

"Yes, that's correct. I'm finally on vacation and I'm spending it at Jolene and Wade's. I'm the pet sitter. They've got three dogs now and a cat. Plus, both my daughters are living down here now." Martine reminisced a bit, "It wasn't so difficult when Alexa got transferred down here to your forensics department, but now Eva has moved into a training facility in Scottsdale to condition competition show horses, so I'm now officially an empty nester."

"Well our good friend Teddy wants to get you over for a poker game when he's back from London. And, we don't have any spellbinding cases at the FBI right now. So, maybe there'll be time for more laughs. You really haven't seen us at our best yet."

Martine nodded, "I'd love that. I was so disappointed he couldn't make it to the wedding. You and Teddy are the only two adults I really know here in Arizona." She was really akin to the way he identified Teddy as 'our good friend' since Teddy was most certainly John Mahoney's buddy that she'd met a few years ago while consulting on a very unique case.

"Not to worry. I'm arranging a poker tournament. So, how 'bout a dance?" Mahoney took her hand and led her to the floor.

Chapter 5

Contrasting the illumination of an Arizona sunrise in the morning dawn, evil rose at sundown where Tom and his current girlfriend Janice were busy commiserating with a group of pleasure seeking hedonistic criminals that hung-out in a low-rent neighborhood in the Phoenix area. Fumes from various drugs plumed the air as the pathetic group of dysfunctional misfits schemed together. Plotting an attack was exhilarating especially for their hyped-up leader Tom.

Spewing his arrogance, Tom boasted obnoxiously, "We've just won the lottery. Now to collect." As the level of drug consumption increased, so did irrational behaviors and distorted judgments.

Brewing the plan like a coven of witches, commonsense left the station when Vic recommended his solution to getting into the safe, "Hey, man, I got some C-4 that can blow anything."

"Shut-up you insect," Tom blurted. "Nobody's gonna hear that—are they," his cynical irritation flared. Thirty-six year old Tom drained his bottle of beer and flung the empty at thirty-year old Vic. "We've just decided that guns are too loud. Do you do anything else with that head besides hang a hat? You can't even do that right."

Vic's head dodged the brunt of a flying Budweiser bottle. "Shit, man." After deflecting it with the rim of his black baseball cap which was always worn backwards, he snatched his bottle of whiskey to engage in mutual combat with Tom.

Eddy took the palm of his hand and hit Vic's head with a thunk. "Don't think anymore, it makes you dangerous to be around. You're already sweating like a drug mule crossing the border."

Vic's unpredictable explosive temperament simmered down, "I'm just saying I can get us in and out fast."

Pacing inside the den of vipers, Tom gestured at Vic like an angry rapper, "You be quiet while I think through the plan. Ya got one job—make sure there's no one around, and no one sees us. You're just a two-bit career thief, so don't get in the way." Edgy and hyperactive from the methamphetamine he had consumed earlier, Tom's squirrely collection of random thoughts was escalating his tendency towards aggression, paranoia, and violence.

Indignant, Vic jumped off the sofa, "Don't call me that, man."

Big Eddy, a large muscular, over-thirty, drug dealer, tried to stop the cockfight, "I'll take care of ya myself if ya don't sit down, Vic." Eddy's euphemism didn't stop there, "I'll rub-out anyone that gets in the way, and I won't need a gun." Ponytailed, and tattooed up and down his arms, Big Eddy found it ordinary to enforce drug control when they were using *his* drugs. Managing the situation like a business man, he was protecting his turf—his trade.

"We just need a way into a safe," Tom stated.

"We need Jake," Bo piped-in.

"I don't trust that guy." Tom's meth high was boosting his suspicions. "Why do we need him anyway?" Moving back-and-forth, pissed-off Tom called-out his youngest co-conspirator Bo, "We don't need more people around to screw this up."

"Hey, it was his idea. It's his mark and he can crack a big safe," Bo argued. "He said he can get in any safe and he needs a job now or he's leaving the state. He's operating here on borrowed time— gonna get found and arrested if he don't keep moving."

"Well, if he needs us I want more money."

Bo, the timid underling stuttered, "I . . . I don't know if he'll do that. I swear he's sure it's a big haul." Bo was Vic's twenty-year old kid brother. Eager to be included and accepted in the world of his older experienced sibling, he would willingly follow commands without question.

Janice slid up to her man Tom with desires of her own. "Hey, baby, let's just use this guy if he can do it. You said we would have everything we need if there's a lot of money in this dudes place."

Vic and Bo looked at each other and agreed with Janice. Inseparable cohorts in various petty crimes and drug dealings, the two brothers preferred to follow behind a master.

Bo reassured Tom, "He's just gonna meet-up for the job. He's not staying around. He takes what he wants and we get the rest. He needs us and we need him."

Emotionally strung like guitar strings, Tom pounced on Bo and pinned him back on the sofa. Scrutinizing Bo with jaundice eyes, he seethed, "Don't tell me what to do—lounge lizard." Tom fed his inflated ego by tearing others down and keeping them there. Constantly high on some drug substance caused unpredictable extreme mood swings. Cruel to others one day and chummy the next kept his socially parasitic associates following him like the pied piper that promised a big score. "I need to meet him."

Being a habitual Meth user can create evil in even a good person, but when you already have an evil predisposition like Tom, it magnifies that evil without limitations.

Craving acceptance, Bo appeased, "I'll call him, Tom."

Horribly addicted to smack, Janice was devouring the treat that Eddy brought to the party. Taking a series of deep breaths, she paused, "Where'd you get this stuff from?" Tossing her head seductively, she added, "It's really fine."

More random than a pinball machine, Tom temporarily calmed down from his antagonistic rant, "Yeah, this is good stuff. Get some more for later." Tom and Janice were both hooked on the ecstatic rush they got from their drug addiction. The incredible high they maintained on a daily basis was more powerful than any sexual orgasm they experienced together. Mutually dependent on narcotic substances, their lives quickly became driven by increased drug usage and bolder crimes.

Eddy was mellowing out on his drug of choice. "Got it from a new source. I'm telling you this guy is connected, man."

Eddy's young girlfriend Rachel, who had been quietly indulging in the drug-fest, addressed Vic, "While you're drinking your weight in Jack and Coke, I wanna know how you're going to make sure no one's home?" Rachel's shrewd dark side surfaced with her drug consumption. "If you screw this up we'll need to hide in Afghanistan." Always on the prowl for the next reckless relationship that got her what she wanted, the voluptuous-blonde addict had solid taste in picking bad-boys. Eddy was the perfect man that could support her six-hundred dollar a day heroin habit that seized her psyche. Rewarding Eddy with extreme passion was her choice of adhesive that bound them together. Stimulated by the fantasy of drugs and wealth, Rachel used her benevolent feminine skill-set and postage-sized type dress to charm Tom, "Let me take care of Jake. I'll stay with him the whole time. I know how to use a gun if we need to get rid of him."

Tempted by Rachel's proposition, Tom succumbed to her laxadaziel assurednesses. "Call him, Bo."

Chapter 6

Martine, a lawyer, and John Mahoney, the Arizona FBI director, spent the evening visiting and sometimes dancing with a group of FBI and Scottsdale Police Investigators. Kindred spirits from years of working with difficult and unusual cases placed them in a league of their own. Martine's legal and psychological background sparked an intriguing conversation when she debated the recent apprehension of the Grimm Sleeper serial killer in California with Investigator Jones, "He's probably a psychopath and more," Martine explained. "Psychopaths are not mentally intelligent—they're emotionally intelligent at manipulation—they screw up when smart meets stupid. That young female reporter was amazingly tenacious, but mostly very smart," she was saying when she heard her daughters voice.

"Mom!" Eva interrupted with a penetrating screech.

Startled, Martine looked around for her daughter. The bride and groom had departed from their reception and only half the guests were still mingling or dancing in the room. Scanning the dimly lit banquet hall, Martine caught sight of Eva as she stormed towards the table. Sensing the perfect Arizona evening had just been blown to smithereens, she gathered up her long dress and stood. "What?" Martine answered.

"Seriously, this is horrible," Eva sounded frantic.

Pulling a chair up for her daughter, Martine asked, "What happened? Is someone hurt?"

Eva's shocked expression almost said it all, "Yes, there was a fire or explosion at the training facility tonight. I just looked at my phone and there are texts and voicemails from the girls I ride with. Cops and firemen are everywhere. They don't think I should go home tonight. I gotta go now. I need to see what happened. Will you take me?"

John Mahoney strained to hear above the loud disco song YMCA. "Eva, can I help? Tell me what happened," John's professional presence sounded almost protective as he moved his chair closer to them both.

Eva rattled off more news to John, "I just started working there a few months ago. I don't know if the horses are okay. I don't know if anyone is hurt. I need to go right now."

"We can go together," Mahoney announced confidently. "I've got a driver and he can take us all there. Nobody should drive after this reception."

Festivities of the evening disintegrated as Martine, Eva, Alexa, the two groomsmen, and Mahoney gathered up their belongings and took off in his rented car service.

Within a short time they arrived to witness the horror and destruction of Eli Morgan's private residence. Conversations were temporarily paralyzed as the six stared in dread at the monumental estate being consumed by the fires wrath.

Imaginary barricades constructed of yellow-caution-tape printed with 'CRIME SCENE DO NOT CROSS' quarantined the compound. Scores of firemen battled to control the roaring inferno as smoke and flames poured from the building. Water sprayed on the home from several positions tried relentlessly to break through the walls of fire that prevented anyone from entering or searching for occupants.

Chapter 7

Dirty, sore footed, and exhausted from a long wedding day followed at midnight by a horrific sweltering crime scene, left Martine numb. Eli Morgan's home was burnt beyond recognition, and no one had a clue what happened. Unable to access the building at the time, there was no way to determine if there was a crime or what the crime could be.

Martine only had sleep on her mind and went directly to bed, like Eva had already done—who chose to stay at Jolene's with her mother.

Falling asleep quickly, she began to dream of roaring thunderous sounds uprising above her—drawing her attention to the high ornate ceiling of a Spanish looking cathedral. In a state of sleep, her blurred vision came into focus she gazed upon its details until her concentration was broke by the voice of an older Spanish man who surreptitiously appeared in front of her as another loud clap of thunder crashed. Directing her attention to the man she instantly recognized as a priest dressed for a formal religious ceremony, she contemplated his purpose.

"Who gives this woman to this man?" A priest asked in a Spanish dialect.

"I do," a distinguished grey haired gentleman standing next to her proudly said in the same foreign tongue. Formally dressed, and of prominent Spanish descent, he kissed Martine on the cheek before departing.

With the words and images interacting, she suddenly realized a wedding was in progress—and she was the bride—a bride dressed magnificently in an elegant double tiered ivory silk gown with off-the-shoulder bodice and extreme pointed "V" at the waist. Generous accents of ruffled-lace, pearls, ribbon, and fringe on the dress implied she came from great wealth. Given the extravagance of her wedding dress that somewhat resembled a Victorian lamp shade, and the Spanish chapel with desert motif, she surmised the event was somewhere in the southwest during the late 1800's. Moments after making the connection of where she was, gunshots rang outside of the chapel. Before the formal wedding vows could be exchanged the entire congregation of people became alarmed and the happy ritual ceased.

Young men leapt to their feet and followed the groom and his father out of the chapel. Martine went after the procession and out the front doors where she witnessed a stampede of Indian warriors engaging in an aggressive uprising.

Alit by the setting sun the deeply dark-faced leader galloped up to address the unarmed men. "I take her," he said pointing to Martine.

"No," the groom yelled as his friends held him back.

"Then we shoot," the Indian organizer said as he raised his weapon. His long black hair with a thick leather head band framed the strong classic features of an Apache Indian determined to have what he came for. Dressed in a white cotton tunic, dark vest, and pants tucked into knee-high moccasin boots made it obvious the Indians and Spanish had been trading and interacting for years.

"What do you want with her?" The exasperated father of the groom asked, who appeared to be equally respected as a spokesman for the Spanish dwelling community.

"We want you to deliver the guns you promised. We brought you gold—you give us guns now."

"You stole that gold. We will give you guns when you pay. Don't take the girl," the groom's father pleaded.

"We take her till you bring guns, or kill her now," the warrior said defiantly as he signaled his men to grab Martine.

Dragged away from the chapel by three savage Indians, Martine was roughly flung on top of an Indian Paint horse and her hands tied before being led off at a gallop—wedding dress pluming out from currents of air.

Speeding through the desert terrain at a full gallop with the large band of wild Indians took her thoughts and breath away. Watching in awe as they approached a mountainous cathedral of peaks, Martine saw the world dramatically transform from barren wasteland to hills and valleys with foliage and boulders. Becoming conscious of her horrendous vulnerability with these strangers—a pawn in their exploits, she instinctively sought a way to escape. Still tethered to the leaders horse made it impossible for her to try and breakaway until they reached their destination.

After weaving through the forests sheath they stopped before the side of a red rock cliff. Without words, the leader conveyed to his followers to remove Martine from her mount. Awkward and disheveled she landed on her feet and adjusted her huge wedding gown. Disgusted, Martine demanded, "How can this possibly work to your advantage?"

The leader ignored her and forced her to move forward toward the entrance of a large cave. An older Indian in more traditional dress came out of the cave and up to Martine. Large and fit, the warrior chief looked upon her. "The time has come for one to speak for our people." Nodding at the others that were gathering around, he continued, "Our people fight now to keep their land, their homes, their hunting. Spanish take our land and then promise weapons for our peace agreements. Whites take our land if we can't fight war-wagons. Now, Spanish do not honor weapons because we have nothing to trade."

"I do not like war," Martine replied adamantly. "Who really wins when there is war? How will you serve your people if they are all dead? Who will lead them if you are gone?"

Seriousness spread on his face. "You cannot know that my people or I will perish."

Martine argued back, "Two wrongs do not make a right." Equal in their convictions she tried again, "I was not the one who offended you, yet I must pay the price?"

"Someone must," the chief maintained with a stiff face.

"No," Martine returned bluntly. "Your boundaries are set, your mind is stone, and that limits you. How will the scales balance when there is no movement?"

Instantly, the older Indian transformed into his angelic state-of-being. Eminence came from him as his white wings sprung, protruding out of his back. "You are strong in Spirit and they have chosen wisely. Even under these circumstances you do not choose to fight, but defend the quest for enlightened action."

"I don't understand," Martine said with shock in her voice.

"You will," he humbly replied. "You were taken on the innocence of your wedding day—forced to leave your land and your people." The chief stepped closer. "You do not fight me, but challenge my reasoning. You show strength of wisdom. Like a Shaman you saw my soul was too rigid—limiting me to old ways." Looking around to his people he announced, "We give you first decree." Retiring himself on one knee, he gazed up to the skies. Drawn to the magnificent parting clouds, he hailed a winged messenger that descended down to meet them, "Welcome, friend," he said. Taking seven scrolls from the angelic messenger, he thanked the visitor with a noble nod.

Martine had become more attuned to interacting with Native American Spirit guides. In the past they had come in her dreams to impart wisdom and etheric direction, especially in difficult areas where a greater concept could be mastered. She acknowledged the messenger with a slight nod before the guest departed.

Unrolling the first sacred scroll in front of Martine, the Indian instructed her to read the decree aloud.

Breaking the seal, she unrolled the parchment and read,

"Before you wish time was more
Expose how few provoke a war
Truth and justice are divine
Greed and gluttony for the blind
Chart will lead you on our Quest
Your Job will answer and speak of rest."

Apprehensive and amazed by the sudden turn of events, Martine strained her senses to grasp the carefully worded rhyme. "I don't understand."

The regal Indian Spirit opened the hand sown leather pouch. "This may help." Pausing, the Great Spirit approached Martine to gift her with a nugget of gold hanging from a long leather cord. "You will wear element from our mother earth that bears mystical powers throughout eons of time." After placing the sacred necklace around her neck, he dissipated like a vapor.

Awakening early in the morning with the images from her dream penetrated deep in her mind, she quickly reached for her journal and jotted down the pertinent parts she remembered. In the earthly quest for knowledge, our souls are often taken from one extreme to another, for the sole purpose of eventually achieving a higher awareness. Dramatic illnesses, injuries, or experiences have the ability to significantly alter and advance a person more quickly than any lesson learned in a class room. Bringing a concept through from the spiritual to the physical world is a gift that assists the soul's progression.

Though the darkness of the night receded, the memory of such an intense dream would not be forgotten. Minute details, however, could fade within days. Her experience has shown that if she loses aspects of the original dream she can lose the destination.

Chapter 8

Cruising on easy street was always the pattern until Tom and Janice ran out of money. Luckily, their friends had the same dilemma, making theft the logical solution. Bo's connection with an unidentified man provided the opportunity to conveniently rob the victim of a specific treasure. Anything else that was stolen was theirs to fence. Frenzied beginnings from earlier in the evening culminated into the theft of property, and the unexpected murder of two people. Tom's unholy alliance with fellow partners in crime appeared a success, at least until their exuberant highs wore off.

Saul complained first, "We could have gotten more stuff if we had more time."

"Yeah, guess we should have thought about that before we broke in when the owner was home," Bo agreed.

Irritated with the group, Big Eddy shook his head and readied a syringe for his girl Rachel. "I thought no one was going to be home."

"He wasn't supposed to be there," Vic replied. "I thought I saw him leave in his car. Maybe it was someone else."

Janice tried to control her panic, "Did we have to shoot Jake?"

"He was a risk we didn't want to take. Remember?" Rachel spat as she let Eddy shoot the drug into her arm.

"You're such a bitch, Rachel," emotionally immature Janice nitpicked.

"What if they trace him back to us?" Bo fretted.

"They can't," Tom stated. "That's why we torched the place. They'll never ID that ghost. I took his wallet, and we have his vehicle."

Saul lit a cigarette. "Let's look at what's in the trunk."

"No," Tom said sharply. "That's the deal we made. We get the cash and stash, they get the trunk. Vic, you better get going and deliver that trunk to the drop-off. Take Saul and Bo with."

"I'll go too," Eddy said. "No one drives my wheels. Someone needs to make sure these boys get the job done right and ditch Jake's vehicle."

Desensitized from the drug's effects, Rachel drawled, "I'll go too, Eddy."

"No, you won't," Eddy said emphatically. "You're staying here," he added as stood to leave.

"Shit, I hate it when you boss me around," Rachel sulked.

"Get over it," Janice said as she passed a joint to Tom.

"But, we should at least see what we're giving up. It might be full of gold or something better," Rachel tempted the greedy group. "Could be diamonds," she hinted.

Eddy sneered, "Or, something bigger—like a body."

"I don't care," Tom took a drag and held the smoke in. "It's not even heavy enough to be a body—much less gold. Exhaling, he added, "This trunk is so old—it's probably just an antique."

Chapter 9

Martine and Eva hurried to get ready for their return to Morgan's *Desert Run* equestrian horse facility. It had only been five hours since they were on the scene of Morgan's house fire. Ready to resume her daily work routine that began at sunrise—training competition show horses, Eva dressed as usual in her classic skin-tight riding breeches, lightweight V-necked tee, and knee-high black riding boots with silver spurs.

Martine, invited along for moral support and a scheduled trail ride that Eva had had been planning for at least two weeks, wore jeans and her old lace-up riding boots—clearly not looking like the equine professional her daughter was.

"Are you ready, mom?" Eva yelled out from her bathroom. Tying her shoulder-length blonde hair back with a scrunchy she added, "I don't want to be late today." Popping her ponytail out through the opening in the back of her blue baseball cap, she positioned the hat's brim for balance and maximum shade over her fair complexioned face. Eva was always beautiful whether in her formal evening gown, or her riding breeches. After flipping off the bathroom light she headed for the kitchen.

"I'm ready," Martine answered as she poured another cup of coffee in a to-go container. "Didn't really get much sleep." Though she didn't really want to ride a horse today, she did want to be with Eva during this time of uncertainty after the recent fire at the owner Eli Morgan's premier horse facility. It seemed more prudent to be present if more information was shared and became available at the barn, or if there were interviews conducted. Ideally, the police would question everyone. Absorbing what had happened—what they had witnessed, Martine also wanted to know how and why. She added creamer and asked, "Want one too? I'm gonna need this to perk-up."

"Yeah. I guess I probably do," Eva admitted.

#

Driving through the electronic security gate, past outdoor turnouts where lively muscled horses reared, bucked, paced, and whinnied to their friends, Martine scanned the secured compound that prevented even a mouse from entering. She addressed Eva, "So you have an electronic opener to get in here? Is this meant to keep horses in, or people out?"

"Probably both. We all have an opener or the code you punch in on the keypad," Eva said as she swung her truck into a parking space. "My barn is right over there."

Martine was awed by the sophisticated state-of-the-art equine facility set against the McDowell Mountain vistas. Fortunately, the horse operation appeared unaffected by the gruesome fire. Only the home was quarantined off from the numerous stables and riding arenas that constituted the foremost equestrian complex.

Martine grabbed her water bottle and shut the door. "Think anyone is here yet? I can't believe I am."

"You'd be surprised with the time we all get started. Hopefully Sara is already getting the horses ready."

"You'll have to give me a verbal tour. Doubt if there's time to walk around and see everything."

"Right. I haven't even had a chance to tour this whole place. It's like a horse showcase of *Who's Who*."

"I bet it's like a soap opera too," Martine mused.

Eva quipped back, "You mean like, *As the Barn Door Swings*? There are some really gossipy grooms and trainers. There are also valuable stallions and mares—plus champion show horses."

Taking in the sweet smell of hay and clean wood shavings, Martine marveled, "I'm really amazed how big this is. I've never seen a place like it. I can see what an accomplishment it must've been for you to get this position."

"C'mon. Let's see if Sara and the grooms are here."

Stall after stall of the most amazing collection of horse flesh Martine had ever seen lined both sides of the stable that had to be the length of half a football field. Soft muzzles reached out from their caged apartments to meet and greet as Eva and her walked past them.

"Hi, Sara," Eva addressed the brunette average-sized girl that was busy braiding the bottom of a long horse tail. "I knew you'd be here before me."

Bangs flew off her face as the stunned and saddened Sara dropped the black tail and ran up to Eva. "They won't tell us anything. Do you know what happened?" Her eyes filled with tears she couldn't contain. "Do you know where Eli is? Olivia's not even here yet."

"Who's Olivia," Martine inquired.

"That's who we work for," said Eva. "These are all her horses, or her client's horses. We work for her."

"So, all these horses don't belong to Morgan?" Martine looked around, estimating at least fifty horses were in this stable alone.

"No. He has a barn with all his horses, these aren't his." Eva looked back to Sara. "This is my mother, Martine."

"Hi." Sara shook her hand. "I'm so glad you're both here." She wiped her cheeks and forced a smile. "If I forget your name, I'll call ya mom. I feel like I already know you—you look so much alike."

Eva smiled wide. "Sara's a little on the hyper side. The horses and I love her though."

Martine was still processing the extensive horse operation that housed some of the most valuable equine in the industry. "How many horses does Morgan have?" Martine questioned.

Sara chimed in, "He's got lots. You should see the stallions. I went over to make sure Quest was okay."

"You would, Sara. Everyone else is worried about Eli's house and you worry about his baby stallion."

Excited to talk about her favorite horse, Sara relayed her feelings to Martine, "He's so beautiful and bred from the best mare and stallion. They named him after the Norse God Odin, you know—Thor the God of Thunder's dad. Anyway his name is Odin's Quest. We call him Quest. I bring him horse treats every day. I want to be his groom when Julio leaves."

"Oh, Sara," Eva laughed. "You still think they're going to take Julio away. Don't you?"

"Of course," Sara replied—unable to hide her beliefs. "No way does he have a green card. Quest and I are meant to be together."

Martine was suddenly intrigued as she heard Sara rave on and on about a valuable colt named Quest. Her dream from the night before was poignant, yet meant nothing to her when she awoke with the memory of an Indian Spirit who presented her with a message from beyond. Now Martine wanted more information, "Who's the sire?"

Eva answered, "He is a Grand Prix and Olympic dressage champion. He's a one in a million super horse—the most expensive horse on the property."

Sara butted in, "Until Quest. Quest is the only horse that can hop over any fence to graze on the littlest patch of grass. Isn't his name perfect?"

"Whatever, Sara," Eva shook her head recognizing Sara's naïveté when it comes to what really makes a horse notorious and invaluable. Eva took control of her management responsibilities. "We need to get to work if we're gonna take to the trails before it's too hot. If we all exercise two horses now we can do it. Alisha and Kelly should be here in five. I've got two horses you can ride, mom. They're awesome guys."

Martine haltered and led her first horse to the grooming station where she confidently snapped on the cross ties that secured the horse in place by clipping a lead on each side of its halter that stretched snuggly to the two parallel side-partitions. Brushing the large exquisite horse named Bravo was therapeutic and calming for both of them. Bravo was dark bay with four sizable white-socked fetlocks that accented his handsome seventeen-hand stature. "Did you say Bravo was a Warmblood?" Martine asked her daughter.

"He's an imported Dutch Warmblood. He was bred in the Netherlands, and barely missed the scores in his curing inspection to become an Elite Stallion. That's how these horses end up with owners like Olivia. We're training him for dressage and jumping. We'll either show him, or one of her clients will purchase him. We hope we get to keep working with him because he tries so hard and has the biggest heart. He's calm enough that you can even ride him. He just isn't afraid of anything."

"Well, that's my kinda horse," Martine said enthusiastically. Using a step stool, she began combing the black horse mane. Martine watched and listened as the girls busied themselves with a plethora of champion-bred horses. This was like cat-nip for girls that have dreamed of their plastic Breyer horse collections coming to life. Martine knew she had some responsibility in Eva's enthusiastic love of horses. Rich in lore and mythology, she helped Eva with many school papers and projects where the topic could be connected in some way to a horse theme. Eva aced a paper in college when she showed how no one single animal had contributed more to the spread of civilization than the horse. There's no way that teacher saw that coming when the history lesson was *show the migration of a civilization*.

Sara the busybody was now in the grooming stall next to Martine, taking her next horses tail out of its protective sock. "Eva said you know a lot about horses too. I learned so much from her the day I took a lesson that I applied for a job so that I could be here every day. I never had my own horse like she did."

Throwing a saddle blanket on top of the biggest horse she'd ever ridden, Martine laughed, "Well, Sara, did you know that if a horse shows up in your life, it may be time to examine aspects of adventure and freedom within your life? They are very wise clairvoyant animals known for bringing new beginnings or journeys that will teach you how to ride in new directions. They help awaken your abilities and develop your strengths."

"Wow. That's amazing. I did break-up with a loser boyfriend that used up all my money. I moved out of our apartment and moved in here. I was with him for five years and just finally moved out after I came here for a riding lesson." Sara hugged the big horse she was brushing. "I'd live in a stall if they gave my room away—wouldn't I, Diego?" Sara kissed Diego's silky smooth muzzle.

Chapter 10

Police Investigator Ray Siegel presumed he was called to inspect a routine house fire in an area of wealth that rubs up hard against the scenic wilderness of Arizona's McDowell Mountains. A native to fast growing North Scottsdale, a city under the sun—once an isolated oasis in the desert, he assumed no foul play—on his customary day off.

Arriving on the scene at eight in the morning, Investigator Ray gingerly maneuvered his pounding head out of his black SUV. Moving slowly he entered the shell of a building not only with the usual regulation black sunglasses and professional scowl of a wizened arrogant investigator, but he was also storing vodka in his capillaries where he would normally keep blood. Barely functioning from overindulgence in alcohol, the seasoned investigator supposed this was a typical burn that would not require much on a Sunday. Seeing Mark Beary from the Crime Scene Unit kneeling by a pile of debris in what might have been a living room, he hollered, "Hey, Mark. Got anything for me?"

"Not sure," Soft-spoken Mark replied as he stood up and squinted, looking into the sunrise for Ray's form.

Straight backed with the thick neck of a football player, Ray scratched his head in boredom. "Anyone located the owner?"

Mark rubbed his gloved hands together in order to remove residue from handling burnt rubble. "Haven't seen anyone."

"Any bodies?"

"Not yet. Fire Investigator just got here too, and we have to wait for the all clear to go further. He said it's one of the biggest campfires he's seen."

Ray yawned out loud, "Well, looks like I need to track down the owner if you don't have him."

Fire Inspector Don Simmons shouted from the far back of the cindered home, "Hey. I think I found something."

Walking briskly over the charred remains of a once multi-million dollar home, Ray and Mark found the Fire Investigator in moments. "What'd ya find," Ray asked.

Pointing behind a stack of blackened ceiling timbers that were leaning up against something equally dark—more or less, Don theorized, "There's something behind all this wood. There's gotta be something holdin' these beams up—creating a tee-pee. They should've fallen to the ground." Grabbing his ax with both hands he positioned himself to swing hard. "Move back, please."

Mark and Ray backed out of the way and Don hacked at the skeletonized remains of the once formable supporting shafts that held a tiled roof. The scorched timbers began to crumble to the ground exposing a door to a room.

"Wow," Mark said. "What am I looking at?"

"Think we got us an airtight room," Don replied. Maneuvering the heap of wreckage to find a way to push the door open, Don handled the charcoal-carnage like a husky lumberjack. "Here we go—I'm goin' in," he grunted as he pushed the heavy door to gain access.

Once inside he called out, "All clear."

Ray entered first with Mark behind him. "Are you getting this?"

"You bet," he answered back as his camera clicked a series of photographs.

Ray queried the Fire Investigator, "How'd this room stay intact? Everything else is demolished."

"Door closed, one shut window, small room—basically air tight. No oxygen. Fire had nothing to fuel it—couldn't spread in here," Don explained. "The fighters put the flames out before a slow burn got this."

"So, we know the door was closed not locked—creating an air-tight room and the fire couldn't attack this space from the inside," Ray summarized.

"Yep," Don returned. "Let's see what's in here."

Ray removed his sunglasses for a better examination of the only surviving room. "This was the office," he announced. Drawn to the far wall that was slightly out of alignment, he continued, "What do we have here?" Ray dragged the paneled wall section towards him until it gave, exposing another more secured door. "Get this, Mark."

Don reported on the center of the room where he was examining the chair that was partially barbequed, "We got solvent here. There definitely was a fire started in this room."

"This lock has been opened," Ray surmised. "Looks like it operated with a combination. Need some help here, Don."

Don joined Ray and helped tug on the door till it was ajar. "Let me go first," Don offered. Don squeezed through the small opening into the darkness of a hidden safe room. Only the light strapped to his hardhat revealed the contents inside. Stumbling backwards he shook his head sadly. "Better call the body snatchers. You've got two in here."

Ray sobered-up with the unexpected bleak news. Assuming nothing was discovered the night before, he was unprepared physically and mentally to be assigned a double death. Actively indulging in Wade's and Jolene's wedding celebration the night before left the forty-nine year old divorced detective unprepared to undertake a serious crime scene.

Ray and Mark peered inside the room that contained two corpses.

"Better photo this place quick," Ray ordered Mark.

"You got it," he said.

Ray engaged his phone, "I'll call it in, Mark, start canvassing the employees and find someone in charge as soon as you can."

Mark nodded. "Let me get my notebook." Looking around at the sparse number of folks on the property, except for a few Mexicans moseying around a barn Mark speculated, "This won't take long if I don't find someone that speaks English."

Ray called-in for reinforcements, "I need a coroner, lights, and forensics here." Ray stood outside his car scanning for proof of life. "Better pull up everything you got on this place and the owner. Mark and I are starting interviews here. Oh, and have someone bring coffee."

Desk Sergeant Garcia replied, "I could, or you could do it yourself."

Irked, Ray added, "And keep this under wraps with dispatch. I don't want all the news reporters in Arizona to hear about this on their scanners and show up for a story."

Garcia replied sarcastically, "That's what crime scene tape is for. Better get it up."

"Humor is always welcomed, Garcia. Feel free to keep trying." Ray dejectedly stayed on point, "Just get on it."

Mark looked pissed. "Did he blow you off?"

"You bet," Ray said in disgust.

"What a grouch," Mark vented as he walked away. "I'd like to wrap him up in caution tape like a burrito and feed him to the media. That guy has a chip on his shoulder since he landed a desk job."

Chapter 11

Max peddled an old ten speed bike up to his apartment patio, parked it, unlocked the sliding glass door and nonchalantly headed towards the kitchen for a bowl of cereal. Taking his milk-drenched meal back to his living room sofa, he grabbed the TV remote and turned on the local morning news before plunging his spoon into the floating Fruit Loops.

Exhausted from working the eight-hour evening shift as grill-master for at least two-hundred hungry customers always gave him an appetite, but not until he was secreted away in the privacy of his own home—decompressing from the demands of the outside world.

News cameras were broadcasting footage of the *Desert Run* owner's house fire. Fire crews captured the live blaze that firefighters battled into the late morning hours. It was visibly apparent that the home was destroyed inside.

Detailing the disaster from the scene, the popular investigative reporter forecasted the possible outcome, "Looks like firemen were never able to enter the building when they arrived. The fire was too hot and widespread to allow for any rescue. It is not known at this time if anyone was inside, but if there were the fire and smoke has probably overcome them. Attempts to locate the owner are ongoing. More later on this story. Back to you, Jim."

With his cheeks bloating from the cereal, Max shook his head in sadness as he fired-up his computer. It was always difficult to comprehend the horrendous loss people endured while he comfortably lived his life at a marginal pace. It's all relative, he thought. The less you have the less you probably have to lose or deal with. The more you have the more you have to lose or put-up with. Divorced twelve years earlier from his high school sweetheart, Max found he did like simple better. Some people live to work, Max worked to live.

Logged into his favorite chat room to catch-up with the controversial debaters that were always lobbying their theories, he noticed a recent post by a new blogger—*U.R.Wrong*. A rousing round of chat exchanges on the topic of the sinking Titanic must have lured in a fresh catch for the serious and intense opinions expressed by the regulars that used this site. Max scanned quickly through the dialogue-tread to grasp the gist of the discussion. "What?" Max exclaimed out loud. "I don't care if this guy is in the Air Force." He quickly joined in the conversation using his screen name *Supermax*.

Supermax says: "You don't appear to believe that there could possibly be a cover-up regarding the Titanic? Is that correct, *U.R.Wrong*?"

U.R.Wrong says: "Hell no."

Supermax says: "Okay then. Answer this, if you had two identical space shuttles that were each valued at two billion dollars, and they were built side by side in a special hanger you owned, would you consider switching them around if it meant saving your business?" *Supermax* posed a scenario that the opinionated guest could relate to.

U.R.Wrong says: "How could that save my business?"

Supermax says: "Well, your first shuttle, called Olympic was finished and went to work making a lot of money transporting people and goods to the space station, but it got in a wreck with a small NASA transport shuttle. Your Olympic was seriously compromised and couldn't pass flight tests after you spend months repairing it. You also found out the repairs you made failed, and new ones would be horrendously more expensive, and the courts found your Olympic was at fault making you responsible for NASA's broken shuttle. Your two billion dollar space-vessel was now three billion dollars in losses to your business, and the insurance company

'Lord's of London' rejected the insurance claim because the courts found you guilty—right or wrong, they screwed you. So, without the ability to keep the Olympic working you were now losing almost all your income. You can't afford the three billion dollar loss—and two thousand employees will be laid off."

U.R.Wrong says: "So, you think that I would switch those shuttles around?"

Supermax says: "Yep I do."

U.R.Wrong says: "Why?"

Supermax says: "Because your other shuttle the Titanic is weeks away from being complete, and is the twin sister to the Olympic. The Titanic is insured for two billion and scheduled to fly on time. If the switch is made over one of the weekends when the two shuttles are side by side no one but a corrupt official and some paid-off management would ever no. Their jobs actually depend on it happening. Now all you need to do is make sure the permanently damaged shuttle runs into enough trouble—about twelve thousand miles away—and that a couple of transport shuttles are nearby to rescue passengers before the fire and damage you inflict by hitting a space object blow the thing up."

U.R.Wrong says: "You really do believe the Titanic was sunk deliberately, don't you?"

Supermax says: "Yes. It was still a monumental disaster because the rescue part of the plan got really messed up. And the boat did sink way to fast due to something else they hadn't anticipated. They did intend for it to go to the bottom, but long after everyone was safely saved."

U.R.Wrong says: "What makes you believe this so strongly?"

Supermax says: "The Titanic was already insured, but a week before its first voyage the insurance was increase beyond the cost of its value. The ship California was sent on the same course ahead of time with no passengers, and stopped in the water for two days—probably waiting for the Titanic to flounder. The Titanic ignored every ships warning about the icebergs. Many of the passengers cancelled their trip within a week of departure, including the owner, J.P. Morgan."

U.R.Wrong says: "What else did they not anticipate? You said the boat sank too fast because of something else."

Supermax says: "The steel. They used inferior iron. It became brittle in the twenty-eight degree water. The impact to the iceberg would not have caused enough damage, except the rivets and plates were brittle, thus popping and separating. Doesn't appear they ever found the big gash they suspected."

U.R.Wrong says: "You need to prove that, Max."

Supermax says: "How 'bout you prove me wrong, U.R.Wrong."

U.R.Wrong says: "Shit, man. I'm gonna check your facts and get back to you."

Supermax says: "You do that. Some people wouldn't know the truth if it was dancing in front of them though," Max poked back aggressively. "But if you do figure it out, then I'll tell you about the Lusitania."

U.R.Wrong says: "How's that? You work on a cruise ship?"

Supermax says: "Nope—I'm landlocked at Al's greasy diner in Arizona."

Max loved lively discussions that he took control of and looked forward to a bitter challenge on almost any topic.

Chapter 12

An unfamiliar feeling spread throughout *Desert Run* as the day progressed. Only yesterday the formidable facility was a stunning panorama of athletic horses practicing their moves in the various arenas and round pens that peppered the grounds. Now the horse property is a hot spot of mystery and intrigue.

Martine and Eva were actively engaged in conditioning two horses inside a huge covered arena when Olivia finally arrived on the property. Olivia, the owner and trainer to a plethora of horses came into the arena and observed the workout for a moment.

"Eva, move over to the right rail and canter two ten meter circles before you come down the diagonal with flying changes every three strides," Olivia instructed. "Stay on the right lead to the far right corner and establish your bend for a right half-pass. We've gotta practice this to build up his balance and strength, his weakness is on his right hind."

"Hi, Olivia," Eva said loudly as she swept by the owner at an extended trot. Sitting deep into her saddle she collected and then transitioned her horse to the right lead canter departure.

"Your gaits are good, he's looking light on the forehand, sit deeper for more drive in your ten meters," Olivia tutored. As Eva rounded the far corner of the arena Olivia projected louder, "Keep the collection and balance you've established."

Eva rounded her second small circle and headed down the center of the generous oblong arena. "Ya, boy!" Eva urged her giant steed. The horse and rider looked as one being—Eva effortless and poised as the horse gathered and heightened his gait. Changing his front right lead into the left, a maneuver that looked like skipping, turned her dark bay horse into a four-legged dancer. Eva continued alternating the horse's leads, creating the effect of a springing ballet performance. Upon reaching the end of the arena, they rounded the corner and cantered in a sideways sweeping bend.

"Excellent," Olivia praised. "Now transition to slow trot and then change rein and half-pass left."

Martine stopped loping her horse around and dismounted next to Olivia. "Hi, I'm Eva's mother, Martine."

"I'm glad to meet you," Olivia replied as she studied Eva's half passes. "Repeat it again, Eva, half pass right and when he loses his bend do a five meter circle and then back to half pass. Let's finish on a good note with his most difficult maneuver."

Olivia's tall toned-frame and authoritive voice gave her a commanding presence. Visibly focused on Eva's workout her tanned, weathered face showed driven dedication to her sport. "Eva, I see improvement," Olivia said encouragingly. "This week it's two for one. Two routines on the right lead for each one on the left. He is definitely looking more balanced as we strengthen that right."

"I'm sorry about the fire." Martine started following Olivia out of the arena. "Eva is on cloud nine working for you, she's never trained with an Olympian, or this caliber of horses."

"Thank you. We have some great talent ready to compete."

"I've met some of them," Martine replied as she led her horse into the long stable.

Crime Scene Unit Investigator Mark was inside talking to Sara when Olivia, Eva, and Martine arrived with the two horses.

Sara took Eva's horse to the wash stall, "This is Mark. He has questions," Sara smiled bravely at Eva and cross-tied the horse.

"Good afternoon. I'm looking for any information that might help us in this investigation. Which one is Olivia?"

Olivia answered, "I am."

"Good." Mark opened his small notebook to a fresh page. "I just have some standard questions, like how long you've known Mr. Morgan."

"I've known him for over ten years. Why do you ask?"

"Did he have any enemies?"

"I don't think so." Olivia was caught off guard. "Is everything okay?"

"Did you see anyone or anything suspicious lately?"

"No. Why are you asking me these questions?"

Mark kept firing routine questions, "Any girlfriends?"

Olivia paused, "I suppose so."

"Were you one of his girlfriends?"

"No."

"Can I get some names?"

Olivia interrupted, "Is Eli alright?"

"Not sure," Mark replied dryly. "We haven't verified if he's one of the victims."

Olivia gasped. "What?" Visibly flustered she added, "Victims? Who's hurt? Eli wasn't supposed to be home yesterday."

"It seems that was the consensus until we discovered a body matching his description. We're gonna need someone to ID the body for us."

"Body? He's dead?" Olivia stammered. "Do you need my help?"

"I'll need a statement. Maybe some names of acquaintances. Like business associates and female friends?"

"Right. I'll have to think about it for a minute. I don't know how serious any of these girls were, but he used to spend time with Lana Marsh. I haven't seen her for awhile. There was a girl after that. I think her name was . . ."

"Take your time. Let's have you ID the body first."

Olivia left with Mark leaving Eva, Sara and Martine to ponder the disaster.

# # #

Olivia returned with a shocked expression. "This is unbelievable."

"It was him. Looks like he was brutally murdered with a knife. They won't tell me anything—but I saw another body they asked me to identify."

"What?" Eva burst. "Who was it?"

"No idea. Never saw this guy before."

"I'm calling my sister." Eva speed-dialed Alexa.

Chapter 13

Ray briefed the crime scene techs when they arrived at Morgan's, "We've seen this movie before; robbery, murder, and cover-up. Need a body ID'd fast. Don't think we need to look further to find owner. This routine house fire became a murder scene less than an hour ago. Okay, let's get to work people."

By the end of the day plenty of material evidence had been documented and collect for the double murder at a private, mostly equestrian, community that had never had one before. Scottsdale's overall crime rate was so low that the average of five murders a year meant there wasn't a lot of time dedicated to investigating homicide cases.

Alexa and Wade's bother Dylan Harding, a police officer, stopped by the department to catch up with the investigation on the fire they were a witness to the night before. After a perfect day four-wheeling around the Saguaro Lake area they returned early after receiving Eva's alarming news about the double homicide.

Dylan located Ray after learning he was the detective in charge of the incident. Finding him diligently wrapping up his report for the day, Dylan and Alexa plunked down on the two chairs that barely fit in the small office space.

"Hey, Ray," Dylan greeted the detective cheerfully. "How's it going? Did you get stuck working all day?"

Distracted by the tragic complexities and succumbing to the extreme fatigue associated with a long day at the crime scene left Ray unreactive. His annoyed expression spoke volumes—his comeback matched it in briefness, "Yeah, you should try it."

"Do you know what I heard today?"

"No, Dylan. Do you want me to guess, or do you really not know what you heard today?" Ray's aggravated robotic-voice droned.

Dylan chuckled nervously, "Rumor is you boys found bodies."

"Yep. Got two."

Dylan edged closer. "So, who do we have for victims?"

"Am I working this case? Or, did they give it to one of the Hardy Boys?" Ray satirically returned.

"Oh, no you are. Alexa and I were at Saguaro all day and her younger sister Eva works there. Alexa's with the FBI—remember?"

"Yes," Ray said coolly. "I was at the same party you were."

"Who were they?" Dylan asked matter-of-factly.

Ray's boredom with the underlings sounded in his voice, "Morgan, the owner."

"If you ID'd the first victim as Morgan, who's the other guy?"

"No idea yet. Nothing on him but the knife he used to kill Morgan."

"Have you run prints?" Dylan asked.

"Yep. No hit."

"Really."

"So far he's a ghost."

"I don't believe in ghosts," Alexa injected. "I can't believe you don't have enough to ID him when you got his body."

"Is that so?" Overly-macho Ray sounded indignant.

"Bet I can get you a name," she stated confidently.

"Don't worry, we'll get a name," Ray replied cynically.

"Not if you're waiting for him to post something on Facebook. Show me what you got and let me try."

Ray laced his fingers behind his head and leaned back in his chair. "I suppose you think because you're with the FBI you can do my job better?" Ray's cell phone rang, which he instinctively retrieved from his pocket. Checking to see who the caller was he proceeded to excuse himself, "Yeah, I need to take this—it's real important." Stepping to the side he flagrantly greeted the caller, "Gemma, thanks for the great time last night. We need to get together soon. How 'bout *Finley's* in Old Scottsdale?" Ray paused for Gemma's reply. "Great. See ya in a few."

Alexa opened her eyes wide at Dylan and whispered, "Is he for real?"

"Oh yeah," Dylan chuckled. "Ray's a real charmer, unless you have to work with him, and happen to be a girl."

Alexa challenged Ray as he terminated his call, "Show me what you got on this guy you haven't ID'd. Let's see who finds him first. We'll play for beers at your sports bar."

Competitive like a gladiator and unable to resist the words *sports* and *bar*, Ray caved, "Fine. Here's what we got." He flipped open the file with crime scene evidence and spun it around to Alexa. "Now you know what he looks like. Here's his prints, and description of his belongings. DNA won't be back for weeks. See, I told you it's a bust—nothing to go on till the DNA comes back."

"What's this," Alexa pried.

"The only thing in his pocket was a map. And the map was to the same house he was murdered in," Ray said as he glared at Alexa mockingly.

"All right," Alexa said as she held up the evidence that was carefully preserved in a plastic sleeve. "I'll need a copy of this, his prints, and a photo."

"Okay, FBI," Ray said as he pointed to the copier. "And now that we're done it's time for me to say goodbye." In his dismissal, he added, "Feels like it's gonna be a long goodbye," Rays voice faded as he walked away.

Alexa glanced at Dylan and shook her head. "That guy has sensitivity issues."

Dylan laughed his reply, "Yeah he does. There's definitely a chip on his shoulder, and I don't mean poker chip. He's not a bluffer. Say's exactly what he wants—when he wants."

More determined than ever to prove Ray wrong about her and the FBI, the tomboy in her fumed, "Let's get this done so I can get started. I've got work to do."

"What?" Dylan said dejectedly.

Chapter 14

Martine's cell phone rang louder than the low tones coming out of the kitchen TV. Home alone at Jolene's after a trying day at *Desert Run* left her tired and complacent. Deep in thought about the rapid turn-of-events since she arrived in Arizona only three days ago for her sister's grandeous wedding—that was also meant to serve as her long awaited vacation—left her confused and numb. Needing mind-rest and food, she threw her purse on the counter and opened the refrigerator.

Startled back to reality by the nagging ringtone coming from her jeans, Martine immediately grabbled for the phone that was stuffed tight in her pocket. "Hey, Alexa, how ya doin'?"

"I got something interesting regarding the fire where Eva works. What're you doin' right now?"

"Absolutely nothing. You're not supposed to be working to-day though. You were going four-wheeling with Wade's brother. Weren't you?"

"I did. But, when I got back we checked-in with the police and found they hadn't been able to ID one of the victim's. They let me try, and I got a lead to work with. I need Jolene's computer though. I'll be there in a minute."

Martine heard the phone call drop. Sensing her mild-mannered daughter was extremely electrified about something to do with work—she was relieved that it didn't have to do with the hand-some Dylan Harding.

"Let's feed you guys now," Martine said to the line-up of well behaved animals.

Honey, the Pomeranian, spun excitedly in tight circles expressing total agreement and the Border Collies Pinto and Tonto sat down maturely beside her. As she measured out the food for each pet she continued to talk to them like small children, "Can I get a smile?" She coaxed the Border Collies.

Pinto and Tonto both wagged their tails eagerly and grinned wide—a silent request for food. Pinto's smile was so big and perfect you could see all his teeth. Tonto's smile was crooked which actually made him appear sinister if you didn't know he was a lovable, intelligent, and gentle companion. Martine set all the bowls down on the floor.

"There you go. Maybe we'll take you for a short walk."

Hearing the doorbell chime, Martine went to greet Alexa, "Have you eaten?"

"No. Not since lunch."

"Do you want me to make us something? Can you stay for awhile?"

"Sure," Alexa answered as she switched on Jolene's computer.

Martine walked back to the kitchen to find something simple to make for dinner. "What're you looking for?" she asked.

"I think I saw Jolene use this 'app' on her computer when we were getting directions to Lake Powell."

"Uh-huh," Martine said absentmindedly as she yanked a frozen pizza out from its icy compartment. "You're going to Lake Powell?"

"No. I think the victim got his map and directions from the same 'app' Jolene used."

"Oh," Martine replied as she adjusted the oven's temperature. Walking back over to Alexa for a clearer understanding, she inquired, "How's this gonna help?"

"I got an idea," Alexa returned, "and a bet going on."

Martine spouted loudly, "I knew it. Someone has told you it can't be done, and there you go proving them wrong."

"That's not true," Alexa argued vehemently.

"The heck it ain't. It isn't any different than when we told you that you couldn't go to a kegger when you were thirteen and you snuck out your window anyways. Or, when we told you not to take the car until you had a driver's license, and you went and got a fake ID. Or, when you couldn't get in the college you wanted and you wrote the Dean a twenty page essay that gained you admission. So, who are you defying this time? Not poor Dylan I hope."

"No it's not Dylan. It's the investigator Ray. He's got to be the most vain and arrogant man I've ever met."

"Wow, he really got under your skin. How'd this happen?"

"He's got this whole 'Men-in-Black' thing going on. He also doesn't think the FBI can help, and certainly not a female. He's just like dad's old friend Dennis." Alexa scrolled down the list of programs as she chattered away, "So, he said they didn't have enough to ID the second guy until DNA comes back. I mean he tried to brush me off like a fly."

Martine studied her daughter. "You say he's like your dad's chauvinist friend Dennis?"

"Yes," Alexa returned bluntly. "He's got a big head to prove it."

"Big like Easter Island?" Martine tried to humor her agitated daughter.

Alexa eyed her mother sarcastically, holding in the urge to laugh at her joke. "Yeah—that big."

Martine comprehended the complex relationships that always arise when new ideas meet old ones. "Check the programs on her desktop first," she said over her shoulder as she headed to the oven that was ready for her pizza.

"Right. They're at least titled here," she mumbled. This might be it . . . ChartQuest." After opening the program she entered and searched directions from her apartment to Jolene's house and waited for the data to display. "This is it." She held up the evidence they found from inside the man's pocket—comparing the details. "Now I just need some contact information from the ChartQuest home page," she said under her breath. "Hey get this, mom, ChartQuest just became the newest major mapping site to embrace open-source mapping. It says it recently launched a new site separate from its main site."

Returning from the kitchen, Martine viewed the site with Alexa. "This might be easier than you thought. Morgan's place is such a remote location—not a regular, or populated place of business for shoppers, it might be easy to track the user since ChartQuest was newly launched and unfamiliar to most citizens."

"Exactly," Alexa affirmed with a grin. "If they won't search their records for the users requesting that address, I'll get a subpoena—with Mahoney's help of course."

"Of course," Martine said factiously.

"I might need your help," Alexa turned to Martine and squinted in chagrin.

"Me?"

Alexa's tone had a scolding edge, "Yes. Jolene's not here and someone needs to talk to Chief Mahoney about this. You know that's what you would do for Jolene."

Martine knew she was referring to a complicated case she had helped Jolene with a few years ago. "That was different."

"Not so," Alexa stood her ground. "What would you do if you had this information?"

"What did you say the name of this 'app' is?"

"ChartQuest." Alexa pointed to the computer page that she had printed out.

"Chart…Quest," Martine mumbled—having a psychic revelation.

"I had a dream last night that had something to do with *Chart the Quest*. Today I heard about an important colt named Quest. Is this all coincident?" She mused out loud.

The color rose higher on Alexa's crimson cheeks. "Not a chance," she proclaimed with excitement. "Tell me about the dream."

Chapter 15

The moon rose full before Alexa left to go home and Martine was able to retire for the night. Without much thought, she fought to get out of her tight blue jeans and climbed into bed with an entourage of animals all jockeying for their position near her. With Jolene and Wade away on their honeymoon she became the surrogate pack leader responsible for the lively Pomeranian Honey, the white cat Sugar, and two Border Collies Pinto and Tonto. After hoisting Honey on the bed, and letting Sugar jump up to cuddle herself next to her buddy Honey, she plopped in bed herself for a much anticipated night of rest. With the lights out and the Border Collies sleeping on the floor next to her, sleep fell fast—allowing her physical form to pass through the lower vibrational dimensions that created the dense ether around the planet. Reaching to a higher realm allowed for expanded awareness and travel.

Shrouded in the darkness of time after passing through a gateway into an astral world of shadows, deception, and destructive energies, Martine emerged within the infantry of a civil war. Turning to the captain in charge she listened intently to his orders.

"Start shooting when you're told. Keep firing till I say stop," he shouted haughtily to his regiment.

Infused awareness of the situation caught her up to the harsh demands of fighting during the American Civil War. Few soldiers remained in this garrison due to crippling circumstances associated with, war casualties, disease, and injury. Human loss was staggering in this war compared to all the other wars fought by American soldiers.

Initially Martine conformed to the notion of accepting her duty as a Union soldier, to perform acts of violence and murder, but quickly she felt outraged against the barbarism. When the shooting began she witnessed terror, carnage, dying, suffering and pleading like she had never known before. Terrifying images of injuries caused, wounds sustained, and lives lost, overwhelmed her. Consumed with grief she began sobbing uncontrollably until an Angel Spirit pulled her away and back through the tunnel of time, where she found herself inside a private office, viewing Lincoln's presidential agony.

Invisible to the people she was observing gave her complete anonymity and accesses to overhear an otherwise secretive exchange between two heads-of-state. President Abraham Lincoln, the 16th president of the United States—recently elected as president—is already frenzied with angst and distress. The unmistakable profile of President Abraham Lincoln was consumed with malaise over the financial burdens brought on by the realities of an unexpected civil war. Lincoln was desperately weighing the options available to fund the expense of fighting the confederate states that had succeeded from the United States of America—forcing a war upon the nation when the Confederates fought at Fort Sumter and took it by force.

Realizing she was witnessing a rapid sequence of events, Martine interiorly knew her position was one of accepting knowledge that could be gleamed by the actual experience had she been there and faced the calamities and limitations the highest ranked individuals in the country were themselves left with.

"Sir," a grim faced man addressed Lincoln. "I find our financial resources are an epic disaster."

Lincoln spoke softly, "I appointed you, Salmon Chase, to be Secretary of the Treasury because you are an honest man with conservative views. We have an urgent state of affairs."

"Yes, Mr. President," tall straight-backed Chase replied. "But at the moment the bankers will not approve the pending loan unless we have a peace policy." Salmon cleared his throat nervously. "The bids are very high for the loan you seek. The interest the banks demand is nearly forty percent. We cannot support a war without their funds." He shook his head sadly.

"We can't pay the loan back with interest rates like that," Lincoln said wearily. "What do we have in the Treasury now?" Lincoln asked. "Our soldiers need better firepower—they are being brutalized."

"The Treasury is a tangled mismanaged mess," Salmon reported. "The one thing I can't find is money."

"We need guns, canons, ships, tents, uniforms, horses and provisions for 20,000 men. Where are you going to get the funds, Treasury Secretary Chase?" Lincoln faced-off in desperation with the only man he had trusted.

"I don't know."

Lincoln paced the room. "Then get the money from the European Banks. They don't control us, and won't control the outcome of our cause."

Prim and proper Chase lowered his head slightly. "The English market is essentially closed to the Union. They most likely don't want either side to win."

"Yes. I suppose that is true. Who then?"

Solemn faced, Secretary Chase stepped dutifully up to President Lincoln. "If the banks can loan money, why can't we?" Chase momentarily paused. "They charge the rates they want and are nothing more than 'money changers' in business for themselves. They will bankrupt the country with their rates and fees."

Lincoln stroked his infamous beard. "I see."

"We can't afford not to do this, Mr. President. This is an emergency." Once a pompous lawyer, Salmon Chase continued, "We will create our own 'Bonds' and 'Treasury Notes,' but we will sell them to Wall Street investors like the banks do—and the people. Why should they not make an investment and benefit from the loans like the banks do? Why do the banks always win in war?"

"You're right," Lincoln said as he thoughtfully pondered the idea. "There is money enough in the loyal North and West to pay for suppressing this wicked rebellion. The people will be willing to loan it to their Government."

"You can find the way to their hearts, Mr. President."

"Yes. I should. If I can't have their support, we should resign and give place to those who can. We are going to the people."

"Mr. President, I have supreme confidence in the people. The enemy underestimates your resolve."

Lincoln bowed his head in grief. "I have two great enemies, the Southern rebels in front of me, and the financial mongers in the rear. Of the two, the one in my rear is my greatest foe."

Shooting like a star an angelic traveler plucked Martine way from seeing anymore of President Lincoln's exchange with the Secretary of Treasury. Materializing atop the Dragoon Mountains, Martine was once again a visitor to the Indian Spirit Chief she encountered the previous night. Gesturing his instructions, he handed her another scroll to be spoken aloud.

"History need not repeat the tale
The lessons that it taught
Evil deeds never fail
When treaties are for naught
Pledge of peace that makes one weak
Gives rise to another beast
Life is not a chore ignored
With death no longer sought
Grasp and learn what few explore
Before the war is fought."

Martine awoke to the soft vibrations of Sugar the cat, which was poised like a sphinx across her stomach. After briefly recalling the experience, she reached for her journal and wrote feverishly.

Chapter 16

Alexa was already at work in her cubicle located within the forensics department. Due to the time change from Arizona to Pennsylvania, she anxiously gulped coffee, waiting for ChartQuest employees to return her voicemail message that she left on their phone before even arriving at work.

Younger than anyone else in the Arizona FBI branch meant she was the least experienced who had the most to prove. Alexa had been briefed by her aunt Jolene about how difficult that could make her first few years. Being young and female made teasing her irresistible to some of the seasoned agents, which they demonstrated during her first week.

When a desperate caller reported that there was illegal actively going on in her backyard, Alexa was the agent dispatched to take the report. When she arrived at the home located south of Tucson, a hysterically-enraged old woman greeted her.

Upon inspection of the woman's property, Alexa quickly discerned that the complaint had nothing to do with illegal aliens or drug trafficking. The women's abandoned barn had a herd of Javelinas, described as medium-sized animals that look similar to a wild boar—that were trapped inside. Due to the animal's very poor eyesight they appear to be aggressive when merely trying to escape a noise or threat. Also known as bold looters, they will go anywhere and get into anything that provides a meal.

With the frenzied woman ranting at Alexa, "What are you gonna do about this?" She had no choice but to document and photograph the incident before luring the Javelinas out of the building with table scraps she got from the woman's garbage.

After Alexa successfully extracted all fifteen Javelinas from the building, she secured the door and explained to the woman, that if she continued to leave the door open with any source of food inside the dwelling—the animals would return every day. She recommended a better place to store her birdseed.

Naturally, when she returned to the office, all the veteran agents were eagerly awaiting her reaction to the bogus complaint they had pawned off on her.

At eight o'clock sharp her direct line rang. "Alexa, here."

"Good morning a soft voice greeted her. This is Maggie. I'm returning your call. Are you really with the FBI?"

"Yes I am," Alexa confirmed. "Do you want my identification number?"

"Well that depends. How can I assist you?"

"I have secured a map from your new ChartQuest site that links an individual to a recent crime. I doubt anyone else would have been searching for this address since your site went live within the last few weeks, and this homicide happened within the last forty-eight hours." Alexa sipped her coffee and continued, "If you could search your records for the IP address of the computer accessing these driving directions you will be helping us immensely."

"Well, I can say we've never had a request like this. Give me the address and let me speak with our techs. I can call you back after I check with them."

"Great, Maggie. If they can help, I'd like all the other address searches that originated from this user, and don't forget the IP address." Alexa dictated all the information she had to Maggie.

"Okay. I can't promise anything. I'm just the office manager."

Alexa hung-up the phone and called her mother—assuming she was already up drinking coffee.

"Mom, I've made contact with ChartQuest. They're going to possibly use their IT techniques to search for the information I requested. I'll hear back from them later. Hope they agree to help without complicated subpoenas."

"That's great."

"Anything new with you?"

"Just another interesting dream."

"I've got time. Tell me about it."

Martine recounted the events in the dream that concluded in a rhymed decree that she had written in her journal.

"I don't understand what that can possibly mean in relation to Eli Morgan's murder. Your dream was about civil war money problems. Is that right?"

"Exactly. But I believe from experience the dream is about a concept, and the decree is about the clue."

"Read the decree again."

Martine carefully reread the rhyme. "I think it has more to do about treaties which are an agreement for peace. Not all treaties work well for both sides.

"Is there a treaty that was broken that can explain any of this?"

"I don't see how I would ever be able to figure that out. There've been thousands of treaties throughout history." Martine thought hard about the Indians in her first dream. "And, probably hundreds of treaties made during the American Indian war era." Martine sighed. "But, based on what I experienced from my dreams, those Native American Indians were Apaches from the American Southwest. The Dragoon Mountains is where Cochise and his tribe hid out. It was their impregnable fortress for many years." Martine had another recollection. "In the first dream I was brought to the Dragoon Mountains which are a range of mountains located in Cochise County, Arizona. I should've made the connection then."

"I really don't see what this has to do with those mountains," Alexa sounded disinterested.

It dawned on Martine that the Indian that reportedly was never photographed may be the Indian appearing to her in her dreams. "Alexa, I think we focus on treaties and events surrounding Cochise. He is one of the best-known Apache leaders because of his prominence and fierceness as a warrior. He is remembered for his diplomacy because of his willingness to negotiate and find peace with the American leaders."

"What? I thought he was a savage. I thought he murdered thousands of pioneers."

"Yeah, he probably did." Martine pulled Wikipedia's definition of the famous Tribal Chief. Scanning the brief biography jogged her memory, and her legal training that studied the ramifications of treaties. Considered aborigines and inferior to the European colonists that settled our country, Martine quickly remembered the complicated history that defined the American Indian warrior made famous in history books and museums. Seeing the location of a notable treaty consummated between Cochise and Brigadier General Oliver Howard and Thomas Jeffords, Martine exclaimed, "Oh my, I vaguely recall the little know details of an incident that sparked ten or twelve years of Indian raids and massacres." Reading further she explained, "In 1861 the famous 'Bascom Affair' triggered an end to peace treaties that had been established between the US government and the Apache tribes."

Alexa interrupted, "What was the Bascom Affair?"

"There was a single incident, which occurred in a remote corner of Arizona in 1861. A settler's ranch had been attacked, his cattle run off and his son kidnapped by Indian raiders. The settler blamed it on Cochise, who was one of the Apache leaders. He was probably the most known in that region. But, there were others that were rogue and wandering. The problem was there were many different Apache tribes, and it could have been any of them. Anyways, George Bascom invited Cochise to meet on neutral ground at a place known as Apache Pass. Lieutenant George Bascom, a young and impulsive West Point graduate betrayed Cochise. When Cochise arrived expecting a diplomatic parley he was met with a shocking breach of frontier protocol. Bascom seized Cochise's family and killed one of his companions, though Cochise himself managed to escape."

"Then what happened?"

"The incident led to more than a decade of warfare between Cochise and the US Army. Some say the numbers involved were never large, usually involving just a few dozen fighters on either side, and others say it was thousands. Regardless, the violence was often horrific. Victims of the Apaches were atrociously tortured. One group of hapless teamsters were tied on wagon wheels and roasted alive. Apaches caught by the Army were sometimes lynched, while Indian camps inhabited by women and children were treated as legitimate military targets. Both sides fought brutally."

"That's so gross."

"The repercussions were heinous when Cochise was betrayed. Being blamed and arrested for a crime he most likely didn't commit sparked an Indian uprising. He literally went on the war path."

"That's interesting, but what does it have to do with our investigation?"

"Maybe a historical agreement is connected somehow to your Morgan case. I also know the Apaches went from peaceful terms with us to hatred and distrust of Americans during that ten year siege. It was a historical blunder that movies were made from. I think I just realized which Indian may be guiding me."

"Cochise?" Alexa remarked. "What happened to Cochise?"

"Well, I'm not sure, but the new treaty was finally executed in 1872 at a secret location in the Dragoon Mountains of Arizona. After he signed the permanent peace treaty with General Howard and the Apaches, he retired to the Chiricahua Reservation in Arizona. He died about two years later.

Alexa summarized, "Indians, treaties, war, history, armies, and betrayal. This should not be difficult," she said sarcastically.

Chapter 17

Sunday faded into Monday as the morning dawn broadcasted another day. Jubilation of her sister's wedding was now a memory after the souring effects of fire and death. It was clearly apparent to Martine that Eva was fighting the feelings of panic and uncertainty regarding the future plans of a famous and established horse operation that she loved and felt privileged to be associated with.

Silence was broken when they entered the stable and encountered an angry exchange between Olivia and Adam Keen, *Desert Run's* facilities manager. Startled out of their solitude, they overheard an argument in process.

"You can't shut this down, Adam," Olivia's reddened face squared off with him.

Adam shook his head in disagreement. "Without Eli around there is no one with authority to conduct financial transactions."

Olivia's voice quivered, "I thought that was your job, Adam." She wiped sweat forming on her forehead. "You've acted like *you* own this place since you arrived. Now do something about this."

"There's nothing I can do," he returned coldly.

"Is that it, or do you have something to hide?"

"What the hell does that mean?" His eyes bore into her.

"I heard that a lot of stuff was stolen from Eli when he was murdered. Any idea what they were really after?"

Adam snapped his fingers in Olivia's face. "Are you suggesting I had something to do with this?" Contempt in his voice stung.

"Well, people are talking a lot right now. The cops are asking a lot of questions."

Adam gritted his teeth and glared in disgust at the pile of horse shit Olivia's horse dropped next to him. "These people spread stupid like its manure. What do you think? Or, are you just parroting what Julio and the others are saying?"

Olivia grabbed Adam's arm when he turned to leave. "I thought Eli was a multi-millionaire. Where's all the money? I have interests in all these horses in this barn."

"Put your hand on me again—you're not getting it back."

Olivia released her grip as Adam tore her arm away. "You can't just evict me."

"Eli was a stingy, greedy old German," Adam huffed heatedly. "This place was a multi-million dollar gamble. Without him, everyone loses. What did you think would happen when the old man was gone?"

"Gee, Adam, I don't know what I think since you just informed me that I have to clear-out. Sounds to me like you're not interested in anybody but yourself."

"Got a cell phone, Olivia?"

Olivia sounded an, "Aah . . .," having a momentary loss of words, "Yeah."

"Call someone who cares." Waving her off with a chuckle, he turned to leave—his eyes slipping from Eva's face to Martine's.

Olivia flung a curry brush at Adam, missing him by a hair. "You're an ass," she screamed after him.

Eva sprang tears as she ran up to Olivia. "Did he really kick you out?"

"Yep. I think he's clearing everyone out."

"I'm sorry we overheard that," Martine said as she approached. "Do you have any agreements regarding your arrangements here?"

"Yes, I guess I do." Olivia turned to face Martine.

"I'm a lawyer. I could look at what you've got."

"We need to act fast," Olivia responded as more sweat surfaced and trickled down her cheeks. "He gave me two weeks."

Sensing the mental gymnastics Olivia had been subjected to was compromising her normal routine, she offered more, "We need to have a quick consultation in private."

"Right," Olivia complied—blinking away stingy tears. "Eva, will you take over for me this morning?"

Eva nodded valiantly. "I will get everything going the way you would." She then mouthed to her mother, "Thank you."

Winking back at Eva, Martine whisked Olivia out of the building before anyone else arrived. Just yesterday Olivia appeared to have the strength and composure of an Amazon woman. Now she was falling apart like a pair of cheap sandals. "I'm going to need some information from you. Is there somewhere we can talk?"

"Yes, we can sit in the pavilion outside the show arena."

After they were seated across from each other—away from everyone else, Martine began questioning Olivia as artfully as she could, "Please explain what Adam meant when he said, 'This place was a multi-million dollar gamble?'"

"Eli was a purist when it came to breeding champion blood lines. According to Eli, back in the eighties, a ten year old stallion named Nero's Hero was bred to a twenty year old mare named Ashkenazi's Quest which produced a filly named Nero's Quest. Nero's Quest became a successful show horse, but she wasn't the breeding stallion he had hoped for. After she retired from showing in 2006, he bred her to his standing stallion Royal Wonder, and got his long awaited grandson to Nero's Hero and Ashkenazi's Quest. Nero's Quest has been his best champion so far—until he got that colt Odin's Quest. Odin's Quest is the quality of breeding stock he has been trying to formulate. He wanted a colt out of Ashkenazi's Quest, but she died after Nero's Quest was born and she had no other offspring. That's what his main passion for horses is all about. He wanted the best breeding stock in the business. I've been getting the ones that don't make the cut."

Familiar with horse breeding, Martine inquired, "Where is the breeding facility? Is it here?"

Olivia finally forced a laugh, "If you consider refrigerated semen a breeding facility."

"It's all artificial?"

"Of course. It's preferred in most breeding arrangements now."

Proprietary Product Law is huge, and Martine knew it. "Who owns the semen? And where is it?"

Olivia searched the air for an answer. "I was not privy to any of his horse breeding business. I guess I don't know where the semen is stored, or how it's sold. I did hear Eli say, 'I could lose every horse in this place except you.' He was admiring his new colt Odin's Quest. Do you think Eli's agreements are frauds?"

"I don't know, Olivia. Here's what I need from you before I can advise you of what your circumstances may entail. Bring me everything you have in a written form detailing your agreement with Eli. If there were any oral alterations or arrangements made that you have evidence of, please bring that too. It can be a conversation, but I need to see notes. I'll be back tomorrow morning. Let's not focus on the possibility that Eli could formulate bad agreements, or that Adam is telling you he's broke. When we look for the worst in someone, surely we will find it."

Chapter 18

Relieved to be home from another unfulfilling nightshift at the greasy diner, Max flattened the cushions on his sofa as he settled his bulky frame for comfort in front of his TV. Logging onto his favorite bloggers site, his moderate attention span warped into overdrive when he sped-read the posts between his new blog-buddy *U.R.Wrong* and two new screen names—*Sharonlove* and *Richmann*. The three conspiracy enthusiasts had become embroiled in lengthy heated posts that spanned over eight hours—after Max had posted the recent test results of a DNA study that was finally released to the public.

U.R.Wrong says: "DNA does not lie. If the scientists are calling each other liars and frauds, something very sensitive is at stake and is big enough to cause a division. Someone just proved their theory is more correct than age old beliefs."

Richmann says: "Someone does not want the truth exposed. If old propaganda is challenged with real scientific proof it could change everyone's perspective by biblical proportions."

U.R.Wrong says: "It could change world powers, and the course of future wars."

Sharonlove says: "Why is this not being publicized?"

Richmann says: "1 guess."

U.R.Wrong says: "The media is controlled and censored."

Richmann says: "Do you see how this actually validates writings and prophecies in the bible?"

Sharonlove says: "How does it do that?"

Richmann says: "In Genesis, Abrahams' grandson Jacob had twelve sons which became the twelve tribes of Israel. Judah was one of Jacobs's sons. After wars and divisions, ten tribes became the Northern Tribes referred to as Israel, the two Southern Tribes became known as Judah. Only the Israelites from the Southern Tribes became known as Jews."

Sharonlove says: "Are you Jewish?"

U.R.Wrong says: "Does it matter?"

Richmann says: "Ezekiel talks about how the House of Israel and House of Judah shall become one in God's hand. Hosea was told that the Northern Tribes of Israel would be scattered amount the Gentiles until the latter days. So, you see that the Jews can't be the only decedents of Israel, or account for all twelve Tribes of Jacob, and DNA advances are going to prove migration ancestry. Some Jews don't want that exposed and never saw this coming."

Sharonlove says: "Who could possibly care?"

Richmann says: "Jews that are Zionists, or not genetic descendents of Palestine or the Middle East Israelis."

Sharonlove says: "Like who?"

U.R.Wrong says: "You don't have to prove you have Jewish blood to be Jewish. It's a matter of Orthodoxy. The only thing that the whole Jewish community accepts is being Orthodox. It's been that way for thousands of years. DNA cannot open a door to prove one's Jewishness. It is a religion."

Richmann says: "That is not even close to the issue being exposed with the new DNA studies that are being reported."

Sharonlove says: "What is it?"

U.R.Wrong says: "Does it have to do with persecution?"

Richmann says: "It has to do with money."

U.R.Wrong says: "What are you talking about? Everyone knows that Jews control a lot of the finances and banks around the world. That is not new news. How else could they get their control of the Federal Reserve? We all know there's nothing Federal about it."

Richmann says: "It might if they really aren't the Jews they claim to be. The ones destined to rule the world. The ones promised their own state when their Messiah comes."

Sharonlove says: "What?"

Richmann says: "Huge populations of Jews, both here and abroad, are called Ashkenazi Jews. They are primarily from Europe, Germany, Poland and France. Jews migrated from the Middle East thousands of years ago, they intermarried, they settled in many places. Just about everywhere. Did you know that?"

Sharonlove says: "No not really. But what does that have to do with DNA?"

Richmann says: "The Jews that claim to have settled with the Khazars, located between the Black and Caspian Seas, are claiming to be Ashkenazi Jews but, most have been suspected of not having genetic lineage to the Middle East Jews."

Sharonlove says: "How is that possible?"

Richmann says: "The Khazarians had Mongolian and Turkic origins. They compromised one of the largest medieval states. The Khazars were a Pagan civilization, and in a short period in history, became the largest and most powerful kingdom in Europe, and possibly the wealthiest."

U.R. Wrong says: "Is this the kingdom that was forced to convert?"

Richmann says: "Yes. They brought with them their religious worship that was a mix of phallic worship and other forms of idolatrous worship practiced in Asia by other Pagan nations. This form of Pagan worship continued into the seventh century with vile and disgusting acts of sexual excesses and lewdness indulged in by the Khazars as part of their religious beliefs. This form of worship produced a moral degeneracy that the Khazarian King could no longer endure. The King claims to have had a dream where God appeared to him and promised him might and glory. He decided to end the practice of phallic worship and all other forms of idolatrous worship and to make one of three world religions, the new Khazarian state religion."

U.R. Wrong says: "I remember reading about this. After a historic session with representatives from the three major religions, the King decided to adopt Judaism over Islam and Christianity."

Sharonlove says: "How did they do it?"

Richmann says: "King Bulan and like four thousand feudal nobles were converted by rabbis imported from Babylonia. Phallic worship and all other forms of idol worship were there after forbidden."

U.R.Wrong says: "Did you know large numbers of Rabbis from Babylon were invited to come and open synagogues and schools to instruct the population in the new state religion?"

Sharonlove says: "Did everyone have to convert?"

Richmann says: "Convert or leave."

U.R.Wrong says: "After the mass conversion of the King and his empire, none other than a so called or self-styled Jew, could occupy the Khazarian throne."

Richmann says: "The Empire became a virtual theocracy with the religious leaders being the civil administrators as well."

Sharonlove says: "It is hard to believe they could accomplish that."

Richmann says: "Hard to believe, but true. During this time the Talmud was added to or altered to protect their state religion from any other outside religious influence and to prevent a return to previous vile worship."

Sharonlove says: "So you're saying that because of this particular king's belief in finding the most proven and powerful—infallible religion, he made his entire kingdom convert to Judaism?"

Richmann says: "Yes. And those are the Jews that are not genetically connected to Palestine, Israel, the near east, Judah, or any of the ten missing tribes. They are not related to the Ashkenazi Jews in Germany. Ashkenazi means German. They are not related to the Sephardic Jews which originally migrated to Spain. They were never Jews in exile from their homeland."

Sharonlove says: "So what is the big deal? Who really cares? You sound prejudice."

Richmann says: "Here's the big deal. The most powerful family in the world claims to be Ashkenazi Jews from Khazaria, but does not want to make claim to their Mongolian genes. Since the DNA studies are showing that the gene markers found in the Khazarian Jews are completely heterogeneous from genetic DNA markers found in ancient Judea, their pious Jewish claims to fulfill bible prophecies of world domination would be laid to rest."

Sharonlove says: "So how does this make them less Jewish or not Jewish?"

Richmann says: "They are Jews religiously, but not racially. An Iranian Jew can be a Catholic. A catholic can become Jewish."

Sharonlove says: "Right. So why pick on those Jews?"

Richmann says: "Because their claim to Palestine would disintegrate."

Sharonlove says: "Are you sure you're not an orthodox Jew?"

Richmann says: "No. I have my bible right here. And it says in The Book of Revelations Chapter 2, *'I know your works, your labor, and your endurance, and that you cannot tolerate the wicked; you have tested those who call themselves apostles but are not, and discovered that they are impostors.'* Or Chapter 3, *'I know the slander of those who claim to be Jews and are not, but rather are members of the assembly of Satan.'*"

Sharonlove says: "Okay I believe you. So now you're saying this is all prophesied in the Bible?"

Richmann says: "I do now. Check out Chapter 3 *'Behold, I will make those of the assembly of Satan who claim to be Jews and are not, but are lying, behold I will make them come and fall prostrate at your feet.'* Or, Chapter 4, *'For you say, I am rich and affluent and have no need of anything, and yet do not realize that you are wretched pitiable, poor, blind, and naked'* . . . would suddenly make sense. Ninety percent of the bible would make sense."

U.R.Wrong says: "This is like cracking open a perfectly white egg shell and seeing what mysterious contents it has been hiding. Before the DNA testing studies, these claims have virtually been unchallenged. Questioned, but unchallenged. This clearly changes a Jewish Zionist narrative, which views the migration of modern-day Jews to what is now Israel and their rule over that land, to a deception of non-religious imposters masquerading as real Israeli descendants that fled Palestine after the Muslim conquest."

Sharonlove says: "So what's the big deal about reclaiming Palestine anyways?"

U.R.Wrong says: "I totally get it. The elite Zionist Jews rule in a dictatorial manner. This type of information might wake up the modern Jews that don't agree with the Orthodox Jews who have questioned this ambition of the Zionists. Together they could challenge these dictators. The Zionist movement brutally suppresses any dissents."

Sharonlove says: "What's a Zionist movement."

Richmann says: "Zionism is a movement founded in 1896 whose goal was to return the Jews to the land of Israel and establish a government. They believe it is their right to fight for their ownership of this land. There are probably twenty to forty million people in the world with DNA linking them to one of the tribes of Israel. They were not meant to literally migrate back to this land. The bible says their nations will be joined. The bible makes more sense."

U.R.Wrong says: "I agree, my orthodox friend."

Sharonlove says: "I think you need more proof than DNA if you believe imposters are taking over Israel."

Max could not resist weighing in on the battled debate. Tapping on his keypad at an accelerated rate he authored his opinion.

Supermax says: "I think DNA will help prove a lot of theories, but if you do your own research the evidence is already apparent. Start with the Israeli flag. Find out whose crest is on their flag."

Chapter 19

Alexa strode confidently up to Detective Ray's desk. Dropping a single page of paper face-down on top of a tall pile of dishevel documents, she greeted Ray, "Hey. How ya doin' on identifying that John Doe body?"

Ray slowly glanced up to see who was invading his space. "Okay."

"Really?" Alexa pulled a chair to the desk. "Not what I hear." Composed, she sat down slowly.

"What's this?" Ray eyed the paper that sat on his work. "It's blocking my pile of files," he said, as if he had something more important to look at.

"Nothing much," she said meekly.

"Yeah, you appear about as innocent as a dingo running away with a rabbit hanging out of its mouth. Cough it up, girl." His gaze wary, he added, "What da ya got?"

Drawing a ragged breath, Alexa flipped the page over and handed its contents to Ray. "I got this from ChartQuest this morning."

"Okay, now I know who you got it from—but I still haven't established a motive why you brought it to me. So . . ." He stopped.

"Motive? In our business we call that a clue. I told you I could help and here is your victim's name." Alexa's irritation waned, as she handed him another document. "His name is Jake Monroe."

Examining the information he started snapping his fingers in the air, signaling his associate over. "Miguel," he sounded loudly. "Come over here."

"Yeah, Ray," Miguel answered as he entered the office. "Whatcha need?"

"Run this name."

Alexa butted in, "That's not necessary. I've done that and there's not much on this guy. He's from Coeur D'Alene, Idaho."

"Sounds like we're done here then." Ray motioned to the door. "I owe you a beer."

"Actually we're not done here," self-assured Alexa objected. "I think we can help you with this case. We're the most advanced criminal agency in the world—specializing in hard to solve cases—think ya got one here."

"We got this, chica," Miguel said flagrantly. "This won't be hard."

With calm disappointment conveying nothing more than the secret's in her lap, she said obstinately, "We got this too."

"Yeah, but, it's our case," Ray protested quickly.

"It's ours too," Alexa gave Ray a fortuitous grin and handed him another document. "I also researched other places Jake Monroe has been and where he was possibly going. You have a likely 'gun for hire' turned murder victim that has crossed state lines. That kinda traffic thread means you need us and our resources." She clutched her files and felt a rising frustration each time Ray blocked her support.

Miguel moved behind Ray and looked over his shoulder to view the document Ray was studying. "What you make of that, boss?"

Irritated by another person invading his space, Ray gave him a preposterous look, "What are you doing?"

"What you mean, Ray?"

Ray tilted his head towards Miguel. "We gonna share a 'Happy Meal' or something? Get over there."

Miguel looked lost for a moment, and backed away. "Sorry, Ray."

Ray looked back at Alexa—it was obvious he didn't want her around. "Alright. What else ya got?"

Alexa handed Ray her closing article and tried to keep her voice steady, "Once I tracked this down with ChartQuest, I got his computers IPO address. I next accessed his e-mail traffic. His e-mails connected repeatedly with an IPO address in Phoenix." Alexa paused for effect. "I'll bet you that address will probably get you a killer, or at least an arsonist."

"Ya think," Ray said springing to his feet. "Let's get a warrant and roll." Moving towards the door before she could gather her things, Ray clapped her on the shoulder.

Alexa reacted to Ray's eureka moment, "I'm coming too."

"I think not," Ray said over his shoulder. "You'll be unnecessary and in the way."

Annoyed at the brush-off, Alexa spouted, "Funny. My mother said you'd say that."

Ray replied mockingly, "Right. What does your mommy have to do with this?"

"You'll see," Alexa said slyly as she followed them through the open office area.

"Yah," Ray said impatiently. Commanding directives to uniformed co-workers, his voice dwindled as he moved away from her, "Thanks rookie."

Miguel winked at Alexa as he dashed out the door behind Ray. "Good job, chica."

Chapter 20

On a street like any other with rows of lightly packed one-story homes, pandemonium ensued after a mechanical barricade quarantined a single house. Eddy and Rachel's front yard was bathed in flashing lights from at least a dozen police vehicles. With the hallmarks of a Greek tragedy playing out, neighbors looked on as rumors snaked through the community like a *Mardi Gras* parade. Police, clad in full swat team armor, drew their weapons and surrounded the couples rented home located in the infamous dark and seedy part of Arizona. Foreign, like a strange third-world country for most people, the area was no place for the faint of heart.

Ray signaled his tactical team to position themselves around the home, hoping to catch the occupant's off-guard.

Pounding loudly on the front door, Ray yelled loud, "Open the door we have a warrant to search the place."

No one answered or stirred inside the residence so Ray hollered again, "Open the door, or we're coming in." When no one complied with the demand, Ray shouldered the door open and let members of his tactical team file-in before him. Observing the odors of marijuana as well as the thin layers of smoke floating in front of the west window, Ray order the occupants to surrender, "Either come out now, or we shot on sight."

Rachel put her hands in the air and stood up behind the sofa. "Don't shoot."

Two officers rushed to apprehend the suspect and remove her from the home as the others continued to search. One of the team moved down a long hallway towards the rooms furthest away from the front of the home. Ray joined the officer who racked his 12 gauge pop-shotgun, making the easily identifiable sound as to what it was. "Anybody here? Come out now," yelled the officer.

"Yes," Janice answered. Followed by Tom, Janice came out of the back bedroom and surrendered.

"Cuff them before you read them their rights. Anybody else here?" Ray steadied his weapon as he kicked open the last door.

Tom grunted, "No," as the officers forced his arms behind his back and cuffed him.

"Your name," Ray asked.

"Tom."

"Where is Eddy?"

"I don't know. He's not here."

"When's the last time you saw him?"

"Couple days I guess."

"He hasn't been here for days?"

"That's what I said, now let me go if that's all you came here for."

"One of you boys read him his rights."

Ray shook his head in disappointment and called into the station, "Put out a BOLO for Eddy. See if there's a car registered to him and 'Be On the Look Out' for either."

Outside next to a squad car an officer was questioning Rachel as Ray approached. With great satisfaction Ray spun her around and addressed her, "Well, Rachel, we meet again. Miss me?"

"Yeah, like a Mexican parasite," she said metaphorically.

"Gee, I love your dissimilies. Do you know why we're here?"

Angrily Rachel answered, "No. What're you taking me in for?"

"Did you recently try to extinguish an old flame?"

"No," she shot back.

"Looks like you folks are connected to some serious criminal activity. Anyone you know that might be involved?"

"Nope,"

"How 'bout your friend Eddy? Or, is he your boyfriend now?"

Rachel shook her head. "Nope. He wouldn't be involved."

"What do you know about Eddy?"

Rachel shook her head again. "Nothing."

"Know where we can find him?"

"Nope."

"When's the last time you saw Eddy?"

Rachel smiled snidely. "This morning. We had breakfast together."

"If you're going to lie to me you could at least have the decency to be a good liar. What'd ya say I take you to our turf, Rachel girl?"

"Tell me the truth, Ray. You're not taking me in, are you?" Rachel's smirky grin collapsed.

"Gee, Rachel." You kinda handcuffed me with the whole 'tell me the truth' part, because I am taking you in." Ray pushed her into the backseat of a squad car. "Do you know Eddy's rap sheet is in pounds—not pages?" Ray allowed a moment to pass, waiting for her response. "Is that a yes, or is your neck broke now?" Ray rapped on the top of the squad car twice. "Take her in, boys."

Chapter 21

Prior to finishing a late dinner of leftover pizza, Martine received word from Alexa that the raid had succeeded in apprehending three suspects. No further information was available until tomorrow. With that bit of good news she decided to retire early.

Sleepless, her mind ricocheted three days of intense activities that drew her into a murder mystery that hit close to home. Opening her journal to review her last two dreams she first read an inscription she recorded on the inside cover. About a month ago an angelic visitor inspired her to begin another journal when her other one was completely filled. At the time it just sounded wise and logical. Now, as she rereads the words, it appears prophetic. *'Truth has many layers. The epiphany of all knowledge cannot be obtained in limited human form, nor in a state void of experience.'* Pondering the relevance of this profound proclamation bestowed to her, she rested her eyes for a moment. Before she could begin examining the puzzling clues recorded from her recent dreams, Martine was put to sleep and lifted out of her body.

Plummeted into the body of woman from the late 1800's, dressed in a blue dress with matching bonnet, Martine found herself blending into the sea of people that surrounded her. Raising her head high to look around, she surmised she was a traveler on a slow chugging train. Outside her window she saw endless landscape of barren land, tumbleweeds, rock, and distant hills. Lumbering sounds of clickety-clack combined with the rolling rhythm of a coal-driven train had lulled all of the passengers into a relaxed or sleepy trance—except for a couple of gentleman sitting in front of her.

"Did you see all the soldiers that arrived before the train departed," the older man asked his neighbor.

"Sure did," the younger man seated by the window replied. "Any idea why they were here? I haven't seen them on the train."

"I think I saw them get in one of the cars down from ours."

Suddenly, without any advanced preparation the train braked and violently jolted everyone. When the natural momentum of the moving train unexpectedly ceased, every individual aboard experienced a disturbing shock—awakening them to some unforeseen state of fright. Screaming followed as the startled commuters reacted to the shift in tempo and heard the loud screeching sounds of metal on metal.

More mayhem ensued when the travelers responded to the fast riding bandits disguised behind cloth masks that scooped-in alongside the train—keeping pace as the locomotive slowed to a stop. Women cried in horror, and men began yelling orders to lock the doors and get their guns.

Halted on the tracks, the train became a prison to Martine and the trapped occupants as the pistol carrying robbers demanded to board the train, "Open the doors," one of them ordered the engineer.

"No," an elderly conductor yelled back.

Jumping on the train, they took the engineer by force. "Open the door to the express car," a second masked stickup man demanded.

"I can't do that," scared, the conductor's voice shook.

Angered by the engineer's refusal, the bandit struck him on the head with his pistol and forced the old man out of train. "Where's the express car?" The masked intruder hollered as he shoved the conductor. "If you don't tell us now we blow up every car till we find it."

Terrorized by the brutal assaults, the old engineer pointed to the second car. "It's locked tight. Only Pinkerton can open it."

"Find the Pinkerton man on the train, boys," ordered the leader.

Shooting the lock off the passenger car door, the threatening thieves' barged in yelling, "Which one of you's Pinkerton?"

Martine's wits finally caught up with the drama conjured-up by the hostile sleazy gang of thieving raiders. Looking sideways to the man sitting next to her, she beheld an older gentleman nervous and sweating profusely. His labored breathing indicated he was suffering from either an anxiety attack or heart attack. Seeing his briefcase was resting securely on his lap, she hypothesized in a whisper, "Are you Pinkerton?"

"I . . . am," he stammered.

Standing up she grabbed his satchel and stepped into the isle—shouting, "I am. I'm with Pinkerton. I'm right here." Unable to see more than the eyebrows raise on the leaders face, Martine stepped forward to meet his gaze. "What do you want?"

Walking towards her he replied, "What do we have here? A lady dressed in blue," he laughed. Grabbing her by the arm he hauled her out of the train car unto the sun-drenched wasteland. "Which car is the express car?"

Lacking the knowledge, she bluffed, "The one without windows."

"Open it," he demanded.

"Open it yourself. You might not like what you find."

"What's that suppose to mean?"

"Soldiers—I'm guessing. I'm not allowed entrance into this car."

Snatching the briefcase out of her hand, he threw it on the ground and shot it open with one blast. Inside the case were papers and no keys. "Where are the keys?"

One of the robbers lewdly addressed Martine, "Maybe they're under them petticoats."

"Of course they're not," Martine scoffed angrily, "The doors are opened from the inside," she deduced.

"I don't believe her. Let me look, boss. I've got a good heart, and I'll be gentle," he said perversely. "Let me do it," the degenerate thief begged.

Appalled by the notion that this outlaw could violate and harm her, she fired back, "You gotta good heart?" Martine spat on the ground. "Rotten brain and putrid thoughts though."

"Leave her alone—don't have time for this," his boss snapped. "Blow it open boys. Let's see what they're hiding."

Martine couldn't help but try and delay the attack, "You're making a dumb mistake, and you can't fix stupid." Interfering with the heist she continued to aggravate the gang, "Soldiers have bigger guns than you."

Laughing at her oddness and hell bent on stealing what wasn't theirs—two of the other gang members fixed dynamite to the car's door and lit the fuse. "Run for cover. It's gonna blow," a gruff voiced warned.

Hauled off to a safe distance by the gangs ring leader, Martine waited the silent moments in the company of five notorious train robbers. Still masked and incognito, she couldn't know who they might be. History told her train robberies were very common in the past, and often occurred in the American old west. Trains carrying payroll, and gold shipments were a major target. These shipments would be guarded by an expressman whose duty it was to protect the cargo of the express car. Expressmen, conductors, and other personnel took enormous pride in their duty and had no problem with risking their lives for a shipment.

Crouched a far distance from the train tracks, Martine could now identify the train that was under siege. Union Pacific was boldly displayed on the trains' locomotive.

After the explosion, four of the thieves ran up to the car that had its side door blown apart. "Hee haw," a raunchy thief hollered. "Let's see what we got."

Held back and still under the grip of the gang's leader, Martine squinted to observe the results of the dynamites destruction. As the smoke cleared from the detonation, she saw a hand-full of guns pointing out of the car.

"Kid, get back," her capture called. "You got company. We'll take her instead," he yelled loud enough for everyone to hear. Positioning Martine in front of himself, he used her as a shield and hostage. "Get out of the train, boys," he ordered. "Or, we take the lady." Pointing his pistol to her head, he forced Martine forward towards the train, clearing passage for his gang to board the express car.

"What're they guarding," the man named Kid asked.

"Just get everything," his boss yelled.

Several soldiers jumped out of the car and were herded at gun point away from the train. Kid and the other bandits removed the contents of the guarded cargo, including a small wooden trunk marked 'US Treasury.'

Once out of range from the soldiers the bandits ran as fast as they could to their horses that were stabled behind an outcropping of rock—dragging Martine with. Two of them handled the trunk that didn't appear to be heavy.

"What's in here, boss?" a young one asked.

"None of your business right now."

"It sure ain't gold," the young one commented.

"Mount up fast," one of the other men shouted with zeal. "They can't catch us without horses."

Kid hurriedly pulled out a map and handed it to his superior—who was still holding Martine close. "Which way do we go?"

"We go where we were told."

Kid's voice had doubt, "You sure you can trust 'em?"

"We split up." Pointing to an X on the map, he instructed Kid and two others to head west. "You take the trunk here and meet back at our place."

Releasing Martine from his hold, the man whom held her captive swung himself into his saddle, tipped his hat at her, and said cordially, "It's been a pleasure, ma'am." Racing off in two directions at the highest speed their horses could take them caused a cloud of dirt that temporarily blinded Martine.

When the dust cleared from the galloping horses, blurry-eyed Martine was met by the vision of the Indian Chief that had appeared in her previous dreams. "White woman very brave," he said with a nod. "I bring message from great beyond." Unrolling the scroll, he handed her the words to read.

"Track the path few could do
Justice springs inside of you
Confirmation comes in two
Follow branch and know what's true

Disillusioned you are not
Now remember what's forgot."

Martine's mind was temporarily emblazoned with the intense dream episode. Every part of each etheric experience was transposed by her into the leather-bound journal she kept near her when she slept. Vivid night-dreams were not unusual for her during times of great turmoil, sometimes leading her to an obvious conclusion and other times to an extraordinary experience with a learned lesson. Catholic and faith driven, she secretly kept the nightly encounters to herself—doubting anyone else would benefit or believe. Just as her worldly life incidents matured, so did the intensity of her 'out-of-this-world' journeys.

Martine finished noting the events of her etheric vision and reflected on why some of the thought provoking dream-experiences took her to such dire places—but after all isn't that where negative minds operate? Their impertinence took her breath away.

Chapter 22

Martine's cell phone rang as she finished grooming one of Eva's horses in training. Noticing the call originated from a blocked number, she answered discreetly, "Hello?"

"Good morning, Martine. John, here."

"Hey," she replied. "How's it going?"

"Well," he paused, "I'm not sure, but it's getting more interesting by the moment. It's always a bit of a challenge when you're in town it seems."

"I'm not sure how to take that."

"I think you do," he said facetiously.

Avoiding the insinuation, Martine suggested, "We should meet."

"I thought so. Where are you? I actually expected you to be at my office this morning."

"I'm at *Desert Run*—barn five." Martine went still.

"I'm on my way. Should I bring anything?" He offered.

Hesitant, she replied, "An open mind."

"I was referring to pastries or coffee."

"That'll be nice too."

"I'll be there shortly."

Martine continued tacking the leggy grey Trakehner gelding, Jazz, as she contemplated how to engage Mahoney's support in the criminal investigation she found herself doubly involved with.

Eva, who had been turning antsy horses out for a morning romp in the large paddocks, returned flushed-faced. "Julio just told me he's been fired."

Hearing Eva's voice raised, Martine turned her head towards her approaching daughter and gave a dismayed sigh, "Oh no."

"What's going to happen next?" She flung the lead rope over the stall rail she had stomped up to.

Martine's frown deepened as she hoisted the black dressage saddle on Jazz's back. "I have no idea." Walking around the horse to adjust the saddle and underneath padding, she asked, "Which bridle's his? I'll finish tacking him up if you need a break."

Handing Martine the English headstall with a double bit, and double reins, she fessed-up to her mother, "What if I'm evicted too? How could someone murder a famous Olympic Champion like Eli? And it was so gross? And it just keeps getting uglier."

Fumbling with the complicated bridle, Martine listened and swallowed her apprehension for the sake of her bewildered daughter, "Sometimes we need to focus on how they lived and not how they died. I wouldn't focus on the worse possibilities, or the notion that something better won't become of these circumstances."

Eva's sun-flushed cheeks popped when she exchanged a grateful smile with her mother. "Thanks. I realize that there's nothing either of us can do right now."

"That's not true," Martine said firmly, handing the tangled leather mass to her daughter. "You can put this on your horse, and I can cinch-up the girth."

Eva forced a laugh and took the bridle, "I guess I found something I can do better than you."

Adjusting the saddle to balance perfectly on Jazz's back, Martine offered a little consolation, "I know it feels like Pandora's Box couldn't have contained this much negative energy, but if things are really about to get worse—it also means they can be made better. Give it some time."

Eva effortlessly lifted the complicated bridle up to Jazz's young Araby face and coaxed his mouth open for both of the bits. "I guess I'm already better. If you weren't here I'd probably be crying alone in my room. You can always talk me off the ledge."

"Exactly," Martine grunted as she used her strength to tighten the buckles on the leather girth. That's the Eva we all know."

Pulling down the stirrup leathers on each side of the saddle completed the process of tacking the muscled athlete that once stabled at Windsor Castle. Over many generations, the best genes from the Thoroughbred, Warmblood, and the purebred Arabian were combined to create the noble pedigree found in Jazz's high-strung Trakehner bloodline.

Ready and anxious to get his workout, Jazz started pawing the ground and clanking the metal of his bits as Eva readied herself to mount-up. "Wait till you see what he can do. Don't forget to take some photos." Eva gloved her hands in black leather and lifted her knee high to get a foot into the stirrup. Pulling herself up into the saddle made Jazz more excited.

"Of course," Martine replied as she steadied the horse, straight-ened the set of reins, and buckled the chin strap that had been overlooked.

Arriving behind her, Stetson clad Mahoney whispered, "Am I late?" Jiggling a bag, he added, "I brought coffee and rolls."

Jazz swished his long thick white tail and reared his front legs—demonstrating his power and eagerness to strut his stuff. "Gotta go," Eva's voice trailed as she trotted off to the arena.

"Well, this looks exciting," Mahoney nodded positively. Himself a cowboy at heart, and capable of herding cattle across the state of Texas when he lived there in the past, scanned the surroundings. "I must say this place is impressive. I only noticed the burning home the night of the fire. It really is a showcase of the grandest horse flesh I've ever seen."

"You're right about that," Martine agreed as she grabbed the camera.

Mahoney, dressed in jeans and cowboy boots, kicked a dried horse turd out of the way before Martine could step on it. "It makes my little ranch look like a spec in comparison to this spread."

"I felt the same way when I arrived. Thanks for coming by. Let's go sit down under the pavilion. No one's ever there in the morning. And . . . I'm here to watch Eva's favorite horse train for his big show coming up."

Mahoney sat across from Martine and gave her a friendly smile. Situated comfortably at the high top table next to the private Olympic sized arena, he started in a scolding tone, "Well, you're only here a few days and you're involved with a murder investigation—aren't you?"

"Feels like old times," she laughed, cradling the coffee cup he handed her. Reminiscent of her last long visit, that resulted in their meeting and working together on a two week criminal manhunt, Martine added, "Feels like I never left."

"I'm really not sure what is going on here, but I suspect you know more than me already." He drew her into his gaze.

Martine bit her bottom lip. "I'm torn. It does appear to be a murder for money, but I can imagine something bigger too." Martine glanced slightly to her left as Eva walked by on Jazz.

Mahoney also looked over as Jazz moved past them. "Like what?"

Martine cleared her thickening throat. "I think we're dealing with a cold case."

"How cold?" Mahoney sipped his coffee.

"Oh, 1865."

Humored by the answer, Mahoney chuckled out loud. "How's that possible?"

Martine looked away dodging his inevitable doubt. "Well, sometimes buried secrets have a way of resurfacing."

"Well, I bet all your witnesses and their DNA is buried. Will that be resurfacing too?" Mahoney played along.

"No." Martine smirked at the tease and pulled out a sweet roll. "That's when we look to the living for more information."

Accepting the sweet breakfast roll Martine handed him, Mahoney replied, "You're talking in riddles, aren't you? And if there's an extremely old cold case, why's it important now? And here?"

Hearing the sounds of Jazz approaching, Martine turned again to see the horse dash by at an aggressive trot. "When we don't admit there's an enemy they're left to prosper—over and over again.

I don't know what was stolen, but I think it was more complicated than just money and jewels," she finished.

Pondering the abstract conversation, Mahoney rubbed at his mustache, keeping his eyes on Martine. "So you think this is more than theft, arson, and homicides—don't you?"

"Yes. Relationships kept secret are always riddled with deceptions." Looking sideways again she studied Eva and Jazz as their speed increased to a canter.

Mahoney observed Martine. "And that means you're onto some unusual relationships, doesn't it?"

"Probably." Nodding jerkily, she added, "I'm sure."

"Do you think it's an affair?" He asked, wiping his hands on a napkin.

"If it is—it's a foreign affair."

"Geez, Martine, what are you talking about?" He asked impatiently.

"Well, if we follow the money—way back, it might expose more than the murder of this one man." Based on her dreams, she stretched the truth.

Mahoney thoughtfully stared at Eva as she schooled Jazz in cantering loops and serpentines that showcased the bond between horse and rider. Focusing back to Martine he shook his head. "Oh no, you're talking about conspiracy—aren't you?"

"I'm suspicious." Distracted again by Jazz's next transformation into light airy dance moves, Martine raised the camera, looked away from Mahoney, and took a few photos.

Tipping his head to get her attention, Mahoney commented, "You're tight lipped—as usual."

"Only because if I'm right, the truth is stranger than fiction." She felt his hand cover hers for a moment.

"How strange?" His voice dropped as he took his hand back.

"I'll admit I can think of a couple angles that could potentially intersect with this crime. I fear they're racy theories that need more investigation." Her vague explanation was the best she could do at this moment.

"I have to ask, is this because this homicide has affected both your daughters?" He lifted his dark eyebrows.

Admiring Eva's ability to instigate graceful, airborne, moves out of a four legged hay-eating giant gave her pause before answering, "I'm not going to say that it doesn't affect my interest, but my experience is also weighing in on this. I'm literally on the inside looking out, and I don't like what's going on here. There's not a lack of suspects—there's too many."

"Okay, Martine," he relented, "say I'm intrigued, what do you need from me?"

Flooded with relief by his acceptance, she suggested, "Since we don't need a search warrant because it's an active crime scene, let's investigate where the police aren't going to bother to look."

"I'm okay with that I guess," he proffered.

Taking a few more photos of Jazz and Eva doing flying lead changes, she added, "And, get me some credentials to participate in the criminal investigation that is underway with Scottsdale Homicide Detectives."

"That won't be hard since Alexa already flexed her muscles there. I'm beginning to see how that could've happened."

Averting his comment, she continued on, "And, I'll probably need to have clearance to question the ones they brought in—due to Alexa's work."

"Done." Mahoney grinned. "Anything else?"

Martine stood tall to photograph Jazz spinning in tight circles on his haunches. "Access by tomorrow?"

Mesmerized by Jazz's dizzying pirouette moves, Mahoney stood next to her. "Why not? I have all day to set it up. Any specific time?"

"Good one." Martine lifted her face to his and smiled, acknowledging Mahoney's sense of humor. "I really appreciate your support. I won't let you down. Nine would be great though."

"Is there more?" He probed.

Jumping at the invite, Martine thought. "Everything you can get on Eli Morgan."

"Like what?"

"Business dealings, women, finances, holdings, insurance policies, phone records—you know, the usual forensics background stuff. Oh, and anything you've got from Scottsdale Homicide."

"I don't have anything for you right now. The Scottsdale Homicide Detective in charge doesn't like sharing too well—you know—why give away the cow and keep the manure? I'll do what I can. Anything else I should know now?"

"I believe we may be venturing into dangerous territory. Are you up for it?"

"Always," Mahoney stood to leave. "I can't believe you're not in sales."

"Let me know if you need anything here from Eva, or me."

"Like riding lessons for me and my horse?" Shaking his head he started to walk away. "Don't get into any trouble here. You call me if something happens that I should know about."

Chapter 23

Max waited in his apartment for Gordy to return his call.

"Gordy," Max said excitedly when his friend phoned him back. "I have no doubt what really happened to JFK. I know who and why—I've been right all along."

"You don't know what you're talking about."

"Of course I know what I'm talking about," Max spouted to Gordy. "I can prove President Kennedy was assassinated for the same reason Lincoln was."

"How can that possibly be?" Gordy laughed his words, "A lone Communist gunman hunted Lincoln down in 1865?"

"Sure, if you believe that's who really killed JFK," Max said callously to his friend.

Gordy guessed again. "The Protestants?"

"No, you dweeb. He was highly principled and educated—enough to discover the financial abuse America was being subjected to by the elite business men and bankers."

"How do you know that?"

"On June 4th 1963 Kennedy signed Executive Order 11110 which returned power to the U.S. government to issue money without going through the Rothschild's Federal Reserve Banking System. Less than six months later on November 22nd, President Kennedy is assassinated."

"You think they trusted and hired Oswald to kill the famous JFK because of banking?" Gordy's voice pitched with disbelief.

Max impatiently waived off Gordy's ignorance. "And more importantly he wanted to end the Vietnam War and be pulled out by

1965 just like Lincoln wanted to end the Civil War. They both found out how hard that was if certain people didn't agree."

"You're assuming a lot, Max. I don't buy that," Gordy debated. "I've never met anyone that wants us to be at war. The boys in Nam with me hated it."

"Not those people," Max clarified. "The elite rich—the shadow government people that make money off of wars. Like its big business, man."

"You think that's a reason to kill JFK?"

"And possibly the fact that Kennedy wouldn't agree to Israel becoming a nuclear state," Max said evenly. "He was adamant about that. Look what's happened in the Middle East since then?"

"Well that makes JFK my biggest hero," Gordy flashed enthusiastically.

"I feel the same way. I think when certain business men, bankers, crime bosses, and politicians realized he was honest and decent, they got scared—they got mad. When he appointed his crime-busting brother Bobby to be Attorney General they knew he meant business. Abolishing organized crime was Bobby's battle cry. Bobby also was committed to getting us out of Vietnam."

"His enemies were really stacking up," Gordy injected. "It could've been any of them. Don't forget he fired a lot of people after the Bay of Pigs."

Max could never completely agree with Gordy. "Or, all of them together. Think about it, what did they all want more of?"

"Power? I mean money makes sense, but how do they get rich off of killing JFK?"

"Think about it, Gordy, our country has to borrow money from the Federal Reserve Bank at a price. It's a high price when you're at war. As soon as JFK is buried, the over four-billion dollars Kennedy was putting into circulation—interest free—was being pulled out and destroyed forever. Everything he did to avoid going through the Rothschild's Federal Reserve Banking System to create money for the American people and pay for the war was undid after his death."

Gordy sounded puzzled, "I just don't get how this is such a big deal that someone would murder JFK over it."

Max interrupted, "And probably his brother too."

"Yeah, I never understood how both those brothers could both end up assassinated," Gordy reminisced his sadness. "Bobby hadn't even been elected yet."

"Gordy, they wanted JFK dead so bad. Listen to this, when I study all the different independent investigative reports done in the last few years that took into account, the wounds, photos, eye-witness testimonies, audio recordings, and other film footages—there more like six to eight gunmen and eight or more shots. I think the fatal one was from the storm-sewer drain in the streets' curb. That's the only way the head shot could have occurred if you consider real forensic trajectory analysis."

Gordy butted in, "Wait, you're saying someone was under the street?"

"I think so. The storm-sewer drain that resembles a gunner's portal was located in the street almost straight out from where Zapruder stood and that's where the fatal head shot was sustained. No one can deny it entered the right temple and blew the right side of his head off—throwing debris back and to the left. There were four gunmen tucked in the building behind Zapruder. He said he heard the shots from behind him. That's when he jerked his camera. And, that's before the fatal shot. The first bullets he took in the upper back, and neck, probably wouldn't have been fatal. Even after they blew the side of his head off his heart was beating and he was still struggling to breathe when he went into surgery."

"How do you figure there were so many shooters?"

"Makes more sense. Each sniper could get in maybe one shot during the time frame allowed. Governor Connelly took three hits, Kennedy took three hits, a bullet hit the grass, one went through the car's windshield, one hit the chrome on the back seat and ricocheted, one hit the curb, one hit a tree, and one hit the dashboard. They said Oswald only got off three shots and had a magic bullet. Zapruder's famous film wasn't the only film footage taken, and there were lots of photos too. Why did the Warren Commission wait twelve years to release Zapruder's film to CBS? Why did they only rely on his? Why wouldn't they release it sooner if they didn't have something to hide? Why did they release it years after Zapruder passed away? Why did they let LBJ head up the investigation?"

"Stop, Max, so why not Lyndon Johnson? Was he in on it?"

"If I'm right, when the privately owned New York Federal Reserve Bank was facing Kennedy's solution of putting them out of business in this country, they had no choice but to eliminate him, and let every president since then know what would happen if they tried again. Lyndon and Kennedy didn't get along or like each other. Johnson was unscrupulous with a horrific temper and very shady background that connected him to the events. The Vietnam War certainly raged on while he was president for over five years. And there were no attempts on his life. You do the math."

"I get what you're saying. But how did they really get away with this? How did they keep this a secret?"

"Here's a better question." Max was getting really steamed. "Why did they appoint John J. McCloy to serve on the Warren Commission? What is a banker doing in a homicide investigation? I mean the guy was connected to the Rockefellers. He works for the banking and business elite."

"Are you kidding?" Gordy said in shock. "I just don't see how they could've covered this up for so long though."

Max repeated Gordy's words, "You have no idea how they've been covering this up? Because most people—like you, won't believe anything else. So listen, there's a pattern here."

"What are you talking about?"

"Well, President Lincoln created his own debt free money to fund the civil war. When he professed to continue doing this, he was reelected and then assassinated. Even President Andrew Jackson was reelected in 1832 under the slogan 'Jackson And No Bank!' After an assassin tried to shoot President Jackson with pistols that misfired, he completed his promise to throw the Rothschild's Central bank out of America. But they got back in and called themselves the Federal Reserve. There's nothing Federal about them."

"I don't know," Gordy said with skepticism.

"How 'bout President Garfield?" Max raised his voice. "After his election in 1881, he lasted about six months before an assassin shot him. Any guesses why?"

"No. But I bet you do," Gordy smarted back.

"Yeah. Two weeks before he was assassinated, he reportedly said, 'Whoever controls the volume of money in any country is absolute master of all industry and commerce.' Why do you think Nixon resigned, Gordy?"

"Everyone knows that, Max, Watergate."

"Nixon was angry about the Vietnam War, and believed the Zionist Jews were running the country. He complained they were all over government and most were disloyal. I think he figured out who was really running the show here."

"I gotta go, Max," Gordy explained, "I'm on the clock here."

Chapter 24

Martine waved goodbye to Eva as she left *Desert Run* for the day. Before getting in her car to leave she dialed her daughter Alexa. "Hey. What're you doing?"

"Working on a new case involving drugs at the border. Big surprise. I got cell-phone detail on this one. These guys think that deleting text messages kills the evidence. They're going to really talk fast after we show them the hundreds of communications I'm reconstructing. What are you doing?"

Martine started her car. "Heading back to Jolene's. I'll pick up dinner for both of us if you want to come over. Eva has plans tonight with her friends at the barn."

"Sure," Alexa's voice perked up. "I'll be there within an hour."

"That's perfect. I'm picking-up food right now. I'll take those dogs for a walk and see you soon."

Within minutes Martine was driving up to Jolene's home. As she was parking her car her phone rang. "This is Martine," she answered.

"John, here."

"Hello," she said as she grabbed the to-go dinners from the backseat.

"I have your interviews all arranged for tomorrow. I'm confirming you'll be there."

"Absolutely."

"I don't think they're too excited about getting any assistance from you, or me. Possibly the opposite."

"That's to be expected. It can work in our favor though. When they don't want to cooperate with us it also means they won't be assisting, which translates into me being in control if the opportunity arises. Unless you wanted to do the interviews yourself."

"No. I'm probably not going to be there at all. Which is why I thought I'd see if you wanted to grab dinner tonight."

"Sorry, but I've already made plans." Martine's phone indicated she had an incoming call. "Hey, I need to take this call. I'll get in touch after the interviews. Thanks, John."

Martine took the incoming call as she walked to the kitchen, "Eva?"

With tears in her voice Eva sputtered, "There's been an accident. Adam was shot. He's dead."

Hearing the news, Martine stopped in her tracks, "What? Where? When?"

Eva vaguely expounded, "The airport I think. Yeah, I'm pretty sure they said it was at the airport. I don't remember. He was shot this afternoon I guess. We just found out."

"The airport? Who shoots someone at the airport? There's hundreds of people around."

"I don't know the details." Eva sniffled. "What is happening?"

Martine instinctively wanted to know more. "Did anyone see it?"

"I don't know, mom." Eva sounded scared, "I don't know what to do."

Martine was still on the phone when Alexa walked in. "Eva, are you alone?"

"No," Eva sniffed.

"Do you want to come over and have dinner with us?"

"Are you with Alexa?" Eva sounded more relaxed.

"Of course. Who else?"

"I don't know. I don't want to leave now. It's Sara's birthday party and I would ruin it for her if I left. I just wanted to talk to you."

"Good. That is the best way to process shocking news. Please don't talk to anyone else about it though. It might not be too safe to talk about anything related to Eli, or Adam. Keep your ears open and your thoughts to yourself. Call me when you get home if you want to talk some more." Martine said goodbye and hung up.

"What happened?" Alexa asked in alarm.

"Another death related to *Desert Run*," Martine said in bewilderment.

"Whoa. That can't be good. How's Eva taking it?"

Martine sat down at the kitchen counter. "Not well."

Grabbing plates and utensils, Alexa dished up the Mexican entrées for each of them. "Let's eat while it's still warm."

"You're right," Martine dragged her words. "I've had one roll today. I was starving till I got that phone call."

"Is there anything I can do to help?"

Martine sounded perplexed, "I don't know where to start. I'm so confused now. How can these two incidents not be related?" She let all the dogs outside.

"I agree." Alexa eagerly took a bite of food. "They probably are. Maybe I can look into cell phone records on this case too."

"Sure," Martine said absentmindedly. "Provided we get all the correct phone numbers. This situation is most likely more sophisticated than the drug trafficking case you're digging into."

"Let's say it is," Alexa sounded confident. "I just need one good phone to start the thread. I'm getting pretty good at it. If they're all disposables I'll hit some dead ends though."

Martine continued eating in silence for about a minute. "There's something else that might help."

Alexa looked up from her enchilada. "What?"

"You know I don't like to talk about it," Martine sounded secretive.

Alexa gulped her food down. "You're having more dreams. Aren't you? Have you told me everything?"

"Probably not, because they don't make any sense," Martine looked and sounded like a defeated soldier.

"I don't care," Alexa said forcibly. "You just told Eva that the best way to process something is to talk about it with the right person."

Hearing her own words repeated back to her was impressive when they came from her own daughter. "I don't know how these dreams can help. They're so abstract."

"You told me last time this happened that the more abstract the dreams, the bigger the subject matter." Alexa's eyes opened wide as she glared at her mother. "Remember? And, you just kept following the clues in those dreams and solved a crime nobody else would've ever figured out. And, it was big. It was complicated. And, you did confide in me."

"Yes I did. You also weren't employed then." Martine thought back and laughed. "And you didn't give me a choice."

"What does that have to do with anything?" Alexa shook her head in amazement. "I think I can help more now. Just try and tell me what you dreamt."

"I'll get my journal." Martine left for her bedroom and returned with her leather bound diary. "The first dream was the night of the wedding and the fire at *Desert Run*. It was about a Spanish wedding and an Indian uprising." Martine recounted the whole dream and concluded with, "That was the first dream the Indian Spirit guide left me with a detailed message."

"What was the message?" Alexa inquired thoughtfully.

"It was one of seven scrolls. Here's the first one." Martine read directly from her journal entry.

"Before you wish time was more
Expose how few provoke a war
Truth and justice are divine
Greed and gluttony for the blind
Map will lead you on our Quest
Your Job will answer and speak of rest."

Alexa shook her in disappointment. "I have no idea what that means. What about the other dreams?"

"Yes." Martine turned a page. "I had a really interesting experience the next night." Summarizing the dream experience she had with the Civil war and President Lincoln, she ended with, "And here's the second decree I received."

"History need not repeat the tale
The lessons that it taught
Evil deeds never fail
When treaties are for naught
Pledge of peace that makes one weak
Gives rise to another beast
Life is not a chore ignored
With death no longer sought
Grasp and learn what few explore
Before the war is fought."

Alexa shook her head slowly. "Gee. What could that have to do with *Desert Run?*"

"I told you," Martine said sadly. "I can't make anything of it either."

"Do you have anything else?"

Martine shrugged. "Last night I had another dream in the old west. It was a train robbery."

"A train robbery?" Alexa expelled in surprise. "Well that might make more sense than a wedding, or a visit with President Lincoln," Alexa attempted to sound reassuring. "Tell me about that one."

Martine described the events of the dream and finished with, "Then I was given the third scroll to read." Turning pages in her diary, she cleared her throat and read.

"Track the path few could do
Justice springs inside of you
Confirmation comes in two
Follow branch and know what's true
Disillusioned you are not
Now remember what's forgot."

"They don't make it easy," Martine finished.

"No. They don't. But, I can see how ChartQuest was important. What else is there? We just need to figure it out and I bet it will make sense when we are on the right path," Alexa tried to sound encouraging. "Just like last time."

Martine raked her fingers through her hair. "Well, it doesn't sound like we have a lot of time. And, it certainly alludes to some type of warring action that needs to be averted if possible. Greed and gluttony implies money and power."

"It clearly has to do with history," Alexa added." "All the dreams have to do with historical events."

"And money," Martine reiterated.

"I'm thinking Eli Morgan's murder had nothing to do with horses per se," Alexa deduced. "It has to do with money."

"Lots of money," they said together.

Martine snapped her fingers. "That doesn't mean his horse business wasn't involved though."

"I'm thinking drugs," Alexa came up with her own premise. "There's so much corruption with drug money and finding ways to launder it. There's a war on drugs because of what they do to good people, but mostly because of the corruption of money."

"Yeah," Martine countered thoughtfully, but they don't seek death. Who does that? Who benefits from people dying?"

"Besides morticians, I have no idea," Alexa responded.

"Follow branch," Martine read aloud. "What branch?"

Alexa looked confused. "All I can think of is a tree branch."

"Oh my God," Martine exclaimed. "Listen to this line. 'Your Job will answer and speak of rest.' That verse had the word Job capitalized. That means it's not referring to my job, it means it's a name. Job—like The Book of Job in the Old Testament."

"It could be," Alexa said as she scooted up to Jolene's computer and began a search for The Book of Job. "I can't imagine how that can apply to any of this stuff so far."

Martine joined Alexa at the computer. "I know what you mean." Skimming her eyes down the page as Alexa steadily scrolled the screen she added, "This is going to take forever." Martine walked away and paced in frustration. "I don't have time to study the bible right now."

Alexa calmly addressed her mother, "Give me a minute here."

Martine muttered out loud as she went back to the kitchen for her glass of water. "I don't see how that old book could have any relevance."

"You didn't last time either," Alexa reminded her.

Martine recalled how The Book of Genesis was used to communicate knowledge to her regarding an equally complex case. "Yeah, but this book is a story about a man that is tested to the brink of extinction. It's miserable."

"Not entirely," Alexa rebuffed. "I studied this book in my Theology class at Regis University. This was classified as unique because it was poetical, and God spoke in this book."

"Really? Martine said with interest. "What else do you remember?"

Alexa explained her recollections, "Job was a wealthy family man that was devoted to God and lived a righteous life. Satan didn't like Job and argued with God that Job is only good because God has blessed him abundantly. God boasts to Satan about Job's goodness. Satan challenges God to test Job, and God accepts . . . accept, Satan is forbidden to take Job's life."

"Yeah," Martine put in, "I remember that. Am I being tested?"

"No," Alexa declared adamantly. "I really doubt it. Let me finish. After Job loses everything, his friends come to comfort him and offer wisdom. They believe Job's agony is due to some sin he has committed and he must deserve God's punishment. Job argues with his friends that God lets wicked people prosper while he and countless other innocent people suffer. Job wants to confront God and complain, but he can't physically find God to do it. Even though he thinks wisdom is hidden from man, he still wants to pursue wisdom by fearing God and avoiding evil."

"Sounds like the same thing everyone still complains about at one time or another," Martine injected.

"Of course," Alexa concurred. "That's what we were focused on in the course. We examined how God is not punishing good people, but allowing Satan to test us."

Martine calmed down. "That's right—we're always being tested about making the right choices. Satan's been messing with us since the Garden of Eden."

"Anyways," Alexa continued, "that's when a young man comes and tries to straighten Job's thinking out. That's what I'm trying to find. This young boy is very advanced for his age, and sounds like a wise prophetic messenger. He was considered much wiser than the three friends that visited Job first. Here it is. His name was Elihu."

Martine retrieved her journal and returned to computer screen that Alexa was busily studying. "Give me the Chapter and Verse."

"Chapter thirty-three is where Elihu speaks to Job," Alexa announced. Reading quickly through the short verses she recalled, "My professor said the young Elihu believed that Job spent too much energy vindicating himself, rather than God. Elihu explained to Job that God communicates with humans by two ways—visions and physical pain. Here is what Elihu tells Job."

> "Behold, in this thou art not just:
> I will answer thee, that God is greater than man.
> Why dost thou strive against him?
> For he giveth not account of any of his matters.
> For God speaketh once, yea twice, yet man preceiveth it not.
> In a dream, in a vision of the night, when deep sleep falleth upon men, in slumbering upon the bed;
> Then he openeth the ears of men, and sealeth their instruction,
> That he may withdraw man from his purpose, and hide pride from man.
> He keepeth back his soul from the pit, and his life from perishing by the sword."

Martine interrupted, "Stop." Her stomach clutched. "What verse is it that speaks of dreams and visions of the night?"

Alexa skimmed the passage. "Verse fifteen."

Martine honed in. "Read fifteen and sixteen again, please."

Alexa reread the passage.

"In a dream, in a vision of the night, when deep sleep falleth upon men, in slumbering upon the bed;
Then he openeth the ears of men, and sealeth their instruction."

"Alexa, in my first dream it says 'Your Job will answer and speak of rest.' I'm receiving instructions through my dreams at night. Well apparently everyone does—I just get to remember them clearly."

"I wish I could." Alexa turned to look at her mother.

"Alexa, you realize that you're probably receiving your own promptings at night too. When I need help it quickly resonates with you. We sync up really fast. Just because you can't bring them into your physical memory, doesn't mean you're not being guided too," Martine said. "So is that the gist of Job?"

"Well," Alexa went on, "when we analyzed this book we found the dominant theme to be the difficulty of understanding why an all-powerful God allows good people to suffer, until God came to Job and Elihu and spoke to them about how people should not discuss divine justice since God's power is so great that humans cannot possibly justify his ways, or judge him. Oh, and that Job was simply a contest between Satan and God."

"Naturally," Martine figured. "This whole thing we're dealing with could amount to another complicated struggle of *good versus evil.*"

"Well, I think that's what this specific bible passage is saying," Alexa said in contemplation.

"Logically speaking," Martine processed her understanding out loud, "we can't overcome challenges without facing fears and hardships. We can't grow and expand if we're closeted away in windowless rooms."

"Can't argue with that," Alexa agreed.

"We're going to have to call it a night," Martine said with a slight yawn. "I have an early morning commitment in Scottsdale."

Alexa shut down the computer. "I heard. Are you doing it alone?"

"Yes I am. It's best that way. It takes too long and becomes unproductive if others are involved in an interview."

"Okay. Good luck. I'll talk to you tomorrow."

Chapter 25

Martine retired to bed almost immediately after Alexa departed. Feeling more conviction after exchanging information with her daughter, she pondered the seriousness of the mysterious mission she was embarking on. With a renewed sense of awareness she also remembered she was not alone in this and must rely on promptings, and ongoing insights that will assist and guide her. Like many saints and mystics that possess spiritual gifts, it's not the spiritual talent that denotes whether the person is good or bad—it's what they do with the gift of insight.

Realizing she was a warrior who humbly worked for the good of others, and like a soldier that goes to war, she would need the strength of an army.

Stroking the soft fur of the white cat that lay beside her in bed, she spoke a prayer out loud, *"God eternal I ask for your intercession. I call upon the Arc Angel Michael to assist and guide me. Surround me with pure Christ light where I call upon the Ark Angel Gabriel to seal this shield of light, and I ask the legions of Arc Angel Michael to guard me on this night. I call forth all my saints, angels, and guides to protect me on . . ."*

Losing consciousness in midsentence, Martine's mortal thoughts and body underwent a voluminous transformation that allowed her to travel through a brightly lit tunnel at the speed of light. Shimmering gold dust particles surrounded her in the passageway that connected her to a land of mystical enchantment. Filled with wonderment, she found herself occupying space in a realm alit by glorious rays of rainbow-hued lights.

Approaching from above was a glowing golden-colored chariot pulled by two large felines. As the airborne phenomena descended to meet her, Martine could make out the figure of a beautiful blonde Goddess wearing the winged helmet of a Viking warrior and armor that eerily flickered like the Aurora Borealis lights. Large in stature, sheathed sword at her side, and a wondrous golden necklace adorned with jewels that glimmered like a constellation of stars in the night sky, illustrated who she was.

Freya, the Norse Goddess from the Germanic mythology of the Viking Age positioned her magnificent chariot in front of Martine. Old Norse literature, Scandinavian tradition, and Martine's own Swedish ancestors held Freya and her brother Freyr to be historical deities titled "Lady" and "Lord" respectively. Pre-Christian Germanic religions present Freya as the possible surviving spouse of the God Odin who traveled far and wide throughout the nine worlds.

Hearing the loud purring of the two large cats that were matched in appearance further designated her as the Goddess Freya described in centuries of Eurasian folklore. It is her dealings with Odin's famous son Thor that she is most remembered for.

Legend has it that boisterous Thor woke Freya one morning when he was nosily preparing to "go fishing" for a sea dragon. Angry Freya chastised Thor for rudely waking her. While he was on the way to his fishing spot, Thor kept hearing beautiful song-like noises that seemed to be lulling him to sleep. When he stopped to investigate the source of the odd sounds, he found them coming from a nest of mewing little kittens being tended to by a tomcat. The hypnotic sound that Thor had heard was the male cat singing to the kittens, "Sleep, sleep, my dear little ones."

Thor forcibly ordered the cat to stop singing the lullaby. The tomcat sassed him back, suggesting that Thor had no idea how difficult it was for a single-male cat to rear his children alone. Thor had no interest in the cats' dilemma, but when the cat asked Thor if he knew any women who would take the kittens in, Freya immediately came to mind. Thor agreed to take them to a good home. Before the tomcat released the kittens into Thor's care he instructed Thor that they were unique cats that deserved an especially fine home. Freya was enchanted with Thor's present and did the kittens honor by letting them accompany her on her daily rounds in the sky.

Thor and Freya are also remembered well in another tale where the Giant Thrym stole Thor's hammer, and as the ransom for its return Thrym demanded Freya as his wife. Loki, who was brokering the deal, agreed to the Giant Thrym's terms, but Freya was extremely angry at being sold like this and refused. So, Thor borrowed her wondrous necklace, dressed like her in a lovely dress and long veil, and went to the Giant. Thor played the role of Freya long enough to get his hammer back and kill the Giant Thrym with it.

Stepping out of her chariot she walked towards Martine and extended her arm in a gesture of friendship. "Welcome, friend," the radiant being said with a broadening smile.

Flabbergasted at the sight of a mighty supernatural apparition, Martine took her hand and was led to a nearby garden of fragrant flowering essences where they both took a seat at a marble-honed table. Situated among lush growing foliage with colorful blossoms in brilliant blues, purples, pinks, reds, and more, she introduced herself. "I'm Martine."

Dressed in feminine warring garments that were neither ancient nor modern in appearance, signified she could slay an enemy with ease. "I'm Freya, keeper of secrets and knowledge."

Filled with wonder in a land of unfathomable brilliance, Martine returned an apprehensive smile. "How is it I'm in your enchanting garden?"

With an air of authority and seriousness in her voice, the host explained, "You would not be here if it was not ordained by the wise ones that oversee your world. In this place I can share knowledge and insight that will assist you in your earthly calling."

Serious-faced, Martine seized the opportunity. "I welcome your insight. I have asked for it. Please tell me what I should know."

"I cannot tell you any secret," Freya relayed, with her glittering dark-blue eyes focused on her guest. "You must discover this on your own. We cannot interfere directly with a human or manipulate an outcome, but I must always be truthful."

Dismayed, Martine probed, "Then how will you assist me?"

"I will tell you a story from my time," Freya said, offering up this bit of her past. "Eons ago when the world was young and being discovered, many different types of inhabitants dwelt here and fought. Even my family and I came to live here as part of an arranged peace agreement."

Martine acknowledged her own distant experience. "I'm familiar with some of the legends regarding your arrangement within Odin's land."

"Yes," Freya said briskly. "You also know from historical records some of the events that occurred during this period in time."

"Of course," Martine admitted.

"Thor's hammer was stolen by the Giant Thrym. Written accounts of the event leave out part of the story that is better forgotten—according to many. It was Loki who borrowed my robe of feathers so he could fly over the country of the Giants until he discovered the thief—Thrym. After the Giant told Loki that the hammer was buried deep within the earth and that no one would ever find it unless he got what he wanted Loki bargained for its' return to Thor, but the price was great. I must marry the Giant Thrym. I was outraged that the Gods would allow this, but because Thor's hammer was so important and must not stay in the Giants hands—I would be the prize for its return. I didn't want to leave my home and live in a dreary and desolate land of cold."

Martine sat quietly as Freya shared intimate knowledge.

"Heimdall," Freya went on to explain, "the guardian of the bridge Bifrost, suggested that Thor should go to Thrym disguised as me, in the company with Loki disguised as a handmaiden. The Gods allowed this and Thor borrowed my clothing, a thick veil, and my dazzling necklace that I never remove from around my neck."

"I do know the tale," Martine said encouragingly. "It worked, didn't it?"

"Yes. After the wedding feast, Thrym ordered the hammer to be brought in and he himself laid it in Thor's lap as a marriage gift."

Martine recollected the legends she learned as a child, "Then it is all true?"

"Yes," Freya replied patiently. "But, there is more. Loki became attracted to the necklace and its wonderment. He became obsessed with it and determined to steal it. One night he changed himself into a biting insect and came into my sleeping chamber. He bit me on the neck until I turned over—exposing the lock. He changed back into his own shape and gently removed the necklace.

Watchful Heimdall heard Loki's footsteps and witnessed the theft. Heimdall immediately set off in pursuit of Loki and overcame him. When he drew his sword to kill the thief, Loki changed himself into a flame. Heimdall quickly changed himself into a cloud, and sent down a shower of rain to put out the fire. Loki then changed to a bear and opened his mouth to catch the water. Heimdall took the form of a bigger bear and attacked Loki, who, finding that he was being overpowered, changed again into the shape of a seal. Heimdall did the same and fought a long time with Loki until he finally gave up the necklace."

Martine commented on the unusual story, "So you obviously received your beautiful necklace back and wear it always?"

"Yes, but that is not the point. The necklace is not magical. It is merely beautiful and Loki stole a necklace that he did not even need for himself."

Sadness washed over Martine. "Then why did he steal it?"

Freya's expression saddened. "He covets what is not his to take or have. He helps someone if it helps him or redeems him. The Giants would have likely been blamed and a war started if Heimdall had not been a witness that intervened. Loki deceives and steals—acquiring property that only serves his unquenchable desire for possessions, power and control. He is a master manipulator that is never caught—never resting. I tell you of this instance I know of. How many more go unrecognized because no one can see it?"

Martine maddened at thought of greed gone wrong. "Why was he never exposed and tried for what he did?"

Freya explained with gold tears dropping on the marble. "From the time Loki was a little boy the sins of greed, and gluttony were already eating away at him—eroding whatever good he might have had. Who wouldn't expect him to grow out of that?" Freya said as she directed Martine's attention to the majestic landscape that stretch on and on. With graceful movements in the air, Freya brought attention to a world of colored tapestry, fruitful trees, crystal waterfalls, and mighty mountains. "Instead he became an instrument of growing evil that went unchallenged, allowing him to become a master deceiver."

Martine remained confused. "I must look for someone with these qualities. Is that it?"

"Like the essence from a beautiful flower filling your soul with joy, the essence of something putrid can permeate a soul with darkness. Your sight, like mine, can see this."

Recognizing a connection finally, Martine sounded encouraged, "If I ask questions can you give me answers?"

"Yes, but I can give you something better," Freya said with a lilt in her voice. Signaling to her exquisitely gorgeous Eurasian Lynx cats, they both stood up at the command. "My beautiful Lynx will be your guides. They are watchful and highly aware." Strong bodied and long-legged the burnt-orange colored tortoiseshell tabbies rubbed up passionately on Freya's thighs.

Studying the physical features of the two exotic creatures, characterized by their short tails and tufts of fur that sprout out of the top of each ear, Martine asked more, "How can you let your cats be my guides?"

"Because Animal Spirits choose you, you do not choose them, and it's their medicine they share. They will be with both of us now. You can ask questions about them."

Seizing the opportunity to obtain more information about her own mission, she artfully queried the beautiful Goddess, "Why would these precious cats choose me?"

"Powerful guardians like these are aspects of the human psyche resurfacing from the pre-conscious ancient mind. They can only serve and protect a formidable soul that has the gift to see another's true nature, has the knowledge to see the truth through walls and dimensions, and can perceive the heart of others."

"How will they help me?" Martine asked.

"These Lynx have powerful eyesight that can see through mountains, and the false identities others hide behind. Their medicine aids in revealing everything that his hidden from most other souls. With uncanny instincts they recognize secrets, agendas, and guilty actions. Their great abilities of stealth and cunning will track where others would not go. They possess the power of good silence. And with their medicine you will be able to hear the higher purpose intended by the Creator. They will provide powerful double protection wherever you may tread."

Wide-eyed with this revelation, Martine looked down at the cats. "I'm honored."

"Yes. These are supernatural cats with powers held only for those who have earned them. Their energy oversees and teaches the truth of all things and the wisdom of eternities. You will also need . . .," Freya's voice faded and her body dissipated as Martine was pulled out of the ancient dimension through the tunnel of time.

Transported back to the Dragoon Mountains, she faced the Old Indian Guide she had encountered previously.

"Greetings, friends," the wise man said. Noticeably younger in appearance, the familiar Indian continued as he approached Martine, "You and your guides are now ready for another decree."

Confused, she looked down to see both the cats had traveled with her between the realms. Smiling with satisfaction, she confidently relayed, "Yes, I believe we are."

Handing her the scroll he cautioned her, "When you read the words out loud, know they are heard and celebrated by everyone that serves the Creator. The words that are written will travel back with you when you return home."

Martine carefully loosened the scroll and read it aloud.

"Knowledge grows like a tree
Never staying just a seed
Nations wait on bended knee
Seeking peace to be free
Twofold meaning in a crest

Has misled all the rest
Roll the stones Chart the Quest
Find the ones that suppress."

Instantly Martine's spirit was returned to her own physical existence before waking up to a glorious sunrise—squeezing it's rays of light through bedroom mini blinds.

Squinting at her clock for the exact time shocked her back to reality—she had overslept. Martine sprang from her bed, looking for her clothes and a quick fix to her hair and face.

Chapter 26

At eight-forty-five Martine arrived at Ray's office. Begrudgingly, he invited her in and explained his procedures, "The interrogation rooms have been arranged to sequester Tom, Janice, and Rachel. I can assist if you want."

After cordial introductions with Ray and his staff, Martine asked to be briefed on any information he had recovered from his efforts since their apprehension.

"This is a group of gaudy gremlins," Ray explained dryly. "I've already grilled them like overcooked burgers." Summarizing a rap sheet, Ray explained, "The girl in the first room is Rachel. She resides with her man, Eddy, at the home we raided. She's not cooperating at all. Tom and Janice are in the other two rooms, and like Rachel, they're not talking either. They say they don't know anything, and they weren't involved. This is a waste of time until we get back some forensics on prints, ballistics, DNA, and the Medical Examiners findings. It's a wrap with these three. They might be out by the weekend."

Martine listened intently as Ray continued to discourage her from interviewing the only possible witnesses at their disposal. Unable to accept defeat without trying, she remained complacent as he reiterated his defeatist inclinations about the three suspects.

"This is most likely a botched robbery or drug deal gone-bad. Until we find Eddy and figure out who's who in the zoo, we won't have those answers," Ray finished—tightly crossing his arms in front of his chest.

"I'll take that file," Martine said as she reached for Ray's folder. "I'll need at least a dozen more folders, a black marker, and post-its."

"Don't think I can prove rain is wet—do you? Or, that I'm organized enough for the FBI?"

Ignoring his comeback, Martine replied cordially, "No, not at all. I'm actually counting on the fact you are." She forced a smile and accepted the office supplies Ray had gathered from his credenza. After speed-reading through Ray's folder she quickly wrote on the blank folders and threw a few documents in each one. She then scribbled notes on the post-its and plastered them on the fronts of each file. "Okay, I'm ready."

"Miguel," Ray summoned. "Let's get this over with."

"Are you coming?" Martine inquired.

"Sure. I'll be there in a minute." He dismissed her off with a wave.

Twitchy as a fly-swatting horsetail, Miguel scrambled into the little office and introduced himself. "This way to the interview rooms," he directed in a fast speaking Spanish accent.

Escorting Martine to the first interview room, Miguel presented her to Rachel and shrugged his shoulders as he departed—indicating his doubt that anything new would be forthcoming from Martine's involvement. Dressed in the seductive clothing she was wearing the night she was brought in, Rachel appeared smug and aloof.

"Oh, I thought Ray wanted to see me. They told me I could dress the way I want for our meeting. Is he coming?"

"Probably not," Martine answered, shaking her head in amazement. "But he can watch if he wants."

"Good." Rachel smiled big and waved into the camera mounted in the corner of the room. "Hey, Ray," she said alluringly.

"My name is Martine and I'm with the FBI. Can you tell me what you were doing last Saturday night?"

"Sure. Me and Eddy was watching TV."

Setting down her newly prepared stack of file folders, Martine pulled her chair out and sat down across from Rachel. "Based on all the drugs, cash, and gold coins, recovered at your residence, it's hard to believe you were just watching TV all night."

"I swear—that's all we did. Eddy makes a lot of money."

Resting her arms in a folded position on top of the files, Martine leaned forward and replied sarcastically, "Right. Can you explain where any of those expensive items were purchased?"

"Sure," Rachel replied, "Eddy's friends."

"Which friends? And where's Eddy?"

"Well, everyone's Eddy's friend, and I don't know where they are. Boys night out I guess."

Amazed by her candor, Martine sat back. "You know, Rachel, it's easy to live in denial until you're exposed." Martine fanned the pile of files so Rachel could see the quantity of them in front of her.

"Exposed?" Rachel replied coyly.

"Well of course." Martine picked up the first folder. "You've been fingerprinted." While dropping the folder in front of Rachel, Martine looked at her hard until she saw her shift her weight for more comfort. Snatching the next folder, she added, "You're DNA is now on record." Letting that folder drop on top of the one in front of Rachel, she held up a third folder. "This is my favorite. Wanta guess what's in here?"

Rachel looked nervously at the third folder. "I don't care. None of them items they found have anything to do with me. If they're stolen it was Eddy's friends who did it. Eddy doesn't have to steal."

Martine raised her eyebrows in speculation. "Even if its drugs? Doesn't matter—if I can connect you to this evidence you're a party to the crime—a really big bad crime."

"How you gonna connect me to the evidence?"

"This is an order to have your blood drawn," Martine said as she dropped the third folder on top of Rachel's growing pile.

"No way. You're not sticking a needle in me," Rachel flipped her hair, flaunting her flagrance towards any forced intrusions that law enforcement could impose.

"You're right. I'm not," Martine said emphatically. "A nurse will—with an orderly, if that's what it takes."

"What do you need my blood for?"

Martine picked up her fourth folder and proceeded, "This is a dictation of all the illegal items recovered by the investigators. There's a unique prescription drug called Ketamine that's listed here. I find that drug to be the most interesting in this laundry list of illegal substances."

"I don't know anything about that."

Martine conjectured, "You probably know it as 'Special K' out on the streets. They recovered enough vials to sedate eighty horses."

Rachel's smirky grin withered. "It's for horses?"

"You bet." Amping up like a fire storm, Martine implied the bitter results she had acquired, "And, this drug is illegal without a doctor's prescription. It also would be a script from a Veterinarian. Do you own eighty horses? Or, did you use it, and plan to sell it as a club drug?"

"Even if I did use it, you can't prove it's ever been stolen by me or, anybody."

"Can't I?" Martine pulled a page out of the folder. "Even if we prove these lot numbers can be traced to the prescriptions filled by the deceased?"

Agitated by the notion she could be linked to this drug and then to the stolen items, Rachel snapped back at Martine, "My Eddy is a good man. He would never kill anyone. I hope you never catch him. You're not gonna pin anything on us because we're good people."

Unable to control her annoyance towards Rachel, Martine's blue eyes flashed as she used her words like a weapon, "Most people don't use drugs that turn their minds into Jurassic brain-matter. While you remain in denial and contemplate another excuse—do consider this, your limitations are a result of bad, lazy, and selfish choices—probably drug induced and smothered with ignorance. When you're ready to talk—wave at the camera. I'm late for my other appointments. They asked to see me." Martine pretended. "Maybe I'll get the information I want from the other two guests residing in jail with you." Looking at her watch, she added, "Guess I might not see you again until your trial—in about three years. The drug charges are gonna hold you till then."

Rachel seethed at Martine, "I'm not going down for this, bitch. You got nothing on me you can prove."

Martine leered at the riled Rachel. "Complicity to commit murder, Rachel. I suspect they'll have enough to expose you like a stripper on a pole."

"You can't talk to me like that."

Martine ended the cursory interview. "And, you can't break the law and get away with it."

Rachel sat speechless with her mouth open as Martine gathered her folders and left.

Outside the room, Martine was met by Ray and Mahoney. Surprised, Martine greeted the FBI Chief, "Hello. Did you think I needed some help here? Ray is doing a great job. I think it's going well—don't you, Ray?" Martine said as she breezed by to the next interview room.

Somewhat overwhelmed by Martine's interviewing technique, Ray's perplexed face bobbed up and down. "More entertaining than I thought it would be."

Mahoney grinned and patted Ray on his shoulder. "It's been my experience, to use Martine when you think you've hit a dead end. She'll at the least point you in a new direction or, scare up some new leads. And no matter how hopeless the clues are, she'll have an opinion. Let's see what happens next."

Martine let herself into the room where Janice was held. Determined to keep the momentum going and stir up some action between the perps being contained, she introduced herself and got down to business. "Gee, Janice, I can't tell what's longer, your work resume, or your rap sheet. You obviously can't keep a job, or stay out of trouble."

Janice kept her face turned away from Martine.

Martine looked up from the report. "Why don't you tell me why you were found at Eddy and Rachel's with possible stolen goods?"

Plain looking Janice stayed tight-lipped and defied Martine's presence with complete silence. Resting back in her chair her body language demonstrated intent to not cooperate—letting her personality of resentment and hate simmer underneath.

Ignoring Janice's demeanor, Martine deduced behavioral evidence found in Ray's folder. "Appears you've been on your own since you were thirteen. You're a reported runaway. Says here your mom's boyfriend was eventually charged with raping a little girl in the apartment building you lived in. I'm guessing you were molested by him too. Wonder why you're mom didn't press charges. Ever talk to your mom about that?"

Breathing hard like a swimmer coming up for air, Janice broke her silence, "How do you know that?"

"I told you, we have your rap sheet and it's as long as the Mississippi River. At your age, you don't get that without some real deep seated issues. If you were conditioned as a child to prey on others to survive, it would explain why you won't cooperate and why you always choose the wrong people to live with. Do you play well with others? Doesn't look like it here."

Janice's eyes flashed with hostility when she bellowed, "What do you mean?"

Martine's serious face darkened. "I bet you buck anyone's attempt to control you. You apparently had a wicked dependence on prescription drugs when you were still a Juvenal. That would be the perfect time to start a bad habit that you never kicked. I think you were involved with drugs to initially dull the pain, and then had to deal them to others to support your lifestyle. You're like a poster child of pain and self-loathing because of a disturbing childhood."

More alert due to Martine's frank observations, Janice barked, "You bitch, that's not in my file?"

Struggling not to react to Janice's aggressions, Martine fake-smiled. "More or less it is. Janice, you've had a good run for about two decades. The free fall's over now. You've been caught and will be investigated for the theft, arson, and the homicides of two people. You're going to be prosecuted this time for at least the possession of the drugs and stolen items."

Less obstante now, Janice huffed, "I would never kill someone."

"Well, unless you want to wear an orange tunic that spills over your baggy orange pants you might want to tell me who did."

Martine scrunched her forehead. "And tell me why, or you're going to be the one languishing in prison for multiple crimes. It only takes one of you to speak-up and turn states evidence. Only one of you will get the chance to reboot your life."

Startled by the realization she was about to squeal, Janice sucked in her cheeks and shook her head briskly. "I don't know what you're talking about. I wasn't there."

Martine shrugged her irritation. "Okay, we're done here I guess. I'm going to put through my orders for a blood test, phone records, and polygraph to go along with your DNA and fingerprinting results. You're going to be registered in every criminal database around the planet. If you think of something you want to tell us I can come back. I'm late for my last meeting today—with Tom. Maybe he'll throw you under the bus and we won't need to talk again."

"Don't hold your breath, lady," Janice said haughtily.

"Why's that?"

"Because I wasn't there. I was out of town."

"Great. That might help clear you. Where were you?"

"Tucson. I went to see a friend."

"Really. Since you haven't given that information to the detectives, I'll take that now. Need names, dates, and times to check this out."

"I don't have to tell you anything. I'm innocent until proven otherwise."

"You're a suspect until you prove otherwise."

"You're a bitch," Janice barked.

"I bet your alibi has more holes in it than a flyswatter. But, you've given us something to verify. Hope you weren't lying. It's a crime to lie to a Federal Agent."

"No way am I talking to you anymore."

Martine absorbed Janice's words and emotions before provoking her again. "That's okay. You've talked enough. Oh, by the way, you've been a resourceful gal till now. You're probably relatively intelligent too. Wonder if you'll know how to save yourself this time? Oh, if your cell phone was used near the crime scene and not Tucson, you go to the top of the suspect list."

Janice raged at Martine with a litany of illiterate and uncouth words.

Martine poked the lion in the cage again. "Janice, how do you like your new living conditions?"

"They're good," Janice smarted off. "I'm just fine here till you have to let me go."

"Great. Let me see what I can do about that."

Janice started raving again, "You can't keep me here, pig."

Martine ignored Janice and left for Tom's interview room in a hurry. She had left him alone the longest and saved him for last. A puff of air followed her as she moved quickly past Ray and Mahoney.

After a brief introduction, she started-in, "Tom, I think you know why I'm here. Can you share any information regarding the fire and homicides at Mr. Morgan's home?"

"Lady, why am I here? I don't know anything about it."

Martine set down her file folders. "Looks like you're facing some serious charges. If you help me I can see about reducing some of them."

Surly and defiant manners reverberated through his loud vocals, "Told you, I don't know what you're talking about."

"Let's see here. One of the victims was shot with a 9mm pistol . . . that's just not sexy for a guy like you. Who do you think shot this guy?"

"You're right." Tom shrugged his arrogance. "I wouldn't use a gun like that if I needed to kill someone."

"Exactly." Martine lifted her brow. "Who brings a switchblade to a gunfight?"

"Not me." Tom's bloated ego remained in control. "Must mean I didn't do it."

"Right. But the other guy was repeatedly stabbed to the hilt. That was done by a strong man. Know anyone that could do that?"

"Nope."

"Someone with as much anger as strength would drive a knife into a victim all the way to the handle."

Tom's forehead buckled into a deep frown and froze. "Why would I murder anyone?"

"There's a saying that for every one person that dreams of making a million dollars, there's a million people that dream of having a million dollars. There's no shortage of people willing to kill for love . . . love of money. Why don't you tell me where you got the jewelry you were wearing?"

"Sure," Tom said, pointing to her chest. "After you tell me why you wear that stuff around your neck?" Martine glanced down at her crucifix and other medals worn daily for her protection.

"Why don't you explain why you're wearing that hardware around your wrists and ankles? Checkmate."

"Now tell me where you got the items found on you during your arrest."

"Lost-n-found."

Martine's irritation swelled. "Lost-n-found. Who loses Gold Krugerrands? 22-Karat gold bullion coins were found by you?"

"Sure were," he claimed.

"You know, Tom, pumping gas into someone's car, don't make it your car. Those items link you to several serious crimes."

"You can't prove that. Like I said, I found the stuff. You can't charge me if I haven't done the crime. Am I free to go or not?"

Martine's voice thinned, "You were until you made a false police report. Says here you got these coins from a guy who bought your car. Doesn't appear you had a car."

"Well, I'm telling you the truth now."

"Looks like we need to clear you of this offense. I'll arrange that polygraph you wouldn't submit to yesterday. That should speed things up and get the truth out."

Tom's dangerous temper boiled to the surface. "I'm not taking a polygraph. You're just setting me up to take the fall for a crime I didn't commit. You're just trying to pin something on me I didn't do. I've seen you guys do this to anybody you pick-up."

"Gee, Tom, though you could use my help. That's the fastest way I can clear you—for now. Guess you'll just have to sit tight here while the investigators do their job."

"None of you are doing your jobs, or you'd be out looking for the real guys that need to do the time. Tell them to get off their asses and start looking. You can't prove anything, or you would've charged me by now. You're going to have to let me go if you know what's good for you."

Perturbed by Tom's threatening arrogance, Martine shook her head. "You know what the difference between you and a puppy is, Tom?"

Tom scoffed, "I don't care."

Martine got up to leave. "A puppy stops whining when it grows up. I hope your own defiant arrogance doesn't rob you of your life."

"Never has," Tom said.

"I see you're from Michigan. In Arizona convicted murderers get the death penalty." Leaving Tom alone with some hard truths, Martine joined Ray, Miguel, and Mahoney in the hall.

"I told you . . . you're not getting any more information out of these three than I did," Ray bragged.

"Not yet," Martine replied confidently.

Ray added, "Was that part of your torture sequence? I doubt if you were the threat that was going to break them. I'm out of here." Unimpressed, Ray snatched his files back from Martine.

"Actually," Martine said as she flicked a loose hair from her cheek. "I gave you legal reasons to keep all three of them detained while you check out their stories and sequester the records you need. Put a rush on everything. You just need to catch them in a lie."

"Damn, Ray," Miguel exclaimed. "She's good. I didn't see that either."

Grins faded as Ray gave Miguel a perturbed look. Thrusting the load of files at him as he turned to leave, Ray spontaneously uttered, "What is wrong with your Chihuahua-sized brain?"

"Ray," Miguel called-out as he chased after his boss.

"That man burns my toast," Martine commented.

"He certainly is fascinating," Mahoney replied.

"I want to thank you for getting me cleared to work with you on this case," Martine said appreciatively.

"Yes, about that, your boss couldn't believe it took this long for me to ask for your help. You have quite a reputation in your office up there. Is this what happens every time you go on vacation?"

Martine made a dissatisfied frown, "No. This is why I don't go on vacation."

Mahoney chuckled, "Have dinner with me tonight."

"Gee, I don't know if I'm in a position to do that right now."

Mahoney paused a few seconds, "Are you in a position to eat? I might have something you want by then."

Chapter 27

Martine felt stuck after her three interviews. Desperate to find some direction to take the investigation, she headed back to *Desert Run.* Olivia and Eva were focused on conditioning a horse inside the arena and the rest of the grooms and exercise riders were wrapping up their chores for the day that began at seven—due to the extremely hot afternoon heat. Restless in thought, Martine looked for Eva's energetic prodigy.

"Sara," Martine announced herself as she walked up to the girl. "I could really use that tour today if you have time. You should introduce me to your favorite horse."

More enthusiastic than normal, Sara cheered, "Absolutely." Coaxing the horse she was leading into a trot, she hurried the stocky dark bay gelding into its stall. "Let's go."

Together they walked out of the stable and crossed the driveway to the next long barn of horses. Each building was so large in itself, that Martine felt like she entered a foreign land with new; faces, customs, and language. "Is everyone in this barn going to be speaking Spanish?" Martine whispered discretely as she observed a dozen or so Mexican workers cleaning stalls and forking woodchips.

"Yeah, probably. Even if they know English they pretend they don't." Sara waved at a couple of boys that were staring at her. "I get to visit this barn because Julio and I are friends. I don't know what I'll do when he's gone."

Martine stopped at a stall decorated with ribbons and plaques. "Who's this?"

"That's Quest's famous daddy, Royal Wonder," Sara clarified proudly. "He's retired."

"Where's Quest?" Martine asked.

"He's down here," Sara said as she headed down the aisle. Stopping in front of another large stall with a private horse-run, her voice beamed with admiration as the horse trotted up to her, "Quest, you beautiful boy. Isn't he magnificent?"

"Wow, he is handsome," Martine marveled as she walked up close to the colt's stall. "So this is Odin's Quest, hah? Words don't describe him." Petting the lovable horse's nose, she added, "Where's his dam?"

"She's with the mares and foals."

Martine studied the many achievements and awards posted on the young colts stall door. Already it was apparent that Odin's Quest was on the road to greatness in the competitive world of horse breeding. Among the numerous accolades' was a pedigree diagram boldly tabled *Chart Odin's Quest Ancestry*. Presuming this information may be relevant to Olivia's horse interests, or Eli's estate, she carefully examined the horse's family tree.

"I'm going to go get Quest's horse treats," Sara broke the silence as she dashed off to the tack room where she became predictably distracted by the attention of numerous stable boys.

Realizing Sara was engaged in the gossipy barn-talk in a trade unfamiliar to anyone else—Martine resumed scrutinizing the pedigree chart like a Last Will & Testament that named the legal heirs to a horses famous bloodlines. Every established breed has certain prominent sires and dams. These names will indicate an exceptionally well-bred foal, and usually be reflected through identifying names—which are passed down through the generations that follow. Knowing bloodlines help predict a horse's suitability as a performer or as future breeding stock, Martine grabbed one of the horses breeding brochures.

"I'm back, Quest," Sara said eagerly as she dropped a horse treat into his feed bucket. "I'll be back tomorrow too."

Breaking Martine's concentration brought the title of the horse advertisement *Chart Odin's Quest Ancestry* back into focus. "What is this?" She looked closely at the chart.

Glancing at the information Martine was reading, Sara answered, "I don't understand that stuff either. You'll have to ask someone else."

Bewildered, Martine rubbed the colt's nose before saying her goodbyes, "See ya later, Quest."

Martine's mind churned as she exited Eli's barn. Was this horse's pedigree what she was supposed to be charting? Possibly ownership issues were unresolved. As they approached their barn they were greeted by Olivia.

"Do you have a minute?" she asked Martine.

"Of course." Martine motioned towards the same table they sat at the day before.

Pulling some folded papers from her back pocket, Olivia strained a smile as she handed them to Martine. "Here's what I got on my arrangements with Eli."

"Great. I'll look this over tonight and get back to you. Do you have a minute? I've got a couple questions about that colt Quest."

"Sure. I know a little."

"Do you have any arrangements with Eli regarding this colt?"

"No," Olivia said fervently. "I'm not in that business. Too expensive for me."

"I'm glad, because I'm more interested in Quest's pedigree history and what makes him so valuable."

"That's easy," Olivia responded matter-of-factly. "His parents, Nero's Quest and Royal Wonder were both champions and qualified breeding stock. They both retired late in their careers and had little time left in the span of breeding offspring. The sire, Royal Wonder was already twenty years old, and the dam, Nero's Quest was twenty-one years old. She's probably never going to carry a foal again. But, it's the third generation that matters in the studbooks. Nero's Quest was out of Nero's Hero and Ashkenazi's Quest. They were the solid breeding identifier Eli sought. Eli told me it was because the great grand dam was Ashkenazi's Star and considered to have the purest bloodline available at that time."

"I'm assuming Ashkenazi's Star was the primary bloodline he was preserving," Martine said with a clarifying tone. "That would be indicative in naming the offspring Ashkenazi's Quest, which would carry her name forward."

"Yes," Olivia said enthusiastically, "you're right."

"I also assume these two horses have passed."

"We can assume that because of their age I guess." Olivia agreed with a questionable tone.

"What do you mean?"

Olivia thought hard. "Eli told me a story about that. He said that the horses vanished during WWII. He apparently searched very hard to find this bloodline when he got into breeding. Horses were stolen and traded back then. He never explained how he finally located the horse he got." She pondered the memories in her mind. "Eli did say it was a miracle from God that he found an off-spring from Ashkenazi's Star. He said he'd tell me the whole story someday and I would be extremely fascinated."

"He must have trusted you very much, Olivia."

"I guess he did. He's been so good to me. Oh, he also said the missing horse became a famous mystery story that was never solved, but he knows what happened. He said it was too dangerous to tell anyone what he knew. He was very private and secretive."

"No doubt," Martine said grimly. "German men tend to be anything but chatty. More like guarded with few words to say."

"He did sorta imply that when he found the horse, the owner had no idea of its real value."

"Did he ever locate anymore horses from that bloodline?"

Olivia searched her memory. "No, not that he didn't try. I know he was convinced he had the only surviving offspring to Ashkenazi's Star."

Martine recapped, "Eli was successful in breeding the bloodline he considered pure. He also hasn't found any other horses from that bloodline that he could acquire. Is that correct?"

"Yeah," Olivia agreed. "That's pretty much the story."

"That's what makes this colt valuable like a Picasso," Martine surmised.

"I guess it does," Olivia raised a brow. "Maybe more. The first foal he bred was a filly. Eli always said that Nero's Quest could change everything. She was a champion throughout an intense Olympic career and consistently proved she was in a league of her own. By the time Eli acquired the perfect stallion to breed her with, she was eighteen. She finally had her own foal. And she had a stallion colt," Olivia said with pride.

"I can clearly see the importance of this breeding accomplishment," Martine said positively.

"I see you do."

"I'm assuming the sire and dam to Nero's Quest have German bloodlines, since Ashkenazi means Germans."

"You do know your history."

"Law is history—recorded."

Martine's phone rang and she excused herself to take the call. "I think we're done here for now, Olivia. I'll get back to you if I have more questions."

As she hurried out the building she answered her phone, "Hey, Alexa, how's it going?"

"Okay. Nothing new right now."

"Alex," she said hastily, "can you check something for me?"

"Did you find something out today when you met with Ray?"

"Yes, and no," Martine sounded downtrodden. "I didn't get anything helpful, and he's not going to make it happen."

"Excuse me? Isn't that what I told you?"

"Yes . . . maybe," Martine replied.

"What did you think was going to happen?" Alexa scolded.

Martine didn't really have an answer. "Let's just say in an area of over four million people we could use the support of at least seventy, state, local, and federal law enforcement personnel. Today, we got you and me—oh, and the watchful eye of John Mahoney. Needless to say the only people interested in this case are the local news reporters. We are flying blind under the radar."

Alexa laughed as Martine vented. "Well, tag I'm it then. What can I do to help?"

"I believe that there're more people involved in this crime. I know Ray's guys haven't located the renter-slash-drug dealer Eddy. I think the gang split up. What if you could pin another address down from Eddy, or Jake's computer?"

"I get it," Alex exclaimed. "I only requested information on who searched for directions to Eli Morgan's address. I didn't have ChartQuest look for every address searched on Jake Monroe, or Eddy's computer—which of course we didn't know about at the time."

"Exactly. Move fast on this, please."

"Of course. I'll call you if I get anything."

Chapter 28

Martine walked up to John Mahoney's booth where he was keenly engaged in a phone conversation. Looking up to her as she approached, he nodded eagerly for her to be seated across from him. "Okay, Brian, that's just great. Thanks for moving on this so quickly. I'll be back to you tomorrow." Mahoney hung up and smiled like a Cheshire cat.

Martine returned a quizzical grin. "What've you been up to?"

Mahoney smiled. "I called in a favor on your case."

"You mean the one on life support?"

Mahoney smiled reassuringly. "Yah . . . that one. Well, when you interviewed the elusive Tom, I couldn't miss your observation that a knife had been used that cut through the victim to the 'hilt.' I haven't heard that term used for quite awhile, but it reminded me of a case I worked twenty years ago where we nailed the guy based on the location and angle of the stab wounds found on our victim. Tom was left-handed like our assailant was. The cuts and angles proved a left-handed guy committed the attack. Tom was left handed—right?"

Martine thought, "Yes, he was. When he pointed at my necklaces he used his left hand to point."

"Exactly," Mahoney said. "That was Brian Lane the coroner. I asked him to examine the stab wounds on Eli and give me his initial report on those findings. He said the wounds are on the left and the angle of the cuts is from a left-handed individual."

"Wow. That should take the bloom off Tom's rosebush. Thanks for pulling in that favor. That might make him squirm. We just need one to cave, and we begin dismantling their alibis."

"That's my thinking." Mahoney affirmed with a nod. Handing Martine a menu he continued, "Everything is good here."

"Great, I'm starving. Trying to keep up with Eva and all the work at that barn is exhausting."

Mahoney studied the three page menu. "I think you can relax now. We can probably get Tom when we get the corners report, cell phone records, and property loss reports from the insurance carrier."

Martine cut him off, "You know that Tom didn't have any cuts on his hands, or blood on his clothes. Right?"

"Yeah, but, that doesn't exclude him."

"Yep," Martine said absentmindedly as she read her menu. "It should definitely help scare him into talking or pointing the finger." She smiled ominously. "Pretty sure you can get all of them to start talking soon. Cravings for the next 'high' have dominated their lives and actions for so long they'll all wanta talk and cut a deal by the weekend."

Mahoney laughed and set his menu down at the end of the table. "From what I've reviewed, the fire obscured a great amount of evidence. They haven't found any weapons that could have been used in the commission of the crimes, and there may not be much else to use from the crime scene," he cautioned. "Even all the security equipment was destroyed."

"I know," Martine acknowledge as she placed her menu on top of his. "That's why I need an intense background-check done on Morgan."

"What?" Mahoney sat back. "We're going to get these three to confess."

A friendly waitress approached the table. "Are you ready to place your orders?"

"Confess to what?" Martine said to Mahoney. Acknowledging the waitress, she answered her politely, "I'll have the cheeseburger and fries with lots of ketchup."

Still focused on their conversation, Mahoney ordered without looking at the waitress, "I'll have the same." He leaned towards Martine to whisper his words until the girl was gone and out of earshot, "Murder, theft, drugs, and arson. Isn't that enough?"

"Don't think so." Martine swept her hair back from her face.

"You don't think so," Mahoney repeated. "What are you saying? What else is there?"

"I don't know yet. I know Morgan is a mystery to everyone all by himself. What's the connection that made these degenerates think he was worth robbing? Where is Eddy? What else was in that big walk-in safe?"

"You're serious. You think this case is bigger than it is? You want something challenging to work on while you're on vacation? I gotta very complicated case I could use your help with."

Martine shook her head in doubt. "Let's just assume this case might not be as advertised, and it's more complex than some petty criminals that botched a murder and theft with an arson cover-up. How'll we know for sure without doing a thorough job investigating? So far it's a crime with murder and arson. That's all the police are focused on."

Mahoney gave a protesting glance. "You're a lawyer, Martine. Not an investigator. This really isn't even your case."

"I know that, John. You're not going to find anything you're not looking for though."

"Like what? I wasn't going to look for anything until you handed me this case. What else can it be? A hate crime? A drug ring?"

"Again, if it were a hate crime it's still under your jurisdiction. The FBI is the sole investigative force for criminal violations of Federal Civil Rights Statutes—he was from Germany."

"What?" Mahoney laughed out loud.

"Get me everything you can on Morgan, Eddy, and that Jake Monroe. I want to know Morgan's life history all the way back to his great great grandparents."

"Is that a joke? What the heck are you trying to do?"

"That's how we bring our victim back to life."

Mahoney made a thoughtful pause, "That's interesting. I don't see it, but I'm listening. I've been down this road before with you. You didn't follow my directions then either—did you?"

"We might only have one chance to get this right. I'm on this now while it actually has a chance to be solved."

"Were you serious about this being connected to a really old cold case?"

"More now than ever."

Their cheerful waitress arrived with two charbroiled cheeseburgers with heaping sides of crispy fries. "Here's two bottles of ketchup. Can I get anything else for you folks?"

"No thank you," they both said together.

"Tell me what you could possibly be looking for."

Martine calmly regrouped her thoughts and laughed at an old memory. "You have been down this road before with me. I know you don't think I listen, but maybe I listen too well. When the girls were very young—preschool age, we were all in the car driving home from mass. Alexa was listening to James and I discuss the sermon which was about which path to take when you meet life's difficult challenges. She heard us referring to the 'fork in the road' metaphor. We were both surprised when she asked us to explain what a 'fork in the road' was. We had no idea she was tuned in to our conversation. After I explained the concept we came to a split in the freeway. I pointed out to her what a real fork in the road looked like and how it compared to choosing the correct path—versus the easy path in life. Suddenly her little sister Eva—probably no more than two years old yelled, 'did you run over it?'" Martine laughed again at the little girls' innocence. "Anyways, I have never forgotten the lesson I taught my own daughters. They made a lasting impression on me that the correct answers will come from searching outside the box. For taking action when the requirement is greatest and not taking the easy road." Martine finished with an acknowledging nod.

"Well, from what I've seen, you are a testament to that," Mahoney laughed with her.

Martine cut her burger in half. "Jake made the critical mistake of communicating long distance which means the case is inter-state. That status alone means it should be turned over to the FBI. Because the conspiracy and solicitation started out-of-state it constitutes Federal jurisdiction. You should be driving this investigation."

"What else is there to investigate? How 'bout you fill me in this time. Maybe I can be of some real help. I already know what you're capable of if I don't get involved."

"Well, when you put it like that." Martine managed a smile. "I'm looking for the architect, not the carpenter."

"What does that mean? We're not looking? Everyone is working on this. Are you taking this too personally? Trying to find something that isn't there?"

Martine's body began to stiffen. "Of course not."

"You know that I'll have to rescind your involvement if you are," Mahoney sounded official. "I don't want you to interfere with an on-going investigation and make a mistake because your daughter is personally involved in this case."

Martine's smile vanished. "Seriously?"

Looking stoic, Mahoney nodded. "Yes."

Martine took a deep breath and threw her napkin on the table. "Fine," she said as she started to leave.

Mahoney grabbed her wrist. "I wouldn't do that. Not to you. Please sit back down. I'm gonna help."

"Okay." Martine bit her bottom lip and sat back down. "I just know in my gut there's more to this."

"Let's say you're right." Mahoney resumed eating. "Let's review what we know, and don't know."

"We need to find Eddy, Martine said without hesitation as she snatched a fry and dipped it in ketchup. "He knows what happened, or he's a victim too."

"I see." Mahoney contemplated the idea. "He may not be hiding."

"Right," Martine said ardently as she eyed her dinner companion.

"That's easy." Mahoney smiled. "We let Rachel out and put her under constant surveillance. She'll lead us to him. The only thing she might be guilty of is a lecherous eye and illegal drug use."

Grinning at the humorous thought, Martine chuckled, "She'll lead us to Eddy? Rachel couldn't find water on a Caribbean cruise."

He laughed out loud. "Then we'll let Tom out, and I'll nail an agent to his butt."

Martine's phone rang as she set down the bottle of ketchup. "Hey," she greeted the caller.

"I got something. This is good," Alexa sounded encouraged. "ChartQuest came through again."

"Really. What'd you find out?"

"There was another search for directions in the Phoenix warehouse district. An abandoned warehouse. I got the address."

Grabbing a pen and napkin, Martine said eagerly, "Great, let me have it."

"Only if you promise not to go there without me tomorrow."

"I promise." Martine grinned confidently. "I won't go there alone tomorrow." Writing down the information Alexa relayed to her, she ended the communication, "Good. I'll get back to you."

"Who was that," Mahoney asked.

"Alexa. I think our case just grew legs."

Interested, Mahoney raised his eyebrows, "Really? What did my new recruit find now?"

"She got another address for me to check-out."

"For you? What're you looking for?"

"Something about this case bothers me. I think the three they have in custody are just the low hanging fruit."

Mahoney swallowed a big bite of his burger. "In the drug world, of course they are. They still did the crime though."

Martine stirred her ketchup with a fry. "Yes, but if there are more people involved it would explain why Rachel, Janice, and Tom are so tight-lipped, and unwilling to save themselves. There has to be more to this. There has to at least be Eddy and someone else out there."

"Yes, I suppose there is," Mahoney said slowly.

Anxious, Martine devoured her food faster. "Actually, I'm really sure."

"I'll have a couple agents check it out tomorrow," Mahoney offered.

"Tomorrow?" Martine objected.

"First thing tomorrow," he said quickly. "I just heard you tell Alexa you promised not to go until tomorrow."

She shook her head quickly because she couldn't speak until she swallowed her food. "That might be too late."

"But I just heard you . . ."

Martine interrupted, "I said I wouldn't go there alone tomorrow. I didn't say I wouldn't go there now."

Mahoney winced. "Semantics? That's how you do it. Very manipulative, Martine."

"Is it?" Martine shrugged.

"We don't exactly have a patrol unit that operates at night." Snatching the address she had written down, he added, "It's not in Scottsdale's jurisdiction, and we don't need to involve Phoenix police before we check it out. Right?"

"Right." Martine shoved the last fry into her mouth.

Mahoney chewed with a widening grin. "You're going there now, aren't you?"

Guilty-faced, Martine looked away. "Of course not."

Mahoney nodded dejectedly. "We're going together to look around if that'll help you sleep better tonight, and give me one less thing on your list to do tomorrow."

Chapter 29

Under the veil of darkness Martine and Mahoney pulled into the parking lot of the abandoned warehouse located in the impoverished part of Phoenix. Driving around to the back of the run-down property brought them closer to total obscurity. Without streetlights, only the headlights of the car provided any visual aid in the back-lot which once operated as a tractor-trailer loading zone.

"Look. I think there's a vehicle parked between the last bays," Martine said excitedly as she glimpsed the roof of a black car.

Mahoney stepped on the gas and pulled up close to the vehicle that had been backed-up tight to the loading docks concrete base. "That could be it. Fits the description. Let's check the plates in the back."

Martine muttered, "Yeah, I don't understand why Arizona only has license plates in the back of the vehicle."

"Wait here." Mahoney grabbed a flashlight and went to the rear of the car for a visual of the plate. On his way back he scanned the inside of the vehicle with his flashlight to inspect the condition of the interior for possible foul play. After getting seated back inside his car he reported his findings, "This is definitely Eddy's registered vehicle. Inside looks clean."

Martine grabbed the flashlight from him and opened her car door. "We need to get inside that building." Exiting the car, she flipped the light back on.

"You can't do that," he said as he got back out of his car.

"Sure we can," Martine shot back without expression.

"Not without Probable Cause. You should know that."

"We have it." Martine pointed to the abandoned black-muscle car. "He's wanted for questioning—his vehicle has been located in a suspicious place. I'm thinking trespassing, or evading arrest." Martine's voice pitched defiantly, "We need to go in."

Mahoney shook his head vehemently, "Not you with me. We need back-up then."

"Fine." Martine hesitated a moment. "That's a great idea. Shouldn't take long once we call it in," she dared Mahoney sarcastically. "The only reasons you're calling for back-up is because you're guys don't patrol, or work at night, and I'm with you. You wouldn't call for help if I wasn't here. Screw that."

Mahoney stood with his phone engaged, and his eyes locked on Martine as he processed what she implied. Shrugging weakly, he back-pedaled before he finished dialing 911. "That might not be the best way to handle this." Terminating the call he looked back to Martine and stroked his mustache thoughtfully. "Let's look in the windows first for signs of suspicious activity."

"Sure," she said. "Maybe someone will let us in if we knock. But," she said slowly, "there might be an open door, or broken window."

Mahoney put a hand on her arm, restraining her. "No wait. You keep the light. I'm bringing my gun. You stay behind me," he directed as he proceeded to the first window on the side of the building nearest Eddy's car. Mahoney looked long and hard through the window. "Okay, give me the light for a minute," he whispered.

Too short to see inside herself, Martine waited a few seconds in silence. "Tell me what you see."

"Not sure, but I think I see a lot of stuff in there," he reported.

"Sounds like Probable Cause," she fired back. "Any people in there now?"

"Not that I can see."

Impatient by nature, Martine grabbed the light from Mahoney and went to a window that had an elevation advantage for her height. Shining the flashlight inside the window exposed the insides of an unkept decrepitated building. Rows of artwork propped against support columns could be seen in the distance. Other decorative pieces like statues and vases where resting on shelves. "Did you see the trash? There's fast-food type garbage. We need to get inside. I'm going in. There isn't anyone here right now. It's too early for bedtime, and too late to be working." Before Mahoney could argue, she hit the old glass with the flashlight. "Oops. I accidently hit this broken window looking for Eddy—I think he's in danger." After pushing the glass out of the way she asked Mahoney for assistance, "Leg-up please."

Left with no choice, he had to follow her through the opening. As he tried to pull himself up he cursed, "Son of a bitch."

"Hurry," she ordered in a hushed tone. Inside the warehouse the abyss yawned wide. Barely visible with the aid of a single beam of light, a great confirmation spread through Martine's being—alerting her to its importance. Not far from where she entered the building a dusty painting of a civil war battle scene rested against the wall. Next to it was another piece of historical art—depicting a train robbery with horse riding bandits.

After hoisting himself up to the window-opening he was able to jump into the building. Once inside the expansive space he warily pulled out his gun, clicked the safety off and assumed a defensive position—keeping his weapon aimed in front of them. "Make sure we're alone, do a three-sixty now," he said quietly.

Protectively bunched together they proceeded to turn in a circle. "Look," Martine huffed hard, unable to catch up to her adrenaline rush. Directing her light to a pillar in the center of the building—her eyes widened in disbelief when she observed what appeared to be spilled paint. "Well—looks like you got yourself another dramatic crime scene." Moving towards the colored splatters, the scene grew grizzlier the closer they got. "If you had enough luminol I bet you could light this place up like Times Square."

"Yes. I think you're right. No bodies though. Without them we won't know whose blood, or when something went down here."

Martine's mind quickly assessed the importance of locating this warehouse in connection with the Morgan case and her dreams. Like clues on a treasure hunt or answers to a test, the two paintings matched her dreams of a gang-style train robbery and a

Civil War dilemma. Insight and instincts alerted her to the fact it was more than a coincident, and she couldn't leave empty handed. "That's right," Martine answered Mahoney. "But when the dead don't speak or show themselves—our job begins." She wondered what other correlations she could gleam from this finding?

"You still sure this has to do with the Morgan murder?"

Martine's heart pounded with excitement. "More now than ever." Keeping most of her confirmations to herself, she added, "DNA will tell us for sure, but I think this case is like Iran—not everyone that signed up for that tour returned alive either."

"You seem pretty sure of yourself, Martine. If there was a murder, it's just not that easy to dispose of a body though."

"Let's just say I feel strongly about a criminal connection between this property and Morgan's." Martine used the flashlight to locate the nearest service door. "See there?" She flashed her light on the steel-grey door. "I'm gonna see if there's any power on in here." Leaving Mahoney in the dark, she trotted down to the wall with a door in it. As she navigated around empty pallets, metal shelving, and old display cases, she realized that the place was probably used to store items from a business that was no longer operating. While approaching the door she shinned a beam of light on the wall in search of a bank of light switches. "Found it," she reported. Flipping all the lights on only produced the glow from a sixty-watt bulb down where she had left Mahoney. "Damn. They must have taken all the bulbs out."

"Yep, or they're all burnt out." Mahoney frowned slightly. "This still does help a bit."

Disappointed with the lack of lighting, she resumed using her flashlight to snoop around the cluttered area she was passing through. Suddenly, her foot made contact with an object on the floor. She screeched as the item loudly rolled on the concrete like a bowling ball finding the pins. Startled, she held her breath until the empty glass bottle of beer hit the wall with a clang.

Mahoney spun around. "What was that?"

She struggled to regain her composure quickly. Picking up a single piece of paper for closer inspection, she hollered to Mahoney,

"Oh, nothing. Hey, this place hasn't been in operation for years. This receipt is from 1999," she added as she walked up next to him. "Who owns an abandoned building for eleven years?"

Mahoney shirked with his shoulders. "Maybe the city or the bank got stuck with it."

Martine looked away—searching for some tangible clue. "Not likely. It would've sold for back-taxes by now."

"Why do you care?" Mahoney asked. "I'm calling this in now. It's time we at least get this building secured for processing tomorrow."

"No. Don't do that yet." Martine stared towards the far corner of the building that still remained mysterious and murky. Swallowing her fear, she forced herself to separate from the safety of Mahoney's presence and forge through the bowels of the dirty storage shelves and containers. Hearing only her own movements was little comfort when surrounded by dark menacing shadows cast by the flashlights beam.

"Martine, where are you going?" Mahoney shouted.

Refusing to be discouraged, Martine kept walking. "I'm looking for another light switch," she lied.

"Get back here. I'll arrange a tour for you tomorrow."

"Sure. Let me just see if this door goes anywhere," her voice fading as she moved farther away from him. "I just want to find something that makes sense of all this."

"I don't see how this building can make any sense other than a drop-off place to beat someone up," Mahoney offered loudly.

Martine reached the door. "Well, if it doesn't make sense, maybe I need to be looking harder."

"You can't look harder in the dark," Mahoney's raised voice echoed in the high-ceilinged building. "We won't be able to see anything else till morning." He took his phone and started dialing again. "I'm calling this in so the building is secure until morning. Once they're here, we'll get going. Let's get outside quick. We were never in here—remember?"

Martine was now a significant distance from where she left Mahoney and the little light bulb. "Ugh," she yelled after opening the door. "I may not be able to see very well, but I can smell something's very wrong over here."

Before he could hit send, Mahoney headed toward Martine's voice. His loud footsteps reverberated in the building as he raced off to find her. Seeing her standing with the flashlight pointed towards a room didn't slow him down. "What is it?" He went past her towards the opening. It was the next breath he took that halted him. "Oh." He stiffened. Wheeling around to face Martine, he exhaled. "I smell it too."

Martine's face of shock and disgust mirrored Mahoney's as he looked into her flashlight. "What is that?"

Moving quickly back to her, he gasped, "Death."

Their eyes locked for one terrifying moment—both with frozen expressions of horror. "This can't be good," she said with a puzzled expression. Backing away from the room, she had to make a conscious effort to hold back the urge to vomit.

Using the hanky from his pocket, he pushed the door closed and cleaned the handle. Desperation to leave was mounting as he walked towards Martine. "I'm calling this in now." He grabbed her arm and led her away.

Unnerved by the appalling odor, Martine held her hand over her mouth, suppressing another involuntary reflux to gag. Her words smothered, she agreed, "Yeah, let's get out of here."

With composure melting, they both rushed down to the service door. Using her elbow, Martine flipped the light off and hurried out the building with Mahoney—letting the door lock behind them.

Words poured out fast and random from Mahoney, "Don't tell these cops anything. We need to process this whole site with our guys. I don't want anyone to go inside and disturb anything. Did you touch anything? Did you leave your prints or DNA on anything? We were never in that building. We found a suspicious car."

"That door handle." Martine moaned and grabbed at the wrench in her stomach. "Did you touch it?" she asked hurriedly.

"No. How 'bout the light switch?" Mahoney pressed her.

Crouching down, she struggled again with the urge to toss her dinner. "No, I used my elbow. I held that receipt though." Checking her back pocket, she found it tucked safely in her jeans. "We're good. I still have it."

"I guess we're good then," Mahoney said flatly. "It'll make it a good clean crime site for them to process. Much less complicated."

Chapter 30

Honey, the Pomeranian, scurried around Martine's legs as she prepared to get in bed. Concluding the process and pulling back the bedcovers, she hoisted the little dog on the bed. Sugar leapt stealthily onto the mattress while the other animals settled in their appropriate places for the night.

Relaxing comfortably under the hypnotic spin of an overhead ceiling fan, Martine fell into a deep sleep almost as quickly as she lay down. Momentarily, her spirit was lifted from her body.

Given entry into a dark and mysterious layer of ether after passing through the throes of deceit and temptation, Martine found her human form materializing in a despicable place with dark walls and floor. Violent, decadent, deviant and primitive energy dominated the space that generated despair and fear.

Cutting through the dense dark matter like a laser, Martine's energetic signature-form had entered the place where the sacred lesson of greed emerged. Absorbing knowledge with ease and joy is preferred—but takes too long. Walking through the fires of hell quickens the conveyance of awareness.

Swarming towards her was a black cloud of dust with an audible hum that grew louder as it approached. Hundreds of bat-winged creatures flew out of the dark cloud when it made contact with her. Foul stench emitted from the reptilian looking creatures brought waves of nausea, causing her stomach to clamp. Martine screamed as the vermin began attacking her physically.

Instantly her two Lynx cats jumped to her aid. Positioning themselves in front of her, they hissed and growled at the attackers until they disbanded and she was free from their demonic strong-hold. Acknowledging her animal guides, she stroked them till they purred their approval and slowly dissolved away.

Having no idea where she was exactly, she decided to investigate the sounds she heard coming from a room which was only feet away. Opening the door cautiously, she observed a parlor-styled room from the 1800's.

Invited by a tall turban-headed man to take a seat at the table, Martine found herself interacting with a clearly demonic looking ghost who was already sitting at the table. Appearing as a mixture of smoky gray matter which formed the shape of his once human body, the beings medium-length grey hair stood on end as if held by electricity. Remaining calm she looked down at an octagon-shaped game table that held an object cloaked with a black cloth.

Unsettled by the notion that the game these unholy ghosts wanted to play was anything but *Go Fish*, she resisted and attempted to excuse herself, until another player emerged that demanded she stay and he would be in charge. Appearing in human form, he projected a powerful presence of arrogance and superiority. Dressed in early nineteen-hundred attire, the man with a top-hat and mustache claimed he was more than qualified to assume the role as Auctioneer.

Growing more suspicious of the game to be played, caused Martine to object again, "No thank you. Please show me the way out."

"No, young lady, you can't go until the game is over," the static-charged ghost replied, his currents of electricity darkened as he spoke.

"Where are the other players?" The distinguished being with a top-hat asked curtly.

"I'm here," a tall vaporous gentleman with a black derby hat announced. As the form of the pointy-nosed man materialized more clearly, his old puckered looking face held an emotionless expression.

Manifesting next to the man with a derby hat was the fifth player. "I'm here," the apparition of an eighteenth-century European man replied. Fully bearded with a mustache, the formally dressed ghost barley acknowledged anyone at the table.

"Be seated," the top-hatted man ordered Martine.

"I don't know this game. I prefer to watch," she rebuffed.

"Sit," he ordered firmly. Pulling the black veil off the object like in a magician's act, he added, "You have played this game before. Let's see how you do in our parlor."

Centered on the face of the game was the graphic depiction of a skull and crossbones—denoting it's secretive alliance with an elite brotherhood that separates them above others. Martine further detected its meaning to mean piracy. *Pirates of what?* She thought as she contemplated her purpose for being in this place.

Astonished to see the unveiling of Monopoly—undoubtedly the most complicated and quintessential American game with origins that date back one-hundred years, she strained to inspect the authenticity and significance of ceremoniously revealing the fast-dealing property-trading game. Familiar with playing Monopoly she recognized the distinct board squares denoting the names of early railroad lines, real estate properties on fashionable Atlantic City streets, and a couple of utilities.

"You know the rules," Top-Hat barked sternly. He narrated the object of the game, "Wealthiest player wins, and everyone else goes bankrupt. I'll serve as the Banker and Auctioneer." Distributing the $1500 allotted to each player, he continued, "We roll the cubes to see who starts first."

As Martine began to participate in the long competitive game, her being began to receive an energetic influx of knowledge regarding humanities many advances in industrial technology that were historically significant—playing out like a Monopoly game. Dating back as far as Atlantis, when all things were working together for the one, an uprising occurred when people in political and controlling positions became greedy and power-hungry—leading to the total destruction of a civilization. Even Ancient Rome fell under the burdens of heavy taxes, excessive military spending, natural disasters, and political corruption—all causing financial ruin. Over and over again the people that manipulated a civilization so they were in possession of great power and financial control would ultimately become increasingly greedier for complete control—until the mighty kingdom is destroyed. Ancient beliefs were 'kill or be killed,' until their demise.

When each player had finished rolling the stones that were chiseled to resemble the modern dice used in the traditional game of Monopoly, the player with a top hat was declared the winner to kick-off the game.

Shaking the stones in his hand first, Top-Hat released them in the air where gravity took them down in a loud thud. "That's a six." After moving his game piece—the hat—six places he said, "I'll buy it. I now own Oriental Avenue."

"You can have it for now. You'll still never beat me," the figure with a derby hat said smugly as he tossed his dice onto the game board. "Five." He moved his game piece—the horse—five places to Reading Railroad. "I'll buy it," he declared without emotion. He passed the dice to Martine.

As Martine's dice tumbled on the board, she couldn't help but notice how the ghostly players watched her dice like hungry vultures stalking their prey. "Seven," she announced as she moved her game piece—the iron—seven spaces. "Ah, Chance," she uttered. Drawing a card from the stack of cards that were all stamped with a big gold '?' and the word Chance boldly printed below it, she grinned as she read her prize out loud, "Advance Token to Board Walk. I will purchase it," she announced with confidence. Familiar with the benefits of owning the premier property on the board, exalted her.

Anger fumed from the European ghost who now held the dice. "That was just lucky. You still have no way of beating me," the nasty man said with a scowl. Releasing the dice onto the board with a quick snap of the wrist expressed his aggressive nature. "Eight," he said as he advanced his game piece—the ship—eight spaces. "Vermont Avenue. Well, I'll buy it," he said without emotion.

Anxious for his turn the static-haired ghost threw down the dice. "Eleven," he laughed. "I may have played last, but I'm ahead of you three," he gloated as he moved his game piece—the canon—to

St. Charles Place. Distorted energy blitzed out in every direction when he spoke this time.

As the next round progressed, Top-Hat rolled a six and bought the Electric Company, Derby-Hat rolled a nine and bought Virginia Avenue, Martine rolled a ten and bought Connecticut Avenue.

Looking at Top-Hat she reminded him of his obligation, "I believe the bank owes me two hundred dollars for passing go."

Handing her two one-hundred dollar bills he said, "I see we have a problem already. We should trade, only one can own all three of these properties if you want to expand and develop." He was referring to the fact that he owns Oriental Avenue and she now owns the adjoining property Connecticut Avenue. "I'll trade you Oriental Avenue for Boardwalk." He stared at her like a vampire lusting for blood.

Martine shook her head. "That would not be a balanced trade."

"But you'll never get a monopoly with just one of these. Surely you want the first monopoly." He tried to coerce her.

"No. Not yet," she replied without hesitation.

Angry at the rejection, he blasted her with profanity, "You don't know what you're doing, whore. How will that help you win and control all four corners of the world? A piece of land can't do that for you or anyone. You need to create a monopoly before someone else does. I may sell this to that player," he said, motioning his grey decayed-looking finger towards the European."

"All four corners of the world you say," Martine repeated back to him. "I never understood that—isn't the world round. And No, I really don't want to trade Boardwalk," she said firmly.

With Martine's turn completed after the purchase of Connecticut Avenue and collecting two-hundred dollars for passing go she handed the dice over to the next player.

As the ghost dramatically shook the dice in his hand the game board magically changed like a traffic light going from red to green. Unexpectedly the board squares were populated with more advances from the Industrial Revolution that manifested rapidly throughout the 20th century.

"What just happened?" Martine asked in surprise.

"Every time you pass go, the board will change," the European ghost replied with a snicker. "You were the first one to pass go," he grumbled his words.

"It's just a game," Derby-Hat added slyly. "See how easy it is to play?"

Filled with disgust towards the incredibly dark souls that inhabited the dungeon they played in, she spouted back, "You call this a game. You think this is entertainment?"

"We call this practice," the bearded European ghost said with a snide grin.

Martine looked over the modified game board that now had squares with names of bridges, ships, banks, and products. "What happened to all the properties that were on the board before it changed?"

"You can buy them at a premium, or wait for the auction," the banker replied with an impatient tone.

Confused by the transformative game, Martine participated in another round. Each player accumulated larger properties for their portfolios—including her. She now was the proud owner of a trans-continent railroad, a cotton plantation, a large television network, and an Atlantic shipping fleet. As she rolled a nine for her next turn, she passed go and landed on a community bank.

As the European scooped up the dice for his turn, he barked at the banker, "What are you waiting for? Give her two-thousand dollars for passing go."

After receiving the money—the board supernaturally changed again. Now visible in the individual squares where the names of, large corporations, oil companies, manufacturers, franchises, and airlines. Each ghostly participant that took a turn played more aggressively as the game progressed. Greed fumed from them as they competed for prized possessions.

When Martine's turn came, she rolled a six, passed go, and landed on a high priced steel manufacturer. "I'll buy it," she stated coolly.

"It's a good thing you have the advantage of passing go first. If you hadn't had the good fortune to land on that steel company, you would've run out of tracks for your trains. I would have bought it before the auction," he said meanly. "Pay her," he snapped intolerantly at the banker.

With Martine paid two-hundred thousand dollars this time, the board changed again. Within the squares were positions of power found in various countries. Completely bewildered each time the board changed, she tried to comprehend what to do when she landed on a square this time.

As her eyes swept around the newly configured board, her mind breezed through a series of epochs in the life of humanity. Reminded with visions of horrific centuries of brutality, war, hardship, torture, and enslavements—numbed her. She could literally see some countries on the board bulging from the effects of tyranny and human suffering.

It might not be an advantage if she landed on the appointment for President of Africa. Buying leadership in a vulnerable country could cost her everything in this game. Knowing these players were like vultures that pick at the bones of the less fortunate made Martine rethink what to do when she took her turn. After nervously blowing on the dice she shook them hard in her hand and rolled an eight. During this round she landed on President of Mexico, Prime Minister of Egypt and President of Cuba—she passed on all of them.

For her next turn, Martine took in a deep breath as she moved her iron to President of the United States. "How much?" Martine looked at the banker who seethed with hatred.

"Here's your two-hundred million for passing go. The price is two-hundred million for that position. You could buy many more positions of power—in richer countries than this one if you save your money," the banker said persuasively.

"That's not why I bought it," Martine returned quickly. "I didn't buy it because I want power. I bought it so none of you would have it."

"There are many other ways to control your country. I don't need to be president to do so," Top-Hat bragged. "I'll trade my publishing companies for your network of television stations."

European ghost boasted, "Do you know how many times I have saved that country you're so proud to protect?" His words brought a sudden wave of discomfort to Martine. "You will either need me to bail you out of a crisis, or make you strong enough to avert one. Either way, it will come at a great price."

Derby-Hat smiled like a master manipulator. "With my resources it will be easy to be the super power you think you are." His exact words were, "It's easy to control all of them." He motioned his hand across the board that was populated with rich countries around the world. "We just make sure they never trust each other. With your media anyone can be manipulated."

Martine lifted her eyes to his cold stare as she processed his words. "Military threats?"

"And more," he added. "I have the resources you need to make any army."

Top-Hat butted in, "But I have the means to fund it."

Before Martine could say more, the turban-headed ghost called out, "Time."

Derby-Hat howled loud, "What? It can't be. She wasted our time with her worthless chatter."

"She played by the rules," Turban Head said rigidly. "Your rules. I called the correct time."

"Let's start the auction, boys," the banker said bitterly without acknowledging Martine.

Martine watched a moment as the demonic figures aggressively bid on properties, entities, resources, corporations, banks, mines, pensions, and positions of power. The more they accumulated the uglier and more corroded looking they each got. Gorging themselves liken vampires for blood, they fed on gluttony and greed to satisfy their thirst for negative energy. Crushing out competition and controlling monopolies was like regular feedings for the damned.

"I now own the counties with untapped oil reserves and the refineries in 70% of the world," Derby-Hat bragged. "I told you the best way to control is to buy the biggest share and crush the rest of them out."

"Well," European ghost said with a sinister laugh. "I have control of the pipelines. You should have bought what I have. No monopoly for you this time."

Static—haired ghost rubbed his hands together. "He doesn't need your pipelines. He needs my trucks."

"I need one of you, and I will have a cartel," Derby-Hat said in a demonic tone. "How 'bout you, deary?" Only his eyes moved sideways to look at Martine. "Are you ready to trade or become allies with me? Just say the word. Keep in mind," he said in a threatening tone, "my publishing companies can make you or break you."

Slack-jawed by the thought of being cohorts in crimes of greed and gluttony with any of these fellows, Martine shook it off as fast as she could. "No, never. I wouldn't want to taste the words."

European ghost fastened his gaze on her. "If we amass our wealth and power together, we will control market prices and become an industrial giant. We will be worth more than most of the countries in the world."

Top-Hat butted in, "With my banking resources you and I can control all of them. They can't buy us out, and we can eliminate anyone that gets in our way. We can squash all the competition whenever we need to. It's easy. We can crash their monetary system and take them down without using a bullet."

Shocked by this bold proclamation, Martine blinked her surprise. "How do you do that?"

"Let me count the ways, Madam President." Spewing his words, Top-Hat boasted, "Interest rates, threats of war, and financial ruin—to name a few. Fear binds people through collective aggression. War is merely an effective tool we use."

"You're in a great position to be my strongest partner. I can make sure you're the most powerful leader in the world. You will control everyone and everything." Derby-Hat tried to entice her with false promises.

Martine cringed at the thought. "Aristotle said, 'The good of man must be the end of the science of politics.' I can see you're all drooling over who has more power and money. You think you can buy my position—my country." Going on, she added calmly, "Your spirits are stuck here with this reoccurring nightmare of a game because you can never move on until you make reparations for what you've done unto others." Martine felt a charge of energy as she spoke out. "You must lower your greedy desires, and relinquish all these things that you lust for." She noticed energy was fizzling out of the static-haired ghost. "How will you restore what you've done to innocent victims? How will you repair the damages that you are accountable for?" More dark energy drained out of the others as she gained strength and stood up. "You have so much to make up for—and you waste your time practicing how to defeat everyone. I ask you—who will you play with when no one is left to defeat?"

Still sounding like a Mafia thug, European ghost roared furiously with his last bit of diffused strength. "Yes. We are the masters at this game. No one can ever beat us—they fear us."

Martine held her hand up in defiance. "Oh, I don't think anyone would fear you if they knew you. You hide your existence and true nature like termites living inside darkened walls. I think we fear what we don't know." She saw their demon-looking human forms become increasingly vaporous. "Exposed, no one would easily follow you, or be manipulated. Enlightened people would unite and reject your selfish game—a game with one agenda and the same winners. Who will play with you if you never lose?" Her voice trailed as she was pulled away from the low realm void of light.

Materializing in front of the Indian Guide she was now familiar with, she looked around to take in the new location.

Finding herself on the fringe of a battlefield, she gasped at the horrors of death left behind in the aftermath of men murdering men. "What happened?" She asked the Indian.

Opening the scroll, he read out loud.

"Greedy men horde this lot
Precious resource always sought
Wars are won and battles lost
Evil spreading like a moss
Star is scared with double cross
Deceiving leaders for a loss"

The Indian nodded in agreement. "You are to read the rest of the decree," he replied stiffly. "Time is not on your side." Handing Martine the scroll, he instructed her, "Read out loud."

Martine looked upon the scroll and read slowly,

"Unholy alliance starts with Brew
Leaders rise and fall askew
Find the ships that sailed on east
In northern waters they lie in peace
Watery graves hide the truth
Tyranny growing more aloof."

When she finished, she asked the Indian guide, "If time is critical I need a sign. Can I have exactly what I need in the physical world to help this cause?" Flustered and impatient, she added, "I feel blind and I can't see what it is."

The Indian stood stoic for seconds. *"Search a place the price was paid—legal means pave the way."*

As suddenly as she'd been taken to an unearthly realm, her soul shot back to her sleeping body, returning to humanness and all the limits that come with it. Lying still for a moment, Martine blinked her eyes opened as she acclimated to her surroundings in Jolene's home.

Chapter 31

Mahoney and Martine convened again at the warehouse first thing in the morning. Less than twelve hours ago the dank abandoned building resembled something scary and intimidating. In daylight the destitute infrastructure of the warehouse, now alive with teams of law enforcement coordinating a forensics assault on everything inside and out, looked like a movie set getting ready for an epic production.

"Chief," a young man called from over by the black car that was presumed to belong to Eddy and be associated with the death and arson of Eli Morgan.

Mahoney headed towards the man haling him. "Yeah, Clint, find anything?"

"Maybe," he replied evenly. "We ran a check on this camper parked around the corner, and can't find it registered or licensed to anybody. Its pretty snarky looking inside—like someone might be living in it."

Following Clint to the camper, Mahoney peeked in the side window. "Dust for prints on the outside first and see if they match anybody's prints on file."

Careful not to touch anything, Martine inquired, "Are the doors locked?"

"Everything is locked," Clint answered incisively.

Mahoney looked at Martine—like he could read her mind. "Dust the door, Clint. With two flat tires, this is probably an abandoned junker."

"Or, some homeless guy didn't want his bed stolen," Martine injected.

Clint laughed. "You got it," he said as he returned back to his team, ordering a sequence of protocol to them as he joined them.

Mahoney turned his attention to Martine and lowered his voice, "Let's see this place in the morning."

"I've been looking forward to it," Martine said with a sigh.

Handing her sterile gloves he instructed her, "Put these on before you go in."

"Absolutely." Martine put the gloves on and followed him to the service door.

Mahoney motioned to his lead agent. "Ken, what do we have so far?"

"Limited crime scene," Ken reported, acknowledging Martine whom he already knew. "They didn't leave much in here to look at except spent casings, and empty bottles of acid. We can't open the drums up until the coroner gives the okay."

Ray walked up to Mahoney. "Thought I'd check this scene out. Thanks for letting me know about Eddy's car."

"Sure," Mahoney nodded. "We might have the car, but you got his girlfriend," he said with a smile. "Looks like our boy Eddy has a lot of baggage if he ended up in this place."

Ray took a sip of his coffee, "Eddy needs no introduction in the Scottsdale or Phoenix precincts. He's a one man crime wave when it comes to dealing and stealing. But, I thought he'd surface by now."

"Well, his car did. I think it's time we get his associates rounded up," Mahoney suggested.

"Been working on that," Ray reassured. "Seems those boys are missing too."

"Really," Mahoney said.

"We just keep hitting dead ends," Ray complained. "Wish we could get some Intel we don't already have."

"Well, Ray, there's a little more going on here than just locating Eddy's vehicle." Motioning towards the far corner of the building, he explained, "We've possibly found the grizzly remains of human bodies."

"What?" Ray's voice echoed loud.

"We're keeping this quiet for now." Mahoney gave Martine a knowing glance. "We have no idea who they are yet, how they died, or who did it." He cautioned Ray with his stare.

"Of course. Can I see?"

"Yep." Mahoney led Ray and Martine through the once abandoned building that was now alive with lights and professional personnel. "Don't touch anything, we're still processing the scene," he warned. Pointing out the blood spills that were being doused with luminal, he addressed Ray and Martine like neither had been inside before. "Down here's a room where we discovered several sixty-five gallon coffins that have human remains decomposing with some acid accelerant. We haven't figured out what to do about retrieving the bodies yet. The coroner's on his way." Mahoney opened the door to the concrete cubicle that housed the sealed barrels.

Ray gasped at the smell and put his sleeve over his nose. "Oh my God. How many?"

"Five barrels."

Cold silence hung for a moment as they all peered morbidly into the room.

"What's that?" There was a pained pause before she made a move. Holding her hand over her nose she ran inside the room and fetched a bottle with her gloved hands.

"What are you doing," Mahoney hollered at her.

Martine ran back out of the room and kept going till she didn't have to hold her breath. "I want to know who purchased this." Carefully examining the bottle like fragile evidence, she explained, "It's a whiskey bottle with a little left in it."

Mahoney who was now peering over her shoulder looked lost. "We'll check it for prints."

Martine zoomed her focus in. "We can do better than that. I want to know who purchased it."

"They'll have better luck tracking down where they purchased muriatic acid." Mahoney pointed to the empty containers.

"Yes, Martine said tensely. "But, why limit the search to one item when you have two?"

Ray's long-standing skepticism about ever really tracking perps through purchases and surveillance videos weighed in, "You got enough here with bodies and casings."

"Not if you don't know who owns the gun," Martine argued. "And not if your in a hurry," she finished.

With equal confidence Ray challenged her, "My guys can track down where someone purchased a pallet of acid. Can you track down who purchased a bottle of whiskey?"

Martine focused on her knowing. Her dream the night before referenced *searching a place a price was paid.* "It's recent. There's still a little alcohol in the bottom. In this heat it wouldn't last long if it was full. I bet this is a very recent purchase."

Ray nodded. "You might get prints and DNA. I don't see any shot glasses lined up. Someone probably drank right out of the bottle."

"Exactly. But that's not why I think we get on this right now. There's a price sticker. That's how liquor stores and convenience stores label their products. They don't usually have expensive scanners. We wait too long and no one will remember who might have purchased it—or worse—erased any possible surveillance tape. Those types of places do have cameras. The big grocery stores where everyone shops don't always have cameras on the cashiers."

Ray looked at Mahoney and volunteered. "Let me and my guys work that. Phoenix patrols would help too. That Whiskey isn't that common. Most people just pick Jack Daniels. This is Dewar's. We'll try—even if it amounts to nothing."

Satisfied, Martine added, "This is traceable if you can find the price gun that made this sticker. When you find the store with the matching price gun—bag it for evidence. You know the rest."

"Well." Ray looked around. "Looks like your people have this under control. Not much else we can do till your coroner starts talking. Keep me filled in. We'll work on these purchases." Ray said his goodbyes and left the property.

"John, we really do have a lot of information now," Martine injected. "Unidentified bodies—lots of blood, Eddy's car, and casings. We know Eddy probably didn't kill himself, or hurt himself and walk away. We ID'd Jake, so we know he's dead and . . .," Martine swallowed hard. "Excuse me," she said. "Let's rush those prints from the camper to forensics and match them with Jakes. He might not have had anything registered, insured, or licensed in his name, but that doesn't mean he walked here from Idaho. If that's Jakes camper, he had a truck."

Mahoney signaled an officer over and gave him the instructions.

"We'll keep working this till we run out of things to do," Mahoney said confidently.

"I think I need to see Tom and the girls today." Martine's blue eyes blinked with zeal. "I gotta an idea. There's nothing I can do here anyways."

"Why?" Mahoney paused for her reply.

"I don't know of anything that can alter and reprogram the brain faster than drugs. He hasn't had any for days. I think I can get him to talk now."

Mahoney looked at Martine like she was insane. "Again, aren't you on vacation? Can't you find something fun to do?"

She smiled. "Not today."

Chapter 32

Max rushed into his apartment after biking home from his late night work shift. As he poured himself a tall glass of orange juice on the rocks and started gulping it down, he called-up his buddy. "Gordo, boy do I got news for you."

"Like what?" Gordy returned with disinterest. "A new record high temp in Arizona?"

Max's voice huffed with excitement, "No. Did you see the latest news today?"

"Of course not," Gordy said, but after more consideration he added. "I told you yesterday I had to go to the dentist. I can't talk or do anything when this dentist uses my mouth like a miner tunneling for gold."

"Yeah, sorry about that. I keep forgetting you had eight cavities. Maybe go to the dentist more than once every ten years."

"Who does that?" Gordy laughed. "So, what's the big deal?"

Max tilted his head from side to side as if weighing out his thoughts. "Guy named Sonnenfeld just released his book and photos on 9/11."

Gordy moaned in discomfort. "What're you talking about? 9/11 was almost nine years ago."

Max plopped on his sofa. "I realize that, but this guy Sonnenfeld is exposing top secret stuff about what he videoed and photographed after 9/11."

Sounding impartial, Gordy grumbled, "Why's he waited so long?"

"He's been a refugee in another country." Max fired-up his computer as he spoke, "Basically, living in exile in . . . Argentina.

Says he's had to be in hiding because he knew too much. He was an accidental witness, or something. He was in hiding until he could finish his book and release the real findings that were covered up."

"That's hard to believe," Gordy commented.

"No it's not," Max argued. "Finally, someone with some balls speaks out and you like everyone else will call him a liar who made it up for money." Max raised his voice in anger, "What if his life is in danger? What if he is like a hero? What if he's risking everything for people he doesn't even know?"

Gordy reacted to Max's emotional state. "Let me pull this guy up on my computer. What's his full name?"

"Kurt Sonnenfeld."

After searching for Kurt Sonnenfeld on-line, Gordy says loudly, "Whoa. This guy is hiding alright. He's hiding from extradition from the state of Colorado. Did he mention that he was the prime suspect after his first wife Nancy died from a gunshot wound to the head in January 2002? It even says he was arrested for the murder. Did he mention that prosecutors dropped the case but still retain the right to arrest him for the death? Colorado wants him back, Max."

"Yeah, I know," Max's tone softened. "If you keep reading, you'll find he had blood on his clothes and face—as reported by responding officers, but the tests showed he had no gunpowder residue on his hands, but Nancy did. He also didn't have any prints on the gun, Nancy did though. They also later found her suicide note. Maybe it all looks suspicious, because it's supposed to. Maybe someone was trying to scare him, or set him up. And they succeeded—so he went into hiding."

Gordy calmly speculated, "Or, maybe he did it. What's so dangerous that he'd go into hiding if it wasn't for murdering his wife?"

"He was one of four FEMA videographers who, for a month after 9/11, filmed the crime scene at the World Trade Center, including the sub-basement levels." Max sat back and put his feet up on the coffee table. "He claims what happened in building 7 World Trade Center is incredibly suspicious. He says he has video that shows how small the rubble pile was, and how the buildings on either side were untouched by building 7 when it collapsed. Remember, it had not been hit by an airplane like the twin towers."

Gordy had a 'recollection' moment. "Oh yeah, I remember you made a big deal about why that building came down in the afternoon of 9/11."

"Yes," Max said with excitement back in his voice, "like seven hours later. It was a complete mystery to me when building 7 of the World Trade Center came down after everyone was safely evacuated. It was a forty-seven story steel-framed sky scraper that came down because of a couple little fires in the building? Come on, man."

Gordy butted in, "Are you hooked on some conspiracy theory again?"

"I don't know," Max sounded perplexed. "I still can't get over how two planes that hit high up on two buildings can cause four buildings to each come down like a stacked deck of cards. One plane hit a tower somewhere above the seventy-eight floor. How can that make the lower floors collapse—almost immediately?"

"Geez, Max, you know why." Gordy's voice pitched a higher octave, "Because the jet fuel blew it up like a bomb."

Max objected, "Well that's what the experts said, but these buildings didn't blow up, they imploded—all of them."

"I just don't believe it was a conspiracy," Gordy said emphatically.

"I know—you never did," Max said dejectedly. "So, how do you explain the melted steel, Gordy?"

"Jet fuel. That'd do it."

"No it wouldn't," Maxed argued. "How do explain molten steel running below ground after the explosions?"

"Jet fuel."

"Is that your answer for everything? That burns at 750 degrees Fahrenheit. That isn't hot enough to bend steel—much less melt it. Molten steel is like 2000 degrees Fahrenheit."

"I still don't believe it," Gordy reiterated.

Max flared at Gordy's stubbornness. "Even if you knew someone who saw this? Plenty of people did. No one ever knew about what witnesses saw or heard because lot's of testimony was left out of the final 911 Commission Report. Why's that?"

Gordy became defensive. "Because it probably wasn't true. They must not have believed them. There's lots of crazy people out there that just want to get in the news. Especially in New York."

"Like the ones that were jumping out of windows to their death because it was so bad, or burnt alive? How 'bout all the first responders that experienced multiple explosions after the planes hit? How 'bout all the people that felt the lobby explosion in the second Twin Tower? The windows were actually all blown out in the lobby before the plane hit it."

Gordy rebuffed Max again, "I think it can all be explained."

"How do you explain almost 3000 people being murdered on the same day?" Max took a deep breath. "Gordy, you're delusional if you only believe the rational dealt out by the media. They've had you and everyone else focused on everything but the whole truth. Just because you pour syrup on a box of rocks, it doesn't make them pancakes."

Gordy tried to diffuse the conversation, "Well, it sounds like you don't think the same airplanes that hit the Twin Towers could've taken down building seven. Is that right?"

Max settled down a bit. "Or, building 6. After everything I've read all four buildings just came down too perfectly."

"But, they'd been hit by planes or debris, which had ignited big fires in them."

"Sure, and many people assumed this combination of causes to be sufficient to explain why they came down." Agitation rose in Max's voice, "I just didn't buy that building 7 could be affected the same way. And I certainly don't now."

"I don't know, Max, everyone said it was the planes that caused it."

"Gordy, why don't you just go back to sleep like everyone else has? Or, you can listen to me and learn something. What if something else made this happen? You don't need to look at the moon to know it's there—do you, Gordy? Someone had to cause these buildings to detonate. It's the only way they can come down on their own footprints."

Gordy was finally grasping Max's theory. "So you're saying building 7 was only forty-seven stories tall, it wasn't hit by a plane, it imploded seven hours later because of a fire, and that isn't possible."

Max resonated relief in his voice, "It would be the first time in high-rise building history that a steel-reinforced building collapsed because of a couple small fires. Actually, it imploded and there is no time in history I can think of that four steel framed buildings all imploded on the same day, in the same way. Even buildings bombed in wars never completely come down. Their shells still stand."

Docile, but interested, Gordy inquired, "Why then?"

Max speculated, "I always figured somebody wanted something in that building. Something so big they would have to destroy it, or steal it. Why else would something of this magnitude be orchestrated like a sophisticated fireworks display on the Fourth of July?"

"I think it was a terrorist attack," Gordy spat back. "Everyone knows it was a terrorist attack. They caught the terrorists."

"But, Gordy, that's my point. The terrorists didn't take the buildings down—explosive charges that detonated four buildings did."

"That's not what anyone has reported," Gordy said evenly.

"Gordy," Max raised his voice in irritation. "Like everyone else, you get your information from the liberal media that reports the buildings came down because of fire—not detonations—and it enters the American History forever. Here's a real shocker if you don't believe me. When anchor woman Jane Standley from the BBC was in New York reporting live on the Twin Towers bombing, she said on the air that building 7 had come down."

Gordy said, "So."

"So, that was at 5:00pm before it came down. If you watch the video you can see building 7 is still standing, even though what she's reporting and what the ticker tape on the screen claim says it's collapsed," Max said roughly.

Gordy cleared his throat before arguing, "Right, but I feel like they may have just said the wrong buildings name, or showed an old picture. You know, used footage from earlier in the day as a backdrop."

"The footage is irrelevant," Max was growing impatient. "It's been proven they reported this building collapsing twenty-minutes before it happened. Don't you remember?"

"You do?" Gordy said in amazement.

"Yes," Max sparked. "They broke the live feed and blamed it on a satellite timer. When she came back on the air, it had just come down at 5:21pm. Don't you think that's a huge blunder? Twenty minutes before it collapsed she reported it live."

"Maybe," Gordy returned.

Max sounded loud—taut with anger, "Maybe? Well, here's another shocker for you. Do you know who operated the electronic security company for the World Trade Center, Gordy?"

"Shit no," Gordy said coolly.

"None other than Marvin Bush—brother to President George Bush. Their cousin Wirt Walker III was the CEO. And why weren't any of them in the buildings when they came down," Max sounded infuriated. "Does it really sound like a coincident that power in the South Tower was out for thirty-six hours on the eight and ninth? Is it really a coincident that the bomb sniffer dogs were removed from the buildings days before the bombings?"

"Geez, Max, take it easy." Gordy tried to settle his friend down. "You're going to have a heart attack."

"Gordy, you just gotta listen to me." Summarizing information found on-line, he simmered down and went on, "This guy Kurt says FEMA put out a report in 2002 that increased the mystery, thanks to an appendix written by three professors at Worcester Polytechnic Institute. This appendix reported that a piece of steel from WTC 7 had melted so severely that it had gaping holes in it, making it look like a piece of Swiss cheese. They pointed out that the fires in the building could not have been hot enough to melt steel. Think about it, Gordy, even if 750 degree jet fuel could melt steel—which it can't—there wasn't any jet fuel in building 7 late in the afternoon."

"That actually does make sense," Gordy relented slightly, exhibiting some support to his friend. "What else?"

Max skimmed through the article. "That building contained sensitive and undoubtedly compromising material for the, Secret Service, Department of Defense, FBI, IRS, Securities and Exchange Commissions, Office of Emergency, and other federal agencies," Max paused. "Oh, it was found to be the largest domestic station of the CIA outside of Washington, DC."

"Wow, somebody really wanted to take down our government. Did he say who?"

"I don't know. Maybe in his book he will." Max hesitated before he read further, "Listen to this, Gordy, his job was to document through film the entire crime scene and most of what was eventually uncovered was subterranean—especially beneath building 6 World Trade Center. Seventy feet below the World Trade Center buildings there was about sixteen acres of warehouse storage, and vaults. Fortunes in gold, silver, Godiva chocolates, assault weapons, furniture, bricks of cocaine, and other items confiscated by US Customs Service officials, were held and contained under these buildings." Max paused briefly. "The point he makes is that it appeared a lot of things of value within the vaults had to have been emptied before the attack. No one could have gotten to these areas until they were excavated. So, how else could they have been nearly emptied? He was one of the very first ones in."

Gordy injected, "But, they did recover gold bullion, didn't they?"

"Yeah," Max concurred as he scrolled down the page on his computer. "Probably a couple hundred million dollars worth. But, Kurt says the rumors around him were that there were billions of dollars stored beneath the World Trade Center, and it wasn't all ours. The couple hundred million dollars worth of gold bricks they did recover belonged to Nova Scotia. I want to know where all the rest went," his voice revealed his deep sentiments of distain for government cover-ups. "I want more answers to why about three-thousand people lost their lives. It's just unforgivable. Gordy,

Joseph Stalin said 'one death is a tragedy, a million is a statistic.' I just don't want this to be a statistic in world history."

Gordy interrupted, "What can anyone do about this stuff now anyway?" Hearing no answer through his phone, Gordy continued, "As a matter of fact, Max, what can someone like you do about it?" Gordy waited in silence for the friend that was never tongue-tied.

Max finally responded, "Accept the truth." He took a big sigh. "I need to get going. Talk to you later."

Chapter 33

Martine let herself into the arranged interview with Tom. Armed with the first-hand news that bodies were discovered in the most ghastly condition she'd ever been exposed to could possibly be exactly what she needed to get Tom to open up. Presenting the discovery to him before he heard about it through other sources would be paramount in reading his reaction, and garnering information directly. Shock-value gave her an advantage she didn't want to pass up, or hand-off to someone else.

"Hello, Tom," Martine said nonchalantly. "How're you doing today?" Tempering her own emotions, she assumed the role of an advocate or mediator, hoping Tom was ready to make a deal.

Tom and Martine were alone in a plain solid-walled interview room—no mirrors, windows, or onlookers—so they thought.

"How do you think I'm doing?" He didn't bother hiding his distrust for her.

"I have some more questions for you? Can we talk?"

Tom remained silent a moment. "Do I need a lawyer?"

"I'm not here to press any new charges," Martine tried to sound friendly and use a 'sales' approach. "You'll want to talk if we can share information that can help us both."

"How's that gonna work?" Tom refused to make eye contact with her. Confrontational—the rubber band started to pull. "Gonna trick me into saying something that'll get me charged for something else?"

"No, I won't have to trick you if you're guilty. The detectives will be dealing with those types of issues. What if we talk about something that helps with the investigation that may become use-ful in negotiating your sentence? It's not looking good for you, and I don't see you going home for some time."

Tom's hazel-colored eyes blazed with hatred. His belated an-swer came-off like a snake coiled in a defensive position before it strikes, "Don't try and get me to rat on anyone I know—you can forget it." His fury flashed again—the rubber band pulled tight. "I wouldn't stand a chance out there, or in here if I did that."

"I would expect you to say that. I want information about what you stole, who you stole if for, and where did it go?"

"I thought you were nailing me for murder?" Tom said with a short smug laugh. "If you can't figure anything out yourselves, why should I help you? Maybe you can't even make my charges stick."

"Again, I'm not here about that. I want to know what the theft was really about. We already know you were involved. Let's get past that, and the arson."

Tense and infuriated—the rubber band broke. "I'm not telling you anything." His head-snapping defiance was directed to Martine. "You're just trying to find more shit to pin on me." Tom looked away trying to ignore her.

"Do you disagree that there are more people involved than you, Janice, and Rachel?" Martine waited patiently for his response.

"I don't believe any of us are involved," Tom scoffed. "And don't try and tell me they're telling you different."

Martine held her gaze. "We think Eddy was involved."

Tom remained defensive. "And you think I'm going to tell you if he was. Get a grip, lady."

"Did you do something to Eddy?"

He looked back at her with a mean-smile. "Of course not."

"What if I told you I think we found Eddy?"

Tom broke-off eye contact. "I don't believe you unless I see a mug shot."

"I might be able to arrange for you to see him, but it won't be pretty and it won't be a mug shot."

"What are you talking about?"

"I'm talking about the condition we found him in today."

"What condition?" Tom now sounded genuinely interested.

"I'm not in a position to tell you anything unless you answer some of my questions. I suggest you take this opportunity very serious."

"Not unless you tell me if he's dead or alive."

"I'll do that if you'll tell me who else was with him the last time you saw him."

Seeing no harm in divulging information about the other guys he didn't care about, he contemplated briefly how much hinged on whether Eddy was still alive. "He might've been with a few of his friends."

Martine asked nicely, "Can I get their names?"

"Vic, Saul, and Bo."

"Can you think of anyone else?"

"No. Now tell me what you know about Eddy."

"I know Eddy appears to be dead."

"What do you mean *appears* to be dead?"

"I mean we're awaiting the Coroner's report to determine conclusively that we have recovered *his* body."

"What about the other guys?"

"Probably the same. We will now try and determine if we can match those three to the other bodies."

Tom appeared genuinely alarmed. "Why did you need me to help you identify those people?"

Martine finally hit her stride. "Because the bodies were not recognizable and we haven't found anyone alive that can ID them," Martine sounded dramatic. "Now for the real reason I'm here. What were those guys involved in? What was so important that they all had to die?"

He rejected her question. "How should I know?"

"You see, Tom, the only reason you may still be alive is because you're in here. I'm taking this very seriously—maybe it's time you do too. You may actually want more protection than what these walls provide."

Looking frightened and defenseless, Tom hit his fist on the table. "I'm not going down for all these murders. You're just trying to scare me and pin this on me."

"I'm not, but someone else might be interested in getting to you." Martine added a little more fear. "I wouldn't meet with anyone you don't know right now. I'm focusing on the possibility that what you guys lifted was dangerous—especially, if they resorted to eliminating all witnesses. Were you a witness? The only thing that may protect you is telling me what really happened."

Struck hard by the notion that nothing had gone right, Tom's body went cold. "Okay, I'll tell you what I know. But, I want immunity."

"I can't promise that, Tom." Martine stared at him with stubborn firmness. Then she thought of a question, "Are any of you left-handed?"

Tom pondered his mind. "Yeah, me and Saul."

Relieved, Martine informed Tom, "Investigators notice things. Like someone left handed stabbed the victim. You see what I mean—you're left-handed. Did you do it?"

"No. I told you."

"Did Saul?" Martine pressed him hard.

Tom just looked at her—not responding. "I guess it doesn't matter now," Tom's deflated voice replied. "Saul killed him."

"Good," Martine said with satisfaction.

Tom tried to bargain his way out again. "If I tell you what I know, I want immunity and protection for all three of us."

Martine hesitated—shaking her head slowly. "I don't have that authority. But, Tom, helping us now is the best way to help them." She waited for his reaction until her cell phone broke the silence. "Yes," she said without greeting the caller. Listening intently for a moment to the person on the other end of the phone call, she willingly concurred before hanging up, "I agree, thank you."

Directing her attention back to Tom she explained, "I was just told they recovered four bodies, and Eddy one of the deceased. I was also given authority to work on an arrangement between you and the investigators. I strongly suggest you consider this now before I contact the girls with this same offer. Apparently Eddy wasn't easily recognizable. That's all I can tell you right now."

Tom breathed deep and reflected on her words. After experiencing the series of highs and lows, Tom conceded. "So I guess we're not really alone in here." Tom looked up to the ceiling where he spotted a tiny camera device and acknowledged it with an 'I should have known' nod. "We were recruited. They said there was a rich guy who owed someone a lot of money and had something that wasn't his. I don't know what else you want to know."

When she realized that moment when the truth was about to come—the room seemed extraordinarily warm and quiet. "Tell me who recruited you," Martine said matter-of-factly.

"That I can't tell you."

"Why?"

"I never knew his name. I borrowed a lot of money. This is what I had to do to repay it. I needed help and everyone wanted in."

"You owed a loan shark?" Martine speculated. "How much?"

Tom hung his head in shame. "I owed a hundred grand." He shook his head slowly and admitted his mistake, "I couldn't pay it back unless I did what they wanted."

"I presume drug-use got you into this mess," Martine stated.

"It wasn't just me, it was me and Janice."

"It's both your faults then. Your dependency opened the door for someone to exploit you to the point you could never pay them back without risking your life."

"I know," Tom's voice whimpered. "They would kill anyone that didn't pay them back." Tom attempted to justify his actions. "But, I was told how to just break in and steal back what wasn't his." Tom lowered his chin. "I was told he'd never report it because he couldn't tell the police what he'd already stolen."

"So," Martine recapped, "you believed what a criminal told you—making yourself expendable—because you had to pay for your drug abuse."

"Yeah—drug abuse," he repeated under his breath. Lifting his head, he amended his confession, "I didn't kill anyone thought."

"I'll need the name of your loan shark."

Tom provided the contact information he used to communicate with the loan shark that subsequently aligned him with the man that ordered the theft at Morgan's home. "I never met the guy that ordered the job, and I don't know his name either. Loan shark gets paid, and we take want we want. Nobody gets hurt. That's what I'm told."

"We'll call that guy the contractor," Martine offered a solution to the man's ambiguous identity.

"What else can you tell me about the contractor?"

"Not much," Tom returned. "If we broke into this safe we could take what we wanted, but, we had to deliver something he wanted. It was gonna be heavy—that's all I knew. The owner was supposed to be out of town. No one was gonna be there. I was even supplied all the codes we needed to get into the house. We just had to find the safe and break into it."

"Jake, explain who Jake is?"

"I was told to use Jake if I couldn't crack a safe. We needed a safe cracker. That was all he was. I didn't want anyone else involved, but none of us knew how to break into a safe that was complicated."

"What did the contractor want in the safe?"

"Something in a trunk."

"A trunk?" Martine repeated. Instantly aware that the trunk had to be significant or she wouldn't be dreaming about it, she pursued more information. "Is that all the contractor wanted?"

"Yeah—that's all he wanted."

"What was in the trunk?"

"I never found out."

Listening to every syllable coming out of Tom's mouth, Martine's mood changed. "Why?"

"Because it was locked, and we weren't supposed to open it."

"Why couldn't you open it?"

"It was locked with an old-fashioned looking padlock."

"How old? How old was the trunk?

"Really old . . . old like the old west."

"What else can you tell me about the trunk? How big and how heavy was it?"

"It was like an average-sized trunk that would take a couple guys to move. But whatever was in it made it really heavy."

"Heavy like gold?"

"Not that heavy and nothing moved around in the trunk."

"Like what then?"

"I didn't lift the trunk myself. It took four of us to carry it out of the house. It wouldn't fit in a car, so we had to use Eddy's vehicle. It was made out of metal. The handles on the ends were metal. It was dirty, weathered, and old looking. Really ugly. That's all I remember."

"So it wasn't a fancy old-time steamer trunk that people used for their clothing?" Martine surmised out loud. "Were there any markings on the trunk?"

Even though Tom was no longer evasive, he didn't have good recollection. "No—it wasn't anything like one of those. Everything happened so fast, I can't remember much about the trunk. I only opened the door, and it was dark in that house because we couldn't risk turning lights on." Tom thought a moment. "I did see something stamped in the metal."

Martine held her breath in contemplation. "Can you remember any words or symbols you saw?"

"I think it said 'treat' on the lid," he told her with uncertainty. "The trunk was so dirty and tarnished looking I can't be sure it didn't say something else."

With her keener senses and knowing prevailing, Martine pondered the meaning of the word that initially seemed to be a frivolous clue. Then she recognized that she may figure out its possible significance—something that no one else would or could. "Anything else you can possibly remember?"

"I thought I saw the word 'moth,' but, I can't be sure."

"Okay." She quickly changed the subject. "What happened to Eli and Jake?"

"Is this where you tell me I get immunity if I talk?"

"This is where you get charged as an accomplice to first degree murder—unless you can help us prove someone else did it without your willingness to help. This is where you get to try and clear your name. I cannot give complete immunity for murder if you performed the act. You will have to deal with the detectives on that. I can make sure that your help weighs heavily on how much your cooperation was valued and necessary. I want to remind you that your four friends were probably murdered. Did you do that?"

"Absolutely not."

"Cooperating with us completely will only help prove you might not be a mass murdered. It will also help greatly in reducing your sentence if you have committed a serious crime."

Tom thought a moment. "Then I'm ready to tell you what happened."

"An investigator will be in to take your statement." Martine advised Tom of the formalities that would follow.

With Tom's willingness to cooperate established, he gave a lengthy account of what transpired the night of the robbery. He described how the gang arrived in a couple vehicles—Eddy's muscle car, and Rachel's car. Rachel, Janice, and Vic were in charge of the getaway vehicles and stayed parked in the back.

After Eddy, Jake, Saul, Bo and Tom entered the home—believing it was unoccupied, they disarmed the security system and broke thru the locked office door. The loud disturbance in the home woke up Mr. Morgan. He discovered the burglars and surprised them. Mr. Morgan had a small handgun that he threatened them with. When Jake saw the gun he tried to overtake Mr. Morgan—Jake was shot in the process but, Mr. Morgan was subdued by Eddy and Tom. With Jake—the safe cracker—dead, Saul used his knife and forced Eli to open the safe. After the safe was open and they tried to remove the trunk along with everything else of value, Eli charged Saul in anger. Saul used the knife to stab him. The two bodies were dragged into the empty safe where they were going to hide them from being discovered. Tom and Janice knew their decaying bodies would be found—so they planned the arson.

The trunk had to be dropped off that night at a prearranged location in an abandoned Phoenix warehouse—or the contractor would hunt Tom down and torture him to death. It took four men to handle the trunk—so Eddy, Vic, Bo, and Saul used Eddy's vehicle to transport the trunk. Tom took enough valuables and cash to pay the loan shark.

Chapter 34

Driving slowly through the gated entrance of Frye Manor residence, Martine took in the stately uniqueness of a historical property in the Phoenix area. Mature with an old-world façade suited the character of its owner, Teddy Frye.

Teddy and Martine had become fast friends years ago, and her go-to person when confronted with old world issues. He was well versed in history and in possession of publications that rival a common library.

After absorbing the verses, *History need not repeat tale, the lessons that it taught. Evil deeds never fail, when treaties are for naught*, she engaged Teddy's help.

"Hello, Martine," Teddy's aristocratic English accent greeted her warmly.

Martine exchanged a pleasant smile. "Hello, Teddy."

"Come in out of the heat." Teddy was sporting his signature bow tie—indicative of his age, nationality, and refined heritage from prominent English ancestry.

"Thank you for seeing me on short notice. Could really use your resources on a project I'm involved with."

"You came to the right place. It certainly was intriguing last time you were in town."

"Yes. I remember. You don't mind keeping this confidential for the time being—do you?"

"Absolutely not. It's my pleasure. And my curiosity is already peaked."

Seated at a table within the labyrinth of books held in Teddy's personal library, Martine pulled out her notebook and pen from the satchel she borrowed from her sisters' closet. "I'm interested in tracking the History of a man named Eli Morgan. He came from Germany, and seems to have shadowy origins that connect him to a valuable horse named Ashkenazi." Seeing no reaction from Teddy, she continued, "I'm trying to determine if his death is connected to his horse business, or another business he may have been involved in. Being relatively new to our country the trail goes cold on his ancestry when we tried to get information on his parents and his childhood. He seems to suddenly exist when he entered into the world of competitive horse shows and breeding."

"I see," Teddy said with a thoughtful tone.

"You know that historically many Europeans changed their names readily."

"Yes, of course. Families changed their names to disassociate from something that they aren't apart of and don't want to be identified with by their last name, or they're connected to something they don't want anyone to discover."

"Exactly. So, given those possibilities, where can we start?"

"His horse," Martine replied sharply.

"Really?"

"That's all I got on him so far. He had a horse called Ashkenazi's Quest that foaled in 1967. His business associates assure me it's an offspring of an acclaimed horse. He seems to have been dedicated to breeding this lineage—perhaps obsessed. Recently he was successful in breeding a colt which was considered his pride and joy. I only know that this new colt's great grand dam had one foal before she was stolen—or went missing for some reason. It's the great grand dam that would hold the most genetic value in the world of breeding. So, it's that horse that I'm tracking. The great grand dam was Ashkenazi's Star and it foaled in 1938. I believe that is where I find the names and correlations that connect with Eli Morgan. His family owned this horse and he would've been about two or three when the horse was born."

"Well you know how to make a challenge."

"I do. The FBI and Scottsdale police would never consider this a viable lead, nor do they have the resources to track this. I can only assume its Europe—probably Germany. I'm thinking a little European history is going be relevant."

"Well, Martine, that suits me just fine. Where do we start with that?"

"Well I know the name of the horse, Ashkenazi's Star, is as far back as I can go with the pedigree. The name of the registered owners was not provided, but the location of birth was Frankfurt, Germany."

Teddy reiterated, "Horses name is Ashkenazi's Star and in 1938 it foaled in Frankfurt, Germany. My that's interesting."

Martine could sense Teddy's wheels were spinning. "It's a history mystery. I just couldn't think of anyone better than you to help me."

Teddy rubbed his dense graying hair, "Yes. You have a riddle. And you picked a fascinating time to explore the likes of poor Germany." Teddy walked to his wall of books. Selecting a few he returned to the table. "I suggest we focus on the obvious events happing during that time."

"How can I help?"

"Well, as you recall after WWII a few major upsets took place. The allied forces secured Western Germany. Your horse appears to be proudly named Ashkenazi because the Jewish family that owned the horse may have been proud of their heritage."

"That would be correct."

"Most German Jews who survived the war in exile decided to remain where they were, however, a small number returned to Germany. Additionally, some German Jews survived the concentration camps or survived by going into hiding. These German Jews were joined by a couple hundred thousand Eastern European Jewish survivors—namely Ashkenazi Jews. They came to Allied-occupied western Germany after finding no homes left for them in Eastern Europe. When Israel became independent in 1948, most of the European displaced Jews left for the new state of Palestine.

However, 10,000 to 15,000 Jews decided to resettle in Germany. If that's where he's from, we start there."

"Excellent. There wouldn't be too many to consider then," Martine said facetiously—unless this horse went to Israel."

Suddenly scooting her chair back, Martine rose and briskly walked over to a display of bronze statues that were housed in a curio cabinet. "That's where we start," she said scanning her eyes over the various replicated heroes memorialized in Teddy's study. "But, we keep in mind they may have most likely come from Eastern Germany," Martine reiterated.

"Got it," Teddy acknowledged as he walked over to Martine.

Bending down to look closely at a tall female figurine, she added, "Oh, I believe the family was wealthy. Olympic horse champions require a lot of funds to go down that road. Owning champion horses is the sport of kings. Since his entire career was most likely devoted to horse competitions on the best equine money can buy, he had to come from a prosperous home."

"I see," Teddy said as he stood next to her. "Let's look for some rich and famous parents first. Hopefully, they had a child with the first name Eli."

Martine's gaze settled on an eighteen inch high statue. "Teddy, is this the Goddess Freya?" Surprised by the similarity of the goddess in her dream and the miniature replica displayed in Teddy's library gave her pause.

"Why yes it is." Teddy opened the cabinet and took out the sculpture. "This piece has been in my family for some time." Handing the heavy artifact to Martine he continued, "I might have known you would be able to identify her."

Instantly embarrassed, Martine exclaimed, "Why?"

"Because you're Swedish," he said with certainty. "Most people recognize all these other statues like Hercules, Thor, Zeus, Aphrodite, and Apollo. They're not so familiar with Freya."

Martine's body vibrated with excitement when she used her fingers to examine the likeness revealed in the statute's form. "I guess you're right," she returned—admiring every detail in the artist's depiction that captured the attributes of the Goddess Freya.

Like in her dream the artist depicted her with thick long wavy hair and the lengthy legs of an Amazon beauty. Tucked in her left arm was her winged helmet. Leaning against her right leg was a large shield used in battle, and sitting at her left were two cats. Gripped in her right hand was her sheathed sword. Other than a cape that touched the ground and a beautiful necklace that hung to her cleavage, her attire appeared to be made of leather and metal. Reminiscent of how her dream ended abruptly with Freya trying to convey something else she wanted to give Martine, she seized an opportunity to sequester more information from a learned scholar like Teddy. "Since I don't read or speak German, do you have any authentic publications on the Norse Gods?"

Teddy chuckled. "Are you going to research your ancestry while you're here? That's taking history back about as far as we can go."

Ashamed to be looking up something so meaningless to Teddy, she fibbed, "No, not really. My friend gave me a beautiful gift of the Goddess Freya. Thought I'd take advantage of your resources before I thank her properly."

Clearly more excited to discuss this with Martine than some German family ancestry, Teddy hurried over to his collection of ancient texts from medieval times. "Freya appears in the writings before the Viking age," Teddy paused and selected a book. "Let's try this one." Leafing through some pages he hesitated. "My Norse is really bad. Give me a second here. Right. It says that after the god Njörðr split with the goddess Skaði, he had two beautiful and mighty children, a son Freyr, and a daughter, Freya. Freyr is 'the most glorious' of the gods, and Freya 'the most glorious' of the goddesses. Freya has a dwelling in the heavens. She is daughter of Njörðr, sister of Freyr, wife of Óðr, and mother of Hnoss. It also mentions that next to Frigg, Freya is highest in rank among them and that she owns the necklace Brísingamen."

"Do you have any books that might be in English?"

Teddy put the book back and selected a newer publication. "That might be best for now since neither of us can read Norse very well."

"Exactly," Martine agreed readily.

"Alright. This is more interesting. Freya is one of the major goddesses of Norse Mythology. Equal in prowess to Thor, and nearly the equal of Odin, according to the Icelandic Eddas and Sagas of the Migration Period prior to the Viking Age, she is viewed as a force for good in the world—protector of the weak, healer, granter of magic and source of love and peace. She is the goddess of Love and Beauty, one of the original fertility goddesses of the region. She listens to the prayers of men and women seeking love and helps them when she can."

Pointing to the statue, Martine interrupted, "So, she was definitely consider a goddess, or superhuman. Right?"

"Absolutely." Teddy selected another larger book. "She'll be in this encyclopedia of gods and goddesses." Finding the page he wanted, Teddy read to Martine, "Norse Literature describes her as a fearless expert in knowledge and magical power with no one equal. Considered a Shaman and seeress she was exalted, feared, longed for, propitiated, celebrated and scorned. Like other northern Eurasian Shamans, her social status was highly ambiguous and secretive—according to past records it was the duty of the warband's leader's wife to foretell the outcome of a battle and to influence that conclusion by means of spiritual powers. Insights and wisdom both help and hurt—depending on the person's willingness to accept the truth when told, thus being an oracle alone did not make her greatness. Abilities to foster love, guard sacred secrets, and protect the human race earned her an esteemed position in the hierarchy of the god realms."

"Very interesting," Martine said. "She was very connected to the Asgard gods then."

"Most certainly. The older texts seem to indicate she was married to Odin's brother. Some later theories suggest she was with Odin. I don't think that fits well within the course of the historical stories recorded. Being married to Odin's brother fits."

"Was Loki her adversary?"

Teddy rested his eyes on the statue. "It does seem to imply that in several myths." Contemplating the details on the statue that are meant to convey the characters attribute, he added, "Most interesting are the ones with Freya's cloak of feathers, which she used to enter the underworld. Freya borrowed her cloak to Loki on several occasions—in the spirit of helping Asgard. It does read later that Freya also wrangled with him on many things. She began to see how he instigated and manipulated events that gave rise to conflicts. He later appears to resurface to negotiate and resolve the clash." Handing the book to Martine, Teddy offered, "Please borrow this. There are many chapters to read on the subject in this book alone."

It was not unusual to receive corroborations in the physical world that helped authenticate an ethereal experience, or what some people referred to as—a download. Appreciative of the validation regarding her exchange with Freya and the gifting of her Lynx animal guides, Martine gave the figurine a nod of approval before walking away.

"Thank you, Teddy, I will. Now back to some real difficult subject matter." She sat down and looked at her notes. "We know they were in Germany, we know when, and we know they had money. We know they had to be connected with the same type of people."

Teddy injected, "Besides claiming property back, the Jewish community was still actively involved with banking."

Martine had a visceral reaction to Teddy's comment. "Banking money would explain a lot." Then she suddenly remembered her dream about a treaty. "Wasn't there a treaty imposed on Germany. What was the name of that treaty? I'm drawing a blank," she blurted. "What do you have on that?"

Teddy had an immediate response, "Well the treaty from WWI—was the Treaty of Versailles—wasn't it? I don't believe there was a treaty after WWII."

"Yes, you're right. The first treaty after WWI was already such a burden, I don't believe President Roosevelt went along with another treaty. Can I see what you have on that treaty? I need something that will jog my memory." She tried not to divulge too much. "I haven't studied that part of the law since my school years. My work is geared towards criminal activity," she explained.

Teddy retrieved his resources on the history of WWI. "This is actually one of my favorite subjects."

"I know. You and John are both history buffs."

"Crime-solvers too," he added in agreement.

While Teddy gathered his books, he began narrating some of the events widely known about the war, "This is the war were you Americans started fighting on the same side with us Brits."

"Exactly," Martine confirmed. "The German U-boats torpedoed and sunk your British cruise liner because they believed it was transporting ammunition to your soldiers. So, was it, Teddy?" Martine asked playfully.

"The Lusitania," Teddy said nostalgically. "Ironically, last year divers explored the wreck of the Lusitania which still lies at the bottom of the ocean off the coast of Ireland. That dive with the robotic sub finally answered the long awaited secrets entombed in the oceans bed. It was discovered that the Lusitania was used to transport ammunition to Britain during the war. They found approximately four million US-made Remington bullets. Apparently the Germans were right, but there wasn't a way to prove it back in 1915."

"Well that's depressing. I don't think President Wilson would've gotten into that war if Germany hadn't sunk what he'd been told was a passenger ocean liner with Americans on board."

Abruptly infused with recall, Martine recognized the significance of her dream and the sinking of ships—but stayed focused on what Teddy could help her the most with.

"Neither do I." Teddy set down a few books. "This book," Teddy said as her handed Martine a thin hard covered periodical, "was written by a lawyer who lived during that era. I remember he was logical and concise in his writing about this treaty. These other books are historical facts about everything leading up to the treaty."

"You've read this then?" Martine asked.

"Yes. If you're looking for a treaty that went awry, this may be your answer."

Martine handled the book written by a lawyer. "Let's start with this book and reference those if we need too."

"Well, I can tell you what it says then. You can study it later if you want, counselor. I think his perspective was enlightening."

"Perfect. Tell me what it says."

"The Treaty of Versailles took months of hard bargaining. Remember—Germany was like America back then—strong, sophisticated, and wealthy. The treaty really hammered Germany into the ground and stripped them of land, possessions, and money. It was the enormous 'reparation payments' that the Germans were forced to accept and the discovery that they were betrayed and stabbed in the back by their own German socialist bankers. It truly shocked and devastated the German people. When the Versailles Delegation presented the treaty to the Germans—who were not allowed to participate in the negotiations—they couldn't even find one to sign the treaty."

"Right," Martine recalled, "President Wilson's famous Fourteen Points were mostly ignored. Actually, I don't think our own president signed off on that treaty."

"Yes. Your president thought the terms were too harsh. Germany was a buffer to the spread of communism within the European continent. The treaty according to this author did three things that caused WWII and the rise of the madman, Hitler."

"What did he say they were?" Martine prepared to make notes.

"First, and most humiliating, was the 'War Guilt Clause' that forced the Germans to accept complete responsibility for initiating WWI. Second, because of the 'War Guilt Clause' they were liable for all material damages—which were in the billions. According to this author it would be the equivalent today of over four-hundred billion. Third, was the discovery that the Jewish banking Zionists were responsible for getting the Americans in the war so Britain could destroy Germany—in exchange for Britain's promise to give them Palestine."

"Really," she said reflectively.

"During the peace negotiations in Versailles, Germany's overseas properties were seized as part of the punishment. It was like a grand bazaar where the allies—France, England, and Russia and a couple others bargained for the assets. England took control of

Palestine—which was part of Germany's overseas property. The problem was that from a Palestinian Arab point of view, the same area had been promised to them for siding with Germany in WWI."

"Wow, I didn't really know that part," Martine said admittedly. "I just assumed Britain was already in possession of Palestine. You should teach history, Teddy."

He laughed with her. "I do." Skimming the table of contents, he continued, "This chapter is about how the flaws of the Treaty of Versailles destined Europe to a Second World War. Because the treaty was riddled with revenge instead of balance and fairness, Germany was stripped of its democratic government by the people of the now defeated and destitute country. They opted for an authoritive government—a hero—that could deliver salvation not starvation. They picked Hitler who hated the treaty and despised the Zionist Jews that betrayed Germany. The reparation payments forced on Germany through the Versailles Treaty amounted to three-times the value of all of Germany's assets. Hitler was a proud German that wanted to save his country. He promised to liberate the German people of the dictating treaty that had the purpose of destroying them."

Martine interrupted, "The Treaty of Versailles was like a stick of dynamite, and Hitler was the little boy with a match."

"Yes, but not how you have been taught from the history books—according to this author."

Martine brainstormed with Teddy. "Can you imagine if we lost a war like that and had to pay the winners four-hundred billion dollars?" She asked with a contemplative look.

Teddy nodded poignantly. "Germany's population was so fragile then too. People were dying in famines. Jobs were scarce. There were only about 60 million people left."

"That means there were probably less than twenty-million households." Martine did the math in her head. "Teddy, that treaty cost each German household twenty-thousand dollars."

Teddy smiled affirmatively. "That would be before interest, my dear. Also, keep in mind the average household's annual income back then would've been $1,000-$1,500."

"I never understood why the Jews didn't move to Palestine when they saw their lives were in danger."

"Most people didn't understand that—in hind sight I think we do now. The truth was that after WWI when the Zionists got possession of their 'homeland' where they were going to settle it with Jews and make it their state, they couldn't get the Jews to go. In 1923 German Jews were wealthy and comfortable in their beautiful mansions. They had their symphonies, art, theater, and good food. They weren't interested in leaving that for the Middle East." He raised his brows at Martine. "Would you leave America for that?"

Martine didn't have to think about her answer. "Absolutely not."

"They also weren't interested in being Zionists which were atheist Jews. Orthodox Jews believed their Messiah would come— as prophesized—and establish their Jewish state. Unorthodox Zionist Jews did not accept Christ as their savior. Zionists then re-formed Judaism—stating they could have a Jewish state before the Messiah comes. Of course it was the Rothschild's—with all their money—that said they could buy their own state. If Germany was the least anti-Jewish country in Europe—you have to ask yourself, why in the world would they relocate to Palestine? They already were on top of the world."

Martine stated in contemplation, "The Transfer Agreement. That's why Hitler signed The Transfer Agreement with the Zionists."

"Exactly. The Jews weren't leaving Germany, so the Zionists used Hitler to help create their state. If they were going to succeed in their dream of a Jewish run country of their own, they needed a way to force the Jews to want to leave Europe and find refuge in Palestine. Hitler actually participated in creating the forty train-ing camps that the Zionists used to train their European Jews to survive in their new land, and fight for it in anticipation of the 1948 take over. The same time your Morgan family ancestry probably changed."

Martine surmised aloud, "That's why the controversial Transfer Agreement was implemented by Hitler. The Zionists needed to maintain a Jewish majority in their new state, and the

Jews wouldn't leave their wealth behind. The Transfer Agreement allowed them to convert their wealth into goods for Palestine. The ones that didn't want to be forced to leave and transfer their wealth to Palestine changed their identities."

"Yes," Teddy agreed. "The Zionists used Hitler's new power to do their bidding in exchange for money."

"This gave Hitler his chance to make good on his political pledge to lead Germany out of the Zionist-engineered Versailles Treaty," Martine added.

"Oh my!" Teddy said excitedly. "I just thought of what happened to your Mr. Morgan. The Zionists had to populate their new state, or the Arabs would continue to stake their claim. That's when the Zionists aligned with Hitler. Hitler agreed with their goals to start their own state and leave Germany. It was 'win win' to Hitler. He wanted the Jews gone anyways. So, the mission of the NAZI's was to force anti-Zionist Jews to accept Zionism and deportation to the new homeland. Orthodox Jews did not agree with Zionists— who were considered atheists. They were split sharply down the middle—to the point of riots. One group of Jews fell victim to another, and of those targeted, few escaped. Your Jewish family was probably susceptible to deportation. They didn't want to be forced to go."

"If we presume Eli was from a Jewish family that was subject to the sorting process of that time," Martine joined in, "we could theoretically presume he was from a family of Ashkenazi Jews that wanted to hide their identities before being rounded-up. Right?"

"Yes," Teddy nodded. "It's now more understood that Hitler's training camps were for the young, healthy Jewish population. Zionists were trying to populate Palestine with the young and amenable. They didn't want the burden of the old. They also didn't want the religious orthodox Jews. They relocated about half a million Jews before WWII ended—probably more."

Martine asked, "Wouldn't the wealthy aristocratic Jewish families be desirable for their assets?"

"I would imagine so. Maybe his parents wouldn't have been so safe though. They probably were connected enough to see the handwriting on the wall."

"If Eli was only a few years old back then, they probably kept his first name Eli which may be short for Elijah. They may have only changed his last name," Martine deduced.

"I bet you're right, Martine. That gives me an idea. I could engage my students to participate in an extra credit project. They could do some ancestral research on this family."

Martine barley heard him as she considered what may have happened to this man's family. "You know, they may have just shortened the last name from Morgenstein to Morgan. If I had a young child that needed to keep a secret identity—that's what I'd do."

"Brilliant."

"Whoa!" Martine raised her voice as she lifted her head from her notes and eyed Teddy. Experiencing the biggest adrenalin dump from connecting the sorted details her and Teddy discussed along with her interview with Tom, she blurted-out, "Can you have your students do some 'up to date' investigating on The Treaty of Versailles? Besides what's written in the old history books, I'd like to know what arrangements were made to retire that treaty." Martine just realized Tom may have seen the word treaty on the trunk—not treat.

"Well, my dear, you have just made this project more interesting for me and my graduate students. I can't wait for their reaction to their new assignments."

Chapter 35

As Martine's day dissolved into the dimness of a moonless night, she fell fast into a deep slumber. Without knowing what was happening, her spirit instinctively took flight to another time in the future.

Upon her arrival she found herself inside a military command center with countless TV screens playing live footage of many events throughout our world. Inside the darkened room, she quickly ascertained that this post was the result of terrorist cells being formed by new bold leaders.

Current activities being reported included; bombings, spree killings, kidnappings, and beheadings. Hijackings of various kinds were in progress as the terrorist cells cropped up around the globe.

Observing that the United States officials monitoring this activity were having a difficult job trying to stop the irrational anarchy because the bans of snipers and commandos were targeting innocent civilian people in their homes and workplaces—not on a battle field, she surveyed the uniformed American personnel for the leader in charge. Sighting the General in command she telepathically understood that his normal war strategies did not apply to the enemy groups with strange and difficult names to pronounce.

"This is affecting every country," the General said as he paced in front of the visual displays showing various groups of faceless heads wrapped in scarves. United in their intent to sow terror with barbaric violence, they hoisted their weapons in the air and chanted while the rest of the world braced themselves for surprise attacks.

Martine was overwhelmed as she watched gruesome assaults happening that are normally viewed as motion pictures at the cinema. With real time events playing out like hell on earth, she was frozen in disbelief as these crude militant attacks occurred simultaneously in different regional hot spots. Each time they carried out aggression on blameless citizens they magnified fear and attracted new recruits.

"We are at the point where no one is safe, Sir." An analyst entered the room with a document and handed it to the General. "Here is the latest threat."

Shaken by these words, Martine tuned in on the conversation that related to the terrorist leader that had newly surfaced. As his picture flashed up on screen, Martine found herself looking into the soulless eyes of a shark.

Ordering someone to pull up the visuals on the newest terrorist attack, his face quickly changed from concerned-urgency to panic. "May God have mercy on their souls," he uttered as he witnessed men and women being crudely beheaded and mutilated by Jihad extremists raging out of control in a village of two-thousand people. Gouged out eyes, amputated body parts, and beheadings—remained in the wake of their ethnic cause. Nothing was off-limits in their pursuits of domination. These once barking dogs were somehow banning together like packs of carnivorous jackals. God-fearing in his love for mankind, he added, "Jesus help us."

At that moment the vivid images of angry screaming vigilante terrorists waving guns and knives began to slowly dissipate like rain washing over wet paint—leaving only a few behind—the worst and highest-ranking of their order.

"God have mercy on their souls," another intelligence officer uttered loudly. Those rebels remaining, with absolutely no respect for the lives of man or beast, began to dissolve—like melting snow.

Watered down by his words of prayer, Martine witnessed the power of faith at work. As she watched, totally unnoticed, the workings of evil in ordinary men, she was able to assimilate a higher understanding of how these once commonplace men could operate like blood thirsty assassins. Because no regular human on earth can see the difference between a truly demonic person and a Christian person, they can exist and blend in anywhere.

Most people strive to live exemplary lives. Most are not inherently evil. Sadly, because of this they are not able to readily accept that there are such wretched people in operation.

As the General whispered his words, "God save America," the images of crazed terrorists completely washed away.

Witness to the revelation of how to snuff out more bands of terrorists, Martine yearned to eagerly assist the General in his plight. Being blind to the power of his own faith gave him a disadvantage she wanted to rectify. Faith-filled words spoken in the room appeared to be supernaturally powerful.

With a rush of infused energy, she was whisked away through the tunnel of time.

As if walking out of an elevator unto a Wild West frontier land, she stopped in her tracks when a galloping white horse came into view. Black hair flowed around the riders face, neck, and shoulders as he slowed his approach. Clothed in buckskin and a hat shadowing his face, the rider was not easily recognizable until the familiar voice spoke, "Isn't this disrespectful to the Spirits?"

Instantly aware this was the Indian Chief that had revealed numerous decrees to her thus far, Martine studied his more youthful appearance. "Yes," Martine answered.

"You felt it?" He dismounted his steed and approached Martine.

"Yes, oh yes, I certainly did."

"Did you see and feel it through your eyes?" His voice was soft and soothing.

His question instilled intense compassion in her soul. "Yes."

Taking her hand the Indian lead her to a camp fire surrounded by a group of Native American elders. "What did you feel?" He motioned her to be seated in the circle with him.

"I felt horrible and helpless. I felt foreign, like I didn't belong in the room." Martine breathed in the aromatic vapors of the sage fire. "It felt like a bad dream I wished I'd never had."

"Tell me if you saw a pattern." Lighting his peace pipe, he handed it to Martine in a gesture of sharing.

Pausing a moment to gather her thoughts, Martine tuned into the singing of an ancient Indian chant that was now audibly present at the camp site. "I saw men wrapped in scarves killing people that were defenseless and innocent. It is different than when both sides have a purpose to fight each other. I saw unprepared powerless people murdered." Martine puffed on the pipe and handed it back to him.

Taking on a more serious tone, he asked, "Why?"

"I don't understand why this happens. I don't see the reason."

"What makes you know dark from light?"

"The energy of light is loving." Recalling what she knew about dark, she finished, "Dark is void of light."

"Yes. Void of love."

"Remember, life is greater than you know and is born of love. Ignorant of that—horrible things happen. What are the desired results of the aggressors?"

Martine's mind flashed to the jeering and cheering done by the terrorizing assassins as they celebrated their actions and success. "They were energized. Their adrenaline fed off of their murdering ways." Martine heard the Indian chants increase in volume, almost crescendoing with the progression of the conversation.

"Yes. They are bored without it. Their chants are death to life—death to Spirit."

Wanting a solution to the lesson, Martine asked, "How do we stop it?"

"First, you become aware that it exists. Only then can one recognize that which no longer serves the people. Like the battles your warring General encountered against the ancient patterns of underdeveloped souls, there comes a time when we are expected to reject those old ways and accept what the Great Spirit desires—and its greater responsibilities."

Martine looked into the fire. "We are at war—on the planet. Aren't we? We are all in danger."

"You are protected. Your actions when the requirement is greatest mark your path. Your choices create the protection you require. Take this." He handed her the scroll. "Read out loud."

"All the darkness of the night
Won't snuff out one brilliant light
Battle evil with enlightened might
Using power of birthright
Bearing truth will stop the fight
Righteous ones end the plight."

Without another word being spoken, Martine's spirit was returned to her slumbering body in Arizona.

Chapter 36

Armed with new insights after her interrogation with Tom and a visit with Teddy, Martine arranged to meet with Olivia away from *Desert Run*.

"Hey, Olivia," Martine greeted her as she sat in the booth across from her.

"Hi," Olivia returned, "hope you have some good news. I could use some."

"No, not really," Martine replied. "But, a lot is happening. Which got me to thinking about how you could help."

"Sure. Whatever I can do to help," Olivia obliged.

"Can you give me any information about Eli's family?"

"He never spoke about family. He was an only child and both parents were deceased as far as I know."

"I know that's what's has been explained, but he's clearly European and had financial assets that the average American doesn't have."

"Well," Olivia said thoughtfully. "I assumed it was inheritance."

"Me too," Marine agreed. "If he had family money that he parlayed into American assets in the form of an elaborate horse business—more like an enterprise that would explain a lot. Where did it come from though?"

"The only person I know that knew about Eli's finances was Adam."

"Were they friends?" Martine questioned. "Were you friends with Adam?"

"I don't know if they were really friends. Adam didn't give me the time of day, so we weren't what you would call even friendly," Olivia explained.

Martine pulled out the file she had started on Olivia's business transactions with Eli. "I've read through all your notes and documents regarding the horse dealings you had with Eli. You have good enough documentation to make your claim for varying degrees of ownership in about twenty horses."

"Really?" Olivia sounded hopeful.

"Yes, I believe so," Martine sounded sure. "Did he make arrangements like this with anyone else?"

Olivia replied, "Not that I know of."

"I'm just being cautious in case Eli made similar arrangements with other people to own these same horses."

"I never got that impression," Olivia returned.

"Well then, it looks legitimate that he did execute legal agreements for you to have some or all ownership in these horses—even if he passed away. I didn't see any escape clauses."

Martine held one of the papers up to read the words that created a legally binding contract. Instantaneously, her eyes caught a new detail. "Did you notice how he referenced 'TMFT' after his signature?"

Olivia took one of the documents and studied it. "No. I never noticed that. What does it mean?"

Martine looked puzzled. "Is it a designation used in the horse world, like Dr. is indicative to someone with a medical degree?"

"Not that I can think of," Olivia replied.

"It has to mean something if it was important enough to enter after his signature. Each time he executed an exchange of some ownership over to you he signed his name with 'TMFT' after it." Martine went rapidly through each paper in the file, stopping at the oldest one he had executed with Olivia. "Oh my," she declared in alarm. He wrote the word trustee after it on this one. TMFT is a trust. It's probably code for The Morgan Family Trust. That trust must've controlled the horse assets he was signing over to you. Did he ever explain that to you?"

"Not really. I don't know what a trust is."

"Well, in legal terms, a trust is a relationship whereby assets are held by one party for the benefit of another. An owner placing property into the trust turns over part of his or her assets to the trustee, separating the property's legal claims and control from its equitable ownership. This may be done for taxes or to control the property and its benefits if the grantor is absent, dead, or incapacitated. Trusts are frequently created in wills, defining how money and property will be handled for children or other beneficiaries."

"I guess I understand. Are you saying that now that Eli's dead, I don't own these horses? Now his trust owns them." Olivia looked panicked.

"No, I'm saying there appears to be a trust that owns his assets. It could mean the horses are protected by the trust, and so are these transactions. Adam insinuated there was no money and Eli was broke now. How did he know that? What did he know about the trust? Were they good friends?"

"I only know that Adam was like a business manager here. They weren't friends. Eli was like seventy, and Adam was like forty. There was too much of an age difference."

"Did Eli have an attorney?" Martine probed.

"Not that I know about."

Martine handed Olivia back the original documents. "You need to keep this in a safe place. Do you have a safety deposit box?"

"Of course not. What would I keep in there?"

"These documents. They may or may not be valuable. I have copies, but the originals must be kept in a safe place till the beneficiaries of his trust are revealed. A trust has to have one or more beneficiaries. That much is for certain. When and who created the trust can be a mystery until probate, or until someone in possession of Eli's will comes forward. That trust may have been created out of a family will. Unless you know someone who is familiar with Eli's estate that is still living, there won't be too much to do on this matter. It appears you have a legitimate claim to your arrangement with Eli's trust, and that may be a very good thing."

"When do you think someone will come forward with Eli's will?"

"Usually upon notice of the death, or a death certificate being issued."

"What's notice of the death?"

"There's most likely been an obituary in the newspaper. If there is an executor of the trust appointed, they're probably stumbling around right now getting all the legalities sorted—such as locating the beneficiaries."

"Okay. I'll put these in a safe place. Do we need to pack up and leave like Adam told us?"

"You should be ready to go somewhere in case you're evicted by someone. Adam's not here to do it, but you don't know who's ultimately been left in authority. These horses can't be left without care. I suspect something will be done very soon."

With her quick meeting with Olivia completed, Martine headed out. Calling Teddy from inside the privacy of her car, she filled him in on the name of Eli Morgan's Family Trust. That alone could help in locating details on Eli's infamous family origins. He invited her to stop in to his class room, for a quick chat.

Chapter 37

Teddy and Martine exchanged friendly greetings over the phone before getting down to business.

"I want to update you with some very intriguing information. My students couldn't have been more fascinated with an assignment. If a green-skinned extraterrestrial had moved onto campus I don't think they would've noticed. Their enthusiasm was so contagious—I've got to come up with more assignments like this."

"That's encouraging. Are you saying they found something?"

"Well, it seems there was a family living in Frankfurt Germany with the last name Morgenstein. They did have a child named Elijah who was born in 1936."

"That has to be them," Martine gasped excitedly.

"The parents were Moses and Sarah."

"Good biblical names."

"Most certainly they were," Teddy concurred. "Moses was an Ashkenazi Jew, but Sarah apparently was a convert from a Christian family. Moses family was involved in banking. His father was the president of one of the big banks in Frankfurt and Eli was a prominent business man during that time. Sometime between 1939 and 1948 Moses changed their identities. It is hard to determine if it was to protect the Christian mother, the Jewish father, or the half-breed son."

"Or," Martine injected, "their assets."

"Lest we forget those," Teddy said mockingly. "A rich Jew would not let his wealth go unprotected."

"So, which is it?" Martine asked with bated breath.

"I don't know." He shook his head in disappointment.

Martine probed again, "How did they end up in America?"

"Haven't found out yet."

"Still sounds like the right family," she sounded encouraged.

"Looks like it," Teddy said.

"What happened to his parents? Any siblings?"

"Parents are deceased," Teddy explained. "No other children seem to be in the family."

"Seems simple enough," she theorized.

"Yes, but this is a story about a family in Germany during the most dramatic times in history. This is actually more like a suspense novel where people are never as they seem, or people have mysteries and secrets to hide. I've read a lot fiction that doesn't compare to this monumental time in Europe."

"Go on," Martine said.

"Sarah was a Christian girl that married a much older Moses—twenty years her senior. They had their only child within a year of marriage. Maybe they had to marry."

"How'd you find this information so quickly?"

Teddy looked sheepish. "It was decided by my students that they'd start by searching obituaries—hoping a name or family bio would fit within the parameters they determined would address the family we described to them. Once they located one with the name Morgenstein—the research took off like one of Eli's champion horses. Using everything they obtained from the obituary and the story that accompanied it, they could find more reports, articles, and publications that referenced their names. Anyways, after the death of Moses something happens to change everything for little Eli."

"What was it?"

"The family was religiously observant orthodox. After the mother's death, Moses tried to smuggle Eli and himself to America. That would explain the name change and need for new credentials. However instead of bringing the passengers to America, they were brought back to Germany. Five ships of Jewish refugees from Germany were turned back due to immigration bans during that time. According to more modern research done by my students, they learned Zionist Jews helped orchestrate these immigration bans because they weren't trying to save Jews—you can see by this—they were trying to force them to Palestine. After the ships returned to Germany the passengers were boarded trains to Hamburg. From there they were taken to the Poppendorf Displaced Persons' Camp. On the way to the camp, Moses was shot by a NAZI soldier. Eli remained in this illegal immigrant camp with other Palestinian emissaries until they took control of the camp in 1947.

"Why did they shoot Moses?"

"Probably because he would've been marked as a traitor, or he tried to escape. Moses actually did work for one of the Jewish training camps set up in Germany to prepare the Jewish population for their new lives in Palestine. It can only be assumed he eventually decided against the philosophy of their ideologies, their transfer of his wealth, or the military demands of defending a new state in Palestine. That's the period were Kibbutz's began to assume a more prominent military roll. He probably feared for his very young boy. The Kibbutz training camps were rough. They had to work very hard—make no money, and be separated from their children. It would've been a cultural shock for an older man. It also was the time Moses would've discovered these new Kibbutz's were staunchly atheistic—more like monasteries without God. He would've been a hindrance and rebel if he was practicing Orthodox Judaism. He also would've been aware of the increased Arab opposition to the waves of Jewish settlers coming into Palestine. The Arab-Jewish violence had become virtually constant."

"How did the mother die?

"Don't know."

"What happened to Eli?"

"Moses' obituary listed Elijah as missing. Most likely, the new identity of a young boy eventually put him in an orphanage. He must have been reconnected with some surviving family or adopted by a Jewish family. All we can presume is we are on the heels of connecting his past with his future."

Martine relayed her suspicions that there was a Morgenstein Family Trust, before she terminated the conversation.

Chapter 38

Drowsy from the effects of seven hours of deep sleep, Max lumbered over to his sofa and logged onto his computer for blog updates before getting ready for his Friday night shift at the diner. Still in progress was a hotly debated string of conversation that he eagerly read over after he himself had started the postings hours earlier after sharing a link to a controversial interview.

Supermax says: "Before DNA testing and conspiracy theories, there were whistle blowers. The real story began to emerge back in the 70's after Walter Carl Darrow White published this shocking interview with Zionist Harold Rosenthal," Max had typed to his bloggers. "My ass fell through my socks when I read it."

U.R.Wrong says: "Where is White now?"

Supermax says: "Even after his interview went public, nobody seems to know for sure."

Richmann says: "How is that possible?"

U.R.Wrong says: "He probably had to go into hiding or die."

Supermax says: "I had a source once like that once."

U.R.Wrong says: "What happened?"

Supermax says: "Cooperation lasted about as long as a Canadian summer. In 2 weeks all contact was cut off. E-mails wouldn't even go through. Never heard from the guy again."

Sharonlove says: "What did source say?"

Supermax says: "Said we had all the proof we needed before the interview was published in 1978. Said every group with an agenda has its own fanatic with enough sociopathic tendencies to brag about their world supremacy. Rosenthal was young, arrogant, belligerent, and aggressive."

Sharonlove says: "That made him believable?"

Supermax says: "He was so boastful, forceful, and evil-tongued he sounded believable. He gloated with excessive confidence over the success of a Zionist world order. He considered every Christian a slave to their Jewish needs. You tell me after you read the whole interview."

Sharonlove says: "Who was Harold Rosenthal?"

Supermax says: "Twenty-nine year old that worked in the Senate. He needed money for gambling and agreed to a paid interview with Walter White in 1976. Within months after the secret interview he was murdered in a terrorist hijacking out of Istanbul, Turkey. White said it was an assassination."

U.R.Wrong says: "We will never know how many people have died because of what they know. What killed him?"

Supermax says: "He was so candid and outrageous with his claims to possessing all this secret knowledge about the Zionist plot to rule the world that they had to shut him up. Back then he was nearly unbelievable. Now his claims make more sense than anything else I have found."

Sharonlove says: "Like what?"

Supermax says: "Read the Hidden Tyranny. Signing off."

Richmann says: "Jews control everything like politics, world-trade, banking, and wars."

Sharonlove says: "They do not. I have Jewish friends. They never talk about that stuff."

Richmann says: "Rosenthal was a deranged fanatic like Hitler. Rosenthal said that Jews hate Christians, because of Christ."

U.R.Wrong says: "You do know that they were expecting a warlord that was going to conquer the world for them, and they ended up with Jesus who stood up to their greedy 'money changers.' Jesus was an insult to the Jews in charge."

Richmann says: "Rosenthal claimed there is no God and Jews are actually Luciferians."

Sharonlove says: "That is not true. I've been to Israel. I've been to the Wailing Wall. Jews and Rabbi's do not worship Lucifer."

Richmann says: "Of course they don't. He used his Jewishness to inflate and validate his delusion that an entire race of Jews is behind some agenda he is involved with. Like a small group of race hating White-Supremacists hide behind and within a race of Caucasians. All Jews are not Zionists, and all Caucasians are not White-Supremacists."

U.R.Wrong says: "White-Supremacists are just a terrorist cell who believes that the white race is superior to other races of color and that white people should control people of other races. The entire Jewish race does not hate Christians, or have an agenda, anymore than all the Caucasians in the world hate and discriminate against people of other races."

Richmann says: "A true descendant of an Israeli Jew would never denounced God for Lucifer. Even the converted Jews from Europe would not practice that belief."

U.R.Wrong says: "A Zionist Jew would pretend to be Jewish for political and financial reasons. Most of them have forsaken the faith of their forefathers and were not Israeli by birthright anyways. Modern Jews have been duped by the Zionists. True Torah Jews are not fooled."

Sharonlove says: "Are you referring to the converted Jews?"

U.R.Wrong says: "Yes, and any atheistic Jew that didn't practice, or believe in their faith."

Sharonlove says: "Sounds like Rosenthal was in a league all his own."

B.Frank says: "It is about time somebody talks about this. I read the interview. Rosenthal was so prideful and self-righteous he couldn't maintain any discretion. It obviously got him killed. What choice did they have if they didn't want the secret out. Behind every extremist is an element of truth."

Richmann says: "Edmund Burke said, 'The only thing necessary for the triumph of evil is for good men to do nothing.' Harold Rosenthal along with other truly influential people have been warning us for decades."

B.Frank says: "You mean centuries. It took conceited Harold to expose it."

Richmann says: "Others have. Benjamin Freedman tried to tell people the same thing. JFK was president when Freedman revealed the truth about WWI and why the US got involved. It wasn't our war."

B.Frank says: "WWII wasn't our war either."

Sharonlove says: "What do you mean?"

Richmann says: "WWI broke out the summer of 1914. My parents were not even born then. Britain, France, and Russia were fighting against Germany, Austria, Hungary, and Turkey. By 1916 Germany had won, thanks to the German submarines blowing up all the convoys in the ocean. Britain was out of ammo and food, the French had mutinied, and Russia was defecting. Germany offered England peace terms. They offered to call off the war and let everything go back the way it was."

Sharonlove says: "Germany didn't win that war."

Richmann says: "They should have."

B.Frank says: "They would have if we stayed out. We helped win that war for England."

Richmann says: "Yah, in 1918."

Sharonlove says: "Why?"

U.R.Wrong says: "We are allies with England."

B.Frank says: "Since when?"

Richmann says: "Why are breaking news stories about certain political figures so sensationalized that you need earplugs to avoid them, versus huge court and legislative decisions that become laws and regulations that receive zero coverage?"

U.R.Wrong says: "The media?"

Richmann says: "Of course it is. When Germany was clearly defeating Britain, Russia, and France in 1916 they offered peace terms. England considered it. They really didn't have a choice because if they went on with the war they faced complete defeat. While that was going on the elite Jewish Zionists from Eastern Europe, went to the British War Cabinet and proposed a way for England to win the war."

Sharonlove says: "Why would they do that?"

Richmann says: "Zionists, which were actually in London, Germany, and the United States, saw an opportunity that would serve them very well. They proposed Britain could win the war if the US helped. They said they could get us to join Britain and beat Germany. They used propaganda to convince President Wilson to join Britain and defeat Germany."

Sharonlove says: "Why?"

B.Frank says: "They wanted something they couldn't get on their own."

Sharonlove says: "Religious freedom?"

Richmann says: "Palestine. England had as much right to promise Palestine to the Zionists, as we have to promise Mexico to England."

Sharonlove says: "That is nasty."

B.Frank says: "Before WWI we liked the Germans. We wanted the Germans to kick the Russian Communist's ass. Jews didn't like the Russian Czar and the Czar believed Jews were revolutionary Communists. Jews had to evacuate Russia when the Communist revolution failed. Guess where they went?"

Richmann says: "They went to Germany who gave them refuge."

B.Frank says: "What happens next is the ultimate in betrayal. German Zionists do succeed in persuading our President Wilson into joining with England, we do help win the war against Germany, and our country believes we did the right thing."

Richmann says: "Benjamin Freedman was at the Paris Peace Conference where the Germans found out for the first time why we turned against them and what the game of war was really about. They were defeated because of us and they didn't know why. They found out their own German Jewish Zionists sold them out for Palestine."

B.Frank says: "That is how Germany went from giving refuge to Jews to hating them."

Max was caught up with the aggressive postings that had been going on during his long sleep. He couldn't resist joining in the banter that he had started that morning.

Supermax says: "No. Don't ever say that. Germany did not do that as a people anymore than we would. Hitler was a Jew hating fanatic who became a powerful dictator. Germany was broke, starved and ruined after the war. He would not have gotten into power under different circumstances. He promised the people salvation. That is not what he delivered."

B.Frank says: "I apologize. This is not about a race, religion, or the color of a people. It's about a type of person that wants to control and dominate others for their own needs. They use others, manipulate situations, and implement their agenda at the expense of others. They were International Jewish banksters."

Sharonlove says: "How could this have happened?"

B.Frank says: "Go read the Balfour Declaration. That is Britain's promise to pay the Zionists what they had agreed upon as consideration for getting the US into the war."

Richmann says: "Benjamin Freedman was a prominent Jewish businessman who left the Zionist organization and spent millions trying to expose the truth. And he wasn't alone."

U.R.Wrong says: "Like who?"

Richmann says: "Henry Ford, and General George Patton."

B.Frank says: "Read the Patton Papers."

Sharonlove says: "What did Harold say was the plot?"

Supermax says: "For the Zionists to create a Nation, not a religion, where they will rule and dominate the world. Total extremist mentality—Socialism."

Sharonlove says: "Maybe that is okay."

Supermax says: "A society where everyone is equal? Equally miserable and poor?"

Richmann says: "He also said it is their greatest fear that their agenda will be discovered."

Sharonlove says: "Do you believe Rosenthal was telling the truth?"

Supermax says: "Yes. Too bad the mouthy little shit is not alive. Bet he could tell me if I'm right about why the World Trade Center was demolished."

Richmann says: "Do you know?"

Supermax says: "Next time. Signing off."

Chapter 39

Now—late afternoon in Phoenix, commuters file into every road and highway—lining up to go home. School children are engaged in after school games and practices. Stores are busy with a rush of out-of-school kids and clocked-out employees. On the south side of town Ray and Miguel are checking out small stores that may have been party to selling the whiskey to the possible executioner of four people. As their car inched its way through traffic, Ray's radio suddenly cracked with the sound of dispatch relaying an officer's request at a nearby liquor store.

"We have an Officer at the *Quick and Easy* liquor store. He's looking at possible evidence pertaining to your case. He's requesting assistance."

"Affirmative," Ray replied. "Tell him we're on our way." Ray picked up the pace weaving through traffic until he reached the little corner liquor store.

"Officer, I'm Ray Siegel with Scottsdale police."

"Detective, I believe these price stickers are a good match." Handing Ray a bottle of high priced whiskey, he added, "And there are cameras."

"My, that works well for me. Have you bagged the price gun?"

"No, Sir," he answered formally.

"Miguel, take care of that. Let them know it's needed in an active criminal investigation. We'll return it as soon as possible. See if I can speak with a manager today?"

"This is good work, officer McNeal," Ray said as he noted the name on the policeman's uniform. "We'll take it from here."

Up at the register, Miguel was bagging the price gun and a pack of gum with the price sticker firmly attached. "Can we speak with boss?" Miguel said with a Spanish accent in slightly broken English.

"He's on his way," the busy clerk spoke while he rang up a customer and made change. "He'll be here in just a moment."

"Name," Ray said bluntly.

"What?" The clerk said as he hurried through another customer purchase.

"Your bosses name?"

"Oh! His name is Sam."

"What's he drive?"

"Blue truck."

"We'll wait out here." Ray and Miguel strolled outside to their air-conditioned car—waiting for Sam to arrive.

Within a few moments a blue truck pulled up and a short stocky man with a Cardinals baseball cap popped out. Before he could enter his store, Ray intercepted him.

"Sam?" Ray addressed the man he'd ID'd as the owner or boss. "I'm Investigator Ray Siegel with Scottsdale Police. Wondering if we can get a look at your security footage?"

"Well, we only have certain days. The video rerecords over the tape every few days."

"We always suspect that. That's why time is sensitive in this investigation. We need footage that may go back six days."

"Well that's pushing it. Motion triggers these cameras, so we may have seven days on there, or two."

"Let's get what we can right now then. Can you work on purchase history regarding a Dewar's whiskey purchase made within the last seven days? We'll need that to match with video. Oh, we're in a hurry, so what kinda records do you keep?"

"Well, pretty good ones. We ring up each purchase, but if it's cash—it's cash. There's no accounts here."

"I think we can help make this easy. We're looking for a sale on Dewar's whiskey."

"Good. Dewar's is a blended Scotch Whiskey. Most people choose cheaper whiskeys. We sell four. Do you know which one?"

"Why yes we do, Sam." Ray was grateful the man was cooperating so nicely.

"We're looking for a Special Reserve buyer."

"That helps some. It won't be a typical purchase like the beer and wines. Very specific price on a specialty item like that. We'll get to work on this right away."

"Appreciated. Apologies for taking your price gun. It'll be returned as soon as possible, but must warn you it could become evidence in a case—so I don't think you should count on seeing it for some time."

"It's okay. We can get another one." Sam went to his recorder, ejected the tape, and handed Ray the video.

"Here's my contact information." Ray presented his business card. "I'll be waiting to hear from you."

Ray and Miguel took off into the thickening rush-hour traffic. He put a call into the FBI offices as he maneuvered through the streets. After some consideration, he selected Alexa's extension.

"FBI, this is Ray," he said with pride. "Looks like it's your turn to dance. I got some video surveillance from the store. So, do you have resources to screen this fast?" Ray proceeded to give Alexa the rest of the details regarding the price gun he had secured, finishing with, "And the sales records are being researched by Sam." Swallowing some pride, he added, "I'm bringing this to you now. Don't know how many days are on it."

"I'm here and waiting," Alexa said positively. "I'll get everything arranged for a quick preview. We'll see if there's any footage going back to Saturday. That's what we're looking for, right?"

"It sure is."

"See you in a few," Alexa said with a smile. Jumping to her feet and for the chance to find something substantial for this case, she jogged to the technology center. "Boys we need some equipment and space. Can you set up something for me to screen surveillance video—sounds like old school VHS stuff."

Always willing to assist young pretty girls, the three techs froze and gazed at Alexa for a few seconds—as if someone hit pause on a TV remote. When their brains caught up with their thoughts, they all instantly scurried about gathering up devices and cords. Like the Three Stooges trying to set-up a home entertainment system for the first time, they argued and ran into each other till they finally agreed on a configuration.

About as soon as the techs had a viewing station setup for Alexa, Ray and Miguel walked in.

"Here it is," Ray said, handing the video to Alexa. "Let's see what you can do with this old-world device."

Don the senior tech backed up the video to almost the end.

"Saturday!" Alexa shrieked. "It goes back to Saturday."

"Keep going," Ray instructed. "I want to see all of Saturday."

When the video stopped rewinding, the picture screen froze on Saturday 10:20AM.

"This is great," Ray sounded with satisfaction. "We might get this done so I won't miss happy hour."

As the video played forward they all focused on the type of customer, but more importantly what the customer purchased. Don sped through miscellaneous purchases of beer and wine as they all focused on a customer purchase of whiskey.

"Stop," Ray and Alexa said together.

"Let's zoom and go for some facial recognition," Alexa added.

Swinging into action, Don began running a facial software program that could connect a criminal with the likeness of this customer found on the surveillance video. Criminals' with arrest records and mug shots can be chronicled in a national data base if the arresting police department is participating in the program. "You're getting a facial recognition hit on this guy. His name is Ricky. He's thirty-five years old. He's still wanted after assault charges were filed in Texas. Oh, they've added murder charges too."

"Are you saying he's never been caught and arrested?"

"No, looks like he's been caught plenty, but has only been incarcerated for a couple months."

"What does that mean?"

Don explained as he read, "He escaped while being transported to his court house hearing—that was the first time. He escaped from the prison holding him, and then he escaped from the actual court house during his hearing. He actually shot an officer and is wanted for that murder."

"What were the original charges for?" Ray asked.

"He had forcibly taken his estranged wife by gunpoint on a cross-country rampage," Don said. "Angry about his divorce, he claimed to be winning her back by beating her and raping her for days—until law enforcement apprehended him in a police standoff. He's considered vicious, vengeful, and extremely manipulative."

"Why manipulative?" Ray asked. "It sounds like he's not right in the head. Don't you have to be smart to be manipulative?"

"Probably because when he escaped the first time," Don surmised, "he talked the deputies into removing his cuffs for the ride. Second time he escaped, he talked guards into giving him work related privileges. The last break from the court house—they found out he did it with the help of a female guard. He's on the 'Most Wanted' and has been for five years. Here is says they're sure he's living under the radar somewhere in the US. There've been sightings of him around the country. He's violent and capable of killing his own wife."

"Where is she?" Alexa asked.

Don scrolled down the screen. "She's in protective custody because he's escaped three times now and was only caught when he got within blocks of her house—for the purpose of murdering her. He has sworn to kill her."

"So our guys name is?" Ray asked the open-ended question.

"It was Ricky Kreb," Don obliged with a nod.

"Don't think we're looking for that anymore," Ray said glancing at Alexa.

"Let's look at his psychological profile, Don," Alexa suggested as she squinted to read the fine print.

"How'd you get that?" Ray probed. "Doesn't sound like he ever got evaluated by experts or prosecuted."

"When it becomes imperative to locate fugitives on the 'Most Wanted' list the FBI puts together a psychological profile that detects and classifies the major personality and behavioral characteristics of the individual. This guy made the cut because he has proven to be a most difficult one to track."

"So you think that really does work, hah?" Miguel questioned with skepticism.

"Seriously," Ray added, "if you haven't even caught him in five years, how do you really do that now? Or use this profile?"

Alexa took the question. "Profilers analyze the crimes they committed and how they did it. They look at how advanced their social skills are, they look at how they plan their crimes, or if they are crimes of opportunity. They even analyze how much control they exert over their victims, or if they just lose control. Everything they do is a clue."

"Who does this profiling?" Ray inquired.

"A team of geniuses and growing software," the younger tech replied proudly. "These experts are like always right."

Alexa added, "Trust me, they get it right. These analysts have more degrees than a thermometer."

Ray rubbed his head. "I never really put any stock into figuring out the perps brains."

Miguel laughed. "That's because you don't think they have a brain, Ray."

"This might be all we have to rely on if we want to find someone that hasn't been found by the two or three states looking for him," Alexa cautioned. "When we can't find them, we look at how their mind works."

Don started reading highlights of the Ricky Kreb profile, "He's classified as extremely dangerous and well organized—capable of planning crimes that others can't even contemplate. He has great self-control when he's in charge. Socially, he's a chameleon. Sounds like he can charm a girl, or an experienced Sheriff. He doesn't leave clues or evidence behind. He even hid under mud or water to throw the dogs off his scent on two occasions. He becomes frenzied and obsessive when he rages—and that's only when he can't have what he wants. He has an intermittent anger disorder with psychopathic tendencies. Otherwise he is considered to have excellent self-control."

Alexa elaborated on the diagnosis, "That shows he's emotionally deformed and unstable, but the average person will never see it or believe it."

Don continued narrating the profile, "He had military training until his dishonorable discharge. His father raised him to fight, shoot, and hunt, like an outdoorsmen survivalist. He's skilled in all weapons. When he was trying to track his wife he was covert, invisible, and unstoppable. Looks like the three times he's been apprehended he was within minutes of getting to her."

Miguel asked jokingly, "Does it say what he likes to drink and where he shops?"

Don nodded. "Says he probably drinks good whiskey."

Miguel shook his head in disbelief. "That's pretty good."

"Does it say what made a smart guy turn out like this?"

"Sure does," Don answered. "He was raised by an abusive father and no mother. Father disciplined his boys severely. They would be locked out of the house for days as a punishment. They had to hunt and fish for their food. Lived in the doghouse with the dog. Physical abuse was constant until father died while hunting."

Alexa pondered the profilers report. "This helps explain how and why he can avoid detection. Does it say what his signature is?"

"What's that?" Miguel asked.

"They try and construct what the offender does to satisfy his psychological needs," Alexa explained. "Or, what satisfaction is met when he commits a crime. Remember, we're trying to identify with him—so we can find him. He's not looking for us. He probably has no idea he could ever have been connected to this crime. We have the element of surprise on our side. We just need to figure out what makes him tick."

Don continued reading out loud, "Says his identifiable signature is abnormal sexual behavior and militia lifestyle. Oh, this is scary. Says killing is his method of revenge. He's now suspected in the death of his father and high school girlfriend."

Alex injected her thoughts, "The hunting mishap probably wasn't exactly an accident."

"They are very sure his signature is revenge," Don reiterated. "He is driven by hatred towards law enforcement, authority, and his estranged wife. Locating and killing the wife is what motivates him. That also seems to be the only time he makes mistakes."

Miguel looked back and forth at Alexa and Ray, "What do we do to find him? The FBI hasn't been able to for five years."

"Oh no," Alexa exclaimed. "I just figured out what might have happened." All eyes were on her. "The only reason a guy like this would have been involved in this type of criminal activity is if someone could give him what he wanted."

"His wife," Ray said flatly.

"Yep," Alexa agreed. "We need to warn someone that her location may have been compromised."

"If your guys are right here," Ray was saying, "sounds like he could be the world's biggest asshole."

Alexa turned to Ray. "Well, we are looking for one of those, aren't we?"

Ray jotted something down on a piece of paper and handed it to Alexa. "They can call this guy Sam and tell him we're looking for possible sales information on this guy? We got the date and time of purchase. Maybe he lives in the neighborhood."

"You bet." Alexa looked at Don. "Can you finish screening the rest of Saturday in case anyone else purchased the same whiskey? I'm moving forward on this unless I hear from you in five minutes."

Chapter 40

Martine rushed into Jolene's house after the long day. After setting down the bag of take-out food, she hurried to let the dogs out for a quick game of Frisbee catch. She had promised Jolene and Wade to play this game with their dogs each day since the hot pavement was too much for them to walk on during this time of year.

After the game of Frisbee, she dished up the dinners for all the pets, she let her mind wonder a bit—discerning what she could possibly do next. She couldn't imagine how this case could ever be resolved—given the perplexing complications at every turn. Doubting how her random researches and dreams could culminate in anything relevant to all these murders temporarily stalled her movements.

Alexa burst through the front door—startling her. "Wait till I tell you what happened," she said breathlessly.

"What?" Martine opened up the to-go containers and started serving-up Chow Mein and rice on their plates.

"After Ray found the price gun and we matched a face to the purchase. I had to notify the police in Texas about this guy."

"Yes," Martine said. "I know. You told me you had a hit."

"Well, he's a serious criminal. I'm sure he did this."

"You're kidding." Martine looked perplexed. "Why didn't you tell me when I called you about dinner?"

"Because I didn't know till I was on my way here that something else has happened."

"Like what?"

"The agency in charge of the estranged wife's witness protection called me back after I contacted the agency. When they tried to locate her caseworker they found him bludgeoned to death in his home. He died recently."

"Ricky," Martine calculated aloud. "He killed the man to get her location."

"That's what they're thinking now. What they don't know is if he got it."

With a million questions surging through her, Martine plopped the dinner plates down on the table. "Better fill me in on everything."

Alexa recounted the last hours of her day as fast as she could talk. "Because it was so late in the day, everyone was gone for the day—for the weekend. I couldn't just leave this woman in jeopardy if I'm right about her being in danger."

"You did the right thing," Martine said encouragingly.

"Thanks." Alexa gave her mother a smile.

"What're they going to do?" Martine quizzed.

Alexa looked down at her plate and said slowly, "I think they're going to set up a sting. The only way they believe this Ricky Kreb will be apprehended is to catch him trying to get to his wife."

Martine frowned. "Do you know where she is?"

"Nope, she could be in Alaska. But I bet he's been trying to get to her since he left here. And, he probably got what he wanted before he murdered the only person who could tell him where she lives. This guy has no conscience from what I read."

"I agree." Martine scrunched her shoulders from the chill traveling up her spine. "He might be a house that nobody lives in, but he would never have killed his only source until after he got his wife's location."

"I gave them the latest photo we had from the liquor store. They've confirmed it's definitely him. They'll be in touch if they apprehend him. They're instructed to take him alive."

"Hope their guns shoot tranquilizers then. It won't be easy to get him to surrender this time. If he can't have her, he probably doesn't have anything to live for."

Alexa tapped her upper lip. "Sounds like this could be the big break in the case though."

"It will be if they can take him alive, and he'll talk. You know this probably means that someone with a lot of power and money is involved in this. If they're capable of getting this Ricky guy the information that he wanted—at the expense of an estranged wife, they wanted something very important or valuable."

"I know," Alexa agreed. "What did they want? It would really help to know what was in that trunk."

"Well, let's see what we should do next." Martine paused as she got up to fetch her journal.

Alexa cleared the dishes and joined her mother back at the table. "Do you think this could really help locate this guy?"

"No. I'm thinking that we go back to the beginning and see what we could've missed. That's what we do when we're losing a court case. We start over. The smallest item overlooked in the initial investigation can be the smoking gun. Just because we don't have all the answers right now, doesn't mean they're not there hiding."

Martine started reading from her journal, "*Expose how few provoke a war* means we are looking for people that have the means to start wars." Martine turned a page. "And this one, *Evil deeds never fail—When treaties are for naught.*" She skimmed down the page. "Here it is again." Martine read from her notes, "*Grasp and learn what few explore—Before the war is fought.*"

Alexa injected, "You think this really has to do with some very powerful people?"

"I'm thinking it does," Martine revealed. "Listen to this one."

"*Greedy men horde this lot*
Precious resource always sought
Wars are won and battles lost
Evil spreading like a moss."

"I'm still confused." Alexa looked discouraged. "I don't know anything about war. I don't even know how they start a war. Do you just start shooting at each other?"

Martine laughed. "No not usually. What I'm starting to see is it has become like a malignant cancer that we just can't get cured of."

"Maybe the same type of people keep getting elected."

"Or, the same people have been controlling all the people elected," Martine countered with.

"Like who?"

"I'm not sure. There are theories though." As Martine read on she stopped abruptly. "Listen to this." She looked hard at the words before repeating them.

"Unholy alliance starts with Brew
Leaders rise and fall askew
Find the ships that sailed on east
In Northern waters they lie in peace
Watery graves hide the truth
Tyranny growing more aloof."

Alexa asked, "You know what that means?"

"I think I do now. When I met with Teddy we talked about a treaty—The Versailles Treaty. We talked about the horse Ashkenazi's Star. We talked about the Jewish family that owned the horse. We talked about the sinking of the ship Lusitania that got America into WWI. I just remembered that the word Brew has nothing to do with alcohol. That's what they used to call Hebrews before Europeans started calling them Jews. We talked about Hitler and the NAZI's."

Alexa shook her head in disbelief. "Is this about NAZI's again?"

"I don't think so. I do want to know more about some of this."

"Like what?"

"What other ship? And what is it about a treaty that can cause all this trouble now? And what is the unholy alliance that started with Jews? Ashkenazi's are Jews." Martine kept formulating her thoughts out loud, "Ashkenazi's initially aligned with Hitler so that the Jews would relocate to Palestine. Zionist Jews are primarily Ashkenazi's. All Jews are not Zionists."

Alexa scooted over to Jolene's computer. "Let's try this." She typed in the search box on Google. "How do you spell Ashkenazi?"

Martine pulled up a chair next to Alexa and spelled it out. "ASHKENAZI."

Alexa typed the word in the box and hit search. "Wow. There are over three-million results. You can learn everything you want to know about them right here." Reading aloud several listings on the first page, Alexa commented, "These all read like they're talking about conspiracies. Do you think anyone can prove any of this?"

Martine took in a deep breath of dismay. "Conspiracies born in hell don't have angels as witnesses. That's why they're usually not provable."

Martine gasped as she looked at all the links Alexa scrolled through on the computer screen—some in caps. "This goes on for a country mile." Martine froze. "Ooh. I just noticed something." She caught herself before saying more out loud.

Alexa stopped what she was doing, instinctively drawn her mother's comment of surprise. "What is it?"

Thinking it better to say nothing, than to conclude something unspeakable, she avoided voicing her observation. "Nothing, I just can't believe how much there is on this subject."

"Right?" Alexa said in agreement.

Martine thought to herself. *Did I really see that so clearly, or is my mind playing tricks on me? If I did, that really does give some serious credence to the theory that Hitler was originally working in concert with certain Jews.* Before her mind wandered too far, she suggested, "Let's pick one to read."

Alexa shrugged at the notion of picking one randomly. "You tell me which one. I'm getting tired and can't think right now."

"Okay," Martine said slowly. Her eyes caught the link to a page with a subtitle 'War is a Bankers Harvest.' "Bookmark that one for me," she directed Alexa as renewed energy ignited her insights. "It's getting really late and I'm helping Eva tomorrow at a schooling show. We both need to call it quits."

Chapter 41

Fluffing her pillow first, Martine sank back in her bed before turning off the lamp. Knowing she had to get to sleep so she could get up earlier than the birds, made it harder to do so. Before she could change her mind and get back up, the sounds of the cat purring next to her must have lulled her to a deep slumber.

Once asleep, Martine suddenly found herself inside the bedroom of an old farm house that seemed to be spinning inside a violent storm. Angry clouds and loud roaring winds surrounded her and the quaint house as they journeyed together in the eye of the storm.

Martine struggled with her footing as the house pitched and jerked from the squalls effects. While in the process of leaving the bedroom, she lost her balance again and caught herself from hitting the floor by grabbing onto the dresser. Attached to the dresser was an old-fashioned round mirror were she could clearly see herself donning camouflage apparel. Clothed like a hunter that hides among the trees, she looked downward and took notice of hiking boots she wore as well.

Suddenly her insides felt woozy and tingly like the thrilling sensation experienced in a loopy rollercoaster ride. Feeling like the bottom was dropping out from under her feet, she quickly assessed the house was plummeting to the ground faster than a broken elevator.

When the building landed with a thud she lurched backwards—falling onto the bed. Jumping off the bed, she ran to the window and looked outside. Unfamiliar with the strange surroundings, she made her way through the home and out the front door.

Only fifty-feet away, a wavy phenomenon of strangeness encircled the home. From her position on the deck she could see to both sides and above, which indicated the house had landed in a lush clearing that was surrounded by thick tree foliage. Green leaves were brightened by the effects of the recent rain showers, and the blue sky was deepened by the glowing white clouds that formed after the storm broke-up.

Reluctantly, seeing no one around and only one narrow driveway leading away from the home, she determined she had to go forward through the hazy shimmer that hung in the air. As she timidly passed through the optical occurrence, a contrasting reality emerged.

Martine had been fooled by the hallucination of a heat induced mirage. The kind experienced when looking through a layer of heated air, or viewing an object surrounded by gaseous fumes. Gone were the green leaves and blue heaven that were merely mirrored back to her from the shield of heat radiating from the real surface that surrounded the home she arrived in.

Backing up as fast as she could was futile and made no difference to the place she was trapped in. Confused and unable to reverse her circumstances, she tried turning around and running back through the heat infused veil, but none existed from this side. Only more desolation was observed when she looked beyond where the house once was.

All around her was a horrible endless bog of hot vile slimy mud and rotting marsh. Dirty oily rain fell in the distance, keeping the sky dark green.

As she stood still on the last foreseeable patch of ground, she assessed the soggy, bone-strewn, disease-ridden swampland that would be impossible to move around in. Only an occasional ridge of volcanic rock could be used to avoid the endless terrain of bubbling mire.

Overwhelmed with confusion, Martine remained alone and stranded on the fringe of a, hot, eerie, desolate surface—causing her brow to burst with perspiration.

"Hello, my dear," an elderly plump woman hollered as she waved her hand in the air excitedly.

Martine turned towards the lady who must have walked through the same mirage she had. Waving back, she greeted her, "Hello."

"Are you lost?" Simply dressed like a matronly grandmother, the old woman continued to approach.

"I might be," Martine sounded unsure.

"Good, good," the woman replied with a bright smile. As she neared Martine she eyed her with an expression of skepticism. "I'm sorry I'm late. We weren't expecting you."

Martine wiped her forehead. Trusting that she couldn't imagine herself ending up in a place like this, it was understandable her arrival was unexpected. "Can you tell me where I am?"

The elderly woman thought a moment. "Don't you know?"

"No. I wouldn't ask if I did. I don't even know why I'm dressed in camouflage fatigues."

"Are you hunting something?" The woman asked—evading the other question.

"I don't think so."

"My goodness, I have no idea why you're dressed like this. I'm sure you'll find your answer in plenty of time."

"Maybe you could help me," Martine said. "What is out there?"

"Oh, yes, you would ask that if you weren't familiar with it." Her round face with lines of age looked down in sadness. "Do you know how you got here?"

"Actually, I don't even know that." They both laughed.

"You are deep below the earth's surface. Many layers of the earth reside all the way down to the molten core, each of them containing various realms of what you call hell. You are in a place reserved for the greedy, selfish, and vain." The woman told what she knew. Tightening her lips and tossing her head in disgust, she continued with wary eyes, "We call it *Muddy Flats,* because it is an endless span of crudeness and filth. It suits the souls of the greedy, selfish, and vain. Since it's enclosed like a cave—no one escapes once they enter."

"Oh," Martine sparked. "I think I get it. It's the Second Realm of Hell."

"Yes. You already know it?"

"I know *of* it," Martine corrected her.

"The fact that *you* were not expected here, and were able to avoid the temptation to enter that place indicates that your soul may be ready to take another path."

"Help me, help me," a muffled female voice yelled from a distance as she streaked through the imaginary wall. When she completely materialized, she ran towards Martine and the woman. "Please do something," she begged them.

"My, my," the older woman said in a comforting tone. "What happened, dear?"

"They're turning into corpses or mud dwellers," her panicked voice sounded broken.

Alarmed, Martine grabbed the frantic girl by the shoulders. "Who did that?"

"The man over there." She pointed in the direction she had come from.

Martine looked at where she aimed her finger, but saw nothing. "What happened?"

"I wouldn't take the coins."

"What coins?" Martine asked with a questioning inflection.

"We were each given a bag of coins—thirty coins."

"Oh, my goodness, dear, you did the right thing," the older woman nodded jerkily. "You mustn't accept anything from him, else your fate will be to remain in there as well," she said with a warning tone. "It is not easy to evade such a big temptation."

"Is this hell?" The girl cried.

"Well?" The old woman said contritely.

Angry, the girl pulled back and spouted, "I knew there really wasn't a *God*. Why would *He* allow such a place to exist?"

"You mustn't confuse what *God* is, with what you've become," the old woman said firmly.

Shocked and self-diluted, the girl barked back rudely, "You don't know who I am. My family is very rich and powerful. I've never done anything wrong. You can't judge me. You don't even know me."

"I bet you've said that before." Martine squared-up her stance— putting her hands on her hips. "Sounds like you came from a good family that gave you what you wanted. Maybe they spoiled you."

Tearing up from the traumatic experience, the girl wailed, "I thought *God* was good. My own daddy wouldn't ever let me go to a place like this."

"*God* doesn't want you here either. *God* is merciful to those who love *Him*. Do you love *God* enough that *He* even knows you any-more? Because *God* isn't down here," the old lady scolded, shaking her finger at the girl. "Is *God* supposed to find you even if you're not looking for *Him*, or interested in going with *Him*?"

"My dad would, she returned smugly. "When I ran away he found me and brought me home," the girl said without blinking.

"Is that love?" Asked the old lady.

"Of course," the girl replied.

Raising an eyebrow, the old woman asked another question, "What else did your dad do for you?"

The girl thought a moment. "When my parents got divorced and I flunked out of college my dad came and got me. He said I could stay with him and he bought me a car so I could get a job."

Martine impatiently rolled her fingers on her hips. "Is that re-ally what love means to you? Because I would've told you to get your grades up or buy yourself a bus ticket."

"See—you're judging me. Who do you think you are? *God*?" Agitation sprang out from the spoiled girl.

The old woman spoke up, "Have you considered that you have received gifts through the *Grace* of *God* that you squandered?"

"Are you talking about my car?" She said defiantly. "My dad bought that car."

"And what did you do with it?" The old woman said firmly. "Did you get a job?"

"No," the young girl pouted, "I couldn't find one."

"When a gift is given, it is not meant to be wasted on self-centered attachments," the old woman explained. "*God* allowed you to receive many gifts, starting with generous loving parents. You turned their good intentions into your vices when you took advantage of their support and used many gifts selfishly."

Martine saw the marks on her arm that could only be made by needles. "You did drugs. You must have overdosed." Comprehending what this place represented, she fixed her eyes on the crying girl. "I'm not judging you. You just don't like being corrected."

Addressing the young girl, the old woman clarified, "It is not a matter of judgment, but of compatibility. You have come to the place you are the most compatible with. Because of your actions, this is the place you have associated with." Looking sorrowfully at the young girl, she went on, "Being in *Muddy Flats* indicates you are oblivious to others. You have aligned with selfish and greedy ways. Instead of being self-absorbed you have an opportunity right now to make another Karmic choice."

Martine coached her, "Only you can choose your path—no one can choose it for you." She looked at the girl encouragingly.

"I don't know," the girl replied. "What if it's another trick? I don't know if I can trust anyone."

"You are the only one that can make that decision here, little girl," the old woman said. "Your *Free Will* was a gift that provides an opportunity for you to make your own life-altering-choices. Loyalty to *God* is voluntary. It is completely up to you. You possess the freedom to choose *His* way, or not. *He* does not change you to be with *Him*. Nor will *He* give you thirty pieces of silver to enter *His* kingdom. You alone must choose to walk with *Him*. That is authentic love. What do you wish?"

"I don't know. You tell me."

As usual, Martine kept it simple and cut to the chase. "If someone has to tell you what to do—you can't take full credit for your own bravery."

Older and wiser looking to the young girl, the old woman weighed-in, "You are also accountable for your bad choices—there are no exceptions."

Appearing braver and more empowered, the young girl reacted eagerly, "Yes, yes, I want another chance to be with *God*."

With the girl's words spoken out loud—accompanied by a sincere interior shift, an electrifying spark ignited in her. Like her sudden death, the gift of *Grace* was delivered instantaneously, allowing the wavy distorted-wall to reappear.

"Come quickly, dear," the old woman said without delay. "We must go now." Taking the young girls hand, the old woman led her through a glimmering vortex—away from *Muddy Flats*.

Before Martine had a chance to follow through behind them, the open vortex closed tight, leaving her alone again on the desolate ridge.

When she spun around to face the source of a booming thunder, her eyes fell upon another optical illusion that resembled an ancient castle gate. Assuming the entrance was meant for her—she cautiously pushed open the large doors and stepped inside.

Martine now found that she was in the midst of creepy woodlands that consisted of voluminous tree-branch canopies that completely filtered sources of light. Gnarly limbs protruded from the trees, blocking easy passage. Roaming creatures of the night were mostly heard and not seen. Using quick breaths, she tried to control bouts of panic as she assessed her situation. With only one path to follow, she began a treacherous hike over boulders and fallen trees. Deathly and hideous, not even a green leaf survived in this place of damnation.

Following the narrow path that coiled through the forest, like the grotesque twisted-trunked trees with their blackened moss hanging thick from them, lead her deeper into the abyss. Cloaked in the darkness, winged-creatures soared by her head as she bravely journeyed on.

While pulling apart a prickly-branched barricade, she heard the hint of a conversation. Following another sharp curve in the trail, she soon laid eyes on a decrepit cottage with overgrown thorny vines and dirt yard.

Certain that the sounds were coming from within, she knocked on the door till a short gremlin-looking man answered.

"How can I help you?" Clothed like a woodsman, he stared her up and down. "How did you find us?"

Curious about him and much more, she peered over his crooked shoulder to see a small urchin-creature scurry out of sight. "I'm looking for information," she stated vaguely.

"What kind of information?" He asked with a suspicious glare.

Panning his deformed appearance, she wasn't taken aback until she looked at his eyes that resembled black bee-bees inside of mucusy larvae. "I believe you might be able to advise me how I can get out of here."

Annoyed by her interruption, he tried to dismiss her. "Oh, only the Dark One would be able to allow that." He expelled an evil laugh. "But, when has he done that?"

"Okay." Martine swallowed hard. "Let me speak with him."

"I'm afraid you can't do that." He tried to shut his door.

Martine blocked him from closing it. "Why?"

"You know why," he said contemptuously.

She caught the threat in his voice. "No, I don't," she insisted.

"He only has time for his cohorts. Are you one of them?"

Cautious that it might be a trick question, Martine hymned and hawed a bit. "Define cohort."

"Have you been doing his bidding, or are you a new recruit?"

"Oh, that." Martine started to read between the lines and realized she needed to keep up the appearance that she worked for the underworld king himself. "Yes, I'm tracking souls that have too much light and goodness. I fear they are coming this way."

"That's impossible. They would never get close to this place without being detected."

"Really, how's that," she said.

"We can spot them too easily. They can't fool us like we fool them. They are gullible and easily manipulated because we know what they are, but they don't identify us until it's way too late."

"What would they have to do to trick me?" She tried to sound sincere.

"Be invisible?" He snapped back to her. "And nobody can do that here."

Martine suddenly remembered that Freya had tried to tell her she would also need something else of hers—but the words were lost when she was pull away with the cats. Freya was giving her the magical cloak of invisibility. The one Loki was so fond of.

It made perfect sense at that moment of clarity, when she finally figured out why she was wearing camouflage clothing. She had traveled to a worse and deeper place than *Muddy Flats*. Here she needed to possess the proper knowledge and training to do this, but most importantly—she needed the protection of invisibility. Moving among these dead and damned souls required the ability to not be seen. To remain incognito she had to camouflage her living light-force from the voracious beings of destruction that occupied this layer of hell. Light was their natural enemy. Realizing she was well disguised with the help of Freya's cloak—now symbolized in the wearing of blending-camouflage colors, Martine felt activated to complete her function.

Like a general gathering Intel for his battle strategies, and like Dorothy from the Wizard of Oz who falls from the sky into a strange dimension with a wicked witch that needs to be eliminated for the sake of her friends and the Munchkins—Martine had a mission and she immediately realized her purpose for wandering around in this *God* forsaken place.

Keeping up the appearance of a soldier in the dark army, she convincingly sequestered the little man as if she was one of them, "How will I know if these beings are imposters or not?"

"That's easy, I know exactly how you do that," he boasted. "You are new at this. You can only be sure about their true nature if they have absolute *hatred* of '*you know who*' as opposed to the ones that just don't believe in *Him*. Of course we keep that hidden, or risk exposure."

"Is that it," Martine probed.

"They can't say *His* name with authority. Too bad our enemies don't even know how powerful their true weapon is."

"I'm curious," Martine probed. "How do you stop them from blindly using their true power against us?"

Addressing Martine's attire, he answered, "Mass murder. Like deer being hunted, they never live to figure it out, or to tell. It's the perfect device. We provoke conflict to distract them and eliminate them before they use it."

Martine stroked his ego to get more information. "You are wise and experienced. More than most. Your important position impresses me. Are we winning the battle?"

"We're winning the war," he bragged loudly. "Evil has ruled and sometimes light has ruled. More and more they choose evil. The ones that follow '*you know who*' can't discern between the two forces because they are always sympathizing with us. Even the brave and righteous unknowingly do our bidding. Someone always helps us—they just don't know it. That's why they will never be able to stop us."

"That's it?" Martine questioned.

He couldn't stop crowing, "The only way to control and restrain our own hellish mobs that move through here is to make them fear punishment. Nothing else ever works and nothing exists except the fear of punishment and torment. If we did not implement and instill drastic penalties this whole realm you are in would fall apart and these souls would plunge to deeper and worse levels of hell. If only our enemies knew what we know." He laughed hard.

"Right," Martine said slowly—still pretending to be one of them. "They would rather rehabilitate us rather than stop us."

"Exactly . . ."

His words faded away as she was pulled away back through the Earth's layers to the surface. Now safely out of the dimensions of hell and returned to the campfire of the Indian guide that has met with her consecutively every night since the fire, she expressed her relief with a huge sigh.

"You are brave warrior. Like me," the Indian said with a pleased expression, "you go where Great Spirit cannot be seen."

"I did," Martine answered. "May I never know those places below the earth. Why was I there?" Instantly her question was answered with infused awareness. Facing the Karmic choices a soul makes in a lifetime can be frightening if they practiced selfishness, greed, jealously, and vanity—to name a few. Following a maze of choices in a lifetime, the soul naturally amends to that which most deeply aligns with their inner desires. Subconsciously, a soul such as that would not willingly amend their choice. Only with the gift of *Grace* is an extreme shift possible.

"What do you bring back with you from journey?" He asked.

"The method of operation used to destroy men of goodness."

"Tell me," he said.

Martine gave her best recollection, "Fallen souls would give no thought to traveling to the center of the earth. Those souls' cravings will lead to a familiar route—usually the road easily taken. They feed off of death. Death to man. They, manipulate, deceive, hide their true nature, and take advantage of our compassion—which they only see as weakness."

"Yes." He nodded once.

Martine asked, "Is it possible they are more evil than an earth full of *God*-fearing people can overcome?"

"You have no time to waste," he said, handing her the final scroll. "Please read out loud."

"Distorted truths deceive the wise
Buried secrets hide the lies
Opened eyes remove disguise
Look where no one dares to pry
When evil plan goes awry
Earthly peace is free to rise."

Woken with a start, Martine popped up in bed. Looking around the bedroom like a cornered fox, she realized it had been a dream and she was safe in her bedroom.

Chapter 42

At sunrise evil and mayhem had yet to darken their doorway again. Martine and Eva were frantically loading horses and tack into the trailer that would transport them all to the nearby schooling show.

Martine had just finished securing the last horse in the trailer when her phone rang. "Martine here," she answered.

Mahoney's downtrodden voice dimmed the mood, "I got good news and bad news."

"Why can it all be good?" She wiped her brow in exasperation.

"They caught up with Ricky early this morning. He was located in Tennessee."

Martine finished his sentence. "At his ex-wife's place?"

"Basically. He wouldn't surrender. He wasn't going to be taken alive unless she was dead."

Martine's heart started racing like a jackhammer. "No. Are you saying he got to her?"

"I don't know all the details. But, he was gunned down in a hail of bullets. It's already on the news. They haven't released details on all the casualties. I didn't want you to hear about it on CNN."

Martine groaned in despair. "What did they expect when something evil like him breaks the surface? Couldn't they have stunned him or something?"

"We're talking Tennessee. Hillbilly justice was served. They don't take their time or waste bullets. Guess they all had guns and none were afraid to shoot. Our guys didn't fire any shots. Martine, you may have saved this girl just in time. I do know they put a female agent in as a decoy. Ricky tracked his wife down where she worked. I don't think the wife has been harmed at all."

Reluctantly, Martine conceded, "I guess it was good and bad news. I'm very grateful law enforcement acted on this. If they hadn't taken it seriously she may have been murdered today. I'm discouraged that we were so close to finding the answers to these crimes."

"Let's not give up because of this setback." Mahoney tried to cheer her up. "You helped find a needle in a stack of needles. Now we need to find another one."

Martine's voice went hoarse, "It seems like every opportunity is circling the drain—and another one just went down."

"Sometimes it just happens this way. We don't close every case in a week. Sometimes we just have to move on."

"Right. I gotta go anyways. Horses are loaded. I'll talk to you later." Martine waited to hear him say goodbye before she let her sinking heart moan, "Now what?"

Chapter 43

Alexa found herself waking up slowly on her day off. After glancing at the clock for the exact time she popped up like a spring loaded toaster. Dylan would be coming by soon to pick her up for the planned four-wheeling adventure in the Four Peaks Mountains. As she finished applying the final touches to her hair a thought prompted her to check-out a theory regarding the Eli case and her mother's dream.

Logging on to her computer she began a research on the sinking of ocean liners. In less than a moment, pages of results were accessible to her, referencing the large ship disasters recorded in history. Baffled at where to start reading forced her to refine her search parameters, so she typed in more specifics which included the Lusitania and 1900's.

When the page refreshed, her eyes captured a recurring theme that connected the sinking of the Lusitania and the Titanic in the early 1900's. Clicking on the first link directed her to Wikipedia where she quickly learned the 1912 sinking of the Titanic and the 1915 sinking of the Lusitania were related by none other than J.P. Morgan. With her curiosity peaked, she clicked on the next link that claimed to have historical correctness. Alexa read with fervor the following:

"Furthermore, through holding companies, the House of Morgan directly owned many of the manufacturing firms receiving production contracts for military goods from England and France. (Undoubtedly these firms were the foundation of the 'military-industrial complex' later referred to by President Eisenhower.) Soon, J P Morgan became

*the largest consumer on earth, spending up to $10 million per day.
Morgan was in the privileged position of being buyer, seller, and
producer and amassing profits from all sides."*

Wrinkling her nose at the thought of profiting from war weapons sickened her, but still she read on.

*"However, when the War began to go badly for England and
France, Morgan found it impossible to get new buyers for the Allied
war bonds. There was a real fear in Whitehall at the time that England
was about to lose the war. If the Allies were to default, Morgan's
large commissions would come to an end and his investors would
suffer gigantic losses (some $1.5 billion). On top of that, Morgan's
war production companies would go out of business. Something
needed to be done urgently."*

Oh my gosh, Alexa thought. *What did he do?* Scrolling down
rapidly she landed on more damning accusations.

*"As the RMS Lusitania departed Pier 54 in New York on May 1st,
1915, Morgan surmised that if the cruiser were to be sunk by a German
submarine, the resulting furor would certainly bring America into
the War on the side of Britain and France. Not only would Allied war
bonds be in great demand but Morgan's war production companies
would have to go into overdrive to outfit over four million American
soldiers who would be mobilized for the European War."*

"This is maddening," Alexa muttered as she went on to reading
more.

*"Six days later, on the afternoon of Friday, May 7th, 1915, the
Lusitania approached within 12 miles of the southern Irish coast.
Winston Churchill, the Lord of the Admiralty, knew that German
U-boats were operating in the area after three ships had been sunk
in the previous 2 days."*

Appalled by what she was absorbing, she wanted validation
and proof. Tapping the print button on her computer, she kept
reading while the printer engaged its dormant mechanisms.

*"Unknown to her passengers but no secret to the Germans, al-
most all her hidden cargo consisted of munitions and contraband
destined for the British war effort that included tons of explosives,*

6 million pounds of ammunition, 1,248 cases of shrapnel shells, and some American passengers."

"Knock Knock," Dylan said loudly as he walked into Alexa's house. "Are you ready?" Eyeing Alexa at the computer, he kept talking as he headed for her, "I got lot's to drink. We should go if we want to get all the way up to the mines."

"Sure," Alexa said with a stiff grin resulting from the editorials she was reading. "Listen to this, The Germans placed newspaper ads in 50 newspapers across USA, warning Americans not to travel aboard the Lusitania, which was carrying munitions but masquerading as an ocean liner."

"Sure," he said with questionable doubt. "What're you talking about?" Dylan's grin flatlined. "We're still going aren't we?"

"Of course," she reassured with a nod. "Give me one more minute. There's a big sub in the refrigerator. Can you grab it?" Driven to find one more article before leaving her computer behind, she clicked on another link while Dylan retrieved and examined the giant sub.

"Not much in your refrigerator. You're not a cook, huh?"

"Nope," Alexa shot back. "I only have a kitchen because it came with the rental."

"Me too," Dylan said with a chuckle. "Don't worry—I packed enough food for three days."

Alexa gave a laugh—remembering what happened the last time they hooked up with his friends when they went four-wheeling in the high country. Leaving that memory, she quickly scanned the articles first paragraph.

"The same crowd which manipulated the passage of the income tax and the Federal Reserve System wanted America in the war. J.P Morgan, John D. Rockefeller, Colonel House, Jacob Schiff, Paul Warburg and the rest of the Jekyll Island conspirators were all deeply involved in getting us involved. Many of these financiers had loaned England large sums of money. In fact, J.P. Morgan & Co. served as British financial agents in this country during World War I." Gary Allen, None Dare Call it Conspiracy.

Alexa hit print again just as Dylan returned from the kitchen. "I'm ready," she said as her hand simultaneously grabbed the paper spitting out of the printer. "Just need to make sure I got everything." She gathered her belongs, checked for her phone, and stuffed the papers into her purse before leaving the house.

"So you couldn't talk your sister into coming?" Dylan kept pace with Alexa. "Dan and Dean are going to be very bummed."

Alexa laughed as she settled in the vehicle and buckled her seat belt. "The only way those guys are going to get her to go mountain climbing is on a horse." Alexa was dually aware that her younger sister Eva was an electrifying boy-magnet that was emotionally charged and flirtatious.

"You explain that to them." Dylan started selecting music for the drive to the trailhead.

"Gladly." Alexa changed the subject. "I need to make a phone call before I'm out of cell range. You okay with that?"

As Dylan sped off with his trailer in tow, Alexa excitedly rang her mother. "She's not answering," she proclaimed with disappointment.

"Hope she can call back within the next fifteen-minutes." Dylan shook his head glumly. "There's no service out there and we won't be back till really late."

With Dylan seated next to her, Alexa left a cryptic message. "I think I found a connection between the Lusitania and the Titanic."

Chapter 44

Olivia finished securing her truck's electrical connection to the trailers. "Martine, do you want to ride with me?"

Martine looked at her daughter questioningly, "Eva, do you care?"

"No, I don't care. Sara's riding with me anyways."

"Great," Olivia said with a frantic smile. "Let's go then. We're running a little late and our first show is in less than an hour. That only leaves fifteen minutes for warm-up."

Martine hiked herself into the front passenger seat next to Olivia. "I'm coming along to assist. I know you're shorthanded since the help isn't showing up lately. Just let me know what I can do for you and the girls."

"Of course I will. We're grateful you're helping. Can I ask what just happened on the phone? I know it was important."

"Oh that," Martine said dismissively. "We had a lead on Eli's case and I just found out they got him."

"That's good, isn't it?" Olivia said as she came to a stop at the light.

"I was hoping it would be, but he was killed before he was apprehended. Now we've hit a dead-end again. Since I got here the body count keeps going up. Maybe I should stay home."

"What are you talking about? None of this is your fault."

"How can Eli Morgan, Jake Monroe, four bodies in a warehouse, and now Ricky Kreb all die since I got here?"

"Don't forget Adam." Olivia winced slightly.

"Geez, I forgot Adam." Martine looked out her side window, contemplating the nine deaths connected to her visit in Arizona. "Speaking of Adam, have you heard anything about his death," Martine asked.

"No. I think airport security is handling that. Nobody's come to *Desert Run* to ask about him."

"That's interesting. Does Adam have family here?"

"Not that I know about. He didn't really spend much of his time around any of us."

"Were him and Eli sorta close?"

"I thought so until Eli was gone."

"Why do you say that?"

"He made such a half-hearted attempt at being distraught over Eli's death that I just didn't find him sincere. You saw us fighting."

"Tell me what you mean."

"No tears or questions. If you don't feel like crying, don't you still have lots of questions? He was just out of character from what you'd expect."

"For instance?" Martine asked.

"His comments were strange. Like, he wanted to know what I was going to do when all this is gone. He didn't even know how Eli died until I told him."

"Tearless grief is common if the person isn't close to someone who dies," Martine explained. "But, all lack of emotion—like shock, would be considered suspicious. If he was a friend or advocate of Eli's, at the least, he should have showed genuine concern. You say he didn't do that?"

"Not at all," Olivia sounded adamant.

"Do you know why he was at the airport?"

"Nope," she bluntly replied.

Martine took her phone out and stared at it in contemplation. Deciding who to call took a moment before she dialed. "John, its Martine. I just thought of something to look for. Have someone get hold of Ricky's belongings."

"Okay," he said in hesitation. "Can you hold a minute?" Mahoney dropped his phone in his pocket, planted his feet solidly apart on the ground, bent his knees slightly, and gripped the object firmly with both hands. Positioned in the perfect stance he had practiced, he took aim and swung. As he walked away from the T-box he fished the phone out of his pocket. "Sorry, what're you looking for?"

"I'm looking for a connection between him and Adam Keen. Adam was Eli's manager here. He recently died in a possible car-jacking at the airport."

"At the airport?" He annunciated his words.

"Yep. Maybe he was the one that arranged for this job to get pulled off."

"Well, what good's that if he's dead now?"

"Until we find the trunk, we keep looking. Somebody has it."

Martine started to say good bye, "Oh, can you get some information on Adam?"

"Martine, you know it's Saturday. We're probably not going to get much of anything until Monday."

"Shit. Can someone get me Adam Keen's address and any police records on him?"

"Sure, when I'm done playing golf."

"Golf? You didn't tell me you were a golfer."

"That's because I'm not. I said I was golfing. Big difference. This is the charity tournament for vets. It's a benefit."

"Sorry." Sounding embarrassed she added, "Don't worry about it. I shouldn't have bothered you on your day off. Have a good time." Martine hung-up before more was said.

"I might be able to get Adam's address. Would that help?" Olivia offered as she raked her fingers through her hair.

"I don't know. I was hoping to get a lot more than that, but it's the wrong day of the week. What did you have in mind?"

"It might be in my records. Last year he made me sign a new boarding agreement. His information might be with my leases. We'll look went we're done here."

Martine left the air-conditioned truck and joined her at the back of the trailer where they worked together to unlatched the back door of the trailer. Each horse looked sideways at them in anticipation of moving around freely. Unloading was twice a fast as loading a team of horses.

Martine untied the end horse and backed it carefully out of the slanted stall. "Do you have the records at the barn?"

Olivia jumped in the trailer to retrieve the next horse, which literally lead her out of the trailer. "Yeah, they'll be in my little office in the tack room."

"Great," Martine sounded encouraged again, "we'll check that out when we're done here."

Eva and Sara pulled up next to Olivia's trailer and started unloading their horses too.

After a long and productive day of horse trials that involved judging and points for each horse in select categories, they were soon loaded back up in the trucks and trailers for the trip back to *Desert Run*. Martine was extremely impressed with the excellent performances done with Olivia's horses. High marks proved the horses were progressing in excellence along with riders Eva, Sarah, and Olivia.

After returning to the *Desert Run*, happy giggles from the girls could be heard throughout the whole barn as they recounted the great scores they got on each horse.

"Let's go celebrate," Eva suggested.

"First we braid those tails and feed," Olivia said as she put her horse in its stall. Addressing Martine she signaled with her head to join her in the tack room. "Maybe I have something in this file." Olivia opened the folder with her boarding leases and spotted Adam's business card. "Will this help?" Handing the card to Martine she continued leafing through the documents.

"This might help" Martine surmised. "Seems too easy though. His business address looks more like a residential address. His title is Financial Operations Manager."

"What does that mean?" Olivia questioned.

Martine's cell phone started ringing. "I think it means his expertise didn't have anything to do with horse operations. It had to do with money." Recognizing the phone number, she greeted the caller, "Hey, John."

"I asked a couple guys I was golfing with to help try and get some information on this guy. I'll let you know what I find out. Where are you now?"

"I'm at the barn."

"Can I talk you into dinner?"

Martine considered her options. "Sure. I just need to make one stop."

"Okay. I'll pick you up in a few. Almost done here."

"Great," Martine agreed.

"Sounds like you're leaving us." Olivia frowned slightly.

"Yes," Martine said distractedly as her mind wandered back to Adam's business card. "His card has an emblem like the Israeli flag." *Star is scared with double cross,* she recalled from her dream.

"Yeah, I noticed that too. I just figured he was Jewish."

"Naturally." Martine's thoughts strayed further as Olivia left the room to help the girls finish chores.

"Olivia," Martine rang-out, "what kinda car did Adam drive?"

"BMW. Black."

Chapter 45

Martine couldn't resist the opportunity to locate the trunk, given the window into the world of Adam Keen had just opened wide to the biggest lead in her quest for the truth. If he was such a big player in the world of finance, who would want to muscle him out, or do business with him? The trunk had to be the Holy Grail in this case. With all the witnesses mute, she found herself relying on fragments of evidence—splinters of their lives on this earth.

Martine said her goodbyes and hugged her daughter before leaving the barn with John Mahoney. Once in his car she handed him Adam's business card.

"What's this?" Laughing, he slowly swung his head in her direction.

"A clue?" She wanted desperately to explain her dreams and how the Israeli Star of David on this man's business card represented a clue in her mind's eye.

Still chuckling, he suggested, "Let's grab food and you can explain this to me." Winking for her approval, he added, "I could use a beer."

That might help, Martine thought to herself. "Agreed. I haven't eaten all day."

"Excellent. I know a great Mexican restaurant nearby."

"Super. My favorite. Tell me about the golf tournament. Did you do well?"

John's private personality showed when he shared the buddy stories that went along with military-comrades armed with clubs. "These guys used to talk about bars, broads, and booze. Now I get to laugh at stories about their little dogs being banned from the dog parks for harassing the big dogs, and men without hair jokes. Instead of pictures of girlfriends, they share photos of grandchildren. We are officially the generation that will retire next."

While Martine pretended to listen intently to John, her attention wavered in and out—impatient thoughts wouldn't stop surfacing no matter how she tried to tune them out right now. Her mind was sorely divided as it calculated and weighed each event that had happened since she arrived.

"And then Glen, a helicopter pilot in Nam, told us he's ready to finally settle down after being a bachelor for forty-years," Mahoney was saying when he noticed Martine wasn't following the conversation. "So, I gave him your number. Am I boring you?"

"No—not at all," she said sincerely. "I'm sorta distracted. And, no." She stopped briefly. "I don't want to be fixed up with your bachelor friend."

Pulling into the restaurant parking lot of *Some Like It Hot*, he glanced at her and chuckled. "So you *were* listening. Better tell me what's really on your mind. I always find it interesting."

Martine and John slid in a red leather booth under a thatched cabaña-styled awning. Stings of lighted red and green chili peppers hung around the room, giving authentic ambiance of the Mexican Rivera.

"So what's on your mind?" Opening the menu the hostess had left them with, he cautioned her, "And, I don't want you to do anything like we did at that warehouse."

"I realize that." She lifted her face to his.

"We have ways of getting everything we need. You just have to be patient."

"Patient like a court trial? Those take years," she fired back. "I don't know if you have that much window of opportunity here. I think there's a very short shelf-life in this case."

"What is the urgency?" Mahoney's eyebrows narrowed to a distinct V.

Martine shagged her shoulders. "I don't know," she said after a moment. "If I knew for sure, I'd tell you. I'd tell you before I'd tell anyone else."

"Well what do you have?"

Martine thought back to the crime. "Besides a lot of suspicions, I think whatever's in that trunk is time sensitive."

"Like a bomb?" Mahoney's mouth tilted down with a questioning frown.

"Not like one that can go off, but it might have to do with the military." An odd momentum was building as she spoke about her unanswered issues.

"What?" His narrowing eyes fixed on her. "That makes no sense."

"I know." Martine looked into her menu. "How hard would it be to find out more about Adam?"

"I don't know? My buddy will call as soon as he finds anything out."

"How do you feel about going over to his address?"

"For what?" Mahoney shrugged his shoulders.

"Since no one can tell us anything today—like who has his car—I'd like to look for that of course. Luckily, we at least know what he drives." I also wouldn't mind talking to his wife." Martine stretched the truth. "Maybe she'd let us take a look at his computer before someone else decides to. Actually, I'd like to know everything about what he was up to before and after Eli's death."

"Interesting. What'd you say he did for Eli?"

"He was supposedly his facilities manager. His card says Financial Operations Manager. I don't have good information about that, but I think there might be a clue or two there."

"Sounds like a waste of time. I'll send agents over first thing Monday. We'll see if he has other offices here too. I don't see how you'll get any answers at his house right now that can't be found legally Monday."

"If there is anything there Monday," she pressed harder. "We need more information. We need to collect the clues before we can connect them, and they keep slipping through our hands like sand."

"Okay, we'll drive by there after dinner," Mahoney relented begrudgingly. "We can at least look for his car and see if someone is home."

Satisfied, Martine announced her decision, "I'll have an enchilada."

Chapter 46

Mahoney pulled up to Adam Keen's residential address in a secluded and sparsely populated neighborhood. Parking on the street, they exited the car together, walked up to the front door and rang the door bell like any other couple would. Casually dressed, they blended perfectly in the bedroom community.

Hearing no sounds and seeing no lights, Martine tried the door. "It's locked. Let's try around the back." Before he could object, she walked briskly to the side of the house.

As they walked around the front and headed for the back yard, John stopped to try the service door into the garage. "It's open," he exclaimed.

Exchanging expressive glances of intrigue—Mahoney pulled out his hanky and opened the door carefully. "Now you can see if his car's here or if it was a car-jacking."

With some light coming through the now opened service door the empty garage resembled a racquetball court—it was obvious there was absolutely nothing in it, or on the white painted walls. "Did you notice that there are no cars in the driveway, or in the garage?" Martine relayed as she looked around. "It's never been returned."

"Exactly," Mahoney affirmed. "Did you really expect to find it here? This guy lives alone." Mahoney observed at a glance. "Only one car has been parked in this garage." He was looking at the tracks from one vehicle that drove in and out of the enclosure.

Mahoney used his hanky and tried the door to the house, the one that people usually don't keep locked unless they're leaving for extended trips. "This is open too."

"If no one is home, do you think someone has broken in?" Martine asked.

"No. These doors haven't been tampered with," he assured. "Why do you ask?"

"I'll tell you when I see inside."

Mahoney led the way as they entered into the laundry room that was relatively neat and orderly. As he keep moving into the kitchen area, Martine looked in the washer and dryer—making a mental note of what she observed before joining him in the kitchen.

"Let's find that computer," Mahoney stated. "I don't like being here without a good reason."

"Here's the story, we didn't break-in—that's a fact." Martine peeked in the refrigerator as she followed him through the kitchen. "I had an appointment with a Financial Operations Manager. Got it." She patted her pocket. "I have his business card with me."

"Your mind really does know how to spin a tale." Mahoney scoped the large home till his eyes landed on a room next to the formal living room. "There." He pointed. "That's the office you're looking for. And there's the computer. Will that do it?"

"Almost." Martine breezed past him towards the office.

"You know you won't be able to log-on without his passwords," Mahoney pointed out the obvious.

Martine spun on her heels to face him. "I do know that." Glancing at him coolly, she turned towards the desk and rushed around to the keyboard. "Just let me try something." Wiggling the mouse for Adam's desktop computer awakened the sleeping screen. "Look. It's on," she announced.

"Really?" Mahoney sounded surprised.

Frantically she formulated in her mind what to search for on Adams computer. "Do you know what this means?"

Mahoney shook his head. "Do you?"

Analyzing recent observations, she explained, "Adam was not leaving town or planning on not returning. His doors aren't locked because he simply ran an errand. John, he was doing laundry. And feel that air. He's got this place set at seventy-five degrees. It's like ninety-nine degrees outside right now."

"Then why was he at the airport?" Mahoney questioned her theory.

"I don't know." An ominous tightening in her chest hastened her actions. "But, I'd sure like to figure that out."

"Why is that so important?" Mahoney looked around the home for anything that might indicate what Adam was all about.

Martine opened up his online search engine. "It might help someone figure out what happened to him."

"Do you think the same people that killed Eli got to him?" Mahoney questioned.

"Maybe." Martine pulled up the most recent histories Adam had used on-line. "If it wasn't an accident, then what was it?"

Mahoney moved around the desk to look over Martine's shoulder. "What're you looking at?"

"This is his recent searches on-line. He was looking for cargo flights. He didn't book a passenger flight. He shipped something big." Martine backed out of that link and arrowed down. "Look at this. He was looking at banks in Switzerland, Belize, and CIBC First Caribbean International. These are off-shore banks used to avoid the IRS. What did he need that for?" After exiting out of the on-line searches she looked for his saved files. As she studied the directory of saved documents she sat back in contemplation. "We need to take this, John." She sensed it was more than speculation that Adam started these events in motion.

"You know we can't. You know we aren't supposed to be here at all."

"I know," she conceded. "Someone needs to change those laws so that getting a search warrant doesn't require a legal order from a judge. When I think of all the missed opportunities we've had in getting evidence because of obtaining a search warrant—well that's why I work in a different department." Martine stopped herself from venting. "The point is, evidence has to rise to a certain level to prove guilt, but obtaining it before it's destroyed is complicated by our own legal justice system. This might not be a person of interest, but it's the next best thing and it should be apprehended like a suspect."

"That's why you work with legal documents and jurisdiction matters?" Mahoney exclaimed. "I never understood why they put you there."

"I chose it. Nobody put me there." Scrounging around in the desk drawers, Martine searched for a back-up device. "Crap, he doesn't have one here. I need your hanky." As she wiped her prints off the keyboard and desk areas she had touched, she looked over to Mahoney who was studying personal items that Adam had displayed in his office. "Let's go get one." Martine insisted.

Before Mahoney could respond they heard voices approaching the outside front door.

"Quick," Martine whispered in desperation. "Lock the laundry room door." She hung back to jot down some information. "We need to buy some time before we get out of here." The notion of being caught in the commission of a trespassing crime, made her insides lurched.

Mahoney sprinted back through the laundry room and deadbolted the door. Rushing back to the foyer, he saw shadowy blurs through the frosted side light. "Where are you?" Mahoney murmured.

"Doesn't everyone in Arizona have a patio?" Martine said softly as she cleverly unplugged the computer. As Mahoney signaled her to follow, she shot up like a rocket and bolted outside to a blast of heat on the west side of the home.

After exiting the house they both dashed over to the wall of flowering Oleanders. "Squeeze through here," she said. Disappearing through the thick leafy foliage bought them just enough time to slip into a neighboring yard before they heard the sound of a door being kicked in.

Realizing he didn't have his badge or gun, he hastened her, "We need to get out of here." Mahoney grabbed her hand and pulled her alone. "This way." He pointed to the house next door. Peering around the corner of the neighbors' house, he gave the order, "All clear." Mahoney dashed for his car with Martine next to him.

After they were both safely inside his car, Martine struggled to catch her breath as she jotted down the license plate number. "Recognize that car?"

"Nope," he said casually.

"You know what this means?" Moistening her sunburned lips, she nervously repeated, "Do you?"

He just looked straight ahead as he drove away as fast as he could. "Yeah, they're taking the computer and that's a rental car." Bouncing over the curb and into the busy street, Mahoney was able to lose their car in the crowd of vehicles.

"It means we are only one step ahead of them. We have to find out what Adam was up to at the airport. If they figure it out first, they're going to get what they came for. I don't think it was a computer. Hopefully I bought some time if they need his computer and don't know his passwords."

Mahoney sighed and mimicked Martine, "Fine. We're going to the airport, and we're going to need some help."

"Who do we call when we need help?" Martine broke down and laughed. "We almost got busted back there. I felt like a cat burglar."

Chapter 47

Anxiety set-in and rippled through her as she sat helplessly in the car Mahoney was driving. Powerless to do anything while he drove them to the airport, Martine's mind meandered to what they were running after.

Mahoney hung up his phone as his car lurched into a train of vehicles that clogged every path. Switching lanes back and forth he maneuvered through the dense traffic leading to the airport. "Phoenix police are going to the residence to secure the house and apprehend the intruders if they're still there. They'll contact me when they have someone on the scene. Well, did that go the way you wanted?" Mahoney joked satirically.

She had no answer for that. After a pause she did say, "I do believe we're onto something." Afraid to give voice to more, she asked, "Don't you?"

"I suppose I do now."

Feeling immense relief, Martine smiled—brightening her face. "Go to the cargo shipment terminal. Even if they can hack Adam's computer it's going to take them awhile to figure that much out." She hoped.

"Agreed." Exiting the freeway he merged with slower moving traffic—allowing him to glance at her sharply. "You cannot put yourself in harm's way again. *You* are not armed." He looked ahead to the directional signage.

She eyed his weapon uneasily. "You're right," she broke off for a moment, "I don't have one." Thinking straight, she promised, "I won't get in the way."

"Good." He turned back to her with an affirmative stare.

Before he finished parking, she had her hand on the door handle. "Let's see if this shipment ever left here." Waving the note she had scribbled down at Adam's, she let Mahoney catch up to her.

Their paces quickened when they saw and agent.

When they announced their business to the employee, they were corralled in a private area until a slow moving security officer approached.

"How can I help?" The plump man asked them.

Mahoney flashed his credentials. "We're tracking a shipment that was scheduled to leave here Tuesday. Who do we see about that?"

"What is your business with this shipment?" He looked discerning as his eyes moved between Martine and Mahoney.

"It's involved in a criminal investigation," Mahoney explained in legal vagueness.

"I can look into this for you," the officer obliged. "Do you have a number you can be reached at?"

"We'll need that information now," Mahoney rebuffed without pause.

"Alright," he said slowly as he turned to leave. "I'll see what we can find. Almost everyone is gone for the day."

Martine sat at the table and drummed her fingers nervously. "I can't believe how slow this place operates."

Pacing like an expectant father, Mahoney nodded his agreement. "It just seems like it. Give'm a few minutes, Martine. It's not like we're saving any lives right now."

Somehow his words were not comforting. She did have to question herself though, *what could be so time-sensitive and be contained in a trunk*?"

When the security agent returned, he had a clerk with him who brought flight records. "Hello, Mr. Mahoney. I went through the cargo manifest for that flight and found nothing."

"What?" Martine exclaimed. "That can't be."

"I looked for the name of your sender, and subsequent flights. It doesn't appear that anything matching this description has left through our airport. There were, however, arrangements made to ship a heavy object that meets the criteria here. All I can tell you is that it never happened."

Martine looked conflicted and defeated. "Where and when was it scheduled to land?"

"Oh, that shipment was going to Tel Aviv. It would've arrived Friday—yesterday afternoon, our time." Seeing the disappointment on both their faces, the woman finished, "I'm sorry we couldn't help more."

Mahoney thanked her and gave instructions, "If anyone comes here looking for the same type of information I need you to contact me."

Martine interrupted, "Oh, would you mind letting anyone else that asks about this shipment know that it did get shipped? For security purposes," she intimated, "you want to direct them back to Tel Aviv, right?" Eyeing Mahoney she repeated, "Right?" Watching him absorb the concept that they needed to buy some critical time, she waited for his acknowledgement.

"Right, but contact me immediately," he concurred.

As they walked back to his car, Mahoney tried to appease Martine, "You realize that it's only a theory that Adam had anything to do with the murders, or the trunk. We haven't definitively connected him to any of this yet. We may find out that Ricky was behind all this, not Adam." Listening to his voicemail he reported, "Adam's house was broken into. Computer was taken. Place was tossed."

"Figures," was all she could say. Martine couldn't relay to Mahoney her complete disappointment and that the dreams she was still having made it apparent to her that much more had to be done—the case was not resolved. If Ricky was the only one behind these crimes, she wouldn't have had the dramatic dream experience she had last night. "But, I'm sure there is something that connects Adam to Ricky," she finished with.

Chapter 48

Martine arrived home late and went inside the home with the realization that nothing made sense again.

Eva was in the living room watching TV with all the animals. "Hey, mom. After I fed the dogs we went to the dog park. They had a blast. Honey can run as fast as a Border Collie."

Martine plopped on the sofa. "Great. Thanks for taking care of them. Things got a little more complicated than I expected."

"Yeah. What were you doing? Are you like dating this guy?" Eva teased.

"No. Of course not." Martine filled her in as best she could on what had happened after she left *Desert Run* with John Mahoney. "Have you heard from Alexa? She left me a voicemail, but I haven't been able to get through to her since she left this morning."

"Nope, they won't get back till late. Sometimes they camp overnight. Don't worry, she's done this before. It's Dylan. He's a good guy—reminds me of dad."

"Yeah, I know she likes him. What do you mean they camp overnight?"

"Didn't she tell you? Last month when they went four-wheeling with Dylan's friends they got stuck there overnight."

"Why?"

"His loser friend didn't want them to leave, so when Alexa and Dylan went down to the water to swim with his other buddies the guy moved Dylan's vehicle and trailer to another campground nearby and hitched a ride back. When Dylan and Alexa left the campsite on their four-wheelers to go back to the trailhead where they had parked their vehicle they couldn't find it. It was like ten o'clock. They finally gave up looking and had to four-wheel back to the campsite. His friend pretended that Dylan must have parked in a different area because the keys never left their campsite. He said they'd be able to find it in the morning when there was light. That's how they got stuck there."

"Geez, that was sneaky."

"Dylan is so mild mannered that he actually believed him. There are so many different trailheads with off-road parking, it was somewhat possible. Alexa didn't buy it though she just couldn't figure out how he did it by himself."

Martine's mind processed through the clever trick innocently played on Dylan and Alexa. "Oh my gosh!" She sprang to her feet. "Ricky and Adam both must have had something to do with transporting Eli's trunk to the cargo plane terminal."

"What?" Eva said in surprise.

"It's early in the investigation, but I think we've been able to connect Ricky with what happened to Eddy's gang. If Adam was behind it though, and Adam was shipping the trunk, he would have had to meet Ricky at the airport. Adam couldn't lift the trunk alone and it wouldn't fit in a car. But Ricky wanted his information first, so he parked his vehicle, with the trunk in it, somewhere else until he got what he really wanted. When Adam only gave him the name of a caseworker, Ricky killed Adam and took his car to find the guy. The caseworker was found deceased."

Eva was mesmerized as her mother acted frenzied. "Okay, Ricky is the guy that was killed this morning. You went to Adam's tonight and found information about a cargo shipment. This is actually is making sense."

"Yeah," Martine said excitedly, "so where would Ricky have left his vehicle? I bet it's a van or SUV."

"Somewhere near, but not too close," Eva theorized.

"Oh, what if that was Ricky's real plan? What if he was planning on getting his information and keeping the trunk and cash? He would've parked it somewhere safe, long-term, and where no one would find it suspicious. He needed time to get the wife and wouldn't want to be caught with stolen merchandise. He's a wanted man. Right?"

"Right."

"While he's tracking down his wife, and on the run, that trunk would immediately implicate him in murders—he wouldn't risk that."

"He could've parked it within a ten minute cab ride, right?" Eva contributed.

"And he would have the keys to the vehicle he was leaving behind. He may even have a parking stub," Martine added.

"There aren't a lot of overnight parking facilities like that."

"He only needed one," Martine said slyly. "We find out if Ricky had two sets of keys and a parking stub in his possession." She paused. "Damn and those possessions have already been requested by the FBI. They probably haven't sent them yet since it's the weekend."

"Maybe Alexa can make some calls tomorrow anyways," Eva offered. "So what if it's the weekend. You know how she is."

"Yes I do. That's great if we see her tomorrow. Unfortunately, Dylan's friend might have something up his sleeve again." Martine felt a release and laughed with her daughter.

Not wanting to endanger her daughters or anyone else, she instructed Eva, "Let's not mention this to anyone. It could be dangerous to discuss this with anyone at work. Please don't for everyone's safety. Do I have your word?"

"Absolutely," Eva said as she rose to leave.

Chapter 49

Sleep came fast to Martine once Eva had left and she could curl up in bed for the night. With prayers said, she was whisked away to another dimension where she was met by Freya.

Familiar Freya was now dressed like a goddess in a long white gown with plunging neckline. Gold bands bedecked in jewels wrapped around her hips and bodice. Cuffed wrist-bracelets and a generous headpiece shimmered golden when she moved.

Freya approached Martine as the two cats' moved lightheartedly between them. "You visit me again," she said with charm.

Martine exchanged pleasantries, "Yes. I seem to have found my way back to your beautiful and welcoming land." Martine found she was now wearing a simple gown in this mystical realm.

"Have you journeyed well with your new companions?" Both cats enjoyed rubbing up against her legs.

"I have, but not with just a pair of beautiful cats." Martine petted one that rubbed on her. "I believe I have your cloak."

"Awe yes," Freya said reverently. "Did it serve you well?"

"If I used it as you would've intended, it did serve me well. It provided protection when I found myself within the enemy's lair."

"That is good. Very good." Freya motioned to her garden's table. "Be seated."

"Am I here to return your gifts?" Martine frowned slightly.

Freya smiled. "Do you want to?"

"I'm not sure. I haven't understood what the reason for entering into the dark realms was."

"Do you want to know your enemies as well as they know you?" Her wisdom and knowing radiated.

"Of course, but I don't know who my enemy is. I only know something is wrong. I can't take on all the realms beneath the earth." Martine shook her head slowly. "Do you know who my enemy is, or where I can find them?"

Seriousness spread on Freya's face. "I can only ask you questions, and answer yours truthfully—not less, not more."

"I understand," Martine said, remembering that Freya had already explained to her that she could not advise—only answer questions. "I believe you can tell me more then, if you will."

"Yes. I can do that."

Martine pondered her options. "Did you tell me everything about Loki and the gods?"

"No I did not," Freya seemed to spark at the mention of Loki.

"Tell me how he came to be in your time."

"Loki was born from giants—our perpetual enemies. Odin became friends with Loki. They swore eternal friendship with each other and became blood brothers. He had favor with Odin and chose to involve himself with the gods. He was handsome compared to the horribly ugly giants that he came from. He was a charismatic prankster. His entertaining ways gained him favor. His clever methods and eloquent tongue convinced many to trust him and turn against each other."

"He stirred conflict?"

"The answer is yes," she said soulfully.

"How did he do it?"

"By his words and propaganda he would be helpful when it amused, or benefited him. Likewise, he poisoned relationships and made conflicts for the same fulfillments. Loki ensnared everyone into a complicated problem, to which he would supply the remedy—though his solution often created even greater troubles."

"Why?" Martine's eyes widened.

"Your mind would ask that question. But there is no answer when a *being* has no function or benefit. Manipulation became a sport. His unpredictable behavior became more than merely mischievous, he became blatantly malicious."

"Why did he stay with the gods if he was a giant?"

"Giants were opposed to the gods. So, by birthright he was from a race of natural born killers. But, Loki tried to be good. Loki bonded with Odin. They had pledged an eternal friendship."

Martine thought about the legends. "What happened between Loki and the gods? What went wrong?"

"Ah, the chain of events that revealed the depth of his truly evil and cunning nature. His impulsive actions and mounting pride was determined to trick the gods after that fateful incident."

Eagerly, Martine continued, "Can I know what he did?"

"Yes. I need to tell you a story—a parable of sorts, about love and loss, doubt and faith. In my head I know what happened many eons ago, but in my heart it's as though it happened yesterday." Freya sighed with sadness. "Loki was falling out of favor with the gods. During a feast, Loki forced his way in—despite not being welcomed. Odin found him a place to sit. After the meal, Loki told one bad tale after another. He blamed gods of their past deeds. He disclosed secrets and spread deception. He said horrible things about Heimdall, Thor, Sif and me, to only name a few. Without remorse, regret, or sympathy for anyone, he manifested into an unstoppable master of deceit and lies who could not control his tongue or true nature. Not until Thor arrived could anyone stop Loki from spewing false accusations, and only after Thor threatened to destroy Loki with his hammer did he flee."

"What did they do with him?"

"Not enough," she allowed her words to linger. "More should have been done."

"Is there more that happened?"

"Yes," Freya said flatly.

"Can I know?"

"Loki took his revenge out on the one he truly hated."

Martine guessed, "Thor?"

"No, Odin's other son Baldur. Baldur was unlike Thor. He was gentle, loving, peaceful and most handsome. Everyone loved the brave, beautiful, and kind, Baldur. Throughout the nine worlds, he was the god of light, truth, and reconciliation."

"Why did he have hatred for Baldur?"

"Jealousy. Baldur was loved by the gods and men of our worlds. He was highly regarded and considered wise and helpful."

"What did Loki do if Baldur was so favored?"

"Loki was very obsessed with destroying the gods. He plotted Baldur's death, which caused Baldur to begin dreaming about his demise. When his mother and father were made aware of his dreams, they were able to secure his safety with every creature, disease, weapon, elemental, and being. Because he was universally loved, all agreed to protect Baldur, except the mistletoe. It was believed the small inconsequential mistletoe tree could not possibly be used as a weapon to kill their son."

"Well, who would?" Martine said.

"Loki." She paused briefly. "Through shape-shifting and trickery, Loki was able to learn this information. That's when he masterminded the most treacherous act of all—the one that altered the worlds."

"He killed Baldur with mistletoe?"

"Worse." Freya's sad eyes closed.

"Please tell me."

"Loki used Baldur's blind brother Hodur to throw a mistletoe branch that he had fashioned into a dart. By shape-shifting he disguised himself and tricked Baldur's brother into playing a game with the weapon. With Loki helping aim the dart, it met its mark. The dart pierced Baldur's heart and he died immediately."

"There must have been big trouble for Loki after that," Martine stated. Killing his friends' son would make him a monster."

"Of course." Freya appeared disheartened. "Odin was beside himself that he was betrayed by the one that had sworn eternal friendship with him. This is the event that exposed Loki's true nature. He was a rare defect. Not loyal to his own race or the one he longed to be accepted by. He would and could deceive all of them for his pleasure."

Martine looked sickened. "What did they do to punish him?"

"Because of his shape-shifting abilities Loki was able to hide from the gods for a long time. When he was finally captured, all those he had injured devised the worst punishment conceived. He was escorted down into a damp underground cavern that served as a prison chamber—here he was bound in the most dreadful way possible. Loki was permanently exiled and confined inside an undisclosed cave, where he resides with ugly toads, insects, snakes and creatures that live in darkness. He has vowed to get free to destroy and conquer." Freya gave Martine a concerned look. "What do you say the gods should do to Loki?"

Martine surmised the reasoning in Freya's lesson. "There is no place for Loki to exist. He can never be trusted, and no one can protect themselves from his perverted ways. He must be bound for eternity, or destroyed. However, he is only made worse in captivity though. He would grow more vindictive and spiteful. He will only conceive more ruthless games to play on the good and innocent. From what I learned about darkness, sparing him with the littlest compassion is what we do, and what they abuse."

"You understand well," Freya said encouragingly.

Martine's eyes flitted back and forth for a second as she processed the grave ancient events of Freya's time. With trepid speculation in her tone, she asked with dread, "Where is this underground cave that Loki was bound in?"

Ominous regret washed over Freya's face. With her eyes fixed on Martine, she returned a deplorable look of knowing.

Martine's eyes grew wide as she comprehended Freya's communiqué. "Are you trying to tell me . . . ," Martine was saying as she was swept away from Freya's enchanting presence.

Chapter 50

Anxious and eager to start the day, Martine made her way to the kitchen to let the dogs out and start a pot of coffee. As the brew perked she pulled her phone from its charger and checked voicemails. Disappointed that she hadn't heard back from Alexa, she listened again to the staticky broken message from the previous morning.

"Hey, mom, Dylan and I are going to be out of cell service all day. Found some interesting facts on two ocean liners that sank in early 1900's. You were right—there is a conne . . . shhhhhhhhhh, titanic . . . shhhhhhhhhhhhhh, Lusit . . . shhhhhh, Fed . . . shhhhhhhhhhhhh." The call finally dropped.

With the communication incomplete and no way to speak with Alexa, Martine decided to use this time to check out what her daughter might have found.

With a fresh cup of coffee at her side she started her first search for sunken ocean liners Titanic and Lusitania. It didn't take more than fifteen minutes with Wikipedia to garner excepted facts. The cruise ships were related to none other than J.P. Morgan. So Martine next tried to connect him with the word fed. In less than a second, Google search engines drummed up 33 million results. J.P. Morgan was directly connected to the Federal Reserve Banks. Shaking her head in wonderment, she though, *how is this not a conflict of interest? It is clearly a monopoly when someone that orchestrates the creation of the Federal Reserve Banks in America ends up owning one of the biggest bank conglomerates.*

As she clicked and opened all the links on the first page it became painfully clear she was venturing into the passionate minds of strangers that ranged from learned historians and authors to opinionated Americans. The consensus was there is a problem with the banking and political system in our country.

What prompted her to read on further was she could really imagine and relate to what they were all fuming about. After her experience playing Monopoly with the souls of fallen beings, she could now see how they operated. Participating in the competitive game with the dark-souled beings enlightened her how they feed off of others to satisfy their greedy desires to control everyone and everything. Martine realized she could read this stuff forever and not figure out what she was really looking for. She refined her search again to include; Federal Reserve and Ashkenazi.

Martine fetched a second cup of coffee as the screen refreshed. When she returned 81 thousand results were accessible—all of them referencing the Ashkenazi Rothschild Jews. *Okay*, she thought, *who can help me here?*

As she pumped her keyboards' down arrow to a link dated two days ago she found herself speed reading through an intense dialogue between educated bloggers who used their keyboards instead of picket lines. These activists were embroiled in lengthy threads of communication that spanned a month. Computer technology made it possible to catch up on all their drama and heated debates in less than thirty-minutes.

"Whoa," she murmured, "that's who I need to talk to." As the projector in her head came to life, playing back memories of her dreams, Martine connected what she just read about a publication called The Hidden Tyranny with the warning from her dream— *Tyranny growing more aloof.*

Realizing more and more of the information she was reading on this link seemed to resonate with what she had become aware of, quickened another recollection—*Confirmation comes in two, follow branch and know what's true.* Picking up Adam's business card with the Israeli flag on it added intrigue. She muttered slowly,

"What does he know about a crest?" Her mind had to identify the significance of—*Two fold meaning in a crest, has misled all the rest.*

Cautious to keep her identity secret from crazy fanatics, Martine started to log into their blogging thread using an anonymous e-mail account she often used at work. Before completing the required registration she thought better of it. She suddenly considered that she would be connecting herself with a string of e-mail addresses that may be in a government surveillance watch group. She would also be connecting her sister's computer to the group. If anyone of them were under suspicion with the law or government, they all would all be caught in the net.

Martine sat back in her chair, clasping her hands behind her head in contemplation. *This guy sounds like the Wikipedia of current affairs*, she thought.

Within moments Martine deciphered from Max's blogs where he could be found.

Chapter 51

Martine walked into the bustling diner that was frequented by local residents and young college students. After consulting with the cashier, she was directed to a middle-aged man with a silver-mane pulled back in a pony tail.

After weaving between departing customers and crowded tables, she walked up to the man who was engrossed in the Sunday paper and introduced herself, "Hi, I'm Martine. Are you Max?"

"Yes," Max obliged, putting down the paper. "So you're here for a job?" He slid his dirty breakfast plate off to the side.

"Not really," she confessed, looking embarrassed. "I really needed to meet with you about something else."

Max being considerably more reserved around real people winked his brow in confusion. "What do you need to meet with me about," he said apprehensively.

Martine seated herself across from Max. "Research," Martine said with precision. "I've got some questions about your blogs." Worried this would terminate the conversation because the whole point of blogging was to establish boundaries for privacy and safety, she added, "Of course confidentially." Bloggers felt protected when they were anonymous. Breaching that protocol was a risk she was taking.

"Am I in some kinda trouble here," Max said tightly.

"No," Martine said without hesitation. "Not at all."

Still sounding toneless, Max asked, "Then what kind of research are you doing? Is Big Brother watching me?"

"I assure you, it's nothing like that?" She leaned in slightly. "No one I know is watching you. I'm interested in the same subjects you're blogging about. You know—the sensitive ones."

"Some people might interpret some of our blogging as racist, although I'm not," Max clarified. "How do I know you're not going to cause me any problems?"

Martine knew it would be difficult to speak to each other about any of his topics since they were strangers. "Let's just say whatever we discuss doesn't leave here because anything I've uncovered may be very interesting to you, but sensitive in its raw form," she offered stealthily.

Curious Max straightened up. "Like what? What do you know?"

"I'm working on book about the Ashkenazi Jews."

"Oh," Max mused thoughtfully. "That'll be good. Lots of stuff on that now. Awkward subject matter. Got anything new I don't know about?"

Martine had to get his interest sparked or he'd stay tight-lipped forever. "Well my research clearly shows that Hitler was supported by them initially." Pausing before volunteering some information that would capture his attention, she looked upon his emotionless expression. "So have you ever wondered where the word NAZI came from?"

"Yah, I suppose it's an Acronym for the German Nationalist Party."

"Are you sure?" Martine shrugged her doubt.

Max tried again, "Maybe National Socialist Party."

"Is it?" Martine queried. "Could it be something else?"

Max stared, determined to figure it out if she had. "Could be an acronym for National Zionists."

"That's not really an acronym either," Martine pointed out.

Looking quizzical, Max gave up. "Well if it's not one of those, what do think it stands for?"

Martine scrunched her lips. "I see the last four letters in Ashkenazi."

His eyes flared in brief surprise, processing her words. "Oh my God, you're right. How did I miss that?"

Detecting she finally had his attention, she continued, "In my novel I'm tracking the migration of a particular family and their horse's bloodline. There's money in this family, but everything goes dark on them around 1940. What do you think could have happened to this family's fortune?"

"Do you think they were Ashkenazi's for sure?"

"Absolutely. Frankfurt."

"You picked a very complicated and messy era. Were they Orthodox or Zionists?"

"Can they be both?" She looked at him expectantly.

"Yeah, I guess so, just not at the same time. Back then the Zionist Jews began dictating the European and Israeli Jews—as well as the orthodox and the Zionist Jews. Zionists became boss."

"Based on what?"

"Based on an interview with an egotistical Zionist," Max said matter-of-factly. "Read *The Hidden Tyranny* if you can stomach it. According to this Zionist, their takeover has been dictating world events since WWI." He looked discouraged. "I wish I could prove what everyone thinks is incomprehensible."

Martine reflected in her mind what she had been become familiar with since arriving in Arizona. "Maybe you don't. It could be deadly to learn the truth, or know too much."

"What can I ever do about it anyways?" Max lamented.

Martine had to know what Max was referring to in his blog when he mentioned there was a story behind the Israeli flag, so she changed the subject. "Tell me about Israel's flag."

"Long before the state of Israel, there was an Ashkenazi Jew named Moses Amschel Bauer who was a money lender. The sign on his door was a red hexagram—which interestingly enough translates into 666 because of its six equilateral triangles, six columns, and its six sided hexagon in the center. When his son Mayer takes over the business, he changes his name from Bauer to Rothschild. German translation is, 'roth' means red, and 'schild' means sign. The Rothschild's became the leading force behind the Zionist movement. When the Israeli flag is unveiled in 1948 it is a blue version of the Rothschild's' hexagram. Even though they call it the Star of

David, there are no origins, or emblems that connect the hexagram star to Israelites' or King David. However, it is related to the emblem used by the Zionists dating back to the eighteen-hundreds."

Martine could now understand *Twofold meaning in a crest.* "That might be helpful to me when I write the book. Every picture tells a story—that's a good one."

Martine was impressed so far with Max's insights. "What could they have owned and stored between 1940 and today that would be considered very valuable?"

"Can you describe it?"

"Not really, I've never seen it." Martine found herself straining to hear Max above the noisy families coming into the diner for breakfast.

"Well, money was everything. But gold was the standard." Frank and to the point was his way when Max was on a roll. "They would've converted their wealth to gold and hid it away." He motioned for a waitress to fetch more coffee and water for the both of them.

"I need to let you in on one more thing about this family," Martine lowered her voice, "What I'm looking for is somehow connected to the Lusitania and the Titanic."

Max was spurned instantly. "That can't be good. J.P. Morgan and his cronies the Rothschild's and Rockefellers come to mind."

"Me too," she agreed. "Based on what you've discovered, and what I've uncovered, J.P. scored really well financially from both of those incidents. Now we know the ammunition really was on that sunken ocean liner, and we know it was actually manufactured by him." Like a professional blogger, Martine drew an incriminating conclusion. "It's painfully apparent he wanted WWI to rage on."

"Even when it looks like this guy has lost everything, he really was winning," Max contributed. "And then to add salt to the wounds, he's our representative at the Paris Treaty of Versailles and a founder of the Federal Reserve Bank."

"Exactly," Martine said reflectively—thinking about the most powerful monopoly formed. "So now we know he's connected to the Zionist bankers and the Federal Reserve. We know the Zionists are backing Germany for another World War, and that's the same country they threw under the bus and hit hard with the Treaty reparation payments," Martine summarized.

"You got that right so far." Max sipped his coffee.

Martine continued articulating out loud, "Germany was broke after WWI, but the Zionists needed their help settling Palestine."

"Yep. Zionist Jews couldn't get their new territory settled fast enough," Max threw in.

Martine wrinkled her nose. "Frankly, who else could they get to do that for them? The Zionists needed to create lots of money to fill their coffers and create their own country. The business men and bankers lost all the big war revenues when WWI ended. The only way Hitler could financially raise a war machine was with lots of new money."

"That's my theory," Max said bluntly. "If enemies exist the Zionists know how to provoke a war. And if one or both of them lack military might, money is all it takes to create it. So, they create money to fuel a war, make lots of money while there is war, and grow their money off of the debt service after the war. It's an enterprise to them."

"An enterprise they operate in our country and around the world," Martine said in agreement.

Max shared his deeper insight, "Actually, I think it's a Ponzi scheme because they get investors to purchase a piece of the action. If you think about it, it's a fraudulent investment operation where the Federal Reserve pays returns to its investors from interest payments our tax payers make, or it distributes new capital paid by new investors, rather than from profit earned by them. They really don't have to do anything to earn it, because they'll just print more when they need it."

Martine's mind wandered back in time through the circumstances that may be relevant to her case. "Hitler wanted out of the Treaty payments. That Treaty was equivalent to almost ninety years of hard labor for every working person in Germany. It was an impossible situation," she paused, "unless you're a banker."

"Not completely accurate," Max pointed out. "Hitler didn't agree with the Treaty of Versailles. He wanted to make Germany strong again. He wanted to make an army, and not have debt. He rejected the treaty that made Germany sound weak. He wouldn't pay it."

Martine added, "I know. That was the pillar of his campaign, along with his hatred of the Jews. He used his disgust of the treaty and traitorous Jews to win public favor and eventually rise as the Fuehrer of Germany." She thought a moment. "So, when he did get elected, I know he stopped making the payments. He did do what he promised. He made Germany strong and restored their pride. He still needed the new money, not to make reparation payments, but to build his country back up."

"Agreed," Max replied with a nod. "I just never understood how he was able to abolish the Treaty of Versailles."

Martine responded, "It wasn't abolished as far as I know. When Hitler's actions were allowed and no one stopped him or enforced the treaty, it was abolished in deed, not word."

"You sound like a lawyer or a history teacher," Max said admiringly as he jotted down her words.

Martine went on, "Between 1919 and 1933 when Hitler came to power, the reparation payments were a huge source of contention, but there were payments made. Germany tried to negotiate the, payments, interest, payment plans, and other details—the French wouldn't have it. Germany defaulted on payments many times. Germany faced hyperinflation, starvation and humiliation, but there were many attempts made to restructure the crippling obligation. The reparation payments compounded Germany's problems when they already had a war torn country after WWI. The reparation payments were so outlandish that most people had never heard of a sum that high."

"You know you're right," Max said with a tap of his finger. "Germany did work something out with the allies eventually. I recently read in the paper that on October 4th 2010 they are making their final payment."

"Yep." Martine nodded. "See it took over ninety years."

"So I don't know where you're going with this treaty," Max commented.

Martine channeled memories from her dreams. "Let me think." Searching the air, her mind sorted out the sequence of events. "So, why didn't anyone enforce the treaty when Hitler told them—which he did—that he would not be making any payments and he would grow an army for Germany?" Martine answered her own question, "They either needed him to help them, like you think, or they wanted him to start another war for the purposes of making money."

"Or both." Max rubbed his chin reflectively. "I know what they did." He studied Martine as he voiced his thoughts, "The bankers took on the debt by selling bonds. They sold the bonds in exchange for gold. Someone had to make the enormous reparation payments. It's the only way. The payments and interest would've been unbearable and crippling to the German people. We know Hitler was obsessed with gold and treasures. Maybe He was going to pay the bankers back and be rid of them."

"Of course that would make sense if someone was interested in helping Germany."

"Like the Zionists," Max expounded with certainty.

"It also explains something else, Max, like you said, we know Hitler was obsessed with gold and treasures. He may have planned to pay the bankers back. He certainly didn't want them to own him or his people. He also wouldn't have had any problem double-crossing them as they had done to Germany. And that would have been a secret."

"Okay," Max commented. "That should be easy to track if you think your family was involved with a fortune of gold or war bonds."

"Not really. The problem with bonds," Martine explained, "particularly Bearer Bonds, is that there's no record of them needed. That's the whole point. There is no record kept. They're meant to protect people's privacy and secrets. They're like the dollar bills on that table over there." Martine pointed at the cash tip left by the customers that had just departed. "Once they leave your possession, they're not yours, and there's no record. But, given the outrageous amounts of money Hitler would've needed to fund his operation while rebuilding a country, I can't think of a better way than that to anonymously collect valuable resources in exchange for bonds that are backed by a powerful and wealthy institution."

"Are you sure?" Puzzled, Max rubbed his chin. "There's no form of registry like when you title your car or house?"

Martine sighed. "None required. It's meant to keep peoples wealth private and hidden. It's meant to make great amounts of money easily transferable, easily negotiable, easy to store at home, or in safety deposit boxes, and completely anonymous. The only requirement is that you must have possession of the bond. That's why they're not popular anymore. Governments found it was too easy for criminals to launder and traffic money illegally when their cartels used bonds to do it. Governments also found out how they were being duped out of taxes when Bearer Bonds were in play. Most counties have outlawed them."

"I suppose, but they were popular back then, right?"

"Every country has tried using them when they needed money. Income tax wasn't really born yet. But, Hitler needed more than what Germany herself could raise, so he would need a very big financial backer."

"Exactly. He would need a large investor that everyone trusted," Max said with a conspirator hint in his tone.

"You realize you're probably referring to something like the Federal Reserve Bank," Martine contributed suggestively.

Max replied evenly, "I do."

Martine was ready to leave when she heard Max propose a question.

"But, don't they have to redeem them? Isn't there always a maturity date?"

"Usually there is," was her reply.

"Like sixty years?" He raised his brow.

She lifted her face up. "Not that long."

Martine had struck a chord with Max and he couldn't resist telling her about his recent findings in regards the World Trade Center Buildings. "Well I know this is a racy theory, but I've been researching the collapse of the World Trade Center Buildings and there were vaults underground." Max looked cautiously at Martine for an objectionable reaction. Seeing none he continued, "But, they were mostly empty when they excavated down there. The theory was that the Federal Reserve gathered gold from all over the world in exchange for these Series 1934 Bonds. Back in the 1930's everyone was bracing for a big war and wealthy countries were feeling vulnerable and threatened. The Federal Reserve gathered gold from countries like China, Japan, and most of Europe in exchange for Bonds."

"I've heard a little about that," Martine admitted. There are actually lawsuits because authorities claim they're counterfeit bonds."

"I know," Max agreed. "Did you know that these bonds were meant to be stored secretly underground for sixty years?"

"No," Martine admitted.

"Since the Bonds could be redeemed after sixty years, it's speculated, that China and others wanted their gold plus interest returned after the sixty years. By 1999 they were threatening our country to honor the release of their gold. What if the Federal Reserve Bank used those vaults under the World Trade Center to store hidden treasures of gold?"

Sickened at the thought, she took in a deep breath. "Any proof out there?"

"Not really." Max shook his head dubiously. After sharing his elaborate speculations about the collapse of all four buildings, he presented her with a possible scenario. "Anyone who wanted to protect their wealth and get it out of a vulnerable country was said to have participated in the scheme. If your family controlled great wealth during the rise of Hitler they may have done this to get it away from him, or used it to financially support him."

"What do you know about the series 1934 bonds?" Martine felt a connection to Eli was possible.

"I heard that there were many crates floating around Europe and other counties—totaling in the trillions or quadrillions. Of course they were bullion-backed. They've all been deemed fake when they surfaced."

"Well, Max, even a trillion dollars worth of Bear Bonds would take up more than a crate. More like a warehouse."

"Not if each bond was a billion dollars." He smirked. "FDR passed an Executive Order in 1933 criminalizing the possession of monetary gold by any individual or business. That was the beginning of the Federal Reserve's control over gold. They got the gold, people got a bond."

"I can imagine how Hitler would've been useful in rounding up European gold for the banks," Martine injected, "if Hitler was a madman, what is the Federal Reserve Bank?"

"Exactly, they say the Federal Reserve probably received much more gold from Japan and China."

Martine felt the vibration of her phone go off again. Silenced inside her purse, she figured about five or six calls were missed while the cell was sitting deep somewhere in her purse. "I think it's time for me to get going." She fished her phone out and saw a text from John Mahoney stating the airport had called and he needed to talk. Looking back at Max, she readied herself to depart. "I know I've taken up a lot of your time and I want to thank you for helping me. It's been good information, Max." Every word she had heard struck her like whiplash, and it was time to move forward.

"No, thank you. I've enjoyed our visit." His smile grew. "As a matter of fact—anytime you want to talk is fine with me."

"Great." Martine checked her watch. "I guess I know where to find you now."

Max scribbled his number down on a piece of newspaper. "Here's my cell. Let me know what happens with your book."

Martine got up and waved goodbye.

Chapter 52

Just as Martine was preparing to back her car out of its parking place, her phone went off again. This time she answered it. "Martine, here."

"Martine," John's anxious voice returned. "Where are you?"

"Sorry. I've been at breakfast with a friend," she fibbed a little. "What's up? I just read your text."

"Well, I think you might be right about something bigger going on besides murder and mayhem—as if that wasn't enough," he scoffed. "I've been contacted by the airport, and there were officers that showed up looking for a shipment like the one we described."

"Officers?" Martine said in surprise. "From where?" She waited for an opening in the busy street.

"Federal Reserve Law Enforcement Officers."

"What could they possibly be doing in Arizona?" Martine asked as she pulled into the traffic.

"I don't know," he replied. "I haven't formally met them yet. Can we meet?"

"Sure." Imagining that it might be time to be more discrete, she suggested, "How 'bout *Desert Run*. It won't look suspicious if we're there."

"Is your imagination running wild?" he said humorously.

"Can you please make sure you're not being watched, followed, or bugged?" She retorted.

Mahoney made light of her paranoia. "I'm not being followed or bugged. I'll take extra precautions if you're concerned."

"Please do. Especially, if the lady at the airport told the Federal Reserve Officers about us."

"Right, I presume she did," he admitted.

"They may be looking for you right now," she cautioned.

"Got it. I'll leave immediately."

"You'll beat me there. Need to stop at the house for something." She increased her speed and merged onto the interstate highway. "See ya in a few."

"Wait," he injected. "Why don't I meet you at the house?"

"I don't want you to lead anybody to that house. I'm there alone, or with my daughters."

Mahoney countered, "I'll know if they're following me."

"No. They could have 'eyes in the sky' and you wouldn't know they were tracking you."

He knew she could be right. "I'll meet you at *Desert Run*," he conceded.

Martine disconnected from Mahoney and took another incoming call. "Eva, how are you?"

"Mom, where are you?" Eva's alarmed voice sounded.

"Late breakfast. What's the matter?"

"Everything," Eva moaned slightly. "Olivia's scared. She said a car followed her to the barn today. She's afraid to leave."

"Shit," Martine howled. "Are you there now?"

"Yeah. Olivia and I are tacking up a couple horses in case they come back to find her. We know they can't catch us in the desert if we're on horses and they're on foot."

"Have you called the police?"

"No," Eva sounded distressed, "because they're not here right now."

"Did she get a license plate number?"

"No. They were following her," Eva clarified.

Martine's response sounded rehearsed, "I know, there aren't any licenses plates on the front of the cars in Arizona."

"Exactly."

"I'm on my way and so is Mahoney. We're meeting at *Desert Run*. Please watch for the car to return until Mahoney gets there. Call the police if they show up. Don't worry."

Relieved to hear help was on the way, Eva's voice trembled, "I'm so glad you're down here right now."

Martine finished her conversation as she pulled into Jolene's driveway. Seeing nothing unusual, she ran into the house and logged onto the computer. She couldn't shake the feeling that she needed additional information on the Bearer Bonds before it could be a viable concern in this case. Satisfied that Mahoney would be there with Eva and Olivia by now, she took the time she needed to find specific information on these bonds.

Story's and reports varied slightly, but mostly confirmed what Max and she had discussed. These Series 1934 bonds were issued by the Federal Reserve to countries like China, who themselves moved their gold to the US so it could not be looted by the Japanese occupiers—eight ships to be exact. These iron trunks or crates stuffed with bonds were stored in climate-controlled caves. Similar trunks were found at a plane crash site in the Philippines. Even Swiss banks were reported to have had vaults for the bonds. Dramatic stories and legends of intrigue surround these mysterious artifacts.

One thing was consistent—the way they were packaged and stored. Another major consistency related to the exterior description of certain chests—which made her think of Tom's descriptive words 'treat' and 'moth' that he had seen on the trunk. Another major concern is the connection of J.P Morgan's relationship with the Federal Reserve as one of its founding architects that met on Jekyll Island.

Martine thought deeply, *am I on the right track?* She also processed the seriousness of having possession of one of these chests and the lengths someone would go to keep them covered-up forever, or deliver them into the hands of an enemy. Martine imagined *what would they do to destroy these Bearer Bonds if they couldn't steal them? And whose hands were meant to receive them if they made it to the Middle East?* That thought made her shudder.

Her phone rang again. She answered it absentmindedly while she continued to read more, "Martine, here."

"And where are you now?" Mahoney's deep voice asked.

"Just finishing up at the house. Almost done."

"I'm here with Eva. Her and Olivia are really shook up. I know you've really been working hard on this case. I hope you got something for me. I'm ready to listen. Eva has been very convincing."

Martine chuckled, "That she is. Talked me into raising a squirrel, and tried to get us to raise a skunk."

"You sound very calm and collected," Mahoney commented. "Do you know something I don't know?"

"Not sure, but if those officers with the Federal Reserve contact you, please do not confide in them."

"Wasn't planning on it," was his short response. "This is the FBI's case."

"Likewise, it's my opinion this is not their jurisdiction. They really are not part of our Federal Government. They just act and look the part."

"I know. But it's a cursory relationship."

"Only if you're working together with them on a specific violation that involves both entities," Martine corrected. "As a whole you do not want to associate with them. Please do not interact with them yet."

"Agreed."

"I'm on my way," she stated hurriedly before disconnecting.

Before she changed into her barn boots, she rounded up the dogs to let them out for a quick bathroom break. When they came back in she decided to feed them early in case she got home later than normal. She petted each animal and apologized, "I'm sorry I can't take you with, but I promised my sister I would never take you to a barn because you guys are manure seeking missiles." Feeling guilty she added, "I'll see if Alexa will take you three to the doggie park." She sent Alexa a quick text since she still hadn't heard from her.

As she locked up the house she had a thought that turned her mind like a windmill. She imagined what terrorists in the Middle

East would do with that much money. At the least, weapons could be purchased. At the worst, nuclear war devices of mass destruction could be obtained.

Chapter 53

Within thirty minutes Martine pulled into *Desert Run* where she was met by John Mahoney. She was finally prepared to tell Mahoney what she thought the case was all about. She was not prepared to go it alone where the clues would take them. Dressed casual in jeans and cowboy boots, he walked over and greeted her with a big smile.

"Hey," Martine said.

"I'm glad you're here." Mahoney glanced around. "This place is a ghost town on Sunday."

"Not just Sunday. A lot of people have left the property completely. They don't have much stable help. Eva and Olivia are doing practically everything now. It's been a disturbing week," Martine explained with a shrug.

"Olivia told me about a car following her. I just drove around the grounds and did see a car parked down the road. It left before I could get to it. I didn't tell her that the description does meet the one you and I have from our visit at Adam's. So, this is where you let me in on any theories you have."

"I can't say I have a theory, John. I'm suspicious about everything surrounding this man's life. Too much has happened to make his death just a crime statistic."

"I'm willing to agree with you on that." He rubbed his brow.

"Good, because I could use your help now. Let's not stand in the sun. Let's park our cars over there so they're out of sight."

After both were seated at the pavilion, Martine started, "I might have an idea what has happened, but first I want to know if you do?"

"No. I haven't come up with anything."

Martine began by summarizing, "We know that Eli had a trunk that was taken. We know we haven't found it yet, and we're pretty sure someone else is looking for it. Perhaps more people than we know. That's why I don't think you should talk to the Federal Reserve Police."

"Yeah, why is that?"

"If I'm right, there are Bearer Bonds in that trunk," she said fast, and waited in silence for his reaction.

Without hesitation or acting alarmed, Mahoney asked, "How much are we talking about?"

"I'm guessing their value now would be about a trillion."

"A trillion," he exclaimed loudly. "How's that possible?"

"Well first of all, these are probably bonds that are considered fake. They also may date back more than sixty years. And they would be huge multi-million to billion dollar bonds."

"In that old trunk?"

"Matches the description of what I've found so far," she said positively. "These bonds had to do with the Treaty of Versailles. They were stored in iron trunks so they could be buried and hidden from enemies and aggressors. The ones that have surfaced match the description Tom gave me."

"Tom, Tom in jail, Tom?"

"Yep, he described an old, dirty, ugly, iron trunk. With two words on it—treat and moth."

"And those two words lead you to believe it contains Bearer Bonds?"

"I think it might, especially if you take a little folklore into account. The trunks, or crates, had the words 'Treaty of Versailles' imprinted on the outside. Some of these were called 'Mother Box' because they were very large and resembled a treasure chest. They supposedly had thirteen sealed boxes inside. Twelve had bonds, and the thirteenth was the 'Book of Redemption' that contained the instructions on how to redeem them. Do you see what I'm saying?"

"Maybe, but you have no way of knowing if that's what was being stolen, unless someone told you. Or, you found the trunk. Because as of last night we did not know where the trunk was."

"Don't we?" Martine grinned like she held a secret.

"What?" Surprised doubt rang out.

"We were right about Ricky being involved. I think he holds the key to finding the trunk."

"Martine, he's dead."

"Yes, I know, but I literally think he has keys to a hiding place where he left the trunk. It really is imperative you get his personal effects immediately."

"Well, I know that's how you'd like it to go, but there are three or four states and about five agencies after the same thing you want."

Martine tossed her head. "You know that whoever gets custody of Bearer Bonds becomes the owner of them. It's all about possession. We could never prove these belonged to Eli if anyone else gets them first. Chain of custody is imperative."

"Are you thinking I can find them before anyone else?"

"No, but I think we can. It would make it easier if we had the keys, but if you can't get Ricky's effects, don't tell anyone what you're looking for, because, I'm willing to bet he had two sets of keys on himself."

"Do you now, and how do you think we can find it—with or without keys?" Mahoney said without blinking.

"I need you to swear that you're not working with anyone else on this, and you won't share this with anyone until we're ready."

"Of course. Everything is confidential."

"My daughters are both here and too close to this case. If anyone thought I knew more than they did, it would be very easy to get to me through them." Apprehension spread across her face.

"I do know that and would not put you or them in jeopardy," he assured her. "How did a man like this end up with a treasure of such worth?"

"I don't know yet."

"How did they find him if it's such a secret?"

"It's not a secret if you tell someone. He probably needed to find someone to broker the bond redemptions. Enter Adam."

"Okay, I'm listening."

"If Eli has been in possession of the bonds, or merely came into possession of mature Bearer Bonds, he would need to go through the CUSIP process. Long after those bonds were issued, The Committee on Uniform Security Identification Procedures was formed to identify and assign numbers to redeemable bonds. So before the bonds could be negotiated, sold, or redeemed with the issuer, they would have to go through the CUSIP requirements. I'm guessing the good Adam was a broker Eli had turned to."

"Makes sense."

"If greed got to Adam and he was going to cash in himself, he would steal them before the CUSIP numbers were assigned. Likewise, anyone that found out about these bonds would probably try the same thing. That's why the big hidden safe was in Eli's house."

Mahoney listened and nodded. "That makes sense too. Is there more? I need to figure out a way to find these."

"I think that Adam underestimated Ricky. Ricky was the intermediate he found that operated underground and could be motivated to do his bidding—no matter what. Ricky wanted something really important to him—his wife's location."

"Agreed. Think he proved your idea was correct that time."

"Yeah," Martine said in haste, "so when Ricky met Adam at the cargo airlines he came alone—as in not with the merchandise. He called Adam's bluff somehow. If Adam hadn't been successful getting the information, Ricky would hold the bonds hostage. I can only speculate that someone had to give Ricky something so he'd make the exchange—even if it was the name of the caseworker."

"So far that's probable."

Martine recounted her scenario, "I think Ricky came to the airport without the trunk. He probably used a cab. Kills Adam and hijacks his car. Sets out to get wife, but ditches Adam's car eventually because it's hot."

"I still don't get where Ricky's car is."

"I think it's a van or SUV type vehicle. I think it's within a cab ride. I think it's going to be in a non-conspicuous place where it can't be taken or hauled off."

He looked at her quizzically. "You have a place in mind, don't you?"

"The International Airport Parking garage.

"What can we possibly do to even remotely consider your theory?"

"That's a fair question. We should presume there would never be a parking ticket on him. He wouldn't want anyone to receive his stash before he released it, or confiscated it for himself. It may have just been ransom to him. He could only keep the secret if no one could even have a clue where he left it. That parking ticket is in the vehicle."

"I agree. We do all leave our parking tickets in our vehicles."

"Exactly. So, based on a few premises, like; what he might have been using as a vehicle to transport a heavy trunk, the fact that he's most likely alone in the vehicle, the day and approximate time he would have entered the parking garage, and if he ever exited it, I think we use the airports security cameras to see if anything could possibly match those parameters."

"This is a big maybe. There're many parking options at our airport, which happens to be the ninth busiest in the country. They do have surveillance cameras that monitor license plates, but they have also had problems with new software that has compromised efficiency and reliability. There have been failures reported with this system. There will be so much to look at and consider. This is in a place that has to meet demands for the Department of Homeland Security."

Martine knew the magnitude of finding this trunk was serious enough that this could constitute a security risk for the public. "John," she said in her most serious voice, "what makes you think this is anything less than that?"

Mahoney shook his head in bewilderment. "Because robbery isn't a threat."

"What if it was?" She looked off, trying to find the words to convince him. "I think it is very possible that if anyone else has the same conclusion I came too, they would be willing to use any means they deem necessary to destroy this evidence. I'm not sure they are trying to steal it for its value. What if it is better that it never existed?"

Shaking his head in disbelief, Mahoney said, "Are you serious?"

Strong conviction resonated in her voice, "Enough that I think it is remiss of us to ignore that possibility."

"You're saying that the airport is in jeopardy?"

"I think it is entirely possible," she said. "If we don't get this thing found, and out of there immediately, I'm anticipating that there could conceivably be a bomb threat, or an actual bombing. What if they're willing to do anything to destroy it, or capture it? Time is only briefly on our side."

"We're talking about public safety that requires an evacuation and National support, and we don't even have a legitimate threat," he argued. "You realize we only have your thoughts on this."

"I know, you think I'm paranoid. I feel deeply that there could be a lot at stake if this is left unresolved," she warned.

Mahoney pressed his lips together. "I wouldn't say you're paranoid, but everyone else might. We can't sound the alarms with what we've got. We also would be negligent if we do nothing. Many huge events have happened in history that could have been averted if warnings had been heeded," he rationalized.

"Sadly, that's how I see it too," Martine concurred.

Mahoney relented, "Agreed. That means we need a plan. Any ideas?"

"I might," she said mysteriously. "We don't want you to draw any attention to the airport. That would just lead them there faster. I think you arrange to eagerly assist these Fed guys starting tomorrow. That will buy us time today to start our own search. If nothing turns up we can move onto another place Ricky could have left the bonds. If we do find them we can draw attention to where we have taken them and remove the public threat they pose now."

He sat back in his chair. "You think it's that easy?"

"No. But, reacting quickly is our only bet at this window. If we want to square this circle, we have to do something now. Otherwise, we could be left with another unsolved catastrophe. It will go down as another senseless terrorist attack that no one was prepared for."

Mahoney nodded. "You really are thinking the worst."

"I can't help it." Martine tipped her head slightly. "Right now I can only think of reasons that the Federal Reserve would not want these bonds to reappear in this country."

"So what's the plan?" He asked with an affirmative nod.

"You contact Ray, I'll find Alexa. We can trust them. No phones—no e-mails though."

"Okay," Mahoney said. "How do you propose we do that?"

Martine looked around. "We need to get out of here without being spotted. We need to presume you and Olivia are already being watched, or looked for. To stay in control we need to employ our own element of surprise. We need to be sneakier than our opposition is." Martine's eyes rested on Eva and Olivia who were bringing in a couple of horses that had been in turn-out paddocks. "We leave phones here and find burners. Do you have some?"

"Of course. Narcotics team always uses them. I just need to go to the office, which I can't do inconspicuously. If someone is keeping tabs on me, I won't be able to dodge them if I show up at the bureau."

"I understand, but Alexa could."

"Yes, she could get them. You realize we still have a very complicated task if a few people are going to discreetly look for a vehicle at the airport that has no registered or identifiable characteristics."

"I know. We need to try and narrow this down more." Martine thought a moment. "What were the findings on that old abandoned camper your guys found by the warehouse?"

"Prints didn't turn up anything when they ran them. Prints inside and out belong to the same person."

"Wasn't Ricky's then," Martine surmised out loud. "Did it look like someone had been living in it recently?"

"As I recall, the boys said it looked like the garbage inside could be a week or two old. Nothing was fresh. No identification found.

After they went through everything it was determined that some old Mexican immigrant probably squatted in the camper."

Her eyes followed Olivia and her dog as they went for another horse. "Really?" Sounding upbeat, Martine continued, "That gives me an idea."

"That gives you an idea," Mahoney hooted. "What doesn't?" He shook his head in amazement.

"I've been trying to imagine how to get this done without Ricky's personal effects. But, I just realized it might not be his things we're most interested in."

"Care to explain?" His eyes studied her.

Watching Olivia as she directed her dog to herd a pastured horse up to the gate triggered another dream recollection that played back in her conscious mind—*Track the path few could do.* "I will on the way." Martine stood. "Like Snow White—it only took one bite of the apple to make her go away. Let's see if we can do the same to these guys. Shall we?"

He looked confused. "Shall we what?"

"I have an idea. Let's lock up our cars and cell phones. We won't need them where we're going."

"Where are we going?" He asked suspiciously.

Martine pointed out to the desert. "Those trails will take us to a little town with gas and groceries. We'll call from there. By the time we get back, we'll have set everything in motion, and anyone tracking our positions, or whereabouts, will think we've never left this facility. I really think you and Olivia are on their radar—possibly me too by association with the case. These people are going to be very connected and capable of out maneuvering anyone that gets in their way. I think we let them try."

"Not bad," Mahoney acknowledged. "How far?"

"Might be five miles, but that will not be a problem." She said confidently. "We'll cut through the desert."

"We're going to hike through the desert?"

"And back," she injected. "What do you say to riding out of here?"

- 289 -

Mahoney laughed his words, "Ride one of those?" He watched two seventeen-hand performance horses clip-clopped beside Eva into the barn.

"If I can do it, you can do it." Martine nodded aggressively. "We ride out of here cross-country and make contact with whoever can help us get this in motion."

Mahoney smiled. "I can do that."

"Let's get some help from Olivia and Eva. I know how they can help."

Chapter 54

Seven O'clock Monday morning, Ray, Miguel, Alexa, and Martine joined forces at the airport.

"Well we all meet again," Ray said, shaking his head in disbelief, "Mother, daughter, tag-team strikes again."

"Back at ya," Alexa answered proudly with a smile.

After entering the airport as inconspicuously as possible, Ray presented the security officer in charge with a warrant for surveillance records on Ricky's activities, though they disguised his name to a more well know drug and money trafficker.

Ray pressed for access to the airports parking records, "Which way?"

"This is most unusual. It will take some time for me to check-out all this information for you," a stout security manager objected. "I don't have enough help here to execute your demands. We have not been given advanced notice, and can't possibly comply with this right now. This is not a simple matter, we have procedures like . . .," he was rambling excuses to all of them until Ray intervened.

"Yeah," Ray said impatiently, "I don't need a playback with extras. We're doing this now." He gave the man a wry smile. "Sorry," Ray said bullishly as he pushed past the man, "we don't have any more time to waste."

Dumbfounded, the manager yelled after Ray, "You can't just barge in here. Do you want to guess what's going to happen to you if I report this to Home Land Security?"

Ray shrugged as he kept walking. "Are you sure you wanna play this game with me? No one ever appreciates my guesses."

Once Ray took control, the four of them underwent the rigorous and monotonous task of reviewing garage surveillance footage, and parking activities for the day in question.

Daunting as it was, every suspicious vehicle that entered the parking garages and lots the day of Adam's murder were scrutinized. After identifying potential vehicles that matched the criteria established, they began the process of cross-checking the vehicles' time-stamped tickets with departure dates. No vehicle could leave without completing a payment and being photographed. After a large sample group was completely researched, it was determined that about forty-five percent of the vehicles entering a paid parking location at the airport on the day Adam was killed still remained on-site.

"Keep looking," Martine instructed. "Keep the photos of vehicles for each parking lot in a separate folder. The teams will be mobilizing here shortly. Please keep additional records of the worst looking enclosed-type vehicles. The tackier the better."

Ray motioned for Martine. "I just heard from Dylan. They're about thirty minutes out. How are you guys doing at your end?"

She glanced at her watch. "Mahoney has everything under control right now. He says it's going really well. His guys should be here in fifteen."

"When this starts the media will be here before you count ten. They usually watch from the sky."

"Not a problem." Martine nodded encouragingly at Ray, who had been a stranger one week ago—now they were comrades. "Airport Security is handling the story. It's a drug-runner sniffing sting. I think the public will love it."

"They're not gonna just love it, they're gonna stop working to watch it." Ray laughed with the smirk of a prankster.

"Well that's what we want." She took a deep breath. "There's no better form of protection than being too visible in the public's eye. Don't criminals do their best work when they're hidden from prying witnesses?"

"That's my experience." Rays phone rang. "Ray, here." Listening intently to the voice on the other end of the conversation, Ray looked at Martine and gave her a thumbs-up. "Thanks Sheriff. Bring your boys in. We're set-up in the big lot outside." He hung up and gave Martine an affirmative look. You wanted a show. You got the Sheriff's posse on horseback too."

"When?"

"Thirty minutes," Ray calculated. "When do we call Mahoney?"

"When it's unavoidable. Wish we could do this without being a production, but in this situation the stakes were too high. We're going to recover the property, or at least eliminate it as a public place that could be threatened."

"Remember," Ray used his warning voice, "You promised to tell me everything when it was all clear."

"Ray, we can't wait to tell you."

"That's all I ask," he replied. Miguel signaled Ray over to him. He started to walk away and checked the time. "Fifteen minutes, Martine."

Her stomach started rolling in waves like a nervous bride who was making the decision of a lifetime. She knew this was risky and over-the-top, especially, if nothing was ever resolved. There would not be a good enough hiding place on earth to escape to if she was wrong, but risking humiliation and shame seemed the only way to deal with this under the time constraints revealed to her. Preventing the natural course of crime-solving protocol to dictate the months or years required to maybe serving justice in this case, led her to concocting a dramatic diversion that gave them a chance of possibly recovering the valuable commodity before it fell into the wrong hands.

Ray lifted his wrist in the air and tapped his watch, cueing Martine to the time. "Ready?" He mouthed.

Chapter 55

Mahoney deliberately arrived late to his meeting Monday morning. "Hello, gentlemen, how can I help you?"

Four Federal Reserve Agents stood to acknowledge him. "I'm Randall Owens," formally dressed and bristle-faced, their spokesperson answered. "We're conducting an investigation that we believe has overlapped with yours."

"Really," Mahoney said calmly to the proper sounding agent. "I don't see how. We're not working with any such cases here in Arizona."

"Yes, well you see it's a delicate matter when the Federal Reserve vaults are breached."

"Well, we don't have any of those here that I'm aware of," Mahoney said politely.

"No, of course not. The currency that was taken has been tracked to a man named Eli Morgan. Do you know that name," Randall said in a condescending tone.

"Yes, I guess we do know that name. We haven't uncovered any currency from the Federal Reserve at his residence."

Sounding irritated with Mahoney, Randall explained more, "We're interested in where the stolen items are that have been recovered."

"I'm sorry to disappoint you, but not much has been recovered," he stated matter-of-factly. "Why don't you tell me what you're looking for? I can't believe you're interested in the horse drugs, coins, or jewelry we've recovered."

Randal accentuated his purpose. "We've been dispatched to recover valuable currency."

"You'll have to tell me more," Mahoney said, feigning interest in their plight.

Randall stiffly expounded, "All you need to know is it's of great value and the property of the Federal Reserve."

"Could you use our help?" Mahoney faked a smile.

"Yes, if you believe you have the resources to do so. The amount involved would be very dangerous in the wrong hands."

"On that we can agree," Mahoney said coyly. "Anything in the wrong hands becomes a dangerous weapon, don't you think?"

"Yes, I suppose it does," Randall replied skeptically.

"Let me get some agents on this for you. We'll set up in our conference room. You do the briefing and I'll assign tasks. Our office has excellent detective skills and technology at its disposal." Mahoney excused himself, "Why don't you get some more coffee while I get everything arranged. We'll be meeting in the big room to the right." He left his office to initiate a task force for the visiting officers' currency investigation.

Chapter 56

Martine and Ray left the Security center of the airport and headed outside to the staging area where vans and trailers were proceeding through security into a big lot like train cars on tracks. As the procession of vehicles pulled into the parking lot, police officers assisted in parking everyone in an orderly fashion.

No nonsense Ray had his men maintain order and control. "This should be interesting," he said to Martine as they watched together. "Looks like the Mexican's clothes are here," he added, motioning towards an officer in a squad car. "He brought everything but the camper."

Martine looked on as men and women with dogs and horses emptied out of the vehicles they arrived in. It was no surprise to her when search and rescue volunteers responded to their request for assistance in locating a very suspicious vehicle—known to be associated with the ongoing drug trafficking problems. Though it was unusual to request an extensive search be done on parked cars instead of the natural terrain found in the wilderness areas where people are frequently lost in Arizona, they welcomed the chance to search for anything.

Canine and handler teams spend years in training before field work begins and certification is awarded. Dedicated to their calling, these volunteer rescuers practice drills and devote a great amount of time and effort in search and tracking operations wherever they may be requested. Being deployed to disaster areas throughout the country is expected of these specialized teams. Fortunately, for

Martine and Mahoney, Arizona is home to some of the best trained and certified canine rescuers in the country.

Ray and his officer approached Martine as the assortment of search teams finished mobilizing around the lot. "Here you go. This is a long shot," his voice skeptical. "But it could work."

"Okay, Ray," Martine said apprehensively, "divide them in groups for each area." They looked at the diagram together. "Assign a team leader for each group and someone with the Sheriff's posse to accompany them. We're looking for these vehicles, and a possible scent hit. Make sure each team has their article of clothing left out here. They'll need to use it again if the dog becomes disorientated. It's the best way to keep the animals focused on tracking this smell if the thousands of scents in this place start to confuse them. The officers will have to control the traffic and keep the sections they're searching in as safe as possible for everyone concerned."

"What happens if we get a hit?" Ray asked.

"John Mahoney will have to tell us that," she said without explanation.

Ray shook his head. "I can't believe he's not here."

"He can't be. Let's get this done," she said. Martine held her breath as everyone dispatched out to their respective areas. Alone in her thoughts she waited for the infamous signal from a single search dogs hit.

Chapter 57

Randall was visibly irked by Mahoney's laxadaziel efforts in gathering his records and rounding up in-house personnel for the Federal Reserve's inquisition. "I expect your full cooperation in providing all the information you have come in contact with," Randall spoke with bossy pride.

"Of course, just let them finish getting the room set-up for you." Mahoney went over to his staff and instructed them to hang every photo of the related crime scenes up on the wall. "Stage this room like we do when we work a big case," he whispered. Looking back at edgy Randall, he tried to appease him, "They need about fifteen more minutes."

"There has to be something you've overlooked. It's not listed in this file," Randall complained after his initial review of Eli's property list.

"No, not that I can think of." Mahoney motioned around the room that now displayed convincing photos and diagrams from the FBI files. "Possibly you could've left something out about what you're looking for."

"Let's take this outside." Randall motioned with his head to leave the conference room that was jammed with as many bodies as it would hold.

"Sure," Mahoney said, following Randall out of the room to his office.

"Maybe I've been a bit too vague," Randall started. "We need to find some very sensitive documents. They would be stored in a large container. Did anything like that show up?"

"Oh. I see what you mean. I should check with the Scottsdale detective about that." Mahoney stalled while he pretended to call Ray. "No answer," he relayed with his hand cupped over the mouthpiece. "I'm leaving him a message." He left a convincing voicemail for Ray as he watched Randall fume. "You know that Eli Morgan had an employee that handled his financial affairs, don't you?"

"Yes, of course." Randall's determination got sassy, "But, he can't be of help since he's dead—can he?"

"That's right. I did hear that." Mahoney gave a slow nod.

"I should hope so, isn't this your case?"

"I wouldn't call his death high profile enough for an FBI investigation—unless you have information tying him to something of that nature."

Randall rolled his eyes. "Fine, I'd like to look at what you have on that guy."

Mahoney started to lay his ground work. "His name was Adam, wasn't it?"

"Yes, yes," Randal sputtered in frustration.

"It was a carjacking I believe. He was killed, but no one has recovered his car," Mahoney looked preoccupied in thought. "We presume he had a car."

"His car hasn't shown up anywhere?" Randall asked.

"No. I've heard some theories," Mahoney shared.

"Perhaps you could divulge those now," Randal said sarcastically.

Mahoney began by giving a lengthy dissertation about various investigations involving carjackings and finished with, "We usually don't recover the cars. Probably, because they end up in the desert, or Mexico. You can see why. We're only hours from the boarder. But, I'm very confident that we'll be able to find it eventually."

Randall appeared to have had enough after numerous prolonged, useless, interactions. "I think we're done here."

Chapter 58

Pacing inside the largest parking ramp, Martine watched anxiously as spirited canine with their handlers in tow descended into every parking area related to the airport. With priorities decided ahead of time, the surveillance camera and ticketing review concluded with the least secure outside parking area on site. Special attention was given to the most likely perceived place someone would park and leave a valuable possession—inside the ramped parking structures. Martine heard her name called by Alexa.

"We're done," she announced as she approached her mother. "I brought down the last folder." Her blue eyes raked over the parking ramp loaded with cars. "I hope they find something before they need this one."

"Why?" Martine swallowed the knot in her throat.

Alexa squinted in chagrin as she leaned against a pillar. "Because I didn't see anything suspicious. Just a lot of small compact type cars and pick-up trucks. Not much to consider."

Tension ratcheted inside Martine as she paced in front of her daughter. She was about to respond when she heard the sound she had been diligently waiting for. Echoing through the noisy structure was the faint bark from a search dog—indicating a hit. Excitement ripped through her as she anticipated what they might have found. Before she could react with words, her phone rang.

"Martine," she said quickly.

"We got a hit. Meets all the criteria. It was on the priority hit list."

"Come and get me," she shot back without hesitation. Clearing her throat, she looked at Alexa. "This could be it."

Ray's car pulled up close to Martine and Alexa. "Let's go." While he drove the car through the garage ramping system to the top level, he explained what he could, "Old truck with enclosed back. Expired New Mexico tags. My guys are running registration now. Locked up tight."

"Is someone on site with a slim-jim?" She asked with hope.

"Squad car is probably there now."

Drawing near the scene was comparable to the cornering of a fox after an exhilarating hunt. Canine, horses, police, and rescue volunteers were all responding to the excitement of the chase. Ray parked close, popped out of his car, and strode up to the vehicle in question. He gave Martine a glance as she caught up to him. "We're ready when you are."

"Open it up," she uttered with anticipate in her voice.

Ray's officer slim-jimmed the locked drivers door.

Holding her breath, Martine climbed into the truck and looked into the back. "Oh my God," she muttered. Backing out of the vehicle she looked at Ray, Alexa, and Miguel. "This is a crime scene," she announced. With a grave expression, she added, "Everything is here, but we're going to have to process this like a homicide too."

"Secure the area," Ray ordered. "We want to thank everyone for their amazing work. Please meet back in the lot. We'll brief you all there." Turning back to Martine, he asked, "Did you really find what we're looking for?"

"I believe we did."

"Why is the thing you are looking for always in the last place you look?" Ray looked around at the least used area in the crowded parking ramp.

"Because that's when you stop looking, Ray." She patted him on the shoulder. Can you excuse me a minute?" Martine walked away and called John Mahoney.

Chapter 59

"Mahoney," he said with authority in his tone as he left the room for some privacy.

"It's done," Martine said into her phone. "Everything is here—including the public. Are you okay?"

He sighed deep. "I am now. Finally some fun. You'll have to excuse me." Mahoney hung up and returned to the room.

Randall came up to him. "Was that the detective?"

"You bet. He's working on a hunch. He thinks that Adam was involved in this mess simply by association. He believes Adam's vehicle is parked at the international airport. That's where the detective is. They're going to find the car if it's there," Mahoney sounded convincing.

"What?" Randall spouted in shock. "He's going to search the airport for it?"

"Absolutely. If they locate it, they'll tow it to our forensics lot. He has orders to deliver it right here for you. I told you we're capable of solving this for you boys."

Miffed Randall pushed his doubts back to Mahoney. "What makes him think that someone would carjack a vehicle and park it at the airport?"

"Let's just say this detective is more like a cowboy than an investigator. When I told him Adam may be in possession of a valuable commodity, he thought the airport would be a logical place to store it till the heat was off of him. The detective contacted airport security and did find that they show his vehicle entering the parking ramp the day he died." Mahoney barely finished his sentence before Randall walked away.

"Need to use the restroom," Randall sputtered in a dejected tone.

Mahoney eyed Randall making a hasty call as he took off for the men's room. "Should we order lunch in? Looks like this might be an all-dayer." Mahoney nonchalantly wandered out to the receptionist and gave instructions to order pizza for everyone. While they casually discussed it, Mahoney watched Randall move his conversation outside where he paced like a nervous jackal. Observing Randall as he became more animated and agitated intrigued him. At last, he was able to take pleasure in Randall's much deserved panic attack. "I'm expecting an important call," he advised the receptionist. "Make sure you put it through to me. I'll be in my office."

Randall coincidently appeared in Mahoney's office at the same time an important call was received. "Excuse me," Mahoney addressed Randall as he drew him into the room. "Mahoney," he said to the caller.

With a deeply pronounced Middle Eastern accent, the caller relayed a message in broken-English, "We have bomb at your airport. You have one hour to meet demands."

"Who is this," Mahoney broke-in.

"Islamic Brotherhood. Ten-million American dollars in one hour, or bomb goes off. Call you back in thirty-minutes."

Mahoney listened like a concerned Federal Agent of the Government. "What's your name?" Instantly, he was disconnected.

"So, you have an emergency?" Randall questioned disingenuously.

Mahoney jumped up from behind his desk. "Randall, we have an emergency at the airport. I'm going to be negotiating with a terrorist. We'll have to finish working on your problem another day."

Exhibiting concern, Randall probed as he followed Mahoney into the conference room, "What happened?" He pushed his way into the crowded room to observe Mahoney.

"May I have your attention please," Mahoney said as he waved his hand in the air. "We've just received a bombing threat for our airport. This scare takes priority starting now. Does everyone understand? This is an emergency. The bombers want ten-million dollars in thirty-minutes. If they don't get it, the bomb goes off in sixty-minutes—starting now. We have a big problem. We have not had a terrorist threat of this magnitude."

"What are our options?" A young man asked.

"I don't think we have many, given the time constraints," Mahoney replied. "First we see if the airport wants to pay the ransom to this group of Jihad type terrorists."

Randall butted in, "Don't you need to evacuate the airport and cancel flights for security purposes? That bomb could go off at anytime. You know that don't you?"

"Randall, it was only a voice threat," Mahoney deflected his advice with a cavalier chuckle. "We don't assume there really is a bomb without some proof."

"Proof?" Twisting his lips, Randal exerted the pushiness of a head-butting shark. "Like what kinda proof do you need?"

Mahoney took a tentative approach. "It's like proof of life. We need to know that someone could actually enter our airport and place a bomb there. We have great security measures. This could be a false alert."

"I can't believe what a buffoon you are," Randall said coldly. "Anyone can drive a car bomb into an airport parking ramp and blow people and concrete everywhere."

"Do you now." Mahoney picked up his TV remote and gave a negative glance to Randall. "Not today, son," Mahoney said with pride. After turning on the TV monitor he sat down in his swivel chair as the big screen sprang to life.

"We're staying 'live' today with our eye in the sky," a young handsome newscaster reported, "at the International Airport in Phoenix. Since early this morning we have been reporting on the intense search being conducted in the parking structures and lots at our airport. We've learned from sources that the extensive hunt for a large shipment of drugs and money was underway this morning before most of you had your first cup of coffee. Live on the scene is Natalie who is giving us breaking news. This is where you'll hear it first, folks, so stay turned-in while we go to Natalie."

"Thanks, Bob," beautiful bright eyed Natalie talked into the camera. "We've recently learned that the vehicle has been found and secured. With the help of dedicated volunteer rescue teams, police, FBI, and the Sheriff's Posse, the impossible was accomplished. There isn't enough praise for how these groups came together and pulled off a sting like this. It's estimated that the value seized was more than a billion dollars."

Mahoney watched Randall's arrogance dwindle like a deflating balloon. "See, there's no way anyone got near that airport today with a bomb. If they had gone there this morning with a car bomb, I can assure you they were too stupid to build one anyways. I feel confident everything is under control there," Mahoney said, pointing to the film footage of Natalie interacting with a plethora of dog and horse teams. Visibly, it was the headline story of the week.

Collapsing his cocky grin, Randall roared, "You're not fooling anyone." Scooping up the bogus stack of files and reports that Mahoney had saddled him with, angry Randall hurled them on the floor before he and his associates bolted for the exit. "You haven't heard the last of us," he threatened.

Turning around to face his staff, Mahoney parted his lips and gave a huge smile before bowing. Everyone stood in the room and gave him a standing ovation as he bowed again. "Man that felt great," he exclaimed with jubilation.

"Brilliant two-step, Sir," one of the men said.

Not normally an emotional man, he went around the room and hardily shook the hand of each participant. Men and women that occupied the desks of administrators, lab technicians, analysts, field technicians, and electronic specialists made up the crack team of agents he had assembled for Randall. While these employees masqueraded as agents, Mahoney's bona fide Special Agents were on the scene with Alexa and Martine.

Chapter 60

Mahoney was waiting outside for Martine to arrive with the old truck that housed the precious cargo that was once secretly hidden away in a private built-in safe room. "Hardly the place you'd expect to find something so unique and valuable," he mused to her as she approached. "Is it really in there?"

"See for yourself." Martine took his arm and patted it. "Few men have ever laid eyes on this before." Opening the back of the vehicle, she stood back in silence while Mahoney gazed at the treasure chest. "It is a 'Mother Box' full of bonds issued by the Federal Reserve of New York. Worth trillions I think. It's also a crime scene," she hypothesized. "It looks like Ricky did more that steal this man's wheels, I think he took his life and used his vehicle to haul his body somewhere."

"Wow, what do I do with it now?"

Martine laughed, "That will be a problem. Someone still wants it and people have been killed over it. Just promise me you won't give any of it to your terrorist bomber if he calls back."

He laughed with her. "Promise."

Martine gave her best explanation of what would happen to the bonds. "These need to be safe guarded until all the heirs claim their inheritance. Somehow Eli's family did become the rightful owner, or as I would define it, the guardian for many. You and I proved that, and here it is." She opened the chests' lid for him to see what they'd found. "Eli's family was entrusted with this. They are the largest percent owner, but not the only one."

Opening the Redemption container, she brought out the instructions that literally named all the beneficiaries of the fortune. Each benefactor had created a trust that detailed their designated portion and when the treasure would be safe to distribute. It was abundantly clear that most of the names were of Jewish decent. Each contributor was acknowledged in the document along with their predetermined percent of worth.

"Get this into a secure vault as soon as possible," Martine advised. "After today, if you have any resistance, you have a jury of journalists to protect it, and a gauntlet of reporters ready to document something new for the history books. Keep it safe."

"I've already found a place. Brinks is on their way."

"So is Ray. Hope you don't mind debriefing him. He is owed that, and we wouldn't have gotten away with our somewhat fabricated warrant today without him. He might be a little brazen and rude, but it served us well under these circumstances."

"That's not going to be a problem. He should enjoy hearing what you've found here."

Handing Mahoney the list of volunteers that had signed-in and participated in the airport parking search, she explained, "We want to show our appreciation for these teams. At a minimum, can you send them an Honorary Badge of Service from the FBI? Credits and praise coming from you will be well received. Might even be helpful in the future." She grinned with satisfaction. "I was really impressed with the results." Martine was ready to leave when Mahoney pulled her to the side.

Looking at her with a little sadness, he said in a private voice, "I can't believe what has happened since you got here. I'm not gonna like it when you're gone."

"I have to agree. Jolene and Wade get in tonight. I leave tomorrow. I'll visit at Christmas. See you then?"

"See you then," he obliged.

Chapter 61

With the FBI in her rearview mirror, Martine headed back to her sister's home. As she drove slowly through heavy traffic, her cell rang. Always happy to hear his accented voice, she answered, "Teddy, how are you?"

"Martine," Teddy said excitedly, "was that you I saw at the airport? Have you been working on a case this whole time?"

"Well, Teddy, that's because I didn't know I was going to be working all week."

"I have extremely interesting news for you. This weekend the class found information that you might find remarkable. They searched extra hard to find out more about Sarah Morgenstein."

"Eli's mother? That's interesting," Martine sounded confused at first. "I mean what did they find?"

"Not so fast. You need to know how they did it. They convinced someone working at the cemetery to go look at her headstone. They sent back a photo showing the inscription on the granite. It said 'Survived by Husband Moses, Son Elijah, and Brother Jakob.' Sarah had a brother. The students felt that this family member might be alive, or have their own surviving family members that can provide information."

"Really? That's creative."

"With the cemeteries' help," Teddy went on, "they got her maiden name from the records that were kept. Last name was Albrecht. With that information they found Jakob Albrecht. He did originally reside in Germany. Appears he had already left Germany by 1939 and was in America."

"America," Martine said in surprise. "Is he still alive?"

"He is," Teddy chuckled. "Lives on the east coast. He's ninety-one. He told them what happened to Eli."

"Oh my goodness," Martine blurted. "What happened?"

"Eli ended up in an orphanage. But Jakob could never find him because of the child's name change. Eli got adopted by a Christian couple who raised him in a wealthy home. He became an expert horseman—which of course we know that part."

Martine still wanted to know how Eli might have come in procession of Bearer Bonds. "Was this family extremely wealthy?"

"I doubt it. According to Jakob, Eli's adoptive father owned a textile mill. I think that would make them well-off, but not necessarily filthy rich. Here's what's interesting. In 1990 Eli's adoptive father dies. With both adoptive parents deceased, Eli inherits everything. Among the legal papers were his adoption records and a clue to his past that triggered memories."

Anxious, Martine interrupted, "What clue?"

"One photo of three year old Elijah with a young horse. That photo of him with the horse must have resurrected repressed memories from his youth. Eli used that information to basically find his surviving relative. Eli hired an investigator and found Jakob."

"Did Jakob say why Eli came to America?"

"He certainly did. Jakob and Eli had reconnected, and Eli couldn't get to America fast enough, but that's not the whole story. Apparently When Moses had tried to come to America with Eli, he sent their possessions ahead."

Martine was curious, "What kinda of possessions?"

"Jakob said that Moses shipped a valuable baby horse named Ashkenazi Star on a cargo ship to America."

"The horse," Martine gasped.

"Not just the horse, but crates of horse possessions. One crate had a trunk with implicit instructions to bury it in a safe place. Moses had instructed Jakob to bury it for sixty years if they didn't make it to America. He said it wouldn't be safe to give it to anyone except Eli when he was a grown man and the war had ended. Moses thought the world was going to be at war for many, many years."

"Let me guess, Eli came to America and claimed the trunk."

"Sounds like it to me. He used the credentials his father Moses had arranged for him as a child. He used the name Morgan when he came to the US. Jakob said when Eli came to America he found out he was part of a very wealthy family trust. Which confirms what you thought, and I presumed you were looking for. Which leads me back to Eli's father and grandfather. His father Moses might have been a banker, but it was his grandfather that owned the bank. He was a shrewd miser according to Jakob."

"Are you going to tell me he owned one of the big banks in Europe?" She asked.

"No, it was his own private bank. Martine, I've been researching possible scenarios of what could've been in play during the Hitler era. Hitler's NAZI's worked actively to loot wealth in the nations they occupied. Hitler most likely took great pleasure in destroying the Jews financially. By 1934 Germany's tax laws forced Jews that wanted to flee to leave most of their wealth behind. The 'Reich Flight Tax' increased to twenty-five percent—payable in cash or gold. As the name implies, there was a huge financial sacrifice made if you left the country. Germany needed money, and did not want to be drained of the gold reserves in its economic system. Basically, the Reich had bureaucracies that had the sole purpose of discovering dwellings and bank accounts with substantial assets—that they proceeded to empty. As these Bureaucrats pillaged and stole anything of value in each nation they occupied or invaded, no group of people were left unscathed, however, no group lost as much as the Jews.

With each progressive means taken to strip Jews of their businesses, wealth, possessions, and rights, it would be very obvious to someone of great wealth, or access to it, to find the most protective vehicle possible to preserve it, and not let it fall in the hands of Hitler's NAZI's."

Martine interrupted, "Any ideas how they were doing that?"

"No. But, as we now examine the historical events from that era, we understand more fully that Hitler really hated what the Jewish elite bankers did to Germany. Hitler begins by rectifying the situation by ridding Germany of its financial burdens. With no one stopping him he gets more and more carried away. He becomes fanatical and deranged. What he really didn't understand was that the elite Zionist Jews created all this animosity. It wasn't an entire Jewish race. So, they all became his logical target. And, because the majority of all the racial and financial shifting occurred between 1934 and 1939, I believe the Morgenstein family would have had many reasons for hiding their wealth as secretly as they could. They probably embarked on this before they ever though they'd actually have to change their identities. If it was enormous capital, it may indicate they were part of the one percent Jewish elite that dominated the wealth. Hitler went after the ninety-nine percent that had no influence or huge concentrated reserves of cash and gold because they were defenseless and easily destroyed."

"The primary shift really takes hold in 1939," Martine reiterated.

"Pretty much," Teddy agreed. "The Jews had to register their wealth and property. They could no longer practice law or medicine. Jewish children are segregated and forced out of public schools. Nazis also fined the Jews one billion marks for damages related to Kristallnacht pogrom riots. The danger really intensified in 1939."

She formulated out loud as Teddy listened, "Moses' father would have done what he had to in order to preserve the wealth of his business. Based on what we found today, he may have been forced to accept the terms. He most likely converted many assets into Bearer Bonds in exchange for their lives."

"Based on those possibilities, what Jakob told us next makes your initial presumption that the horse's bloodlines were all you had to go on, even more profound than you realized. Moses told Jakob to never ever sell the horse, and the bloodline must be carried on. Jakob had a horse operation. Moses had sent along written instructions that the only person that could truly claim inheritance to the family would be someone that knew the horse by name and sight. Ashkenazi Star was given to little Elijah when he was a young boy."

Martine felt especially saddened when she realized that the little boy never did see his horse again. It made it clear why his new colt, Quest—the great, great, grandson of his first horse, was more valuable than any other horse on the property. "Wow," Martine said slowly. What a sad ending. But, on the upside, Eli must have heirs."

"Not so fast. Jakob only had one son that passed away from a car accident in 1987."

"Okay, I'm listening," Martine injected.

"Jakob never even knew his son had fathered an illegitimate child. Jakob's son was survived by a daughter. Because Eli was as paranoid and guarded as any Jew who survived the gas chambers, or concentration camps, he did not want her to know who he was. Until it was proven, he believed it was safer that way for her. Jakob felt the same way since there was no proof of her birthright established."

"She never knew her great uncle?" Martine sounded disappointed.

"I didn't say that. She just didn't know they were probably related."

"Teddy, you're saying Eli may have an heir besides Jakob? And that Eli knew her?"

"He does have an heir if someone can prove it."

"That means there really is someone who inherits his fortune."

"Possibly."

"Why haven't they come forward?"

"Jakob is in a nursing home. He didn't even know Eli died recently. But, to answer your question, Jakob's son was deceased before he ever knew that he possibly fathered an illegitimate child. She never knew who her father was. Jakob didn't know he had a granddaughter till Eli informed him. It was Eli who discovered everything. They decided it was better to keep the secret and put her under the younger watchful eye of Eli. Eli supported Jakob in exchange for his secrets."

Martine held her breath in. "Her name. What's her name?"

"Olivia."

"Olivia," Martine repeated with a quick chuckle.

"Do you know her?" Teddy ignited with surprise.

"I do."

"Do you have any ideas on how to prove she's a rightful heir?" Teddy asked.

"I do now. With Jakob alive, DNA testing can finish the story," Martine said with evenness.

"Do you know what she'll do with her inheritance?"

"I do," Martine said reflectively. "Horses. Lots of horses."

"Horses," Teddy said with astonished-doubt. "Figures, won't that be a waste of money?"

"Teddy, horses don't waste money—people do."

Chapter 62

Martine finally got back to Jolene's after leaving John Mahoney with the chest full of bonds. She let the dogs out and sat down outside on the patio for the first time since she arrived. Before returning phone calls to her daughters, she opened the photos she had taken with her phone. One before the trunk was opened that had The Treaty of Versailles Mother Box stamped on it, and the second after the trunk was opened, which showed thirteen sealed compartments inside. On the inside of the tarnished trunk lid was more unique detail. Specifically, a plaque with an American flag displaying forty-eight stars—indicating its historical origins in time.

Entering a phone number into her phone, she attached the two photos and sent them to Max—who never really knew who she was.

The End

AUTHOR BIO

Kathi Bjorkman resides in Colorado and Arizona. Born and raised in Minnesota, she moved out west with her family in 1998 to live and work in the Rocky Mountains. Degreed in Business, she is employed at a Colorado guest ranch that specializes in hosting large wedding events.

Fascinated by the historical significance of the western states, she produced a paranormal clue-solving fiction novel that weaves together, known Indian cultures, ancient religious practices, real historical events, and renowned western landmarks.

Author of Third Eye Witness published 1/11/11
**Finalist in Two 2013 Chanticleer Book
Reviews' Blue Ribbon Writing Contests**
CLUE Awards 2013 Finalist
Paranormal/Supernatural Awards 2013 Finalist
Author of Third Eye Witness-Bearer of Truth published 4/15/15
**Finalist in 2015 Chanticleer Book Reviews'
Blue Ribbon Writing Contest**
Paranormal/Supernatural Awards 2015 Finalist